Stella Cameron

Judith E. French

Linda Lael Miller

Anne Stuart

"*With this ring, I thee wed*"—these are the solemn
words that bind two hearts eternally. From four
of America's best loved authors of romantic fiction come a quartet of soul-stirring and unforgettable stories on the timeless theme of
matrimony—tales of strangers united by
chance, convenience and circumstance, taking
bold leaps of faith in pursuit of glorious
dreams—and of loves, rapturous and true, born
of destiny...and sacred vows of undying devotion.

AVON BOOKS PRESENTS

TO LOVE
AND TO
HONOR

*Don't Miss These Romantic Holiday Anthologies from
Avon Books*

AVON BOOKS PRESENTS:
BEWITCHING LOVE STORIES

AVON BOOKS PRESENTS:
A CHRISTMAS COLLECTION

AVON BOOKS PRESENTS:
CHRISTMAS LOVE STORIES

AVON BOOKS PRESENTS:
CHRISTMAS ROMANCE

AVON BOOKS PRESENTS:
HAUNTING LOVE STORIES

AVON BOOKS PRESENTS:
TIMELESS LOVE

AVON BOOKS PRESENTS

TO LOVE AND TO HONOR

STELLA CAMERON • JUDITH E. FRENCH
LINDA LAEL MILLER • ANNE STUART

AVON BOOKS ⬢ NEW YORK

AVON BOOKS PRESENTS: TO LOVE AND HONOR is an original publication of Avon Books. This work, as well as each individual story, has never before appeared in print. This work is a collection of fiction. Any similarity to actual persons or events is purely coincidental.

AVON BOOKS
A division of
The Hearst Corporation
1350 Avenue of the Americas
New York, New York 10019

Published by arrangement with the authors
Library of Congress Catalog Card Number: 92-97291
ISBN: 0-380-77159-4

First Avon Books Printing: May 1993

AVON TRADEMARK REG. U.S. PAT. OFF. AND IN OTHER COUNTRIES, MARCA REGISTRADA, HECHO EN U.S.A.

Printed in the U.S.A.

RA 10 9 8 7 6 5 4 3 2 1

Contents

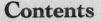

Bargain Bride

Stella Cameron

FOR PHILIP AND LYNN LLOYD-WORTH
WHO LIVE, LOVE AND HONOR

1

London, 1841.

"**M**ARRIAGE? Not an estate I'll readily embrace, by God!" Guy Falconer, Marquess of Rockford, glowered at his companion.

Armando de Silva inspected the outrageous lace cuffs that draped his wrists. "You will embrace it readily enough when the urge comes to fill your nurseries, *amigo*."

"Such an urge shows no sign of occurring. Now, to the matter in hand."

"Willsly's intended," Armando said under his breath.

Guy flexed a hand. "Indeed. And one may be certain our friend Willsly's urge for the marriage bed has little to do with any pressing interest in heirs, and even less with fond feelings for Miss Beatrice Merryfield."

"As you say." Armando pushed back his dark red velvet coat and planted his fists on his hips. "Your plan is audacious, *amigo*. Perhaps I should be the one to—"

"No. The plan is mine and I shall accomplish it. Everything depends upon causing this sheltered female no alarm. One look at your pirate's face and she would surely scream for a constable."

Armando chuckled. "And what of *your* face?"

"One look into my eyes and Miss Merryfield will judge me for the man I am."

"In that case, you had best look elsewhere." A white

grin flashed in Armando de Silva's darkly handsome face. "Or this dull little bird you seek to catch will surely fly away."

Guy did not return the smile. "She will fly nowhere but into my cage. Wait for me in the carriage." Without another glance, he left Armando and crossed Cheyne Walk.

"*You'll know the lady, guv'nor,*" his well-paid informer had assured him. "*The gentleman wot yer told me ter watch calls 'er a dull little brown bird to 'is friends. Probably on account o' 'er manner o' dress and 'ow it matches 'er hair, if yer takes me meaning. 'Er eyes is brown, too. Funny color brown wot looks right through yer.*"

Guy shuddered and bore down upon the tearooms to which he'd been directed. On this clear spring afternoon when daffodils bobbed their sunny heads in every London park and pretty women slipped on their gay and chattering way in all directions, his task was to deceive a plain woman who had already been deceived by a master.

That master was Victor Beresford, earl of Willsly and murderous coward.

Guy was finally moved to smile a little—if grimly. On the night in Hong Kong harbor when Willsly had invited Guy to dine aboard a vessel belonging to "friends," this afternoon's work became inevitable. Left to die in Willsly's stead, for Willsly's treachery, Guy had faced an angry crew who would allow him no chance to defend himself. If the *El Fuego del Mar's* captain had not proved to be Armando de Silva, an old friend made during an earlier skirmish in Turkey, the last marquess of Rockford would be dead.

But Armando had swaggered aboard, barely in time to stop the blade meant for Guy's throat, and Willsly's fate was sealed.

Guy strode on to the tearooms. God only knew why the daughter of a jelly glass manufacturer would be dillydallying over tea when she should be anxiously preparing for her wedding—barely two days hence—to a philandering peer of the realm. However, the woman's apparent wooly-headedness simplified the task in hand.

Despite the warmth of the afternoon, a hint of steam clung to the inside edges of bulbous leaded panes in the shop's bow window. No doubt large volumes of hot tea mixed with female gossip were responsible.

With a hand on the doorknob, Guy paused. No particularly plain woman sat at the table in the window. A handsome blonde and a red-haired beauty smiled over their fine china cups. The blonde's head tilted as she noticed Guy and he was favored with a coquettish smile that faded when the female noted his unfashionably long hair and unremarkable tailoring.

Exactly the reaction he desired. True, he'd been absent from London more than two years, but for a man of thirty-two who was well acquainted with the town's privileged inhabitants, the risk of recognition must still be great. And he could *not* be recognized.

Resolute, he swept off his hat and entered rooms redolent of spices and warm pastry. Prattle and laughter rose and fell all about him. For the first time in his adult life, he wished he were a smaller man. His height and breadth—and the plain dress he'd deliberately affected— made him too obvious amid the expensively attired patrons seated at the small tables.

Much too obvious.

He nodded at a pretty raven-haired female who seemed disposed to ignore his evident lack of wealth.

Turning, he ran his gaze over the clientele.

According to his source, Miss Beatrice Merryfield was definitely in these rooms. She would be seated with a very blonde female of over-thin proportions.

Very blonde and over-thin. Guy saw such a female and felt an unpleasant leap in the region of his heart. He was unaccustomed to counting women as adversaries. This had to be Miss Sibyl Abbott-Smyth. And, seated opposite, leaning forward over the table, her face obscured by her bonnet brim, was a small, brown-haired creature. Brown hair, brown silk dress, brown shawl, brown bonnet. Doubtless any artful decorations tucked beneath the brim of that bonnet would also be brown— if a plain article such as this would bow to even the most insignificant of feminine affectations.

Damn, but he almost pitied Willsly. Almost. A trader in information pertinent to the raging English–Chinese opium wars, Willsly had played the desperate game of double agent and been unmasked. Caught between the Chinese, the British, and Armando's pirate crew, the treacherous coward had all but cost Guy his life and now the time had come for retribution. If he was to keep his grasp on everything he held dear, Victor, Lord Willsly, needed his plain brown bird. To be more true, he needed her wealthy merchant father's money and that was why he intended to marry someone he must despise. Only the wedding would never take place.

Squaring his shoulders, Guy sauntered between tables until he stood beside the women. Without excusing himself, he sat on a chair between the two.

"Oh!" The blonde female turned surprised blue eyes upon him.

Guy smiled, inclined his head and looked directly into the eyes of her companion. Startling light brown eyes that reminded him of an intelligent tiger.

There were no ornaments beneath the brim of her bonnet.

So this was his quarry. This was the woman he would kidnap this very day.

"Good afternoon," he said. "I hope I'm not late."

"Good afternoon," Beatrice Merryfield said in a clear voice that suggested laughter. "Not late at all. Tea is served all afternoon, sir."

Guy found that he couldn't quite remember the exact words he'd rehearsed for this moment.

She turned back to her companion and said, "I really do think we're making progress, Sibyl. Even Mrs. Tyrrel made a remark about Sir Robert Peel and the Reform Act. So she did read what we gave her, d'you see. Most gratifying."

If Miss Abbott-Smyth heard Miss Merryfield she gave no sign. Her small mouth had fallen slightly open while she watched Guy help himself to a lemon-curd tart, and another—and rapidly follow the second with a sticky little pink-sugared bun.

"When we're reaching even those women who have been adamant in avoiding self-improvement through"— Miss Merryfield looked at Guy, at the remnants of the bun, at the plate from which he'd taken it, and pushed the latter in front of him—"the more we can encourage women to educate themselves, the better. But we know that, don't we? Do eat the rest of the cakes, sir. My friend and I have had quite enough, haven't we, Sibyl?"

Sibyl nodded.

"Should you care for some tea?" Without waiting for Guy's response, Miss Merryfield bobbed to her feet and appropriated an unused cup and saucer from a nearby table. "Of course you would. You poor man. Hunger among the struggling genteel is a frightful problem. I do admire your ingenuity; coming in here and sharing our meal like this. After all, we obviously have far too much—much more than we need."

"*Beatrice.*" Miss Abbott-Smyth's gloved hand fluttered. "I really don't think—"

"*Don't* think," Miss Merryfield said promptly. "So much better on occasions such as this."

He would follow the steps he had planned exactly. First, establish without a doubt that he had located the correct woman.

A bright spot of color showed on each of Sibyl Abbott-Smyth's pale cheeks. "There is little time before we must return to Lansdowne Place, Beatrice."

"I know."

"We have not made any final plans." Sibyl's voice held desperation.

"You underestimate me. *I* have most certainly made final plans. I am only missing one key ingredient—the most important ingredient—necessary to my success. And I am confident that will soon be remedied."

"But your father—"

"Oh *do* be calm, Sibyl. I declare you make me quite nervous."

"Please excuse me," Guy said. "May I please ask—"

"No need at all to ask," Willsly's brown bird said before Guy could complete his request for her name. "Eat as many as you like."

"Most kind, but—"

"Allow me to introduce my friend, Miss Sibyl Abbott-Smyth. And I am Beatrice Merryfield." She favored him with a steady, expectant stare from her pale gold, slightly uptilted eyes.

Guy fashioned a guileless smile. "I am Guy Falcon. And I am charmed to make your acquaintance." Now came the second step: his carefully devised excuse to lure her away from her friend and outside.

"Falcon." Beatrice frowned. "What a fine name. A free name. It feels strong and daring on the lips." Leaning closer, she stared at him intently.

"Beatrice—"

"Hush, Sibyl. Are you daring, sir?"

"Beatrice!"

"Hush, Sibyl. I do believe I have found what I need. Are you daring, Mr. Falcon?"

He inclined his head. Damnation, she wasn't silent long enough for a man to say what he must.

"Of course you are. Only a daring man would walk into a polite establishment such as this and join two ladies he did not know for tea."

"Oh, Beatrice, *no*," Miss Abbott-Smyth moaned.

Miss Merryfield spared her friend a withering glance. "You are undoubtedly a resourceful man, Mr. Falcon."

Guy could not help asking, "How do you know this?"

"You were hungry," she said, matter-of-fact. "So you contrived an ingenious method to deal with that situation. Resourceful and audacious. Both most valuable traits and absolutely essential to what I have in mind."

Small certainly described her stature perfectly and she

was no raving beauty, but this brown bird could never be described as dull. Fascinated, Guy watched the way her thick black lashes cast shadows in eyes the color of fine warm whiskey.

"You are not by chance easily intimidated by people of rank, sir?"

"Oh, Beatrice." Miss Abbott-Smyth's voice rose to a wail.

"Mr.—"

"No," Guy said, suppressing a smile. "I cannot say that I am impressed by titles."

"Perfect." She settled the cashmere shawl more firmly over the shoulders of her pleated bodice. "This is absolutely perfect."

"I'm glad you approve," he told her, aware of his own cynical note. Armando would be growing impatient. "Are you at all familiar with—"

"Hush," she told him, looking all about her.

If she would simply give him a few quiet moments, he would ask if she could advise him in a matter regarding his ailing mother . . . might that dimly remembered lady's soul rest in peace . . . He would ask advice in tempting his failing mother to eat—his failing mother who, as they spoke, awaited him nearby. Guy knew that Miss Merryfield's avid support for the education of females was only rivaled by her concern for the aged. She would undoubtedly insist upon accompanying him outside and then the rest . . .

She had said something he didn't quite hear.

"Beatrice!" Miss Abbott-Smyth pressed shaking fingers to her mouth and appeared about to swoon.

"Not *now*," Miss Merryfield hissed.

"I'm sorry," Guy murmured. "What did you say?"

"I said"—she glanced around once more—"I said I need the help of a daring man. I need *you*, Mr. Falcon. And I will pay handsomely for your services."

"Pay?" His mind became temporarily blank.

"Of course. I can tell you are honest and that you need money. This will be perfectly honorable on your part. Even if it will, on cursory examination, appear otherwise.''

''I fear I do not follow you.''

''It's quite simple. Will you be so good as to run off with me?''

His tendency to appear shocked did worry Beatrice slightly. However, she would not allow something so insignificant to deter her . . . even though she must admit to some slight trepidation about the wisdom of the step she'd taken.

''Do stop whimpering, Sibyl.'' She tucked a hand through her friend's arm and hurried along beside Mr. Falcon. ''This will work very well. I have certain insightful powers when it comes to these matters, d'you see.''

''These matters?'' Mr. Falcon sounded cross.

Beatrice looked sharply up at him. ''Some might say I had unearthly gifts. Pure rubbish. I am an excellent judge of character and I *know* when something feels right.'' My, but he was an incredibly large man. Tall, much taller than Lord Willsly, who was undoubtedly also tall, and very strong in appearance. Lord Willsly was also strong . . . She must try not to think of Lord Willsly.

''Do ask him where we are going,'' Sibyl said breathlessly.

''You will be perfectly safe, I assure you,'' Mr. Falcon told them before Beatrice could say another word. ''And I commend you on your instincts, Miss Merryfield—or your *insightful* powers. They have led you on a safe path. I shall make an excellent job of running off with you.''

Sibyl squealed.

''*Hush.*'' Ooh, Sibyl could be *so* annoying. ''This is purely a fabrication, remember. No one is *actually* running off with anyone. I had to find a way to miss my wedding and I have done so. There. Simply stated, that is the fact.

''I know you'll do an excellent job, Mr. Falcon, and I *do* trust you. However, it does seem prudent to inquire about our destination, particularly since we are women alone in the company of a gentleman.''

''And there you have it,'' he said, guiding them around a corner into a small street Beatrice had not previously noted. ''I *am* a gentleman. And you ladies are chaperon to each other. But I applaud your prudence. We will go to my . . . There is a house not a half-day's journey from here—charming spot on a hill not far from the Channel— where you will be safely hidden.''

''Not far from the Channel where?'' Sibyl demanded.

Mr. Falcon waved airily. ''Oh, in a most pleasing place, I assure you. I'm sure you understand that it will be better for my sake if you do not know the exact location—after you go back home, that is—because there can be no question of your being able to reveal where you have been.''

''Of course,'' Beatrice said firmly. ''Mr. Falcon is running a great risk in helping us, Sibyl. He has agreed to do so simply on the strength of seeing our distress. He does not know us at all.''

''Oh, *Beatrice*.''

''*Hush* . . .'' She forgot what she'd been about to say next. In front of them, a few feet from a large, plain black carriage and four fine grays, stood a tall man of most extraordinary appearance. ''Mr. Falcon, that man . . .'' She heard her voice fade.

''An old friend,'' Mr. Falcon said brusquely. ''Armando de Silva. A foreigner.''

''I see.'' That must account for the black curly hair that brushed the shoulders of a claret-colored velvet coat and the cascading lace that dripped from the neck and cuffs of the stranger's shirt. *A foreigner*.

''Armando,'' Mr. Falcon said rather loudly. ''These two ladies are in need of my help. We will travel a little out of our way in order to give them refuge in a time of dire need.''

The foreign gentleman's black eyes passed from Mr. Falcon, to Beatrice, and on to Sibyl. When he looked at Sibyl he didn't just look—he stared.

"This is Miss Beatrice Merryfield," Mr. Falcon said. "And her friend, Miss Sibyl Abbott-Smyth."

The black-eyed man directed a brief nod in Beatrice's direction. With a flourish, he took Sibyl's hand and bent low. "*Señorita*," he murmured softly, looking up at her. "*Muchas gracias.*"

Thank Sibyl for *what*? Foreigners were often so strange. This one regarded Sibyl as one might a heavenly vision.

Mr. Falcon offered Beatrice his arm. "Allow me to assist you into my carriage."

She faltered then. "We have not discussed the, er— your payment."

"Payment?" The man called Armando straightened and his hair swung back to reveal a gold earring. "What payment, *amigo*?"

"No payment," Mr. Falcon said rather loudly. "Of course I will not allow these charming ladies to pay for my help."

"I do not understand." Sunlight glinted on Mr. de Silva's earring. "What is all—"

"Later," Mr. Falcon said. "We will speak of this as we go."

"Certainly I shall pay you," Beatrice insisted. "I have my own means and I insist. This is a business arrangement."

"Please get into the carriage," Mr. Falcon said. "Soon we will attract undue attention and that would be most unfortunate."

The only other person Beatrice could see was the coachman, who stood beside the coach's open door. She raised her chin. "Very well. This is a desperate situation and it requires desperate measures. Come, Sibyl. We shall trust that our goodness will be our shield."

Once they were settled in a surprisingly sumptuous interior, Mr. Falcon rapped the trap smartly.

"To Aldersgate!" the foreigner called before leaping in beside his friend and slamming the door.

Sibyl clutched Beatrice's hand and moved closer. Beatrice smiled reassuringly, although she herself did not feel at all reassured. Perhaps she should reverse this course she had chosen.

The carriage was already rolling on at a good clip.

"This is most dangerous, Beatrice," Sibyl whispered. "And your papa will blame me. I am supposed to look after you."

"Hah!" Beatrice said, much more loudly than she'd intended. "Papa knows I am beyond *looking after*, as you say. Anyway, I've already told you he will be furious with me regardless and I shall insist upon taking all responsibility for my actions."

"It is *not* appropriate," Sibyl continued in her hoarse whisper. "*Two* gentlemen definitely make this quite shocking."

"Mm. Less shocking than the prospect of marriage to Lord Willsly. That is a truly *horrifying* thought."

Mr. de Silva made the most strange noise but before Beatrice could ask if he was ill, Mr. Falcon pounded the poor man's back so hard that Mr. de Silva coughed.

"Excuse Armando," Mr. Falcon said. "He gets these attacks. His health is frequently uncertain."

Sibyl made a small, sympathetic sound and, to Beatrice's amazement, routed out a tiny container of hartshorn from her reticule and offered it to the ailing man.

He regarded the hartshorn, then looked at Sibyl and silently shook his head. He reached to fold her fingers over the vial and gently placed her hand back in her lap. *"Querida Señorita,"* he said, very softly.

Beatrice frowned and looked away—directly at Mr. Falcon, who smiled at her.

"I should explain what has brought me to this difficult pass," she told him. His eyes were dark green. Not a vague shade, but dark, like the ferns that grew near the river at home in Northumberland. "You do not, of course, know Victor, Lord Willsly, because you do not move in his circles—any more than I do. And I don't *want* to."

"Perhaps you should tell me all about this."

"Yes. You will want to know."

Mr. Falcon's wavy hair was somewhat long and very dark—not as dark as Mr. de Silva's, but almost so. And his brows slashed upward. His nose was straight, imperiously so; and his mouth firm, the upper lip thinner than the lower, and the whole clearly defined and tipped up just the slightest bit at the corners. Beatrice took her own bottom lip in her teeth and drew a shallow breath. He was very, very handsome. Yes, Mr. Falcon was the most handsome man she had ever actually met—perhaps even *seen*.

"Why exactly are you anxious to pretend you've run off with someone?"

"Because"—she spread her hands—"because it seems by far the easiest way to deal with an impossible situation."

Mr. Falcon's face was lean, his jaw sharply defined, and his skin was tanned as if he'd spent a great deal of time in the sun. Beatrice studied his extremely wide shoulders in a plain black coat that fitted well, especially over a powerful-looking chest. He'd removed his gloves, and his hands, also darkly tanned, were long and strong with the lightest dusting of black hairs on the backs. And his hands rested on a thigh that also looked most strong where it filled tightly fitting trousers in a manner that showed each hard muscle.

"Miss Merryfield?"

She started and looked quickly back at his face. "Lord Willsly is not a nice man," she said. "My father thinks he is doing his best for me by marrying me off into the nobility, but he is wrong." Oh, dear, surely Mr. Falcon hadn't realized she was studying him so closely.

"Why is he wrong? If indeed he is wrong at all."

"Mr. Falcon," Sibyl said suddenly. "I believe I must take charge here."

Amazed, Beatrice turned to her friend. "Sibyl—"

"No, Beatrice, allow me to deal with this frightful development. I am Beatrice's paid companion and in that capacity, it is my duty to protect her as best I can."

"Piffle!" Really, Sibyl chose the oddest moments to become what she was not—brave. "Sibyl has been my friend since we were children. She is no more responsible for me than I am for her."

"Oh, yes I am. Mr. Merryfield pays me. I am a servant, and—"

"*I* will deal with this." Beatrice looked straight into Mr. Falcon's eyes. "It may not be necessary to actually say that I have run off with someone, d'you see. I'm hoping that if I simply send my father a note to say I am safe and then wait . . ." Surely her bold plan was the right one. "If I send my father a note letting him know I am safe and then wait until the wedding day is past, the . . . desired result will be achieved."

"The desired result?" Mr. Falcon prompted softly.

This was the part that made her vaguely uncomfortable. "There is an element the nobility holds most dear. I intend to rely upon this to save myself from Victor the Bea . . . From Victor."

"Victor the Beast!" Sibyl said stoutly. "Call him by his true name, Bea."

"Yes, well, it is my plan that since my note will not arrive until almost time for the wedding, Lord Willsly will be left standing literally at the altar, d'you see." She felt herself blush. "Not nice, I know, but the only way I can think to be certain of forcing him to abandon his intention to marry me."

"At the altar?"

"Precisely. That will be an event guaranteed to force the bea . . . Lord Willsly to cry off entirely because of that other element I mentioned."

"Would you care to tell me about this element?"

"You probably won't understand—which is very sensible of you—but I will try to explain. The nobility, particularly the gentlemen, make a great fuss about honor, although if you ask me they appear to have precious little."

Mr. de Silva made his strange noise again and promptly moved away from Mr. Falcon before he could repeat the frightful pounding on the other's back.

Beatrice continued, "To save face, Lord Willsly will feel he must renounce me. There will be suggestions of my ruin, but I care nothing for that if it will save me from Victor. Better to end life an old maid than to suffer being used by that man."

For a long time Mr. Falcon stared at Beatrice but his thoughts appeared to be elsewhere.

Beyond the coach windows, the buildings of central London had given way to mean, straggling dwellings that were soon left behind for the open country.

"Why would you agree to so dangerous a venture, sir?" Sibyl demanded suddenly, interrupting the silence inside the carriage. "Try as I may, I cannot understand it."

Mr. Falcon cleared his throat. "I am moved by your need," he said.

"But why were you in the tearooms? You do not appear poor or needy. Why *did* you choose to sit with us in such an inappropriate manner?"

Exactly the questions that were assailing Beatrice now that her head was once more clear.

"I wondered when you would ask me this." Mr. Falcon's smile was . . . It made lines crinkle at the corners of his eyes and showed twin dimples beside his mouth. His teeth were square and straight and white. Mm, a smile became him very well. "Ah, well," he said, turning up his palms. "So I am found out. I am addicted to tea, you see. And I had this absolutely desperate longing for a cup. So I chose to go in."

"That does not explain why you presumed upon us," Sibyl said.

He put a fist to his mouth and looked to the floor. "Simple. Armando despises confined spaces and would not accompany me to the tearooms. And I am afraid of sitting alone in public places."

"Oh." Beatrice frowned. "You poor man."

Mr. de Silva appeared to be in some sort of pain. Finally he covered his face with a hand.

"You did not treat me with disdain when I presumed upon you," Mr. Falcon continued. "And I in turn could not deny you in your need."

"*Señorita,*" Mr. de Silva said to Beatrice. He leaned closer, apparently quite recovered again. "Please, is it possible for you to explain why you chose to approach . . . Mr. *Falcon* with your request?"

"Simple." Beatrice beamed. "One look at his face and I knew him for the man he is."

2

ALDERSGATE looked remarkably handsome at this time of year. In the library, Guy marched from window to window, admiring terraced lawns that swept away from the back of the house toward a walled topiary garden. Even with evening's lavender haze fast upon them, the grounds were grand—if somewhat in need of attention.

"Stop pacing."

"I am not pacing." Guy swung to face Armando. "This is a fine house. I've missed it."

Armando lounged in a gilt Louis XV chair. "So, you've missed Sussex so much that you will hesitate to answer your country's next call for your—shall we say *special skills*?"

"I doubt my particular ambassadorial talents will be needed soon."

"*Ambassadorial?*" Armando shouted with laughter. "A fine word for an intelligence agent's trade, *amigo.*

No doubt there will be other situations where England needs a man with your *ambassadorial* skills. Other situations where only you can pass so easily into enemy camps and bring out information.''

Guy remembered Hong Kong. "I will not be in a hurry to feel pirate blades at my throat again. Willsly was a shock. I had no idea he was dealing with all sides until he sent me aboard your ship to die.''

"It would have worked," Armando said thoughtfully. "My men knew Willsly had betrayed us. They knew he was coming aboard and that I intended to—*confront* him. None of the crew believed you weren't Willsly—which is exactly as he intended. If I hadn't arrived, he would have paid his debt with your life and been free. He still believes he accomplished that aim.''

"Willsly will suffer. His social stature and his pleasures are everything to him. He needs money and he needs it *now*. Without marriage to Miss Merryfield's fortune Willsly is finished.''

"Finished," Armando echoed, drawing an imaginary blade across his neck. "In less than two days that is exactly what he will be. So why are you pacing again, Guy?''

Guy stopped with his back to the windows. "I am *not* pacing. Merely surveying the home I have not seen in more than two years.''

"This is but one of several homes you have not seen in that time, *amigo*. Do you intend to pace them all?'' Armando regarded the fine study in oils of Guy's dead father, which hung above an upright Riesener *sécretaire* that had belonged to his mother. "If I am not mistaken, Aldersgate is the smallest of your estates. The others are likely to wear out your boots.''

Guy chose to ignore his friend's baiting. "The servants played their parts well. Not one slip in front of our lady guests.''

Armando drank slowly from a goblet of red wine. "You may pray no one uses your title until our task is accomplished.'' He swirled the wine. "She is certainly beautiful.''

Guy's frown deepened. "Hardly beautiful. Pleasant enough of face but too small for my taste. Of course, her eyes are quite remarkable. Golden, like some wild cat.''

"I referred to *Señorita* Abbott-Smyth.''

"Miss Abbott-Smyth? She is colorless.''

Armando shook his head. "She is drawn in subtle hues.''

"She is scrawny.''

"Fragile.''

Guy eyed Armando narrowly. "Drab.''

"Tasteful,'' Armando pronounced whilst cracking his crystal goblet down on a marquetry table.

"Shrill,'' Guy said.

Armando uncrossed his legs. "Emotional.''

"Shrewish.''

"Quick-witted.''

Guy hid a smile. "This is fascinating. I do believe we shall continue this particular discussion later.'' Could it be that Armando de Silva, granite-hearted buccaneer, untouchable by any mere woman, had—unaccountably—fallen under the spell of a colorless, scrawny, drab, shrill shrew of a female who, by her own admission, was nothing more than a servant? "We have a simple mission and the sooner it is dispatched, the better.''

Armando rose and stalked to regard the fire. "The messenger should be well on his way to London by now. Miss Merryfield's father will shortly know that his treasured daughter is safe. Even though she does not say as much, he will expect his obedient offspring to return in time for the wedding.''

"Indeed.'' Guy smiled at his next thought. "And at the appropriate moment, when Willsly stands before the altar and Mr. Merryfield continues to pray that his daughter's good sense will return in time for the marriage to proceed—the second letter will be delivered. *Forgive me,*

Willsly, Miss Merryfield will implore in her missive. *With your welfare in mind, I have done the only honorable thing. I have cried off on our wedding day.* Guy laughed aloud. "Our Miss Merryfield does have admirable taste. She positively *hates* Willsly."

"I should like to learn more of the reasons for her hatred."

Guy considered. "So would I."

"She does have remarkably fine eyes."

"Remarkably." Fine gold; amber.

"A sweet mouth, also."

"Sweet." Full and soft.

"She is small, but most femininely shaped."

"Small." Slender. Womanly. Quick of movement, with delicate hands.

"Twenty-two, yet undoubtedly an innocent."

"Undoubtedly." There was a certain charm to the girl, an allure, even. Dammit, he was becoming fanciful. He'd been too long away from England's feminine delights. When this business was safely accomplished, he'd reestablish an acquaintance with a married lady who had made it clear that his return would be more than welcome.

Raised voices sounded in the corridor outside the library and the door slammed open. "Really, Mr. Falcon," Miss Abbott-Smyth said, marching past Guy's old butler, Crivens. "This man insists upon behaving as if you were lord of the manor. We are not to disturb his *lordship*. I do believe he needs a physician skilled in delusions and such."

Guy set his teeth. Crivens must be warned not to repeat his mistake.

"Sibyl, I cannot think what has come over you." Miss Merryfield sidestepped her friend and entered the room. She approached Guy directly. "Sibyl is not herself. Usually she is most meek but these are not usual times. *I* think your servants are dear. They are obviously devoted to you and trying to soften the terrible reality of your reduced circumstances."

Guy crossed his arms and looked down into her upturned face. "Is that so?" A sweet mouth indeed. How would such an untouched mouth feel beneath his own? How would her small hands feel twined in his hair—her soft little body pressed against his own hard need, a need that had unaccountably shown damnably poor timing.

He cared nothing for the feel of the woman. He would never know anything more of her than he did now—would never want to.

"This was once a lovely house," she said.

Guy found himself unable to look away from that soft mouth. "Was once?"

"Oh, you do not have to pretend with me, Mr. Falcon."

"My name is Guy." For an instant he was uncertain it had been his own voice that spoke. Recovering quickly, he added, "Since we are, so to speak, fellow conspirators, it would seem appropriate to be less formal."

She considered only a moment. "And our time together will be so very brief. I agree. I shall call you Guy and you must call me Beatrice." Her nose, when she wrinkled it, was really quite delightful. "Not a name I have ever cared for. Fit for an old maid, though, which is what I am bound to become."

"I doubt that," Guy said, meaning every word. "And I find Beatrice a distinguished name perfectly suited to a woman of character." Whispered in heated darkness, the name would become a sultry caress.

Beatrice turned away, but not before he saw a pink blush slip over her cheeks. "Sibyl and I wished to make certain my letters have been sent. And that our trunk will be picked up from the inn where it was left."

"The messenger is already on his way to London," Armando said, watching Miss Abbott-Smyth intently. "Everything will go exactly as planned."

"I see." Beatrice pressed her hands to her face. "Poor Papa. If only . . . Well, poor Papa. I love him so and I do regret causing him pain."

Miss Abbott-Smyth moved to her mistress's side. "He would *not* listen to us, Beatrice," she said, concern etched in her fine features. "I have considered this rash move you have made and consider it not at all rash anymore."

"That sounds silly," Beatrice said. "My rash move is not rash. What do you mean, Sibyl?"

"Yes," Guy said, studying Beatrice's smoothly coiled hair. "What exactly do you mean, Miss Abbott-Smyth?" Without her bonnet, the Merryfield girl's tresses were revealed as thick and shining, deep chestnut with glints of red rather than merely *brown*.

"You may call me Sibyl if you wish," Miss Abbott-Smyth announced, raising her chin. "And my meaning is that I have changed my mind. Given the extraordinary circumstances, Beatrice took the only course open to her. She threw herself into fate's arms." Round blue eyes flashed.

"Magnifico," Armando murmured.

Good lord. Guy shook his head slightly.

"Now," Beatrice said, patting her skirts. "To the matter of compensation. My mother's inheritance from her aunt came to me when she died and—"

"Miss Merryfield," Guy interrupted swiftly, not quite managing to avoid Armando's quizzical stare. "Beatrice, that is. Are your rooms satisfactory?"

"Quite. The amount—"

"Have you been into the gardens yet?"

"No. We are barely arrived. Money—"

"Are you fond of fine gardens, Sibyl?"

Blue eyes took on an immediate and enthusiastic sparkle. "Oh, yes. Most fond. It is the gardens that I most miss when in London."

Fortune was on his side! "How did I know as much, I wonder?" He felt an unaccountable need to be alone with Beatrice, to discuss the business that was entirely between the two of them in private. "Armando. Beatrice and I need not bore you with the details of our agreement. Would you perhaps care to show Sibyl the gardens?"

Instantly, Armando surged forward. "My pleasure."

"But . . ." Sibyl's newfound determination faltered visibly. "Chaperon," she said faintly.

"Of course," Guy said heartily. "Armando will ask one of the servants to oblige."

Armando gallantly ushered Sibyl, speechless, from the room. Guy waited until the door closed before turning his complete attention upon Beatrice.

Color mounted her neck. "We are alone."

"Indeed." Guy looked around and affected sudden comprehension. "Oh . . . *We* are alone. Forgive me, please. This has been such a peculiar day. But—under the circumstances—we really need not adhere too closely to the constraints of propriety. After all, we have agreed that we are taking extraordinary measures and this changes our situation. Don't you agree?"

She frowned, then squared her shoulders. "I agree. You and I are, mm, *partners*. Partners in a business arrangement. Therefore there is no need to be concerned with, mm, *personal* matters."

"Quite," Guy agreed.

Her words expressed the situation perfectly. Her eyes expressed something different, something that hinted of wariness. Dark pupils grew huge before she turned abruptly away.

He had no experience with women of her type, women who made no attempt at coquetry, at pretty manners or appropriately meaningless conversation.

The silence grew uncomfortable. "Will you answer one or two questions for a curious man?" Guy asked, grateful for a small inspiration.

"If I can." A faint, fiery nimbus formed about her hair.

"You were utterly assured you would find someone to fulfill your needs today? Someone willing to . . . *run away* with you?"

"My need was so desperate I could only believe my prayer would be answered."

"And anyone who came conveniently near would do?"

"No!" She pivoted sharply. "No, no. *You* were the one. You were always the one."

She looked so—so earnest. "How could you know I was the one? How can you know?. . . Ah, of course, I'd forgotten your unearthly powers."

"My *insightful* powers. I just—" for an instant she pressed her lips together "—it doesn't matter."

Such a curious little female. Embroidered trim passed from her shoulders to form a heart shape at her waist, her very, very small waist. He knew she watched him, yet he could not resist studying her longer. A demure white chemisette showed at the open front of the brown silk bodice and, despite the required rigid construction of the gown, Guy saw the rapid and enticing rise and fall of round breasts.

A jolt in his body's most unruly region stiffened his spine and sent him to sit in the nearest chair. He was starved for certain outlets necessary to the healthy male, but he must distract himself at present. "Why don't you want to marry Willsly?"

Beatrice spread her hands and seconds passed before she said, "My, mm, my father wants to make up to me for what he feels I lost."

"I don't understand."

"My mother was of noble birth. The youngest daughter of an earl. When she married my father she was disinherited. Papa simply wants to buy—I mean, he wants to give me what he thinks he took from my mother."

"He did in a way."

"No. She loved him. She would not have changed what she did and I am perfectly happy as the daughter of a man who has made his success with his hands and with his very good mind." She took a deep breath. "I am very proud of my father."

Guy felt an unfamiliar turn in his belly. "Admirable." *She* was admirable, he grudgingly decided. "But you haven't answered my question."

"Papa must be very worried. And—and when the time

comes for the wedding he will be distraught. Oh, dear,
I do wish I didn't have to hurt him.''

"And," he said softly, insistently. "Why *do* you have
to hurt him?"

"Lord Willsly is an animal," Beatrice said in barely
more than a whisper.

Guy moved to the edge of his chair. She was only feet
from him. "Why is he an animal? What makes him so?"

"He . . . He cares nothing for my feelings in this matter
of marriage. He told me so. I am to be grateful for
marriage to a man such as he. I should swoon at the
thought of being . . . of . . . Oh, dear." Closing her eyes,
she buried her hands in the folds of her skirt.

Reaching, Guy caught her wrists and pulled her to
stand before him. "Tell me, Beatrice. It will help to tell
someone. Does Sibyl know everything?"

"No." Her eyes remained tightly closed but she did
not pull away from him. "I could not say those things
to her. She is too gentle, too good."

He allowed seconds to pass before he said, "Tell me."

"Victor . . . He told me the sooner we dispensed with
. . . with . . ."

"With?"

Scarlet stained her redhead's pale skin. "With the,
mm, *necessary*. He meant the . . . The *Necessary* between a man and a woman in marriage." Her eyes flew
open. "He *kissed* me! There. I have told you."

Guy struggled to suppress a smile. "A kiss? And that
was the *necessary* between a man and woman? Was that
so very terrible?"

"You do not understand." Twisting, she tried in vain
to free her wrists. "My mouth . . . bled," she finished,
the final word almost swallowed.

For an instant Guy could think of no response. He
replaced his firm grip on her wrists with gentle rubbing.
"Was that your first kiss?" Somehow he wanted to
know.

Not looking at him, Beatrice nodded. "And my last.
That and the other *necessary* things he wished to do are

absolutely out of the question.'' Her chin went up.

"Will you tell me about the other things?'' Guy asked.
She was brave, different, and he now had another reason
to punish Willsly.

Beatrice blinked rapidly. "I am not sure what the other
things are, but since he . . . since he did begin doing them,
I *am* sure I should not like them.''

This time Guy could not bring himself to push her
further. He let her go.

"Lord Willsly touched me.'' The words were clearly
spoken. Her hand stole toward her throat. "*Touched*
me,'' she echoed in a whisper, unconsciously spreading
her fingers over the tops of her breasts. "Tore at my
dress. And laughed.''

"Beatrice—''

"He laughed.'' She flinched. "The sooner he taught
me my proper place, the better. That's what he said. And
I would come to like what he would teach me.''

"Beatrice—''

"I never could. I thought I should be a good wife, a
good mother, but that can never be.''

Rage rushed through Guy, pumped through his veins.
"Why? Why would your father allow this?''

Beatrice appeared stricken. "He never knew.''

"You should have told him. You say he loves you.
Surely he would never—''

"I tried. Papa thinks Willsly is a gentleman. Victor
has convinced him of it. A gentleman who holds me in
high regard. He has made Papa think I am simply shy
and maidenly reticent. Hah!'' Throwing wide her arms,
she came closer again. "At twenty-two I am a maiden
only in the . . . Oh! Oh, I cannot believe I am speaking
to you of all this.''

"Please do not upset yourself further.'' Humiliating
Willsly might not be enough after all.

Beatrice appeared puzzled. "I cannot understand it.
This is most unusual. I am always circumspect—almost
always—*always* about personal matters. Particularly . . .

You are a *gentleman*. I should not discuss personal matters with you.''

"I am deeply moved that you feel free to do so.'' The poor girl's senses were deeply troubled.

"You are a most unusual man.'' Her voice held amazement. "I do *trust* you.''

He could scarce make himself meet her glowing eyes. "You have been overwrought.'' Standing up, he touched her cheek and, when she smiled, stroked carefully to the point of her chin. "Your instincts are good. I am no threat to you, Beatrice.'' Not in any way she might consider obvious. She was so close he felt her soft warmth as surely as had he held her. *That* thought most certainly held potential danger for Beatrice Merryfield.

Smiling even more openly, she settled a hand on his arm. "Thank you. You really are the answer to my prayers. A truly good man.''

Guy found that smiling back cost him a great deal. He tightened the muscles in his thighs. Beatrice's smile did something marvelous to her face. Pretty. Open, honest, trusting, and so sweetly pretty. Cautiously, making no rapid movements, he brushed back a tendril of hair from her temple and cupped the side of her head.

"I heard Lord Willsly speak most disrespectfully about my father. To some of those unpleasant friends he brought to our house in Northumberland. He despises trade.''

Guy would not try to dissuade her from that notion. Her hair was like thick, smooth silk.

Jerkily, she caught her bottom lip in her teeth. Winding her hands together, she held them tightly at her waist. "Willsly thinks it *vulgar* to work. At least Papa will not now waste what he has made on such a man. My father could not possibly understand that everyone doesn't love me as he does. He thinks . . . To Papa I am beautiful. I suppose that is as it should be. But he has no notion of how others see me—as I really am.''

Guy captured her wringing hands once more. "How are you, Beatrice?''

"I am dull. I have no style."

"You sparkle and you have your own style. Your own special, individual style."

"You are a very kind man. A very good man."

He was an opportunist, a manipulator. "No one could be kinder or more good than you."

"No, no." Unthinkingly, she twined her fingers with his. "*You* will be my inspiration. *You* will be the one I strive to emulate in all things."

Guy's skin crawled. "Nonsense. You are already perfect." Certainly in comparison with him.

"Hush." Rising to her toes, she leaned against him, leaned her innocent, soft, and entirely ready-to-be-taken young flesh against his hard and oh, so willing to oblige body. "You, Guy Falcon are the rarest of creatures, an honest man. I shall always pray for you and hold you in the highest esteem."

Pray? Hold in high esteem?

He ached to hold her anywhere, anywhere as long as it was now.

"Honesty is the greatest gift one can give to another."

What was happening to him? Could abstinence cause this violent reaction to a woman who had, only hours ago, seemed so plain?

"You must never doubt your own goodness, Guy."

Would he not be doing a service if he showed her that not all men were animals? He would not harm her, only teach her the joys a man and woman could find together? Teach her just a little?

"Truth shines in your eyes. How wonderful."

Truth? He took a slow, calming breath. If she only knew that nothing she thought of him was true. "I am glad to be of some service to you. And I must ask you never to mention payment again. If you do you may offend me, and Armando subscribes to old honor codes that abhor payment for voluntary services—particularly to women."

Beatrice bowed her head, rested her brow on his chest. "I can scarcely believe this is happening," she said happily. "You are restoring my faith in men when I thought that could never happen."

He held very still.

"Thank you." Beatrice slipped her arms around him and hugged. "I have met what I did not think existed other than in my father—a man incapable of deceit. You would never use another for your own ends."

When she bobbed up to place a quick, chaste kiss on his cheek, he didn't move. Whirling away, she ran from the room, slamming the door behind her.

Guy touched the spot on his face where he still felt her lips. "Damn!" Spring must be the culprit, spring and deprivation of fleshly needs that rendered him susceptible even to a plain, graceless female.

". . . a man incapable of deceit. You would never use another for your own ends."

"Damn it to *hell*!"

3

"WE ought to be frightened." Standing in the middle of the pretty chamber Mr. Falcon's housekeeper had assigned to Beatrice, Sibyl tweaked a curl loose from her friend's severely dressed hair. "We are two women alone in a strange man's house, a strange man with a flamboyant friend . . . a handsome flamboyant friend who is very probably dangerous."

Beatrice crossed her arms. "But we aren't frightened, are we?"

"No." Sibyl ducked to see her own reflection in the

dressing table glass. "Armando . . . Mr. de Silva has been nothing other than deferential. Really, Bea, he is so charming and so witty and so—"

"I do believe you are smitten."

Sibyl gave an outraged snort, but a flush colored her cheeks and she avoided Beatrice's eyes. "That is ridiculous. It is you who are smitten. With Mr. Falcon."

"Me?" Beatrice tucked her small enameled watch into its pocket in her skirt. "I am a practical woman not given to girlish infatuations. And even if I were of a mind to be interested in a man, he would not be one about whom I know nothing."

"On the evening of our arrival—when I returned from walking in the garden with Armando—you seemed to know a great deal about Mr. Falcon."

"That was then and this is now. And you are calling Mr. de Silva by his first name."

"He asked me to." Sibyl, who had pounced upon their trunk as soon as it arrived, wore an alpaca walking dress striped palest green and white. "Why are you no longer singing Mr. Falcon's praises?"

"I do not wish to speak of this." Beatrice fiddled irritably with a silly bow of ribbon at the waist of her russet-colored gown. "And I merely said that Guy is a good man. Which he is. He is also a bad-tempered boor and the sooner we can safely go back home, the better."

"Tell me," Sibyl demanded. "Tell me what he did to make you so cross."

"I . . . Oh, very well. The night before last he was sweetness and generosity personified. I was moved to think him a kind and caring man."

"Yes?"

"If you had not been otherwise occupied yesterday, you would not have to ask these annoying questions. But you *were* otherwise occupied. *Flirting* with that Armando de Silva who, by the way, puts me in mind of a *pirate!*"

"A *pirate*? Oh, Bea, how could you be so mean? He is dashing, original, completely—"

"Yes, isn't he."

"Why are you angry?"

"I barely caught sight of Guy all day yesterday and when I did he appeared enraged and in a hurry to escape me at once."

"Ah." Sibyl pursed her lips. "Ah, yes, I think I have gauged the situation with you two quite accurately."

"Gauged the situation?" Beatrice tried to poke back the curl Sibyl had freed. "There is no situation to gauge. None at all."

"I think there is. I believe you like Guy Falcon more than a little. I think this may be what is called love at first sight," Sibyl finished with a satisfied flourish.

"Oh . . . Oh, you are a paperskull, Sibyl. And I do not wish to discuss this further. I'm hungry and I'm going down to breakfast." She was also confused and worried. Confused about Guy Falcon's strange behavior following their altogether satisfactory interview on the evening of her arrival, and worried at the thought of her poor, distressed father on the morning of what should have been her wedding day.

With Sibyl trotting behind, Beatrice left the blue chamber and wound her way down an elegantly curving staircase to the flagstoned hall. Guy's relatives—at least she assumed them to be so—stared dourly down from dark oil paintings. Bejeweled fingers and rich attire suggested the Falcons had once been plump in the pocket.

In the doorway to the little parlor where meals were served she stopped, surprised to see Guy sitting at the head of the table reading a newspaper.

A small poke in her back sent her into the room. "Good morning, Guy," she said, casting a glare over her shoulder at Sibyl. "I trust we are in a kindlier mood today?"

The paper rustled.

The man made no reply.

"Good morning, Guy," Sibyl carolled. "And it *is* a delightful morning, is it not?"

The paper was slowly moved to one side and dark green eyes stared coldly at Sibyl, then at Beatrice. "Good morning. I had not noticed that it was a particularly enchanting day.''

With an increasing heaviness in the region of her heart, Beatrice helped herself to a slice of toast from the sideboard and carried it to the table.

"Where is Armando?" Sibyl asked, still sounding irritatingly cheerful.

"London," came the response, from behind the newspaper this time.

"London?" Sibyl raised her light brows at Beatrice. "He did not say he had business to attend to today."

Slowly, the paper was closed and folded. Guy addressed Beatrice. "In case you have forgotten, today is supposed to be your wedding day. As soon as Willsly is safely dispatched from the scene, Armando will report back and you will be returned to your father's loving arms."

Beatrice looked at her lap. Blackness gathered in her head and in her breast.

"You do not appear overjoyed," Guy said softly. "What is this? A change of heart? I fear it is too late for me to rush you to the church. By now Willsly has been made the complete fool and has, no doubt, denounced you as a fallen woman."

Beatrice sighed.

Sibyl gave a small moan.

"The time to change matters is past," Guy said. He set down the paper.

"I have not changed my mind. It is only that I wish I had not had to hurt Papa. If only he'd listened—"

"But he didn't listen. No matter. You have said how he loves you. In time all this will be forgiven and forgotten."

"Yes." Forgiveness was possible, but she doubted that either she or her father would ever forget this embarrassment.

Guy's chair scratched the worn silk carpet and he stood up. "Come," he said to Beatrice. "A little air may cheer you." Not smiling, not bothering to address Sibyl, he opened the French doors and walked onto the gray stone terrace that ran along the back of the house.

"Go," Sibyl whispered when Beatrice didn't move. "It will do you good."

Beatrice shook her head.

"*Yes.* I think there is something of importance he wishes to speak of. *Go.*"

Beatrice hesitated, but only for a moment longer before following Guy outside.

He stood at the top of a flight of steps leading down to a rose garden. "Come here," he said without looking at her.

Beatrice advanced slowly.

Guy looked over his shoulder. "You have nothing to fear from me. I do not bite inoffensive little innocents."

Stung by his words, she hunched her shoulders and drew closer. She raised her face to meet his solemn stare.

"Why are you not laughing, Beatrice? Why are you not singing and dancing and proclaiming your relief to the summer skies? You are *free*, or you soon will be. By this afternoon you can depart for home without fear of encountering Lord Willsly's unwanted attentions."

She nodded and blinked. Unaccountably, her eyes stung.

"What is it?" Guy faced her, his feet braced apart. "Why are your eyes filled with tears?"

The blackness within Beatrice swelled, it swelled until her chest felt about to explode. A small cry escaped her throat and she fled past him. Down the steps she ran, over damp grass that wetted her slippers, between unpruned roses that snagged at her clothes.

He caught her as she flew through a gap between hedges into an enclosed courtyard with an oval pool at its center. Guy reached for her elbow but Beatrice evaded him and tried to dash on. His second attempt to hold her was successful. With one strong hand he almost lifted her from her feet.

"Let me go," she said urgently. Another second and she was swung against his chest. "*Please* let me go."

"I think not." He tilted up her chin. "You do not resemble a woman whose prayers have been answered."

Beatrice looked at his snowy shirtfront. "You could not possibly understand what I am feeling."

"I could try."

He wore no coat. His chest was extremely wide, his waist narrow, and his hips leanly muscled in trousers that fitted too well. "Beatrice," he insisted. "These question games grow vexing."

"All right." She looked at him defiantly and was horrified to see him through a wavering film of tears. "All right. Today was to have been my wedding day and my father—as we speak—is a wretched and worried man. I cannot bear to see another hurt, particularly my father."

Guy's grip on her elbow became gentle. Lightly, he spread his fingers over her cheek and used his thumb to wipe away a tear. "Of course. How could I not expect you to be considering your father. But I feel there is something else that disquiets you."

Beatrice swallowed with difficulty and managed a watery smile. "I am all at sea but I must be truthful—especially with you." Breath rasped in her throat. "I cannot seem to forget that I will never have a wedding day. Not a real one. Oh, I didn't want what was offered by Lord Willsly, not under any circumstances, but still I am sad."

"Hush."

When he cradled her in his arms she closed her eyes and allowed herself to be rocked. For all his moodiness, Guy Falcon was an unusual man, a man capable of great tenderness and understanding.

"You will have a wedding day, little bird. Gentle, pretty little bird. Only be patient and a worthy man will ask for your hand."

"Never," she murmured. Jumbled sensations and images hovered in her mind but they made no sense. She longed . . . She was mad. It was *this* man she longed for—Guy Falcon—generous stranger who must yearn only to be free of the outrageous demands he had uncomplainingly fulfilled.

"Please smile and believe that I know what I tell you."

"The right man will never want me." There was no danger that he would guess her meaning.

Guy raised her chin and smiled down. "I assure you that the right man will fight lions and tigers to secure your love. The right man will look into your golden cat's eyes and challenge any obstacle to claiming you."

Beatrice could not speak. His arms crossed around her shoulders and through her gown his chafing hands warmed her skin. She locked her knees, willing herself not to tremble. He was trying to reassure her, nothing more. He would laugh if he guessed that, even now, she felt herself almost helplessly in love with him.

While she watched, his smile faded and his thumb moved to her bottom lip—so did his gaze. "Soon you will be gone . . . Soon . . ." He placed the lightest of kisses near the corner of her mouth, released her, and stepped back. "You do not think it today, but you *will* be happy, Beatrice. Believe me."

"Thank you for that."

Guy cocked a brow. "What exactly are you thanking me for?"

"For being generous enough to try to revive my spirits." She managed a smile. "Your efforts worked. I agree. Everything will be fine." Nothing would ever be fine again, not after she said good-bye to him for the last time.

Guy glanced past her and frowned. "Armando? How . . . I did not expect you for hours."

Armando strode toward them, resplendent today in a dark green velvet coat. He gave Beatrice a sharp nod and told Guy, "We must speak alone."

Alarm dampened Beatrice's palms.

"Alone," Armando repeated with a meaningful inclination of the head in Beatrice's direction.

"This concerns me," she said, standing firm. "I intend to hear what you have to say."

"Guy—"

"She will learn your news. As well now as later."

Armando regarded Guy then shrugged. "As you say. I fear we underestimated Willsly."

In the silence that followed, Beatrice heard the rapid beat of her own heart.

"The blaggard has generously allowed himself to be *persuaded* by Beatrice's father to make allowances for her gentle nature."

Guy narrowed his eyes. "Continue, man. Finish this."

"It is far from finished, *amigo*. I hid near the coach and heard every word that passed between Mr. Merryfield and Willsly after they left the church. They insist that there is no question of the girl's reputation being sullied. She has *fled*, they assure each other, *fled* because she is so shy and innocent. She is to be given every chance to repent for her foolishness."

Beatrice covered her face. "No!"

"Damn the man's eyes," Guy muttered.

"Indeed," Armando said grimly. "Damn his eyes, but his vision is quite clear. He sees that he needs Beatrice, no matter the whispers he may endure about her character or the sneers directed at him for her betrayal."

Her fragile composure shattered. "What do you mean?"

Armando turned up his palms. "I mean that our plan has failed. At this moment your distressed fiancé awaits your return. He has declared his boundless love for you and is dedicated to helping you become his good and dutiful wife!"

4

"*Dios mío!*" Armando threw back his head and stared unseeingly at the vaulted ceiling above Aldersgate's entrance hall. The morning had been a long hell—a long hell of arguing with a man who appeared deaf.

There were times when Armando de Silva, Spanish adventurer, failed to understand the nature of his reserved English friend. Had good, hot Spanish blood run in the veins of Guy, Lord Rockford, there would be no need for the charade they all seemed doomed to play out.

Striving for patience, Armando breathed deeply and frowned. *Music*. Somewhere in this house a sane soul had turned to a civilized means of putting aside turmoil. He followed the sound of a harpsichord, softly played, to the slightly open door of the music room.

Seated with her back to him, Sibyl Abbott-Smyth stroked forth the sure and subtle notes of a piece he didn't recognize. A surprising girl. A girl with great strength beneath her cool exterior. Strength and . . . *passion*, perhaps?

He entered the room quietly. For now he must do no more than watch and wait in the matter of the fair-haired Sibyl. His efforts must be wholly centered on his foolish friend's blindness to his own feelings and to those of another—and if all was not to be lost to stony denial, his friend's eyes must be most carefully opened to the truth.

Armando shook his head. "*Los Ingleses!*" These cold people could drive a man mad!

Fingers crashing on harpsichord keys ruined any remains of early afternoon peace. Sibyl leaped to her feet.

"Ah, but I am sorry, *Señorita*." Armando strode forward to take her hands. "Forgive my outburst, but I am a man besieged."

"Indeed." Her delicate face radiated concern. "I'm sure you are as concerned as I am about what has happened."

He nodded gravely. "Concerned and convinced that for the good of my dear friend, I must contrive to influence his decisions in the matter of Miss Beatrice's future."

"I could not agree more." She gripped his fingers tightly. "Surely we can help. Surely we do not have to allow them to lose an opportunity for bliss . . . Oh!" She drew back and looked away. "It is not at all like me to be so forward with my opinions."

No, he was sure Miss Sibyl Abbott-Smyth, daughter of an impoverished country squire, was accustomed only to following instructions. That was how she found herself companion to Beatrice. Her family must have considered the position a perfect solution to disposing of a daughter to whom they could offer no dowry, no prospects of an advantageous marriage.

"You and I have talked a great deal in the past two days. I would like to believe we have passed beyond reticence in the area of honesty."

Her smile lightened her lovely eyes. "Thank you."

"Do you know what Guy and Beatrice propose?"

"Not exactly. But I fear I can guess. Beatrice is beside herself with worry for her father. I'm afraid that for his sake she may decide to return and suffer marriage to Victor the Beast."

Armando made no attempt to stop his smile. "A most apt title," he said. This next must be carefully worded. "Do you think there is any possibility . . . No, I'm sure not. No, absolutely not."

"*Please*. Possibility of what?"

He stared at her with deep concentration, pushed back his coat to plant his fists on his hips, and shifted his concentration to his boots. "It is a wild notion."

"We *need* a wild notion or all will be lost."

"Hmm."

"Really, Armando—an *outrageous* notion even."

She had fire, this perfect creature. "Guy is prepared to return Beatrice to Willsly if she so wishes," he said and hurriedly added, "I mean that he will make no effort to dissuade her since she will go to ease her father's distress." And Guy had already begun casting about for an alternate means of punishing Willsly.

"If Beatrice marries that man she and her father will never have *other* than distress."

Armando raised his face and looked down upon Sibyl. "I am going to ask you a question which I should definitely not ask of so sensitive a young lady. Forgive me. And forget the question if it is too upsetting."

"Ask." She leaned anxiously toward him.

Armando cleared his throat. "Do you think it possible that Beatrice . . . I must be direct. Have you noted any sign that Beatrice is . . . Guy is a fine man, an attractive man to women, I suppose, and I wondered . . ."

"If Beatrice was at all drawn to him? Oh, yes, *yes*. And if there were some way to make her admit . . . Do you think . . . Is it possible that Guy . . ."

"*Yes*." He must waste no more time on niceties. "Absolutely. He will fight admitting the truth, but I know he finds Beatrice very appealing. Sibyl, when I came in here I had no idea what to do next. You are a miracle. Now I think that together we can, shall we say 'help' this situation?"

"If you think that is possible."

"I do, indeed. Yes indeed. Let us make plans."

The plan was outrageous, preposterous.

The plan had incredible merit—in the matter of the two most important current issues in Guy's life. He threw down his pen. How in God's name had the second issue insinuated itself—*herself*—into his plans?

He didn't even know if she had a warm drop of blood in her cool, straight-backed body. He had not the slightest idea what would happen if he tried to kiss her. He could not begin to imagine what would happen if he attempted to make love to her.

And why in the name of all that was sane and logical should there be any reason to assume Beatrice Merryfield would not run screaming from him if he tried to as much as *touch* her?

"Please may I come in?"

Guy's elbow slid off his desk. Only Beatrice's head showed around his study door. "Come in or go out," he snapped. Damn, but he sounded like a starving bear.

When her head disappeared, he got up and hurried to throw open the door. With one large, strong hand he caught Beatrice—in the act of fleeing—and hauled her none too gently into the room.

He closed the door and turned the key in the lock.

"Oh . . . I mean, what can be the matter with you, Guy?"

"What?" He laughed without mirth and advanced upon her. "*You.* You are what is the matter with me. Ever since I brought you into my home nothing has proceeded as it did before and I don't know what to do about it!"

"Yes. Well." He saw her swallow. She stepped backward and he followed and when she retreated farther, he followed again until her back collided with his desk. "I realize I have presented you with a quite dreadful dilemma, but I believe I know exactly what should be done to solve the problem."

Guy pressed his lips together, gripped her waist, and hoisted her to sit on the desk.

"Oh!" Her golden cat's eyes held alarm.

"Is that the best you can do? 'Oh'?"

"Oh, I—"

She never finished her sentence.

He covered her mouth with his own, not harshly, not with the bruising force the foul Willsly had used, but with gentle, drawing insistence. Holding her waist firmly, making no more sudden moves, Guy kissed Beatrice softly, sensuously, with closed lips.

And he waited. Waited until he felt the subtle, languorous arching of her body toward him—until her hands hovered at his elbows before stealing upward to sink into the hair that touched his collar.

Then he parted his lips, parted hers—dragged his tongue over the moist, sensitive flesh along her bottom lip—and heard the sigh of her escaping breath.

He opened his eyes.

Beatrice's were closed.

His body was already pulsing, his manhood heavy. This was no duty, no whim—he did want this woman.

A half-sob escaped her throat and she strained to be closer. Still he was careful, slow. When her lips parted wider, Guy tested her readiness for his tongue and smiled with his heart when she shuddered with what he knew to be pleasure.

She wanted to be nearer to him. He wanted her nearer. Carefully parting her legs, he slipped up her voluminous skirts and petticoats until he could stand, cradled into her hips.

Beatrice stiffened and he stopped, his hands cupping her rounded bottom through thin lawn drawers.

Once more he looked at her face. This time her eyes were open, and wondering. She smiled and touched his cheek, his mouth, and whispered, "Thank you. I did not know a kiss could be so."

It was as if she had not noticed where he stood or how he held her.

"It can be so much more," he said and kissed her again.

Beatrice met his tongue with her own. She spread her fingers over his face, ran them to his chest, and silently begged him for more of what she could know so little about.

"Yes," he murmured against her cheek. "Yes, yes, yes." He pressed hard little kisses along her jaw until he could nip the lobe of her ear.

His body no longer wanted to listen to his mind. Guy squeezed his eyes tightly shut, prayed for enough finesse, and went about the tedious task of parting the bodice of her gown.

She only pressed herself more urgently to him.

Damn the stays. So young and firm a body needed no such foolishness.

Aah. Her breasts, round, firm and upthrust, were bared. Holding his breath, he covered and fondled them, used his thumbs to tease the nipples until Beatrice gave a bemused, excited wail and let her head fall back.

"Yes!" His heart thundered. Displayed for his pleasure, she was all he could hope for—no, much more than he had hoped for. Even as some shred of caution flared in his darkening brain, Guy scooped a white breast into his hand and sucked the nipple deeply.

No cry of fear or outrage ripped the air.

Beatrice panted. She panted and rocked—and he read her wordless plea for more of what he had to give her.

She was ripe—just as he had dared to dream she might be. When he found the hot, wet place where her release waited he heard his own strangled groan. He could not give in to his own needs and desires—not yet—perhaps never.

"Guy," she moaned. "Oh, Guy, I don't . . ."

"Yes, you do," he told her, tightening his belly, fighting for control. "You *will*. Let me give you this, Beatrice."

The choice was no longer hers. Barely did he touch her, work the stiffened little nub at her very center, before she cried out. Her eyes opened wide, and her lips drew back. "Guy!"

Her climax rippled in waves through muscle and nerve. "Yes, little one. Yes. Let go. Let me hold you." Almost before he finished speaking, Beatrice slumped against his chest and he gritted his teeth. What he wanted would have to wait. There would be many steps to take before he could truly take her.

Slowly, her breathing calmed. Guy stroked her hair, her neck, rested the backs of his fingers on the sweet, naked swell of her breast. This was a deeply, naturally passionate creature.

"Oh, my goodness."

He stood very still.

"I cannot believe it."

"I think you already do," he assured her.

"That is how it can be, isn't it?" She lifted her face to his and her beautiful eyes glowed. "The *Necessary*. It can—*transport* one."

Guy swallowed. "Yes, it can." It could most certainly transport him from the miserable condition he presently endured.

"And you were showing me that The *Necessary* can be quite . . . exhilarating. You are trying to take away some of my doubts about marrying Victor. How wonderful you are."

Wonderful? "You are wonderful, Beatrice," he said with complete honesty.

"No. I am merely a great nuisance to you. I have put you to great inconvenience."

Guy could only blink. If she but knew the particular form this "inconvenience" took and how simple it would be to alleviate the condition.

She started and glanced down. "Oh, dear. Oh, my. Oh, what must you think of me for being such a helpless simpleton." Fumbling, she tried to rearrange her clothing.

"Allow me." He helped her to stand before him once more and set about the pleasurable, the excruciatingly tantalizing task of covering her breasts. "There. It is done. Now we need to talk."

"I agree." A brilliant flush painted her face and neck. "I should be embarrassed. I *am* embarrassed. But I am also entirely—well, I must admit that I cannot find words to describe how much . . . The *Necessary* can be truly marvelous with someone who does it well. There, I've said it.''

And Guy found himself at a loss for any words at all. She was amazing.

"I quite understand," she told him. "You don't have to say anything more. Allow me to speak, please. You tried to help me prepare myself for marriage to Victor by demonstrating . . . You know what I mean.''

"Yes," he agreed. "I do know.''

"Unfortunately, Victor is not you. He is not, in any way, *like* you. He is a beast and I cannot bear to think of him touching me.''

"No. Nor I. That is why—''

"Sibyl and I have discussed this.''

He stared. "You have?''

"Indeed. And we have worked out the only possible answer to my dilemma. To *our* dilemma, if you will. I think you may agree to go through with my plan. Sibyl thinks so, too.''

"She does?'' In the name of heaven, what *could* Beatrice be talking about? "There is something I wish to—''

"Please, Guy. Let me finish before I lose my nerve. I have to stop thinking about myself and concentrate on saving my father from Willsly.''

"Yes.''

"If I don't, that man will very soon find ways to divest Papa of all he has worked to accumulate. I will not allow it.''

"No.''

She paced back and forth in front of him. "I do think it possible that you may agree to help me.'' Her hair had begun to work loose of its bonds and heavy, dark auburn curls fell about her shoulders. "I believe we could make a harmonious success of it—within the bounds of what is acceptable to you, of course.''

"Beatrice, Armando . . . That is, I had an idea this afternoon.''

"Soon. Your turn will come after mine.'' Warm, trembling fingers came to rest on his mouth. "You have suffered a financial, mm, *reversal*. This is not a matter of dishonor. Merely a fact and one that must be dealt with. You deserve to have this burden removed."

"You are too kind." And too confusing.

"An impoverished man is hardly in a position to court a female with a fortune. Not in the ordinary way in which he might choose to do so."

Guy flexed his shoulders. "Beatrice, there is something I wish to say to you—to ask you." This talk of poverty became very wearing.

"No, I will not hear any more of your selfless protests. Listen to me. Of course, I would not expect you to be a husband in more than name only. Although, naturally, I understand that every man wants sons and I would willingly do my duty by you."

He shook his head.

Beatrice wound her hands together and bit her lip. "I understand that often married men choose to find, mm, *diversion* with someone else, someone they can *feel* for. This would also be acceptable. But, to save my father from Willsly and to save you from penury, could we not marry? . . . *Please?*"

The mantel clock ticked, and ticked—and ticked.

"At first Papa would be furious, but he does love me so and in time I should be forgiven. And he would come to love you, too, and then you would have all the money you need." She rose to her toes and jiggled. "And then there is the matter of my own resources, which came from my dead mother's—"

"Aunt," he finished for her darkly.

"Mm. Aunt Lavinia. I never met her. Anyway, there is that money which will keep us very nicely until Papa forgives us. So it could all work out so beautifully, don't you see?"

Guy pressed a fist to his mouth. The other fist he crammed into a pocket before walking past Beatrice and heading for the door where he paused to free the lock.

"Guy, are you disgusted by my suggestion? I would

not blame you. Only it could work so well. But, if you
are disgusted, please forget I asked such an outrageous
thing.''

"Will you be quiet?" He flung open the door. Before
marching away, he shouted, "Have you *no* sense of the
proper order of things, miss? It is *my* place to ask for
your hand, not the reverse, dammit.

"Yes, I will marry you!''

5

GUY did not like churches. They reminded him of
funerals. Not surprising since his last two visits to
this house of God had been following the deaths of first
his mother and then his father. This was the place where
he had finally looked ahead at a life devoid of blood
relatives.

"Your grin may soon cost you your life, Armando.''
He sent his beaming friend a malevolent sidelong glare.

"Think of Willsly," Armando said. "Think of him
at this very moment, virtually *living* with your bride's
father. Imagine his smug confidence as he anticipates her
repentant return at any moment. *Think* about him making
plans for the swift disposal of her dowry—for his own
purposes alone.''

Guy shifted from foot to foot and continued to watch
the tiny chapel's open doorway. "I had not planned to
be standing before an altar—awaiting my marriage—at
any time in the foreseeable future. If at all.'' Early morning sun streamed through the door, a dust-laden blade of

gold slashing wood and stone. "I can scarcely believe I am here," he muttered.

Armando sighed expansively. "Ah, yes. Well, it is said that only the best of men can readily accept drastic changes in their plans and learn to be at peace with them. It takes true greatness to recognize the positive where some degree of negative may exist."

"Who says these wise words?"

"Armando de Silva."

"It is not Armando de Silva who is about to lose his freedom."

"Perhaps I should be jealous."

Guy aimed a sharp glance at Armando. "You might like to be marrying Beatrice Merryfield?"

Armando shook his head impatiently. "Hardly."

The minister snuffled and clucked behind them.

"Have patience, Cuthbert," Guy said. "You'll be returned to your brandy bottle soon enough." The Reverend Cuthbert Phipps, vicar of St. Philomena's, Aldersgate's minute chapel, owed his living to Guy and did precious little to earn it.

"Not to worry, old fella," Cuthbert said. "My time is yours. Don't s'pose the little lady ain't comin' do you?"

That thought held a degree of appeal. "I haven't set eyes on the girl in two days," Guy said. "D'you suppose she *has* flown the coop?"

"It is a lady's prerogative to keep a gentleman waiting," Armando said, sounding uncharacteristically serious. "I have no doubt she and Sibyl have been doing their best to enjoy the preparations for this wedding day."

Guy's temper thinned. "Where the hell are they? This is farce and you know it. We shall be married in name only." He flexed the muscles in his jaw.

"Is that so, *amigo*?" Armando looked straight ahead. "If you do not make more than that of such an opportunity then you are more a fool than I could ever have thought possible."

Recollections of Beatrice looking up at him with glowing eyes did nothing to assist concentration on his goal. Confronting Willsly with proof that his salvation had slipped from reach; that must be the focus of this exercise. Anticipating the man's shock at seeing Guy, apparently risen from the dead and bent upon revenge; *that* was the joyful moment to anticipate.

The sound of light footsteps on gravel dried any further words in Guy's throat.

"Here they come," Armando whispered.

Guy made no reply.

It was Sibyl who entered first. With measured pace she approached, a bouquet of palest pink roses in her hands. She wore a simple pink tarlatan dress with long, tight sleeves. In the sunlight, her blonde ringlets shone silver.

"*Solo mio*," Armando said reverently.

This was no time to consider another man's apparent infatuation.

Beatrice took a step into the church and Guy, unaccountably, found he could scarcely breathe. Guilt began its assault. He could have asked how she intended to prepare for the ceremony. He could at least have arranged a gown, flowers—made some attempt at a wedding breakfast.

She moved forward through the light and her hair turned to fire, fire ringed by a garland of cream rosebuds. Yards of daffodil yellow muslin shifted gracefully about her legs. As she drew closer Guy saw how cleverly more rosebuds had been tucked into the neckline of a pleated bodice and fashioned to form a sash that circled her tiny waist and swung free to the hem of the gown. Empty, her fingers were laced together before her.

Guy barely noted that a number of his servants filed in to sit quietly in the back pews. He had made no mention of their being welcome to attend.

"Your fair Beatrice has already made friends with your staff," Armando said, as if reading Guy's thoughts.

"She will come to need their company," he responded grimly, whilst pushing aside the question that came again and again: Why had he found it necessary to test the physical delights his bride might hold when she was to mean nothing to him?

"Guy?"

He heard her light, troubled voice and looked her fully in the face for the first time since he'd left her in his study two days since. Her mouth trembled and she pressed her lips together. There was no hint of color in her pale face and her eyes were huge and oddly dark.

"Come." He smiled and found it a simple task. "You are beautiful." And she was.

Finally she stood beside him before the minister. Guy looked down upon her and saw a glistening film on her eyes. He took her hand and held it, not formally but fully, strongly clasped in his. Neither of them had chosen this but he . . . he *liked* her, dammit. A man could do worse in a marital bargain where the bride had been a necessity rather than a choice.

Her fingers stiffened, gripped tightly, and she turned her face up to his. She shook steadily until he feared she might collapse.

Phipps began to drone the required words and Guy responded, heard Beatrice's breathless acceptance of him, and felt the church and the people within recede.

All receded but Beatrice. She sought something in him. Her eyes never left his and she told him in words he could not hear that she was afraid, and something else . . . what else did she say with her heart and soul?

Guy leaned down. "What is it?" he whispered, close to her ear. "Tell me, Beatrice."

". . . man and wife!" Cuthburt Phipps accomplished a resounding ring quite unlike his usual phlegmatic tones and polite applause erupted among the servants.

Beatrice gave Guy one last pleading look before turning into Sibyl's hug.

What in God's name was she asking him? She *was* asking him something. *Women*. He would never understand them and it didn't matter anyway. A day or two and he would confront Willsly with the horrified disappointment that would crush the man. Then would be soon enough to consider how the future with Beatrice should be handled.

"You may kiss the bride," Cuthburt announced, clearly oblivious that this was no ordinary love match.

Immediately, Beatrice turned back to Guy and that damnable plea was in her eyes again.

He looked from her face to smooth, white shoulders, to the rapid rise of pale breasts above the yellow gown's low neckline. How those breasts had filled his hands. How the nipples had sweetened his tongue and sent heavy heat ripping into his groin. And now she was his wife. There was no reason not to fully enjoy the woman who was his.

No reason but an exploding self-hatred for using an innocent; a truthful, caring innocent.

"*Kiss* her," Armando urged.

Obediently, he bent and brought his mouth to hers, intending the briefest brush—enough simply to satisfy onlookers.

The parting of her lips undid him. Softly, she opened herself to him, rested her hands on his chest in gentle trust, and offered him what he could not accept—the promise of an honest union.

But he kissed her deeply, falling into her until the sound of laughter tickled the edges of his concentration and he reluctantly pulled away.

"Thank you," Beatrice said, for his ears alone. "I will try to be whatever you need me to be."

"Let us return to the house," Armando bellowed. He had placed Sibyl's hand on his arm. "This is a celebration. Celebrations make a man hungry."

He was hungry, Guy thought, turning to walk woodenly down the aisle with Beatrice at his side. He was hungry, but not for food. Every nerve shivered like a raw thing and his "bride" was the cause. And she had thanked him!

Crivens and Mrs. Wiffen, Guy's housekeeper, were hurrying the rest of the servants from the chapel. By the time he walked into the fresh air, the two carriages they had evidently used to make the short drive were already departing in the direction of Aldersgate.

Two more carriages remained. Armando promptly escorted Sibyl to one and they drove away, leaving Guy to take his leave of Cuthburt Phipps and take Beatrice home. *Home*. The falseness of what he had done almost overwhelmed him.

Guy willed himself to focus on the night that had almost been his last.

"My friends hope you'll join us for dinner aboard the El Fuego del Mar," Willsly had said and smiled like the generous friend he pretended to be. *"I promise you a singular experience."*

And a singular experience that event had proved to be.

Guy helped Beatrice into the remaining carriage and got in behind her. "Home!" he called, rapping the trap.

Seated opposite Beatrice, he avoided looking at her, concentrating instead on watching the small jewel of an estate that had been his father's favorite before it became Guy's. And while he concentrated he made no attempt to shut out memories of Willsly's voice, or of Hong Kong harbor—or of cold steel against his throat.

"It's very beautiful, isn't it?"

"What?" He narrowed his gaze on Beatrice.

"Aldersgate," she said, a tremor in her voice. "It's beautiful. And it will be more beautiful as soon as we can do all that needs to be done here."

He was tempted to inform her that all the estate needed was more of his undivided attention. Instead he returned his attention to the windows and said nothing.

They rode in silence to the house and he touched Beatrice as briefly as possible whilst helping her from the carriage. He must get away, at least for a while.

"Welcome, your..." Crivens, standing inside the front door, looked confused. Then his expression cleared and he said, "We welcome you and your bride to your home. May you both enjoy a long and happy life together and be blessed with, ahem, many offspring.''

Giggles came from servants scurrying back and forth to the dining room. Guy nodded at Crivens and refused to as much as glance at Beatrice.

"Dios mio," Armando muttered, suddenly close to Guy's left side. "What is the matter with you? You are frightening the girl."

"This has to be over," Guy said shortly. "I have more important matters to attend."

"You will attend to easing your bride's unhappiness or you will deal with me, *amigo*."

Guy set his jaw and murmured. "I will insure she is not *unhappy*. But that may take time. First things first. You knew that when we began this."

"There is time," Armando insisted. "The longer the worm wriggles, the better. Forget him, at least for today . . . and for tonight?"

Further discussion was impossible. Guy had no idea how it had been accomplished, but the rose-colored dining room that his father had ceased to use after the death of his wife had been polished and dusted to its former splendor. Cream roses that matched those Beatrice wore decorated the chandelier and the candelabra, draped the mantle, and clustered in bowls and vases on every surface. And, set about a four-layered cake coated in sparkling white sugar molded into doves, was a feast fit for the wedding of a prince and princess.

With the urge to be free of it all mounting in his breast, Guy dismissed the table with a glance and studied Beatrice. Regardless of the circumstances, she was alone and dependent upon him. And she would continue to be his wife.

He managed a smile. "My dear," he said, patting at his coat. "I have quite forgotten something important. Do not move from this spot. Please." Touching a finger to her lips, he hurried from the room and took the stairs two at a time. He knew what the moment required and this much he would do correctly.

Returning within minutes, he pressed a square, flat

box covered with red velvet into her hands. "This is yours, Beatrice."

"Mine." He saw her tremble afresh.

"Open it."

She did so, watching his face before looking at the array of jewels that lay before her. "No," she said, her voice breaking. "Oh, no, I cannot accept them."

"Yes, you can. They were my mother's and now they are yours. You are my wife."

"Am I?" she mouthed silently.

He took a rope of pearls and diamonds from its velvet bed, turned her around and fastened the necklace. Next he slipped a matching bracelet onto her wrist. Earbobs took concentration, particularly since they required proximity, but he accomplished the task and removed the final piece from the box.

"My mother would have liked you," he said, passing a heavy diamond ring onto her finger. "She would be glad to know you're wearing this."

A sniff caused him to look around—directly into Sibyl's tearful face. She nodded and said, "This is all so wonderful."

"Thank you," Beatrice said, holding his arms while she rose to kiss his jaw. "Thank you so much."

"*Don't* say that again." He stepped away and she stumbled.

It was Armando who steadied Beatrice.

She appeared bewildered. "What did I say?"

"Today we became man and wife," he told her coldly. "In time we will come to terms with exactly what that means to us. In the meantime, let us not pretend I am other to you than I am or that you are more to me than was agreed."

"No." She drew herself up. "No, of course not. What a silly, sentimental goose I am to let you think I believe anything otherwise."

"There is no need to apologize."

"Very well."

"Good." He bowed. "Then we understand one another?"

"We do, indeed."

"Then I will take my leave of you. There is business I must attend to and it has already waited too long."

Beatrice, who, thanks to a hand carefully placed over Guy's name on the special license, did not know she was the marchioness of Rockford, turned her back on him and said, "Go to your business. You need not fear that I may forget the terms of our marriage. We have a bargain."

Women were superior to men in every way. *Every* way. "Women are superior to men in *every way*," Beatrice said distractedly as she reread a sentence in her novel yet again.

"Not *every* man in every way," Sibyl responded from her chair on the opposite side of the blue- and white-tiled fireplace in Beatrice's chamber.

"Every way that matters," Beatrice responded darkly.

"He cares for you."

"Dibble dabble! He needs my money. In that way he is no different from Victor."

"He is not crude and beastly."

Beatrice sighed and rested her head against the back of her chair. "No, he is definitely not crude and beastly. In fact he is gentle and can make me feel—" She stopped abruptly and shut her eyes tightly.

"Can make you feel what? *What*, Bea? Tell me at once."

"The jewels he gave me must be worth a fortune. I wonder why he hasn't sold them to help with his debts."

"Because they belonged to his mother, of course. They would be the very last thing he would part with and I think it was perfectly adorable the way he gave them to you. He is a man who has difficulty showing emotion, nothing more. That is why he left. His feelings for you were overwhelming."

"Rot! You and I both know what this marriage is all about."

"And I know you are avoiding telling me something." A rustle preceded Sibyl's arrival at Beatrice's knee, where she sank to the carpet. "You said he could make you feel something and I want to know what it is. Really, Bea, I shall absolutely *die* if you do not tell me. Has he kissed you before today?"

Beatrice averted her face.

"He *has*. I knew it! Oh, this is so exciting. Look at me."

Beatrice opened one eye. "I shall admit nothing."

"You already have! I am *so* grateful. This is a love match after all. Yes, you have certain things to accomplish together, but you *love* one another."

"Guy Falcon does not love me."

"Aha." Sibyl rose to her knees and bent over Beatrice. "The first truth is admitted. *You* love *him.*"

"I did not say as much."

"Yes you did. By *not* saying as much. And he loves you but doesn't know how to show it."

"I'm tired."

Sibyl held Beatrice's chin and shook it until her friend opened her eyes. "Regardless of your arrangement, you are still married to Guy. Am I right?"

"Yes," Beatrice said, feeling deeply weary.

"That marriage must, by all that's sensible, be made to work at some level."

"I do not see how. My groom has locked himself in his study on our wedding night. I would not say that boded well for a passionate future together."

"Passion!" Sibyl clamped a hand over her mouth and turned bright pink. "For you to mention such a thing must mean that you have already tasted it . . . just a little?"

Beatrice closed her eyes again.

"Oh, I am so jealous," Sibyl said breathily. "If only . . . Well, soon enough for my concerns later. Now we must take care of yours. Look at this book. I put it in the trunk just in case.''

Reluctantly, Beatrice did as she was asked. *"Mrs. Featherwise's Instructions to Brides?* Where on earth did you find this?''

''No matter. It is most instructive. Your first step is obvious. Preparing to receive your husband on your wedding night.''

"Sibyl!"

''Hush. We must be practical about this. See what it says?''

Beatrice looked closer and began to read—and turned pink herself.

''Rather shocking, isn't it?'' Sibyl said. ''But potentially delicious once you get past the surprise.''

''And irrelevant to the situation at hand.''

''Not at all.'' Sibyl thrust the book into Beatrice's hands and went to draw what looked to be nothing more than a diaphanous length of material from a pocket in the open trunk. ''Sooner or later the foolish man will decide to go to bed.''

Beatrice stared from the wispy white stuff to the page before her and felt her eyes grow round. ''And what if he does?''

''Then you will be awaiting him, of course.''

6

Besieged and abandoned. In his own house. By a wife he never planned to acquire and a man who was supposedly his best friend—a man who wanted, as desperately as Guy did, to punish an amoral coward.

"Can't think what Cuthburt Phipps sees in this stuff," Guy said to the brandy that remained in the glass atop his desk. The first few glasses had left a not unpleasant numbness in their wake but now he felt entirely, miserably sober and painfully aware that he was aroused.

And his head ached.

"In God's name! You have no *right*!" He stood with enough force to fling over his chair. The glass shot to the floor and shattered. He had no right to lust after a girl he'd married for no purpose other than to discharge a debt against him.

But he *had* married her. Beatrice was his wife. And he wanted her, damn it.

She wouldn't have him, not until and unless he could give her reason to have faith in their union.

"Threaten me, would you?" he muttered, remembering Armando's litany of what he intended to do to Guy if he didn't *regain his senses and reassure Beatrice*. His world was chaotic and not a friend remained to him.

The drink must have made him maudlin. Sleep was the thing—if he could hope to achieve that happy state.

As he entered the hall the longcase clock struck two. Why was it not much later? It *felt* much later, as if at

57

least a week of sleepless watching had passed, in fact. How many hours ago had he ordered the hovering and visibly disapproving Crivens to bed? Not even his old servant sympathized with a wronged man's plight.

Attempting to make no sound, Guy climbed the curving staircase with exaggerated care. He was a thoughtful man who would do his best to cause his bride no further concern.

His bride.

At her chamber door he hovered. Bringing his ear close to a panel he listened, holding his own breath whilst straining to hear hers.

Nothing. So innocently and deeply did she sleep that there was no sound.

What could it hurt if he opened the door—just a little— and looked at her whilst she slept? Her hair would be thick and shining and dark upon her pillow. Her lips would be slightly parted, her lashes black against her cheeks.

And no stays would hamper a man's access to a body that could not benefit from such damnable restraint.

Guy gritted his teeth and walked resolutely past his wife's door and onward to the west wing. At the end of the corridor he arrived at his own bedchamber.

Not bothering with lights, he quickly entered and shut himself inside. "Enough disruption," he announced to the moonlit sky beyond the casement. "I've got what I need. Use it and let it cause me no more inconvenience."

The words sounded hearty. Guy had discarded his coat and cravat in the study. Now his boots followed, then his waistcoat, thrown onto the window seat whilst he fixed his eye on the band of sea visible from parts of Aldersgate's upper reaches. The black swathe shimmered beneath the moon.

The same moon shone through Beatrice's window.

"Touching your face," he murmured, unbuttoning his shirt. "God's light upon you, *wife*. Your hair, your lips, your eyes—your breasts. Ah yes, moonlight becomes you, Beatrice."

"Thank you, Guy," a small, clear voice said behind him.

Shock locked every muscle in his body and jarred his suffering brain. He spun around and stared. "What in . . ." The moonlight he'd extolled bathed his vast mahogany bed. Sheets and pillows glowed white—so did Beatrice.

Kneeling in the center of the mattress, draped in some white creation he couldn't make out, her face was starkly pallid and her eyes as huge and dark as his very reliable imagination had pictured. "What in God's name are you . . ." He moved closer. "What are you doing here and *what* are you wearing?"

She said nothing.

Aware of cool air smiting his chest where the shirt hung open, he advanced to the edge of the bed and looked down upon her—and caught his breath. Moonlight did indeed become her, particularly dressed in a nightgown transparent enough to present her body as if it were naked yet the more erotic because it was not.

"Beatrice?" The light at his own back was a blessing. If she saw the extent of her effect upon him she would doubtless shriek. Her shriek was not what he wanted. He wanted her drawing him into her body, taking from him what demanded to be released only to arouse him again and again until exhaustion claimed him. He wanted to cover her, to *feel* all of her, to taste all of her, and watch her learn to want him with the same devouring intensity.

He shook his head. "Answer me, woman, what are you doing here?" Her waist was narrow, her hips rounded—and her breasts full, the shaded tips stiff and pressing through thin cotton. She was far more perfect than he could have hoped.

And she appeared to have lost the gift of speech.

If he touched her he would be lost. Bending, he brought his face within inches of hers. "I am waiting."

"Thank you, Guy."

He frowned. "Damn it, madam, will you *stop* thanking me?"

The click he heard was the sound of her swallowing. "I know what I have done wrong. I'm sorry. I am prepared to mend my ways."

Drink had never agreed with him. He'd heard many stories of its strange effects on some men. Squeezing his eyes shut, he waited a moment before opening them again. No, she was not an apparition who spoke meaningless nonsense. She was Beatrice—who spoke meaningless nonsense.

"I came to apologize," she said.

"Apologize?"

"To tell you how I regret my completely inappropriate—my reprehensible earlier behavior."

The shock of what had happened to her in the past few days must have turned her mind. "Beatrice," he said evenly. "We should discuss this matter calmly."

"Oh, yes! Oh, thank . . . Yes. I do wish I had read Mrs. Featherwise's book earlier. So much misunderstanding would have been avoided."

"Of course it would." A pain thumped at his temples. Beatrice's face became fuzzy.

"Unfortunately I had not expected . . . well, of course, you could not know that I was such a peagoose in these matters."

"No." Cautious to make no sudden moves, he sank to sit at the very foot of the bed.

"How I must have disgusted you."

If he turned his head slightly she came back into focus a little. "Disgusted?" He seemed incapable of ordering his thoughts.

"I know. At least I do now, after the book. Wasn't it fortunate that Sibyl packed it in our trunk?"

"Why *did* she pack this—this book? What did you say it was?"

"Instructions to brides."

"Ah, I see." He didn't.

"Of course you do. And I've no doubt you assumed

I had read about or at least discussed such matters with an older female before. But, since my own mother died many years ago and I have no female relatives, well, you do see, don't you?''

"Mm."

"So, dear clever Sibyl packed the book. Wasn't that an intelligent thing to do?"

"Mm."

"When you got so cross with me the other day''— she bowed her head—"in your study when . . . Well, *when*. When The *Necessary,* you'll recall occurred. And my response must have utterly appalled you. *I* am utterly appalled at myself. But I did not know. Honestly I didn't.''

She raised her face again and he blinked to clear his vision. "Perhaps it would be good for both of us if you explained your interpretation of your, er, appalling responses.''

Beatrice sighed and his sight snapped back into focus in time to note the delightful spectacle of her breasts rising. He began to lean toward her. The cotton gown would be soft to his touch, so would the skin beneath.

"I expect it will be good for my character to be forced to voice aloud my disgraceful lapse. It is absolutely no wonder that you were angry at my proposal." She pressed her hands to her cheeks. "To think that I did that. That I breached every rule, even in extreme circumstances, and *proposed marriage to you.* Awful."

"Awful."

"Yes. Naturally I did know it was a daring and amazing thing to do. But what made that the more disgusting to you was my response to The *Necessary.* I had no idea that I was not to like it. Oh, Guy, I'm mortified. If only there had been some warning that I was to be passive and accepting of your actions, concerned only for your pleasure and not, above all, *not* to experience any reciprocal pleasure.

"I think you are marvelous to have answered my plea and married me regardless when you must be completely convinced that I am beyond the pale and could never make a good wife.''

"This is amazing." He knew such nonsense was fed to young females but had never before encountered the bizarre effect it obviously caused.

"I know I am asking a great deal, but I should like to try to be what you need and have a right to expect in a wife.'' She scooted closer until she could take one of his hands in both of hers and draw it onto her lap.

"Beatrice," he said, painfully aware of where his fingers rested. "It might be better if we continued this discussion at another time."

She drew his hand to her breast. "When you approached me that day you were testing my reactions and I failed the test. But, since we are married, can you not allow me to prove how meek I can be?"

"Meek?" He could not stop his bark of laughter.

"I *can* be." She sounded aggrieved. "Preferably silent, the book said. I tried that but you insisted I answer you. But now that you know why I came here tonight I can be silent again, and meek and docile!"

"To what end?" he had to ask, just as he had to move his fingers—just a little.

Her chin came up and silvered light from the night sky caught the pert lines of her face and glinted in her uptilted cat's eyes. "This is difficult to say just so," she told him.

How had he ever thought her plain?

"I shall be straightforward," she continued. "Sibyl and I decided that marital harmony should be promoted in as short a time as possible. So, I shall behave as I should and you may get The *Necessary* over with as it pleases you."

The pain in his head renewed its fury. "This is preposterous, damn it! *Preposterous*." He was to be presented with the fantastic task of educating a thoroughly muddled innocent in the ways of the flesh. He would fulfil his duty manfully . . . when his head stopped aching.

"Guy—"

"Please return to your bed, Beatrice."

"But I thought I could do something for you."

Withdrawing his hand, he stood up. "What I need, you cannot do for me." Perhaps fresh air would help. He went to open the window.

He heard the rustle of sheets and the rapid thud of small feet across the carpet. The door opened, then slammed with enough force to make him groan.

The chill breeze with its remnants of salt from the sea began to quiet the pain. Breathing deeply, treading gingerly, he groped his way to the bed and stretched out. "Ah, yes. Sleep. Tomorrow night will be different." Tomorrow night he would be ready to begin his wife's instruction. The more he thought on it, the more sensible seemed the idea of creating a pleasant bond with her before Willsly was dispatched and the two of them confronted what they were to make of their life together.

Tomorrow.

The door, crashing open once more, smashed Guy's pleasant drifting.

"I tried!"

He struggled to his elbows. Beatrice stood silhouetted in the doorway.

"Mrs. Featherwise says there are men like you, men of naturally unpleasant temper who will not be pleased with any amount of effort.

"It is not easy for a practical, modern female such as I am to bend to the surprises of the past days, but I *did* try. And you have made it clear that you have discharged your kindness to me by ensuring that Lord Willsly cannot make me marry him."

"True." Oh, very true.

"As I thought! Very well. You may inform me when you wish to arrange for an heir."

"Arrange for an heir?"

"In the meantime, enjoy yourself with whatever alternative source of The *Necessary* that pleases you. In other words, now that you have my money at your disposal, it should not be difficult for you to employ a suitable *inamorata*. There, now you know that you have married a woman of the world.''

He was to ''employ'' a suitable *inamorata* with her money? Guy swung his feet from the bed. ''You are too kind, Beatrice,'' he said, making no attempt to keep the menace from his voice. ''*Thank* you.''

''No. *Thank you*!''

And the damnable door slammed again.

Beatrice flew downstairs and through the hall. She spied one of Guy's capes that Crivens had carelessly left on a yokeback chair. Catching up the voluminous black garment, she flung it about her and ran out into the night.

Since her arrival she'd barely had time to walk into the grounds and now she had no idea where she intended to go.

''I will find a place to be quiet,'' she promised herself. ''Quiet and at peace.'' And she would not think about Guy Falcon.

Too soon she remembered her bare feet. She had reached the sweep of gravel between the steps and the parkland that stretched, so she'd been told, to the sea. *Fustian!* Hesitating, she looked back at the house—and clutched at her throat. A tall, broad form stood in the open doorway.

Guy had followed her.

But darkness was her ally. She could see Guy but he could not possibly see her.

Her feet would soon become accustomed to rough surfaces.

Sure enough, by running fast over the driveway she barely felt the clawing of small, sharp stones. Then she was on dewy grass and fleeing downhill toward the massive domed outlines of an ancient sycamore grove.

''Beatrice!'' Guy's voice, well behind, bellowed on the stiff breeze.

Her heart leaped. He sounded so *angry*. She ran faster

and her breath came in great pants that strained her lungs and burned her throat.

How like a man to insult a woman, then be angry because she refused to be completely undone by his despicable behavior.

"Beatrice! Where are you?"

His voice did not sound closer. And what if it did? As usual, the female sensibilities she'd been cursed with were causing unnecessary fear. After all, what could he actually *do* to her even if she should be caught?

She had entered the trees and dashed ahead, holding the ridiculously huge cape and the stupid shift bunched in her arms. Her father could tell Mr. Guy Falcon how swiftly Beatrice could run. Why, when she'd been seven and reluctant to leave a beach to which they'd traveled, she had run away from her poor, dear father and he'd been very hard pressed to catch her.

But he *had* caught her. And Beatrice was much older than seven now, and, she deeply feared, not nearly as fleet.

"Beatrice!"

"Ooh!" She crammed a fist to her mouth to stifle the sound. He *was* closer.

Whirling this way and that, she caught sight of a break in the trees with a paler patch of light beyond. Once there, she found that what she'd seen was the moon's wash through a cut between hills. Beatrice hit irregular ground again and set course for the narrow valley. Grass thinned and gave way to broken rock and she bit her lip as knifelike edges jabbed into her feet.

Beatrice heard the sea, then she saw it and stopped, gasping. On that first evening they had entered Aldersgate by an inland drive. She hadn't guessed the ocean was quite so close.

"By God, woman! I *see* you. This is foolishness, I tell you. *Stop*!"

He sounded even more angry. He sounded enraged.

Genuine fear bounded in Beatrice's breast. Perhaps she had been rash. Perhaps, after all, it might have been wiser to go quietly to her bed and await whatever he might intend to say in the morning.

Oh! Oh, she saw him. Pounding toward her, he approached at a terrifying pace.

At her back was the sea. Before her was Guy. Only the beach offered escape and panic sent her scrunching along sand that swallowed her feet at every step.

"Enough, you little cabbage-head." His hand descended on her shoulder and she began to fall. "I have you now and, by God, you will regret this madness."

"Let me go at once." With a supreme effort, she flung herself forward, slipping free of the cloak, and heard a thump followed by a great grunt.

In the same instant fingers closed like manacles around one of her ankles. There was nothing for it; she must give up and face him. This was made the more difficult because Guy lay, fully stretched out, on his stomach.

Slowly, inch by inch, he pulled her foot toward him. Beatrice hobbled and spread her arms to stop from toppling over.

"You try me too far, madam," he said, his voice muffled but not made less ominous. "Now you will pay."

"Pay?" Her voice slid annoyingly upward. "I have been driven from my own home. I have been forced to beg for help from a stranger. I have been foolish enough to come to trust that stranger only to be humiliated by him and put into an impossible situation from which I cannot guess the escape. I have paid quite enough, *thank you.*"

A hard little jerk almost landed her on her bottom. "Thank me for nothing. Do you hear? *Nothing.* You have not paid enough for this night's work. You have not begun to pay. Do I make myself clear?"

"You do not frighten me."

He laughed. A most unpleasant sound. "I should frighten you, my sweet," he said softly.

"Do not take that tone with me."

Still holding her ankle, he pushed back to sit upon his

heels. "How will you stop me from taking any tone I please with you, Beatrice?"

She glanced down. "Let me go."

"Absolutely not. It will be a long time before I let you go. A very long time."

Something in his voice warned her to be careful. "Don't be foolish. We cannot stay here like this. Get up at once." She had never been good at being careful.

"I wouldn't dream of it. You must be tired after your exertion. It will be my pleasure to entertain and divert you until you quite forget that your feet must be sore from abuse and that you are chilled from standing naked in the moonlight."

She gasped. "How dare you, sir? I am not . . . naked." Another downward glance revealed a horrifying fact: the unsuitable nightgown Sibyl had procured from who knew where billowed in the breeze. The moon shone through the wispy material and for all the world Beatrice might as well be naked.

Guy lifted her foot.

"What are you doing?" Genuinely dismayed, Beatrice tried in vain to trap the flying, gauzy gown against her body whilst wobbling in a most unnerving manner.

"I'm surveying the damage you've done to your person."

Her heel was placed upon his knee and Beatrice squealed. "Stop it. I shall fall."

"Good. Then I shall catch you and I will quite enjoy that."

"No you . . . What are you doing?"

With one hand, he smoothed the back of her leg, very slowly, from ankle to knee. "How soft you are, Beatrice. How smooth."

The little place behind her knee was ticklish. She wiggled and felt a shocking echo of the sensation at her knee in that place where he had touched her when they'd been alone in his study. "Please, Guy," she said, beginning to panic. "Oh, *please*."

"Please?" He passed his fingertips to the inner, soft,

and very sensitive side of her thigh. "You do not have to beg, sweet one. I will gladly persist."

Another plea became lost in a whirl of sensation. Guy released her ankle, but only to find a much more intimate purchase. With her knee trapped against his shoulder, he swiftly slipped his free hand beneath the useless gown to hold her vulnerable bottom.

"The book said nothing . . . Oh!" A further tug brought her close enough for Guy to kiss the tingling skin above her knee. "This will *not* do," she finally managed.

"Not do?" he said with a smile in his deep voice, and placed a kiss an inch higher, and another inch higher— and another. "Mm, I think this is doing very well. Isn't that what your book said you should accomplish—my satisfaction?"

"I do not think—"

"Do *not* think. I believe I heard you utter those words once. *Feel*, Beatrice. Concentrate on feeling alone."

Her breathing became shallow. He could not intend to . . . Desperate, she filled her hands with his hair and held on. "You will *not* . . . No, you will not go any . . . You will stop, I tell you!" Although, and a pox on her wanton nature, she wanted his wretched *feeling* to go on and on.

"I have stopped," he said, brushing his rough jaw back and forth. "You give me no choice."

But he made no attempt to retreat. Beatrice held his head and looked down upon his broad shoulders. Somewhere between his bedchamber and the beach, his fine white shirt had become tattered. The night's ghostly light was kind to powerful muscles beneath gleaming skin. A very strong man, not one to toy with, Guy Falcon was a man any female would do well never to underestimate.

"Beatrice," he said. "Have you already forgotten what your little book told you?"

She began to shiver. "No," she told him in a small voice. Behind her the surf grew louder, rushing over rocks and dropping away again, beginning to send fine spray skyward. Cold, wet droplets pattered against her back.

"You are still pulling my hair."

"I am restraining you. For both of our sakes."

"Not, I assure you, for mine, madam." He drew seared skin between his teeth and also did a scandalous, a deliciously scandalous thing. The hand that kneaded her bottom slipped around her waist. His other hand went surely to her bare breasts.

Beatrice lost her grip on his hair. "Guy!"

He laughed. "What, my sweet? Tell me what you want of me?"

"I want . . . I want . . ."

She never finished telling him, or even deciding on the words she might wish to use. So quickly that she had no time to protest, Guy pressed his mouth to *that* place. He flicked it with his tongue and heat smote every nerve in her body. Her hips pressed toward him, toward the very part of him that should not ever be where it was. She *was* wanton.

The only leg that supported her began to buckle. Noises came from her throat, muddled, moaning noises over which she had no control.

Then, just as she felt herself approaching the brink of that marvelous thing he had accomplished before, his mouth left her and she was eased down to sit astride a hard thigh.

"You are not a bit quiet, sweeting." Guy's eyes were black and they glittered. "Isn't that what we have to perfect here, your ability to be silent whilst I deal with the—The *Necessary*?"

Beatrice frowned, then drew in a sharp breath. He had begun rocking her on that solid thigh, working her back and forth until the searing sensation mounted once more.

"Guy, I . . . Oh, I don't know."

"No, I don't suppose you do." He sought the neck of the gown, bowing his head in concentration. "Blast the thing." With that, he unceremoniously ripped the garment apart from throat to waist.

"Look what you've done!"

He smiled as she presumed Satan might smile. "Indeed," he said. "*Look* what I have done."

Beatrice did look and whilst she did, Guy lifted and pushed her white breasts together with his tanned hands. He sent his thumbs back and forth over her nipples and she clutched at his shoulders. Little streaks of fire tore into places she could not name.

"This is"—he paused to suck a nipple into his mouth—"this is not encouraging." He finished and moved to the other breast.

Beatrice panted and grappled to hold him closer. "Not encouraging?" She hovered so close to that sensation she had tried not to think about.

"Not encouraging at all," he said, nestling his face between her breasts, licking his way back to a waiting peak. "You are supposed to be learning how to do these things correctly—according to your book. Am I not right?"

She could not think. "Yes. Yes, *yes*!" The urge came to move herself upon his thigh and she shifted—and cried out.

"Not encouraging," he said and his voice did not sound quite as it usually did. "Oh, no, not at all."

"So, you will . . . You will give up on me?"

"Give up?" Always there was one more surprise. His fingers, working between his leg and her most private place, tore a shriek from Beatrice. "Worse and worse," he breathed.

"Guy!"

"And worse." With gentle insistence, he pushed his fingers inside her. "But such a ready student."

She would faint. No, she would scream and scream. No. No, she would beg him never ever to stop. "Please, Guy."

"'Please' is so much better than 'thank you.'" Sighing, he buried his face in her neck, kissed the hollows there—and drove his fingers farther into her.

Beatrice felt her mind slipping away. Her body

clamped down on him and she couldn't seem to stop it or decide what it should do at all. "Something is going to happen to me," she whispered. "It is. I feel it. Oh, yes, I *feel* it."

"You will feel much more, sweeting. Very soon."

When he suddenly lifted her she tried to draw him to her. Then she was set on her back atop the tattered remnants of the gown. The surf swished and misty spray rained down upon them.

She was naked, beneath the moon, beside the sea, with the man who was her husband. And her progress was not encouraging?

"Guy! Don't!"

"Ah, me." He had clasped her ankles and was pushing her feet upward until her knees splayed and she knew she was completely, shamelessly displayed to him. "We shall probably be here in this very spot for weeks. But no matter, I shall persevere."

She thought to ask his meaning. But then she forgot her intention.

Once again his dark head was between her legs and he reached up to play with her aching breasts.

"Oh." Too much feeling. "Oh, oh, oh!"

The moon went away, and the sky, and the sound of the surf. The surf could not compete with the roaring in her ears and the moon was snuffed out by the burst of white heat that shot from that magically awakened spot Guy seemed to know so well.

The sky was gone, burned up by a blaze that caressed even as it consumed.

Guy left her hot and heavy and tossing restlessly. "Don't," she gasped.

"Don't, Beatrice?"

"Don't stop. Don't go away."

"Ah, but I couldn't now, could I?"

He stretched out, half on top of Beatrice, and her eyes flew open. "You aren't wearing any clothes."

"Are you sure?"

Tentatively, she touched his chest, the side of his

waist—one extremely hard buttock. "You . . . Your . . . There is *something* large down there."

"I think we should discuss why I can't go away. We must be certain you haven't forgotten your earlier promises to me."

Gazing up into his green jet eyes, she shook her head.

"Good. You'll remember your protestations about your ability to be meek and docile?"

Slowly, she nodded. "It—it's *pushing* at me."

"It is indeed." He stirred and the shaft slipped between her thighs. "It has barely begun. Do you recall mentioning silence?"

Again she nodded.

"You are doing very badly in all these areas, so do you know what I must do?"

"No." Her voice was scarcely audible.

"It's simple. I must ensure that we practice and practice and practice again until you manage—The *Necessary*, in the manner your book has assured you is required. Does that sound fair?"

"It sounds . . . tiring?"

He laughed but did not sound amused. "Such a wonderful reason to be tired. Part your legs for me again."

Obediently, she did as he asked. The piece of him that pulsed and pushed immediately nudged at the opening to her body. "I do not think—"

"Don't *think*," he said, his voice oddly thick and indistinct. "I told you to feel."

She did feel and she was not at all sure she liked what she felt this time. "If you intend to put that all the way inside me I think it's a bad idea."

"Be quiet and relax."

"It will not fit, I tell you."

"Yes it will, sweeting. Trust me."

"I do." He thrust upward and she cried out.

"Hush," he groaned. "Hush, Beatrice. This first time may not be comfortable."

"It is—most—certainly—not comfortable. It's—ooh!"

She felt something within her part and then there was warm, wet heat. He thudded into her again and again and the pain was gone. Then her insides did that clamping thing she couldn't seem to help and the white fire broke over her, wave after wave, while she cried aloud.

Into the night, Guy's harsh yell joined with her shout.

He fell over her, drew her into his arms and held on so tightly she could only lie there helpless. Seconds passed while moisture cooled on their bodies.

"My sweet wife," he murmured into her ear. "The sweetest of wives."

She squeezed her eyes shut and tears trickled down her temples. Tears of happiness. Wriggling, she managed to steal her arms around him and hug with all her might.

"Guy, you said we could not stop until I learned to do The *Necessary* as Mrs. Featherwise says I must?"

"Mm."

"Oh, dear. That means I shall have to work harder on my meekness and docility. And my silence, of course."

"Mm."

She wriggled a little more. "I have always considered education, particularly the education of women, of the utmost importance."

"Hmm?"

"As a woman, I consider it my duty to perfect every facet of my own education—those facets that can be perfected, of course."

"Beatrice, my love, could you perhaps simply think these things—at least until we are rested?"

She smiled. And then she grinned, a very wide and unladylike grin. "Oh!" she cried. "Oh, oh, oh! *Oh, oh, oh!*"

"What is it?" Guy shoved to his elbows, then seemed to remember that he was still inside her. "What are you screaming about, madam?"

Beatrice shook her head sadly. "I'm afraid you are correct, husband. I do not seem to have perfected the required elements of matrimony at all.'' Pulling his head down she kissed him, open-mouthed, long and lingeringly. ''No, Guy, we shall simply have to keep on practicing.''

7

THE carriage bumped over a deeply rutted spot in the road.

''I'm quite worried,'' Sibyl said abruptly, as if the lurching carriage had jarred the words loose.

''Do not be,'' Armando told her. Throughout the trip from Sussex he'd concentrated a dark frown upon Guy. ''This matter with Beatrice's father will be accomplished in a civilized manner. Will it not, Guy?''

Guy ignored the question and turned instead to smile at Beatrice. Just sitting beside him made her swell with happiness. Sitting beside him, remembering last night on the beach and later . . . Later he had carried her back to Aldersgate and his great bed. She would never forget the hours of wonderment they'd shared and could hardly bear waiting to be alone with him again.

''Guy,'' Armando persisted. ''Am I not correct in saying that today's encounter in Lansdowne Place will be congenial?''

Guy held Beatrice's hand openly and he chose this moment to study his ring upon her finger. ''You have nothing to fear, Sibyl. Mr. Merryfield shall learn that you have been a most faithful companion to his daughter.''

Beatrice felt some disquiet. "Papa is a plainspoken man but he is not given to fits of temper."

"Your father has never seen a time such as this before," Sibyl said. "His only daughter, whom he loves dearly, has been run off with!"

"Has been perceived to have been run off with," Beatrice corrected. "And, in fact, he is not yet aware that I have—well, that I have become attached to a member of the opposite sex."

"Very attached," Guy murmured, but loudly enough for everyone to hear.

Sibyl blushed and stole an upward glance at Armando who, predictably, beamed down upon her with frank admiration.

Beatrice poked Guy playfully. "I shall speak to Papa alone at first."

"No." All humor dropped from his handsome face. "That is out of the question."

"It is most certainly *not* out of the question," Beatrice said, withdrawing her hand from his. "I tell you I wish to see my father alone before introducing you."

"You wish me to skulk behind your skirts until it seems safe to emerge? Isn't *that* what you suggest?"

"Oh, you can be such a booby." But there was a hair of truth in what he suggested. She did want to make the path clear for her father to like Guy and to do so without any unpleasant scenes if possible.

"It is inappropriate for a wife to speak to her husband in such a tone," Guy said stiffly. "Particularly in front of others."

Beatrice pretended to be engrossed in the scene beyond the carriage windows. She'd been anxious to become reacquainted with her father. At her insistence, they had left Aldersgate quite early and with the afternoon light slipping away the grand buildings of London's Mayfair were coming into view.

Suddenly contrite, she turned to Guy. "Forgive me, Guy. I am anxious. Surely you can understand?"

He nodded but his green eyes remained narrowed.

"Out of kindness to my father—who is now also your father—can you not see your way to allowing him some time alone with me to become accustomed to what has happened? I shall be frank with him. There will be no more falsehoods."

"Oh, yes," Sibyl said quickly. "Please, Guy, allow Beatrice to speak to Mr. Merryfield alone. Everything will be so much more pleasant."

Guy continued to look into Beatrice's eyes and she saw him trying to decide how to answer.

"Think, Guy," Armando said. "This will change nothing. What has been done, has been done. You have what you want. *We* have what we want."

Puzzled, Beatrice turned to him but he had eyes only for Guy, whose expression underwent a subtle softening. "You could not be more correct," he said finally. "Nothing can be changed. No, there can be no going back now."

She wondered if these two men's words held only the obvious meaning. "So, I may do as I ask?"

"I shall await you. And I shall not be far away, so please do not take long."

"Oh, *thank* you." She clapped a hand over her mouth. "Oh, dear! I said it again."

Laughing, Guy pulled her against his chest. "Clearly it is time for another lesson. More practice is what you need."

She felt her face grow hot and dared not look at the others.

"Beatrice is shy," Guy said above her head. "I understand that adjustment to The Necessary in marriage is quite taxing for many females."

He was *impossible*.

"We're there," Sibyl cried and Beatrice's stomach swooped.

The carriage trundled to a halt.

"Fie!" Sibyl drew back from the windows and flattened herself against the squabs. "Beatrice, Willsly's equipage is here!"

Guy put her from him so briskly, she gasped.

"It will not be possible for you to see your father alone after all," he said, a white line about his compressed mouth.

"Certainly it will," Armando said mildly. "If Willsly is there, so much the better. Another inevitability will be dealt with at once."

"No, I—"

"Guy," Armando said, leaning toward his friend. "You are not thinking clearly. Beatrice will be perfectly safe. We will be nearby. *Very* nearby. And when the moment is appropriate, all will be dealt with to our satisfaction."

Beatrice frowned. Armando sometimes spoke very strangely, but, after all, he was a foreigner.

The coachman opened the carriage door and stood aside.

"Guy," Beatrice said desperately. "I wish to do this alone."

He passed her to alight from the carriage. As he handed her down, he smiled. "You may go in alone, my dear."

"Thank you."

This time there was no ensuing banter. Guy bowed formally and turned to the street whilst Beatrice and Sibyl climbed the steps to the white stone house with its black front door and gleaming brass lamps.

The door opened before she could knock.

"Miss Beatrice?" Ladbroke, butler and Beatrice's lifelong ally, had come into the Merryfield household as a young man. He had grown old in the service of Beatrice's family and frequently mentioned how grateful he'd been to do so. "Oh, Miss Beatrice. Thank the Lord you're safe. And you, Miss Sibyl. Come in. Come in. Mr. Merryfield's in the red parlor. Lord Willsly's with him."

Beatrice and Sibyl hurried inside and the door was closed before Beatrice could steal a backward glance at Guy.

"No," Beatrice told Sibyl when she made to follow

her friend to the parlor. "This is something I really do intend to do completely alone. Don't worry. Papa will be overjoyed to see me and that will eclipse any danger of anger. Go to your room and await me."

"But—"

"*Go*, dear friend." Beatrice gave her a gentle push and walked directly to push open the parlor door.

"There is the little matter of that loan about which we spoke," Willsly was saying. Tall, his smoothly good-looking face and large frame were beginning to show the signs of too much exotic food and drink. He stood beside Ernest Merryfield's red brocaded chair. "That opportunity I mentioned won't wait forever. I do believe that securing Beatrice's complete comfort throughout her precious life is worth our combined efforts to enhance the Willsly fortune."

Her father stared into a flickering fire and she could tell he barely heard Lord Willsly.

How she hated the despicable fraud. *Securing Beatrice's comfort*. "Hah!"

Her father's face whipped in her direction. "Beatrice? Oh, my child—my dear girl—you are come home."

Willsly's fleshy face turned first pale, then a dull, furious red. "Where in God's name have you been?" he said, his lips drawn back in a snarl. "How dare you humiliate me in front of all London. I ought to . . ." He stopped, visibly pulling back from his rush of fury.

"That's no way to greet a child you feared might be lost," Papa said shortly. "Come close and let me see you, Bea."

Keeping her eyes turned from Willsly, she gladly did as her father asked. "Forgive me," she said. "It has hurt me to hurt and worry you."

"And what of me?" Willsly said petulantly.

She ignored him. "All will be well now. I promise."

"Of course it will," Willsly said. "You have seen the error of your ways and that will be good enough."

"There is a great deal to be said," Beatrice told her father, dropping to kneel before him on the silk carpet.

"I know you will understand in time. Understand and accept."

"We have already accepted," Willsly blustered before Papa could respond. "You had a lapse of good sense as many females of your immaturity and shy nature are wont to do. Fortunately you have regained those senses in time. We shall forget all the nonsense you wrote in that disgraceful note. It need never be mentioned again."

"Are you all right, Bea?" her father said as if deaf to the other man.

"Oh, yes. *Yes*. I am more than all right. I am truly happy."

"Of course you are." Willsly's brown and cream checked trousers came closer. "And so you should be for you are a fortunate girl. The marriage will take place at once. There must be no more delay. Your . . . your little lapse has gravely upset my plans, but no matter, we shall make the required adjustments."

Papa leaned toward her. "What is it, my dear?" His eyes, the same gold color as her own, held deep concern and his usually good-humored face was serious.

"Nothing bad," she assured him. "But Lord Willsly and I cannot be married."

Ernest Merryfield was a good-looking man in a flamboyantly broad-featured way. Rather than deepening the worried frown on his brow, Beatrice was certain there was a clearing there. "You cannot?"

"You *cannot*?" Willsly echoed. "Gad! How much more foolishness must a man bear? You can and you will, miss. And you'll be glad of it. It is *I* who will save what is left of your tarnished reputation after this escapade."

"Willsly," Papa said, firmly but quietly.

"No, Ernest. I insist you leave this to me now since it is plain you have no control over your own offspring. Regardless of what pretty stories you may have devised to explain away your sudden absence, miss, I assure you that there is scandal aplenty concerning where you may have been and with whom.''

"Willsly, I suggest—''

"We will marry tomorrow," Willsly said, interrupting Papa yet again. "It shall be quietly accomplished and I'll take you to Hampshire immediately. A honeymoon is out of the question since I must attend to my affairs. You will be comfortable enough in Hampshire—''

"I am already married.''

"Do not interrupt me. I have tolerated all the impudence I intend to take from—'' Willsly stopped. He spread the fingers of one hand over the puce silk waistcoat that covered his soft belly. "Beatrice?''

She looked calmly from her father's puzzled face, to Willsly's startled blue eyes. "I said, I am already married. So I cannot marry you, can I?''

"Oh, my God," Willsly said slowly. He tottered backward a step, located a chair, and sank into it. "What have you done, you little fool? Ernest, she has gone through some damnable sham of a marriage with some opportunist with designs on your money.''

Beatrice tried not to laugh. She failed.

Her father patted her shoulder. "Now, now, my love, don't overexcite yourself. What are you saying? Have you met someone you think you could care for, is that it?''

She shook her head. "No. *Yes*! And you will come to love my husband as I do. I know you will.''

"The poor fuddled creature's been gulled by some bounder, I tell you, Ernest," Willsly said. "We must work fast to turn this about before it's too late.''

"It's already too late," Beatrice said, averting her eyes. "I am well and truly married and that's that.''

"Ignore her," Willsly said, pulling himself to the edge of the chair. He got up and crossed to Beatrice's side. "Come. You have made a foolish error, but I will forgive you.''

"No," Beatrice said, amazed at the calmness she felt. "Please leave my father's house."

Willsly caught her arm and yanked. "Get up you little fool," he hissed. "I will see this person and ensure he causes us no further trouble. Take me to him. Better yet, tell me where I may find him. No man thwarts me and lives."

"Is that so?"

At the sound of Guy's voice, Willsly released Beatrice.

Guy sauntered into the room. "You see," he said, spreading wide his arms. "There is no need for Beatrice to take you to your quarry, or to tell you where he is, for he has come to you."

Before Beatrice's amazed eyes, Willsly seemed to shrivel. Sweat broke out on his brow. "You? No, you are . . . You are not here."

"Am I not?" Guy swung in a swaggering circle. "Then who, pray, is here in this man's boots? No doubt your surprise has impaired your manners, Victor. Don't you think you should congratulate me on my marriage to Beatrice?"

"No," Willsly whispered. "What devil's work is this?"

"A devil with whom you are better acquainted than any other," Guy said cheerfully.

Papa sought and held Beatrice's hand. "What is all this?" he asked.

"Guy is my husband, father. I know you are shocked, but please do not be for he is a very good man."

Papa only shook his head slowly.

"So, there you have it," Guy announced. "I am in, Victor. *You* are out! There is the door. I suggest you use it."

"Swine," Willsly muttered. "You won't get away with this."

"I have! But perhaps it is not enough merely to watch you lose all hope of rescuing your fortunes at Ernest Merryfield's expense. Perhaps it would be best to remind you of my reasons for making certain that your life as you know it is over.''

"Have a care, Rockford.''

"Why should I?" Guy said. "We both know that I almost died at your hands. A word in the right places and you would very soon draw your own last breath.''

Beatrice slowly got to her feet. "Guy—"

"Not now," he said and turned back to Willsly. "When you sent me aboard that ship in Hong Kong harbor, you knew the crew would assume I was you and that they would kill me. They would kill me because you betrayed them and their punishment for that was death.''

"Rockford—"

"You left Hong Kong and returned to England, confident that no one would ever discover that you were a traitor to England, to the Chinese, and to Armando de Silva.''

"In God's name, Rockford, don't—"

"I hardly think you should invoke the Lord's name. You returned to England and discovered your affairs were in a shambles. Even with the handsome payoffs you'd accepted, maintaining your estates and lifestyle was impossible. You needed an advantageous marriage. You needed it quickly and without embarrassing questions. The Merryfields were an answer to your prayers.''

Beatrice stepped forward. "How do you know all this about us?"

"Lies," Willsly shouted. "All lies. Get out, Rockford.''

"Why does he call you Rockford?''

"It is my name," Guy said without emotion. "Do not concern yourself, my love. I would have preferred to explain all this to you quietly, but time forced my hand.''

"Rockford," she said to herself.

"You sent me to die," Guy told Willsly. "For that I have punished you by taking the answer to your prayers as my wife.''

Willsly looked sick. "You are wrong. Honestly, Rockford, I had no idea they would ambush you. I . . . I arrived somewhat late for dinner aboard that night. When I did approach, I heard what was happening.'' He wrung his hands. ''There was nothing I could do and I knew it. I had to leave or we'd both have died. I heard de Silva ordering his men to kill you and I knew it was all over. You've got to believe me.''

Through the door came a dashing figure. Armando's coat was his favorite red velvet today. His blue-black hair glimmered and so did his smile.

''It's finished,'' Willsly moaned. He found a handkerchief and mopped his face. ''I don't know how you've done this and I curse you for it, Rockford.''

''I doubt the marquess is troubled by your curses, Willsly,'' Armando said. ''I gave no order to kill him. It was I who arrived in time to stay my men's blades. Odd that I did not pass you on my way aboard. My hand itches to feel the handle of my knife. It would be better if you were no longer here when I give in to that urge.''

Beatrice held her breath. The figures in the room seemed to recede, then grow very large. Perspiration bathed her back. *Rockford?* Treachery in Hong Kong? Guy knew of Willsly's plan to marry her for Papa's money?

Willsly was edging toward the door. He turned sideways as he passed first Guy, then Armando, and disappeared into the hall.

''It is done!'' Armando said triumphantly, offering Guy a hand.

''Finished!'' Guy laughed and clasped his friend's hand in a mighty shake. ''And now we can put all that behind us. Beatrice, introduce me to your father, please.''

She could not move, could not speak.

Guy frowned. ''You are shocked, my love. Forgive me. I could not tell you everything sooner for fear things would not turn out as well as they have. Sir?''—he bowed to her father, who rose to his feet—''Mr. Merryfield, sir, I am delighted to make your acquaintance. You have raised a wonderful daughter of whom you should be very proud. She is brave and audacious—rare traits in women, I believe.''

Papa was of medium height but he appeared shorter this evening, bowed and older. "This is all overwhelming. I need time to come to terms with so much.''

"You do indeed." Guy kept an eye upon Beatrice and his frown remained. "I am Guy Falconer, marquess of Rockford.''

She scrubbed at her eyes. An arm came about her shoulders and she looked up into Armando's concerned face.

Guy was immediately at her other side. "You have been through too much, too soon, sweeting," he said softly, holding out his arms for her to come to him. "All will be wonderful. Please believe and forgive me. It is poor defense for having deceived you, but the truth is that I never expected to marry you or to discover deep feelings for you. I have done both," he finished simply, beckoning again.

"You *did* deceive me," she said, putting herself from Armando. "Both of you did. You used me to punish Lord Willsly. Surely he is a villain, but you are almost as bad. You toyed with me. Why, I do not even know your true name.''

"It is Guy Frederick Christian Falconer, eighth marquess of Rockford. The last marquess of Rockford if I do not—er—*arrange* for an heir." His smile was charming.

Beatrice was not charmed. "Then we are *not* married. I married Guy Falcon, not . . . not, that whoever you said.''

"I assure you that you did marry me, my lady. If you consider, I think you will have no recollection of seeing my name on the license.''

She thought hard. "No.''

"It was there. You are the new marchioness of Rockford and I am very proud of you.''

"You need not be," she snapped. The outrage of it all became clear. "You, you . . . *you*. I have decided not to be married to you."

He laughed softly. "I hardly think that is something you can argue anymore—no, not at all. Perhaps I should refresh your memory about certain *necessary*—"

"Oh, you are despicable. You lied to me."

Sibyl slipped into the room and went directly to Armando's side. Beatrice looked imploringly at her companion. "Sibyl, please tell Papa how these—these *people* duped us into believing they were generous men helping us out of the kindness of their hearts."

"Are you suggesting you didn't set out to use me?" Guy asked quietly.

"Not to *use* you," she protested.

"What, then?"

"Well, I—" He was muddling her. "I offered you a bargain."

"And I accepted it gladly. I still accept it gladly."

"Beatrice," Armando said. "You have endured a great shock. Guy used you. But you also used him. Perhaps this should be forgotten. How fortunate that your bargain has brought you both love!"

"Sibyl? Help me!"

"Armando is right."

"You are useless," Beatrice cried. "You are besotted with this Spanish pirate!"

Sibyl gasped. "Beatrice!"

"It is true."

Armando held Sibyl's arm. "I very much hope it is true. And I am no longer a pirate, Lady Rockford."

"*Don't* call me that."

"It's who you are," Guy said. His eyes were that dark green she would find ominous were she not so incensed. "We have both been guilty of deceit. I apologize profoundly and I beg your forgiveness. I certainly give you mine."

Beatrice looked to her father and found no help in that gentleman's bewildered countenance.

"Very well," she said. "I am done with all of you. Finished. I will not speak to any of you again. Look at me, *Lord Rockford*."

"Gladly."

She raised her chin. "I concede that we used one another, but I did so in good faith and honesty toward you. I *told* you why I did what I did. *You lied*."

No one attempted to stop her from leaving the room.

8

"WHAT is it that keeps you so busy so early in the morning, daughter?"

Beatrice looked up from the guest list she was compiling. "I'm making arrangements for a gathering," she told her father, who had soundlessly entered her boudoir. "I assume you will have no objection?"

He clasped his hands behind his back and studied his feet. "I suppose I must be glad for any sign of your returning to the world, m'dear."

"I was not aware that I had left it." Part of her had most certainly left, the part she'd briefly, radiantly, held most dear, but her capacity for passionate love had broken her heart and that part must be cut away and forgotten.

Papa pulled a chair close to the writing table and sat down opposite Beatrice. "I suppose I may still not raise the question of—"

"No."

"I thought not. What kind of gathering are you having?"

"Women's minds must be opened. They cannot be left to fall prey to manipulative men."

Papa made a grunting noise. His heavy, expressive brows—more white than black now—rose toward his thick, graying hair.

"Please do not concern yourself that your opinion in any way discourages me," she told him. "After all, you are a man and cannot be expected to be enlightened on these matters."

Papa cleared his throat. "It's been more than a week since you and your—"

"No! Do not mention that man to me."

"Since you and your husband agreed to part."

"I sent him packing!" But *why* had he been so ready to leave?

"You miss him."

"I *do not*!" She *would* not.

"If you insist."

"It astonishes me that you side with a man who dallied with my emotions."

"Beatrice, as we speak, Lord Rockford pines for you."

"Piffle! I have served his lordship's purpose. Now I am an embarrassing inconvenience, nothing more. As we speak he is probably in the company of his *inamorata*."

"Beatrice!"

"I am not a child, Papa. I know about these things. And I intend to work harder than ever to ensure that more women put aside the foolishness of ignorant youth in order to arm themselves with worldly knowledge."

"Men would do well to tremble."

"Do not make fun of me." She slapped down her pen. "And do not treat me like a paperskull."

"Indeed I will not. What exactly will be the topic for your gathering? I take it you do not intend simply to drink tea and discuss needlework, poetry, and the like?''

Men. ''Our subject will be the English, Chinese opium wars and their significance to English women.''

Papa was silent for so long that Beatrice wondered if he'd heard her at all. ''I said—''

''I know what you said. Clearly I am too uninformed to guess at the inferences you ladies may manage to draw. However, I hope the process proves illuminating.''

Beatrice scowled thoughtfully. ''You mean you think it *could* be illuminating?''

''Don't you?''

''I don't know. I only made up the topic when you asked me for one. I suppose I was thinking of how . . .''

''Yes,'' Papa said earnestly and put a hand on top of hers. ''You were thinking of how events in those wars led to a certain evil action against a good man and sent him dashing back to England to settle a debt of honor.''

''*Honor*. Pah! I have no patience with honor.''

''I believe you do. You are an honorable woman and would never betray the values in which you believe. Your husband is also honorable.''

''How can you say that when you know what he did to me?''

Papa squeezed her hand. ''My dear girl, you *did* to one another. You needed him to help you deal with Willsly and he needed you to help *him* deal with Willsly.''

''I was honest about that from the beginning.'' She had revealed to her father the truth about the nature of her former fiancé. ''Guy . . . That man was not honest with me. He let me think he was a chivalrous gentleman in reduced circumstances.''

''Chivalrous, yes. In reduced circumstances, no. He told me how he presented himself to you and I believe him. You decided he was impoverished and he decided not to risk enlightening you.''

Beatrice became hot. ''He made a goosecap out of

me. I cannot bear to consider how I prattled about my fine sympathies for his peculiar circumstances.'' She shuddered.

"You both took false steps. But you are both fine and true souls. Remember, Lord Rockford did not choose to act in violence against his enemy as many men would have done. His punishment was harsh but still merciful.''

She did miss Guy. "There is nothing to be done now.''

"Yes there is. Go to him.''

This time she turned cold. "You jest.''

"I was never more serious. Go to your husband, Beatrice. Tell him the truth.''

"*He* should come to me.''

"You sent him away and said you would never speak to him again. For three days he called and sent flowers and gifts. You would not see him and you returned the gifts. A man has pride. Finally he followed your wishes and returned to his home.''

She folded her arms tightly. "What exactly is the truth I should tell him? If I were to tell him anything. Which I definitely shall not.''

"That you love him.''

"I *hate* him.''

"You love him and you are utterly miserable without him.''

Her eyes began to sting and she bowed her head. "I am not miserable.'' Two large tears slid down her cheeks and spattered the long sleeves of her brown silk dress. "How can I be when I know he would never have noticed me if I had not presented him with a means to punish his enemy? Lord Rockford could have married any woman he chose. A beautiful woman with the best of pedigrees would have been his natural choice. He is burdened with me—a plain nothing.''

Papa sighed. "I cannot know everything that is in the man's heart, but he said he cares for you and, again, I believe him.''

Guy had admitted that he cared for her? "Yes,'' she

said slowly, remembering how young and gay he'd become during their one marvelous night together. "I think he may even like me a little."

"Now you are being sensible. Take your place with him."

"There can be no hope for us—not real hope."

"Beatrice," Papa said in his wheedling voice. "At least try."

She shook her head.

"You love him, child, and you are *desolate* from wanting to be with him. Do as I ask you in this. Go to your husband."

"What if he turns me away?" she whispered.

"He won't. But if he should, it must be your task to change his mind."

Beatrice sniffed. "I am not renowned for prudence in difficult situations. I may make him very angry."

"But you will risk that because you know he is committed to your marriage and that he will eventually forget his anger."

"I don't think . . . Yes I *can* do it." She stood up. When had she ever been a fainthearted chuckle head? "I *shall* go to him. It is time he confronted the true mettle of the woman he married. I am no simpering, swooning, milk and water miss. Plain, I may be. Devoid of splendid taste I most certainly am. But I am also very strong and very *determined*. I shall prepare to go to him."

"Good!" Papa turned in his seat. "Sibyl, you can come in now. Beatrice has come to her senses."

With mounting chagrin, Beatrice watched her friend enter the little yellow and russet room. "You were waiting outside," she said accusingly. "The two of you conspired to force my hand whilst I was in a melancholy mood."

"Conspired?" Sibyl's blue eyes grew round. "How could you suggest such a thing? I've brought your green satin cloak. The coach is ready and our trunks are already aboard. Come along, Bea, we want to be in Sussex well before nightfall."

* * *

Crivens's shoes creaked with every tiptoeing step. Across Guy's chamber to the Jacobean table beside the bed. Creak, creak. Pick up the untouched breakfast tray. Creak, creak, creak. Return to the door.

"Get out!" Guy shouted. "And stay out! I am not hungry, damn you."

Creak, creak. The door closed, but only for seconds before it opened again. Creak, creak, creak, creak . . .

"In God's name." Guy turned onto his stomach in the bed and yanked the covers over his head. They would not leave him alone.

"Luncheon is served, my lord."

"*Enough!*" Guy roared and threw back the covers. He leaped, naked, from the bed and loomed over Crivens. "It is barely eight in the morning, you insufferable ancient pestilence."

Crivens raised straggling white brows and fussed with a silver cover. "If you say so, my lord."

"You brought chocolate at five when the bats were not yet abed. I did not drink it."

"We noticed."

"You brought breakfast at six. I did not eat it."

"True."

"And you returned at eight with *luncheon*. With *luncheon*, man?"

"Perhaps a little something suitable to the early afternoon would tempt you more, my lord. I'll return with a fresh offering at nine."

"Armando shall pay for this," Guy muttered.

"As you say, my lord."

"*You* shall suffer for implementing his design to torture me."

"Undoubtedly, my lord."

"This is mutiny. Mutiny, I tell you. In my own house!"

"We are not at sea, my lord."

"Get out." This had gone too far, much too far.

"And do not return until and unless I call for you. Is that clear?"

"You need to eat and—"

"Answer me. Do I make myself clear?"

Crivens bowed. "As you wish, your lordship."

"You may tell *Señor* de Silva that I am not amused by his interference."

"He . . . That is, *we* wish you to know that you have our deepest sympathies in these trying times."

Guy turned his back.

"The little lady . . . that is, her ladyship immediately became dear to all of us here at Aldersgate. We could not have imagined being so instantly drawn to a new mistress." There was a pause before Crivens rushed on, "And we know you must be mourning the loss of her."

"My . . . If ever a man suffered." Guy fell backward to spreadeagle on his bed. "My wife is not *dead*, damn it."

"No, my lord. And for that we are all truly grateful. We shall pray for a happy solution to your dilemma."

Guy closed his eyes. Crivens left the room again and this time the creak of his shoes did not irritate. *What* was he supposed to do about Beatrice? She was his wife. No matter how angry she was, or how betrayed by him she felt, or how much she might prefer it to be otherwise, Beatrice was the marchioness of Rockford and would remain so.

She had been so angry. Damnation, but she was a firebrand. Truly, a passionate . . . a seductive, tantalizing, lissome, voluptuous . . . a woman quick to learn the most nerve-searing ways to drive a man mad with her every move, with every touch of her small, capable hands.

He rolled onto his stomach, winced, and eased to his side. Simply thinking about the little witch snapped his body to rapt and ready attention.

"Go to your inamorata." Hellfire, she had a mean and inappropriate mouth. *"Find a pretty woman more suited to your taste . . . You did not choose me as a wife,*

you tolerated me out of necessity.'' And that had been the final barb, the thrust that made him give up and leave her—forever.

"Aah." His arousal remained heavy and throbbing. He *needed* her. No other woman would do. And he needed her *now*.

"And I *like* you, you little twit." Again he leaped from the bed, this time to begin dressing. "You have a mind that intrigues me. And I will have you back where you belong. Crivens!"

The man entered at once. "Yes, my lord."

"Where is Baggs?" His valet had a habit of disappearing at the most inconvenient times. "I require a shave. Instantly."

"I'll attend to that for you, my lord. Baggs is with Cook trying to devise morsels to tease your appetite."

"You are all admirable in your loyalty. Hurry, man. I have to be in London as quickly as possible."

Within the half hour, Guy was dressed in his favorite somber tones and striding from the house.

His splendid maroon barouche had been drawn around from the stables and Crivens rushed down the front steps to throw open the door.

Working on his gloves, Guy calculated. "Mm, no," he said at last. "Bring me Trojan."

"But, my lord—"

"I have not forgotten how to ride long and hard and I trust my favorite stallion is still up to the challenge."

The horse was brought and Guy mounted.

"What if there are callers, my lord? Lady Bollington from Nethermill sent word that she's heard of your return and hopes to bring her daughter to meet you."

Guy wheeled the black, drawing him in until he reared. The Bollington girl was pretty and pale, with rouged cheeks and colorless, calculating eyes. The Bollingtons were on the hunt for a husband and had no idea he was ineligible. He laughed. "Tell them I'm sorry I missed them. Tell them . . . Tell them I'm paying a visit to my *inamorata.*'' They would believe that and wait to be invited next time.

With the wind at his back, he rode almost due north. Once the boundary of the estate lay behind him, the next miles were covered through lanes turned into green tunnels by beech trees and wild pear, juneberry, and spindle.

At a fork some miles along his ride he reined Trojan in. Directly ahead lay the main road. To the right was a narrower, less-traveled path used only by those who knew these parts well.

The dry grinding of coach wheels and the whinny and blow of hard-pressed cattle reached him. Someone was in a tear to go in the direction from which he'd come.

The Bollingtons would come that way.

Guy's decision was made. He applied the heel to his mount and shot off to the right.

"I am quite certain my heart is about to leap from my body, Bea."

"Mine, too," Beatrice said, leaning to see the gray stone walls of Aldersgate come into view. "But I am convinced this is the correct course."

"Mm. You don't suppose Armando might have left for Spain, do you?"

Beatrice gave Sibyl a sharp look. "I have no idea. Your infatuation with that gentleman worries me. What do you know of him?"

"Nothing." Sibyl raised her nose in a futile attempt to look down haughtily upon Beatrice. "But I would not allow bliss to escape me if I had a chance to do otherwise. Unlike some people I could mention."

"Touché. However, I am about to put that matter to rights. Sibyl, I must caution you about Armando. He is not—"

"You don't know what he is, Bea," Sibyl said, but she smiled. "Don't worry. I will do nothing foolish."

There was no time for further discussion. The coach swung to a stop before the front doors. Not waiting for assistance, Beatrice scrambled out and rushed into the house.

In the hallway, she turned a circle, gazing happily upward at the vaulted ceilings. Home. She was in her own home—the place where she belonged with her husband.

At this time in the afternoon he would be in his study.

Crivens appeared from below stairs, followed by Mrs. Wiffen.

"Hello," Beatrice said breathlessly. "How glad I am to see you again. Please, do not concern yourselves with me. Or with your master. No, no. We shall probably not need anything more this evening."

They appeared disconcerted. Beatrice smiled to herself and tripped rapidly off in the direction of Guy's study.

Returning to Aldersgate only hours after his triumphant departure—on the back of a hay wagon—stripped Guy of all but simmering frustration.

The untraveled route he'd chosen had foiled him in the end. Had he taken the usual road, a lame horse could have been easily enough replaced. As it was, a farmer's stall in which to leave Trojan and an uncomfortable ride in the farmer's wagon were the best that could be done.

"I reckons that be your place up ahead, sir," the farmer called. "I'm sure as you'll understand if I don't take 'ee closer."

Guy jumped down and jogged alongside until the farmer slowed down. "You've your deliveries to make, my man," he said, pressing a guinea into a weathered and calloused hand. "Many thanks for your kindness. I'll send someone for my horse."

The gold coin in the man's palm rendered him speechless and Guy walked away without a backward glance. Aldersgate's main entrance lay around the next bend in the road.

Tomorrow he'd set off again—with the early morning bats—and in the carriage as he should have done today.

Marching down the driveway, he whistled. Tomorrow would come soon enough and this setback would give him more time to consider how best to woo his lady quickly back into his home, his arms . . . and his bed.

Sunlight flashed on something. Guy squinted against the glare and realized he walked in the path of a swiftly oncoming coach.

Cursing, he threw himself aside, landed half-buried in a spiny yellow gorse hedge and coughed as billows of dust engulfed him.

Twenty minutes had passed by the time he extricated himself from the vicious thorns and finished his walk to the house. The sight of Crivens and Mrs. Wiffen, side by side on the front steps, was surprising but entirely welcome.

"My lord," Crivens said, coming to meet him. "What has happened? Where is your horse?"

"Do not ask me now. I want a bath, food, and bed. And I want the barouche ready by five on the morrow." He climbed the steps slowly with Crivens hovering at his elbow. "Good afternoon, Mrs. Wiffen. Nice of you to greet me."

"Tell him, Mr. Crivens," she said, holding her thin body stiffly erect. "*Tell* him."

Guy stopped and looked questioningly at Crivens who rolled in his lips and executed a strange little sideways dancing step.

"*Tell* him."

"Crivens," Guy said wearily. "Do not waste my time."

"Very well." The man's arms dropped heavily to his sides. "She was here. Your wife. Lady Rockford was here, but she has left again."

"Yes indeed," Mrs. Wiffen said heavily. "And someone ought to find a way to bring her back at once."

Guy stared. "My wife came here and left again?"

"She arrived only hours after you set off, my lord." Crivens resumed his agitated trot. "Went directly to the study expecting to find you there. And when I told her you'd set off, she settled down to wait, so she said.''

"Surely you told her where I'd gone.''

"Not at first,'' Crivens said miserably.

"Why not?''

"I didn't think I ought to.''

"It's a pity you didn't continue to keep your counsel, Mr. Crivens,'' Mrs. Wiffen said. "She'd be waiting yet, if you had.''

"Where is Armando?'' Guy started for the house again.

"Left with the ladies.'' Mrs. Wiffen made no attempt to hide her disapproval. "Said if they were going to insist on traveling into the night, they'd need his protection.''

"But—'' He didn't understand any of this. "What could have possessed them to *leave*?''

Mrs. Wiffen pointed a bony finger at Crivens. "Him. He told Lady Rockford where you intended to go.''

"To London?'' Guy said. "To reclaim my wife? Why would she run away again? I shall leave now. Get the barouche.''

"To . . . You never said that, Mr. Crivens.'' Mrs. Wiffen sounded amazed. "You said his lordship was going to visit his, well, you know.''

Horrified understanding welled within Guy. "You didn't tell her . . . You didn't.''

Crivens nodded. "I did. She dragged it out of me, but not before she suggested it herself. She asked if you'd gone to your *inamorata* and I couldn't tell a lie, could I?''

"You could have on this occasion!'' Guy thundered. "Hell's teeth, I'd better take another horse. I'll never catch them by coach.''

"No, my lord,'' Crivens murmured. "Of course, she did say she'd be stopping at the chapel.''

"What?'' Guy asked with an echo from Mrs. Wiffen.

"The chapel. I heard Lady Rockford tell her coachman she'd be stopping there to pray for your soul before setting out for London again. But she probably won't stay there long.''

''*Crivens!*'' Guy and Mrs. Wiffen shouted in unison.

When he saw the carriage by the churchyard gate, Guy leaned on his fresh mount's neck and gave thanks. ''I am truly grateful that my sins require lengthy prayers.''

Guy dismounted and left the horse untethered and grazing the fragrant hedgerows. The Merryfields' coachman snoozed atop the box and did not as much as stir when Guy passed.

The gate whined on its hinges. Inside, summer-bleached grasses brushed about his calves. Wildflower scents mixed with the soft aroma of warm earth.

A feminine laugh, carried on the breeze, came from the left where gravestones in motley granite and marble hues leaned comfortably wherever winter winds had pressed them.

The laughter had been Sibyl Abbott-Smyth's and the recipient of her rapt attention was Armando de Silva.

Guy stood still and watched, but not for long. Within seconds Armando looked up sharply and, even at a distance, their eyes met. Armando turned Sibyl toward a monument and she bent to read the inscription. Whilst she was distracted, he pointed and Guy followed his direction.

A wild leaping of his heart was like nothing he remembered. The sight of Beatrice, immobile beneath the maidenhair tree in which he'd climbed as a boy, stole his breath.

He spared another glance for Armando, who inclined his head and returned to studying the monument with Sibyl.

The grasses swished against his trousers. At every step he expected Beatrice to hear him, and to run away.

She wouldn't run. His wife was here in this softly overgrown chapel garden because she had returned to him.

Why had she come?

A bird soared from a nearby hollow, its jangling song rushing downward, faster and faster to end with an exuberant flourish.

"You frightened Mr. Chaffinch, my lord."

Guy started, looked from the bird to Beatrice. He hadn't realized he'd drawn so close. "I dislike frightening birds."

"Even dull, brown little birds?" She smiled serenely, showing no surprise at his arrival, and strolled away from him. "Lord Willsly referred to me in such terms to his friends. An apt description, but it did not please me."

He faltered. "There is nothing dull about you, Beatrice. But I would never wish to frighten you."

The folds of her silk skirts spread upon the grass, slipping sensuously with the lithe movements of her hips and legs. "I thought you had gone to London."

"I set out to do so."

She reached another maidenhair tree and paused to snap a cluster of its fan-shaped leaves from a low branch. "This is such a peaceful place."

"It is yours, Beatrice. Just as it is mine. Everything I have is yours."

Bowing her head, she hid her face from him and he waited, as his heart seemed also to wait, for her response.

"Why didn't you go on to London?"

He let out a breath. "I thought it was because my horse drew up lame and I could not locate another in time to make the ride tonight."

"I see."

"That was what happened, but it wasn't the reason I didn't go. Not in truth."

Her head raised a little—enough for him to see her golden eyes steady upon him. "In truth?"

"From this moment there shall never be other than truth from me to you, Beatrice."

Her lashes swept downward.

"I did not go to London because I was not meant to

go. I was meant to be here waiting for you to come home, only I didn't know it."

"Home," was all she said, so quietly he scarcely heard.

"Your home. It must be yours because without you I would have to leave this place, leave my home. I could not bear to remain without you."

He saw her white throat move, and the tremble of her lips.

"You told me I lied to you. I did. I regret everything about that except the fact that it may have brought about our bonding."

"True," she told him. "This morning I decided to come to you and ask what your heart tells you we should do."

"I'm glad."

"Crivens told me—"

"He repeated my exact words. Only he did not know that I jested. I have no *inamorata*, Beatrice. Yes, there have been women in my life, but none that I . . . I have never wanted another woman as my wife."

She looked fully at him. "Yes. I do not know why it should be, but I believe you."

Bending, she brushed a hand over the heads of forget-me-nots and green alkanet, of purple clary and the tender early buds of yellow meadow rue. "There is no time in this place, d'you see. The new and the old, the budding and the dying, only to bud again. Around and around in a circle with no beginning and no end."

"And we are part of that circle," he told her. "Here we were joined. Here you became my own and I became yours. Truly, Beatrice, I became yours."

"By the words man has made law, yes."

"By the words God gave man to take as his law by which to live. To live and make some sense of that life."

She straightened and looked past him. The corners of her full mouth tipped upward, but a sheen came into her eyes.

Guy turned to discover what she saw. A way off, still among the gravestones, stood Armando and Sibyl. His hand was on her arm, hers upon his chest, and there was no need to draw closer to know that they saw only one another.

"I wonder," Beatrice said softly and took her bottom lip into white teeth. The breeze tossed escaped curls across her face but she didn't appear to notice.

"What do you wonder?"

"Foolishness." Shaking her head, she made to turn away.

Guy caught her hands and held her fast. "Tell me."

The sheen in her eyes became the wavering glitter of near tears. "Foolishness," she repeated. "The wondering of all plain women: What must it be like to be loved? What must it be like to look into the eyes of a lover and know that he sees only you and finds in you all that he has ever dreamed of for his life's mate?"

Guy's stomach fell away. Muscles in his thighs locked. She must feel the shaking of his hands yet showed no sign. He had not courted her, told her the small, foolish but good things a woman needed to hear. She thought herself plain!

"Will you let me lead you where I want to go?" he asked, willing her to agree.

She nodded.

Very carefully, he released her hands and set about picking flowers. "Come," he told Beatrice, smiling, leading the way. Bright pink willow herbs and orange poppies audaciously brightened his bouquet and downy roses offered sweet fragrance from the hearts of peach-colored blossoms.

The chapel door was closed. Guy turned the iron ring handle and pushed. He stood back to let Beatrice enter the cool interior before him.

"Wait." Into her arms he placed the bouquet and, before she could protest, he quickly released her hair from its bonds and let it fall about her shoulders. "Beautiful hair."

"Brown," she said.

"Firelight on cinnamon silk. Stand exactly here."

He walked down the aisle, his boots echoing on ancient stone flags. Before the simple altar he turned to face her once more and offered his hand.

She hesitated only a moment before coming to him through dappling shafts of colored light from stained-glass windows.

"Beatrice," he said, once more taking her hands in his. "I came of my own free will to be with you in this place."

Guy pressed her fingers and she searched his face. "I came to this place of my own free will because I knew I would feel you here," she said. "Then you were really here and I'm so afraid to trust what I feel."

"Trust," he told her, unsmiling. "As your husband, I say again that I take you for my wife, willingly, gladly."

"Thank you."

He shook his head. Beatrice smiled and whispered, "Sorry. I am willingly your wife and I gladly take you as my husband."

"You are mine, Beatrice, no matter what good or ill befalls us, and my heart rejoices."

"Whatever comes our way can only bring me joy if I share it with you," she told him.

No longer able to stop himself from kissing her, he rested his lips on her brow and closed his eyes. "Beatrice," he murmured. "I will love and honor you all the days of my life."

The soft sound he heard was Beatrice's indrawn breath. She kissed his jaw. "And I will love and honor you all the days of my life."

When he framed her face with his hands the final rays of the sun through amber glass agreed that her hair was cinnamon silk, her cat's eyes the color of warm whisky, and her skin like peach-blushed cream.

"Now I can tell you how it feels," Guy told her.

Beatrice frowned.

"To be loved. To look into the eyes of a lover and know that you are all she ever dreamed of in a mate. I am beautiful to her, just as she is beautiful to me. Can you feel it, too?"

Her lips curved. "Yes, yes! I feel it, thank you."

"Ah, yes." Laughing, Guy tipped up her chin and kissed her deeply. "It seems I am doomed to be forever helping you practice your wifely skills."

"A shocking burden, my lord."

"Indeed, but all part of an absolutely *Necessary* bargain, my lady."

Stella Cameron

Twenty-six years ago, at this time of year, my husband and I married. The setting was London like the setting of *Bargain Bride*. Like the heroine of *Bargain Bride*, Beatrice Merryfield, I was headstrong and made my own decisions. There end the similarities!

Poor Beatrice. Dependent upon such volumes as *Mrs. Featherwise's Instructions to Brides*, she had to deal with Guy Falconer, Marquess of Rockford, and the pressing question of *The Neccessary*. Mrs. Featherwise is my own invention, but *The New Female Instructor*, published in 1834, did exist and may still be read today.

I've picked out a few insightful suggestions from *The Instructor*—and added my own interpretations:

"Coquetry is, of all female conduct, the most infamous . . . it is an act of barbarity and insolence, that deserves the severest punishment."

Translation: Eyes down, you conceited hussy, or he'll know you're not lusting after his mind.

"Harmless, unmeaning gallantry is one of the qualifications of a well-bred man."

Translation: Insincerity is acceptable if he knows both of his parents.

"It is possible a man may covet your company, without the least design upon your person."

Translation: Optimism has been around a long time.

May you love and be loved—equally. Cheers!

The Bride of
Wildcat Purchase

Judith E. French

Prologue

London, England
1720

*D*AMN *me, but my groom looks much like a frightened
hedgehog,* Lissa thought wryly.

"Elizabeth!"

Her father's reprimand cut through her rebellious reverie and she took his extended arm reluctantly.

"I'll have no nonsense from you today, girl," he warned. "Have you not given us enough grief these past ten years when you've turned down every suitor we've proposed? Sir Edmund is as wealthy as Croesus, and better than a disobedient chit like you deserves."

Lissa, the Lady Elizabeth Rutledge, lifted her chin and entered the chapel of St. Anne's on the arm of her father, Lord Hayden. Slowly, they walked down the wide aisle toward the altar and her waiting groom, Sir Edmund Stiles. And with every step, Lissa felt her heart grow heavier.

The church was packed with highborn guests, so much so that Lissa found it hard to breathe. Elegantly clad gentlemen were standing at the back of the crowded pews and along the walls. Elizabeth could hear the admiring coos and whispers of women as they caught sight of her wide-hooped azure gown of chine silk with its daringly low-cut bodice and pinked open skirt revealing a gold-and white-flowered petticoat.

The Rutledge emeralds encircled Lissa's neck; the matching earrings dangled ostentatiously beneath her heavy pearl-covered cap. Her hands were heavily weighed down with priceless rings: ruby, pearl, and diamond. She felt as though she was entangled in a suffocating web of silk and gold and precious gems.

Her groom turned to meet her. One of his front teeth was missing; the other was capped with ivory. *He's old*, Lissa thought. He's sixty-one. Worse, she towered over him. Even though he wore high-heeled shoes and a russet periwig, she was still near a head taller than Edmund.

"Smile at him," Lissa's father hissed.

Edmund beamed with joy and bobbed from one foot to the other excitedly. His portly figure strained at the seams of his lavender waistcoat; his bandy legs were covered with padded silk stockings.

Oh, God, Lissa thought. He does look like a hedgehog. Her strained smile became a giggle, and for one terrible moment, she imagined waking up every morning for the rest of her life and staring into the face of a grinning hedgehog.

She bit her lip and tried to hold back the amusement. Tears streamed down her cheeks. She jerked from her father's arm and tried to smother the laughter with her hands. But nothing could stop her outrageous outburst.

"Elizabeth!" her father roared. "What is the meaning of—"

"I'm sorry—so sorry," she gasped to Sir Edmund. "But I can't wed you. Forgive me." Still laughing merrily, she tossed her flower-covered prayer book into her shocked stepmother's lap, and ran back down the aisle and out of the church into the bright summer afternoon.

1

Annapolis, Maryland
May 1721

LISSA stood at the rail of the sailing ship and scanned the Annapolis dock for sight of her bridegroom. She was still too far away to tell slave from freeman, let alone recognize a man she knew only by a few lines' description. Nervously, she twisted the plain gold wedding ring on her finger and wished for the hundredth time that she'd married Edmund Stiles and not made a total fool of herself in front of half of London.

Instead, she had wed a total stranger and crossed an ocean to be the bride of a colonial who called his estate by the outrageous name of Wildcat Purchase.

"You are no fool, Lissa Rutledge," she murmured aloud. "You are a raving bedlamite." Unconsciously, she fingered her emerald earrings, the famous Rutledge gems that were the sole item of value she possessed in all the world.

How could she have anticipated the extent of her father's rage when she'd run from the altar? How could she have expected him to strip her of jewels and finery and turn her from his door like a wandering beggar? "You are no longer a daughter of this house," her father had said. And the harshness of his softly uttered words had cut deeper than a whip across her back. The only reason he hadn't confiscated her emerald earrings as well was that her hair had hidden them and he hadn't remembered she was wearing them.

"You have shamed us and Sir Edmund," her stepmother had insisted. "Your father will never be able to hold his head up in proper society again."

She regretted hurting Sir Edmund. He'd never done her harm, and it was scarcely his fault if he resembled an aging hedgehog. Once again her own shrewish tongue and damnable disposition had gotten the best of her.

She was an earl's daughter, of better blood than his royal majesty, German George, and now she was forced to barter herself to an unknown husband like some squint-eyed butcher's offspring.

The wind continued to push the ship closer to the dock. Sailors swarmed over the deck, lowering sails and readying the anchor. Fellow passengers began to assemble on deck, including the Reverend William Parsons and his wife, the couple who had acted as her chaperons on the long sea voyage.

"Lady Elizabeth! Lady Elizabeth!" Mistress Parsons called. "I say!" She waved a gloved hand frantically. "Do take care."

Lissa nodded and smiled dutifully, then turned back to watch the harbor for signs of a tall, well-formed gentleman of means.

He was tall. The letter had stated that. It was the one thing that she'd had to know, once Nanny had assured her that Master Mackenzie was both young and a man of wealth and property. Lissa had spent years looking down on the top of suitors' heads. If she must have a husband, he had to be taller than she was.

Well formed. Lissa pursed her lips. Why would any gentleman describe himself in such a manner? What if he'd lied? What if he was hunchbacked? What if he was a dwarf?

No. She nibbled her bottom lip nervously. She had not only her new husband's word, but also that of a noted London solicitor.

". . . respected throughout the colony as a man of fortune and good sense. He is blessed with a healthy constitution, is not poxed or otherwise disfigured, and possesses all his own teeth.''

She hoped his teeth *were* sound. Her own were white as pearls and perfectly spaced. She'd always been proud of them . . .

No one had ever called her a beauty. She was too tall, and her thick hair was so dark a brown as to be almost black, decidedly unfashionable when blonde was the preferred hair color for a woman. Her hair was too dark, her legs too long, her eyes as brown as Thames mud, and her complexion more olive than fair. She favored her deceased Welsh grandmother. And, truth to tell, Lissa was six and twenty, far past the age for taking a first husband.

If Master Mackenzie expected a pale English lily, with the bloom of youth still on her cheeks, he'd be in for a surprise. Of course, he was in for a shock anyway. She was not the wife he believed he had married by proxy. She was an imposter.

When she'd fled from her father's wrath, she'd gone to the country cottage of her old childhood nurse, hoping that Nanny could make things right as she always had before.

But Nanny had problems of her own. Nanny's favorite granddaughter, Margaret, had strayed from the fold and celebrated May Day with a little too much enthusiasm. Nine months later, only fifteen years old, apple-cheeked Margaret had produced an eight-pound bouncing boy. The child's natural father, the village wheelwright, was a married man and in no position to give his son a name. And because of this illegitimate child, Margaret, now eighteen, had been unable to find a husband.

The colonial Mackenzie had seemed heaven-sent to the shamed family. He had written to England for an educated bride, well-skilled in the duties of a farm wife. He said he wanted a good-natured, sweet-tempered girl of decent background. But he also stated that he did not require a virgin bride. He was willing to have a widow, with or without her own children, and he was prepared to accept in good faith one such as Margaret Bowman, who brought with her the evidence of her own dalliance.

Master Mackenzie had not asked for his bride to provide the usual dowry. He had said that he was "in fortunate circumstances . . ."

Mackenzie had sent hard coin as a gift for the woman's parents. Margaret's yeoman father had accepted the gold; in fact, he'd already spent part of the money on a new team of oxen and seed, when the girl had changed her mind and said she wouldn't marry the colonial.

A tearful Nanny explained to Lissa that between the time of Margaret's meek acceptance and Lissa's arrival, the wheelwright's wife had passed on. Now a widower, the wheelwright wanted to wed the flaxen-haired Margaret and claim his son. Margaret wanted to marry him, but her father was insisting she keep the bargain and take the rich colonial.

Lissa twisted her wedding ring round and round. What had possessed her to offer to take Margaret's place? To go through with a proxy ceremony that made her Mackenzie's legal wife?

She'd always considered herself a thinking woman, despite her stepmother's accusations to the contrary. An unmarried maid was forever under the heavy hand of a father. She must dress thusly and behave in a simpering manner before men. She could not travel without escort, or buy or sell anything not permitted by her father. For the love of Christ! She could not even choose which church to attend—even her path to the afterlife was strictly laid out by her guardians. And if, as in her case, she had no loving mother to shield her from her father's displeasure, she was at a total loss.

After much pondering she had agreed to marry Edmund Stiles to get away from her stepmother's constant attacks. She had reasoned that any home of her own would be preferable to being an unwanted burden in her father's house, always the victim of her ill-tempered stepmother's criticisms.

But she had not reckoned with her own perverse sense of humor. She could not marry a hedgehog, no matter how gilded his burrow.

She only hoped she'd not made a worse bargain in marrying a man sight unseen. Suppose the colonial beat her, or expected her to work like a serving wench? Suppose he was some nasty pervert who would take advantage of her innocence and virtue?

Lissa sniffed. "Hmmph." She was, after all, a Rutledge. One of her female ancestors had pushed a youthful Prince John in a reeking castle moat and lived to boast of the deed. If this Mackenzie was too bad, he'd best look to his own safety. She'd not be abused by any man— father or husband. If this colonial was the devil's spawn, she could send him to meet his master. Better a rich widow than a battered wife, she thought.

"Master Mackenzie . . . Master Reece Mackenzie . . . He had best treat me with proper respect," she murmured. "Or else."

A splash drew her attention, and she saw that the sailors had dropped anchor. Apparently, the merchant vessel that had carried her from Bristol was too large to moor beside the Annapolis dock. As much as Lissa anticipated her arrival in the colony and meeting her new husband, she couldn't help feeling a little sad that the trip was over. She'd never been at sea before, and to her surprise, she'd loved the water. She hadn't been sick once, not even when the ship had been rocked by several days of stormy weather. She'd seen whales and dolphins and flying fish. She knew it was an experience she'd never forget.

"Hallo, the ship!"

Lissa glanced toward the starboard bow. A small boat with two rough-looking men in it had pushed off from the dock and was nearing the larger vessel. The man at the oars was wiry and gray-haired; his striped shirt and tarred pigtail proclaimed him a seaman.

The second man seemed to be some sort of frontiersman. He was dressed in a vest and trousers of fringed animal hide. His hair was so dark as to be almost blue-black, and his features were as rugged as the Indians Lissa had seen on display at the Tower of London. Thinking that this might indeed be a wild Indian, Lissa walked to the center of the deck, where she could get a better view of the boat and its occupants.

"Hallo, the *Provider*!" the woodsman called in perfect, if somewhat accented, English. "Is there a Mistress Margaret Mackenzie aboard?"

It took several seconds for Lissa to realize that it was she the rascal was asking for. Despite her marriage lines, she'd not thought of herself as actually being Mistress Mackenzie. Captain O'Shaughnessy and the Parsons had addressed her as Lady Elizabeth. As an earl's daughter, she had a right to the title of "lady" to be used with her Christian name.

Unable to contain her curiosity, she crossed to the starboard railing and regarded the speaker with no little amusement. "What do you want with the Mistress Mackenzie?" she shouted.

"Lady Elizabeth." William Parsons's tone was slightly censuring. "This is unseemly. Come away from the rail and let one of the ship's officers deal with the coarse fellow."

The rowboat bumped against the *Provider*, and the Indian leaped to catch a dangling rope and climbed agilely over the rail, nearly landing in Lissa's arms. Startled, she backed up a few paces and surveyed him.

He was a magnificent creature, standing well over six feet in his soft skin shoes. His brawny shoulders were as wide as a blacksmith's, and his bare chest bulged with muscle. His well-proportioned arms ended in wide, clean hands with short-cut nails. There was scant body hair in evidence, none on his exposed chest, none on his arms or the backs of his hands—an oddity for one so swarthy.

Coolly, Lissa ran her inquiring gaze up his handsome neck, over the strong jaw and dimpled chin. The Indian's lips were thin but sensual, his large nose straight, his cheekbones high and well defined. His brows were sleek and dark, arching over eyes as shiny as ripe blackberries after a summer rain.

His ears were close to his head and as tanned and red-brown as his face and arms. His thick hair was drawn back into a queue and secured by a leather tie at the back of his neck so that it fell nearly to his waist in a single braid as thick as his sinewy wrist.

Around his neck, the native wore a string of huge animal claws, and as he moved toward her with a fluid gait, she saw that his bulging left bicep was encircled by a band of incised copper. The leather trousers he wore were belted at the waist by a beaded belt, and hanging from that belt was a sheathed knife large enough to butcher a steer.

Lissa stood her ground and threw up a raised palm. "Hold there, varlet," she commanded. "Your master should teach you better manners."

He stopped in his tracks, but his devilish black eyes flashed pure insolence.

"State your business," she ordered. "And show proper deference to your betters, lest I have you physically chastised for disrespect."

He grinned at her, and the sloe-black eyes danced with merriment. "So I shall, m'lady," he replied in a lazy drawl, "once I've met one better than me."

Lissa drew in a deep breath and took a step backwards. A sensation close to fear washed through her as she felt prickles of gooseflesh rise up on her arms and the back of her neck. Sweet Mary! What manner of man was this—to speak so to her? "I—" she began. But she was cut off by the Reverend Parsons.

"You, fellow!" the cleric accused, hurrying to place himself protectively in front of Lissa. "How dare you accost the Lady Elizabeth?" He raised his worn Bible as if to ward off the Indian by the power of the Word. "Captain!" Parsons cried. "Captain! We are in need of succor!"

The savage laughed, a deep rumbling sound that drew Lissa's gaze to his as surely as if she had been bound by invisible chains of affection. "Peace, Black Robe," he said. "I mean you or the lady no harm. I come seeking Mistress Margaret Mackenzie."

"Then you've come to the wrong place," the minister replied. "There is none aboard by that name. The Lady Elizabeth—"

Lissa cleared her throat. "Excuse me," she said, "but I believe I can clear up this misunderstanding. I am—"

Her nervous speech was ended by the arrival of the bosun, the first officer, two armed sailors, and the ship's captain. "What's amiss here?" the first officer demanded.

The Indian turned toward the newcomers without a trace of apprehension. "Captain O'Shaughnessy." The savage grinned. "A swift passage. Congratulations."

Lissa's eyes widened in shock as Captain O'Shaughnessy thrust out his hand to shake that of the intruder.

"Thank you, thank you. Yes, a good trip. Fair sailing, thank God, and a profitable cargo."

"You're a fine master, Sean. I'd have trusted this cargo to none other," the Indian replied.

She was becoming more accustomed to his speech. She could not fault him for his use of the language, and his deep voice was softly lilting. She moved a little closer, not wanting to miss a word of this unusually familiar exchange between the master of the *Provider* and the big native.

"I trust things have gone well in the colony in my absence. You've not suffered another drought like last year's?"

"Nay. We've no cause to complain about these crops." He withdrew his broad hand from the captain's. "I couldn't wait for you to come ashore." He smiled again and nodded toward Reverend Parsons. "I've come for the lady, but yon cleric tells me she's not aboard."

"Not aboard," the captain said. "Not aboard. How ridiculous." He gestured toward Lissa. "She's here, and safe. This is the new mistress of Wildcat Purchase."

It was the Indian's turn to look surprised. "There's

been some mistake,'' he said. ''You cannot be the former Margaret Bowman, now Mistress Mackenzie.''

Lissa felt her cheeks grow hot. ''And why can't I? My name is . . . is . . . Margaret Elizabeth,'' she lied. ''Lady Elizabeth. I am Mistress Mackenzie.'' She held out her hand with the heavy gold wedding ring as proof. ''And I assure you, fellow, that your master shall hear how rudely you've treated his new bride.''

''Margaret is eighteen, and the mother of a toddler, madam,'' he answered coldly. ''You hardly fit the description.'' He folded his massive arms over his chest and stared at her through narrowed eyes. ''You, my lady, will never see twenty again.''

''Jesu!'' The oath slipped from her lips before she could cover her mouth. ''I'll not be insulted by a . . . a . . .'' Anger made her bold. She trembled with indignation. ''A creature in animal claws!'' she declared. ''A common forester who would not know a maiden of quality from a hickory stump.''

The Indian covered the distance between them in a heartbeat. Before she could flee, he'd seized her hands and held her in an iron grip.

It seemed to Lissa as though time stopped. Her heart pounded; she couldn't breathe. She felt as though she had suddenly been plunged into a bath of freezing water. She was icy cold from her cheeks to her toes, yet his fingers burned into her skin as though they were red-hot.

''You cannot be the bride of Reece Mackenzie,'' he said softly.

Lissa swallowed the lump in her throat. ''I am,'' she croaked. Shamed at her cracking voice, she repeated herself in more normal tones. ''I am.''

''You've tricked me,'' he accused.

''Tricked you! I don't even know you.''

''No, but you will. I'm Reece Mackenzie, the man you deceived into marrying you.''

Lissa blinked. Her stomach seemed to drop to her knees and come bouncing back. ''You?'' she stammered. ''You can't be.''

"Easier me to be Mackenzie than you to be Margaret Bowman, yeoman's daughter, wearing emerald earrings that would buy any farm in Kent," he retorted.

"You're lying."

"No, m'lady, he is Reece Mackenzie. I've known him for fifteen years," Captain O'Shaughnessy put in.

"What?" Reverend Parsons asked. "She's not his wife?" Mistress Parsons appeared beside her husband, her round face pale with shock.

"No man would call me a liar to my face and get away with it," Mackenzie said.

"But . . . but, I thought—" Lissa was horribly aware of Mistress Parsons's murmurs of displeasure. She scrambled for a proper answer, desperate to right matters, to put this scoundrel in his place and restore her plans. "I expected Mackenzie to be—"

"Faith and damnation, woman!" he exclaimed. "I am the injured party here. I don't know who you are, or what game you think to play, but—"

"I tell you I am his wife—*your* wife," Lissa insisted. "I have a ring . . . marriage lines."

"She crossed the ocean to live with a man not her husband," Mistress Parsons whispered.

Lissa looked from the angry hawk face looming over hers to the captain's stern features. "This is just a . . . a misunderstanding," she said. "If we could speak in private, Master Mackenzie."

"And so we shall," he snapped back. "Sean? Your cabin?"

"Of course," the captain said. "Feel free."

Mackenzie let go of her hands, tucked his arm through hers, and half-led, half-dragged her toward the master's cabin. "You'd best have a smooth tongue, madam," he threatened softly, "or you'll find yourself staring through the bars of the Annapolis jail."

"You can't do that!" she protested.

"No? If you do have marriage lines, then I am your legal husband. And if I am, I can do anything to you that I like—even sell you to the Indians!"

2

THE cabin door banged shut behind them. Reece let go of Lissa's arms, and she put as much distance between them as she could in the cramped quarters. "Well, woman?" He kept his tone low, but his words contained an edge of acute exasperation. "Who are you?"

Lissa straightened to her full height. "I told you. I am your wedded wife. If you really are Reece Mackenzie—a statement I still doubt."

"I am Reece Mackenzie, and I am the man who paid a marriage portion to the father of Margaret Bowman, yeoman. I also paid for your passage from England."

"No one said you were a red savage. '. . . Respected throughout the colony as a man of fortune and good sense.' So the London solicitor proclaimed." She wrinkled her nose disdainfully. "You are in no position, sir, to cast stones. Why, I doubt that you are even a Christian."

"I'd not have to be a wellspring of piety to be a better Christian than you. I have not lied or deceived anyone. I make no excuses for my Indian blood; my mother is of the Nanticoke people. But I was born in wedlock, and I am my Scottish father's heir."

"Ha!" she scoffed, unwilling to admit that she was on rocky moral ground. "Look at you! My father's game-keepers dressed better than you. You said you owned five thousand acres of land in the Maryland colony. I doubt if you own an uncracked chamber pot or the place to empty it.''

"You jay-tongued jade!" He took a step toward her.

"Can you deny you lied about owning the land?" *How dare this heathen try to bully her!* Lissa thought. She was no ignorant farmer's daughter! She'd read their marriage contract carefully, and she'd bade the London solicitor to tell her of a wife's rights according to Maryland law. His bluff of selling her was no more than that. She wasn't a slave. And if he did own land, she was entitled to an income from part of it, even if they divorced. As for harming her, he'd not dare to lay hands on her aboard the *Provider*. "I know not how the natives treat their women," she added, "but I am of gentle birth, and I resent being shouted at."

"Am I shouting at you?" he asked between clenched teeth. His features were so taut, that were his skin not so tanned, she was certain he would be as ruddy as a beet.

"Answer me this simple question, sir. Have you five thousand acres of land?"

His fists clenched at his sides, but intuition told her that he would sooner strike the furniture than her. Unwillingly, she began to feel some bit of sympathy for Reece Mackenzie. Most men would have withered before her sharp tongue.

"It is not quite the whole truth," he managed.

"Ah-hah." She gave a satisfied smirk to put him in his place, but inside, her hopes sank. A tiny part of her had wished . . . She seized the weapon he had given her and drove it home. "You lied about owning the land, then?"

"Aye, in a manner of speaking."

"Either you do own five thousand acres, or you do not. 'Tis not a difficult concept, even for an uneducated colonial."

"Madam, I'll have you know that I received a proper schooling."

She smiled again. "Then you should certainly be able to express yourself concerning the land."

He swore beneath his breath. "I do not own five thousand acres, I own fifteen or twenty thousand—God knows exactly how much since the land grants are written in such a whimsical manner."

"Oh." She brought the tips of her fingers to her lips. "Oh, I see." He was not a pauper. He was a man of property, despite his appearance. She allowed herself a quick glance at those brawny shoulders, then dropped her gaze modestly to the deck. For a man dressed like a rough servant, he did exude a certain virile charm . . .

She turned toward the single cabin window to give herself a little more time to gather her wits. Her situation was desperate. She had no money, not even enough to keep herself for a month at the most modest inn. She had no skills to market, save those of a wife. Of her own clothing, she had only the gown she stood in and the garments he had provided as part of the marriage contract. A wealthy husband who had been educated as a gentleman—a man with such an admirable body—did seem the lesser evil. Even an eccentric husband might be softened by the right woman's attention.

"Woman."

Lissa prided herself on her chess playing. As a student of the game, she had always had the ability to assess her own strengths and weaknesses and those of her opponent. She was an offensive player; her instructor had taught her to consider all aspects, conceive a plan, and strike hard.

Besides, she liked the tingly feeling that made her breathless when Mackenzie got too close.

She turned back to him without a trace of shrewishness in her voice or manner. "I owe you an apology, sir. You are right. You are the wronged party. In my defense, I can only say that the fault is not mine, but the wheel-wright's."

The tension drained from his face. "Who in hell is the wheelwright?"

Lissa's explanation of Nanny's granddaughter's romance with the village wheel maker, and Margaret's change of heart toward Master Mackenzie, lasted all during their boat ride back to the dock and dinner at the Gilded Pigeon, a local inn.

She concluded her sad tale over a goblet of decent red wine and a delicious helping of wild strawberries and scones. "So you can see that I felt obligated to assist my old nurse and come in Margaret's place," she said. She had been careful to omit the story of her own canceled wedding to Sir Edmund, simply telling Reece that her stepmother's ill wishes had driven her from her father's home.

Reece leaned back in his chair and took a sip of water. She'd noticed that he had ordered wine for her, but none for himself. Could it be that he was cheap? That would explain the rough deerskin trousers and shoes. She sighed. There were worse things than a man who watched his pennies—at least she wouldn't have to worry about being married to a tosspot.

"Your kindness to a stranger leaves me speechless," he replied. "Unfortunately, you won't do. You aren't what I ordered or what I need in a wife. You'll have to go back."

"Go back?" Her eyes widened. "What do you mean, go back? What of my reputation, sir? As a divorced woman—"

"In this, it seems to me there can be no need of a divorce. A simple annulment—"

"I consider myself a wedded wife. I've left home and friends, I've sacrificed everything to—"

"Madam, lower your voice. You are attracting attention."

Lissa glanced around the public room and saw that heads were indeed turned toward their conversation. The buxom barmaid was listening so hard that her head was tilted sideways and her mouth was gaping open. "Close your mouth, girl," Lissa said sharply to her. "Flies are getting in."

"I can see why you've gone so long without finding a husband," Reece said quietly. "An aging spinster soon turns as sour as four-day-old buttermilk."

"I hardly qualify as a spinster," she retorted. "I may not be the child bride you asked for but—"

"I wanted a young wife, yes," he admitted, "but only because many English women find it difficult to make the adjustment from home to the colony. I felt that one younger in years would be easier bent to—"

"*Bent*? Do you feel a wife is a sapling to be molded at will, sir?"

Reece felt his temper rise again. "Stop calling me *sir*. I have a name. It is Reece. Under the circumstances, I believe we may address each other by our Christian names."

She sniffed and wiped daintily at the corner of her mouth with her napkin. It was all he could do to keep from grabbing her and shaking her until her teeth rattled. The woman was exasperating!

He'd gone to the ship expecting a plump yellow house cat, and instead, he'd found himself with a spitting black-maned lion. It was unsettling. He'd gone about the entire business of finding a wife logically, so that what had happened between his parents wouldn't happen to him—and this was the result.

He patted Margaret Bowman's miniature in his pocket. Margaret was a plain, no-nonsense farmer's daughter, a young woman with a fatherless child to fend for. She would have fit into his and his daughter Jilly's life with the ease of a worn glove. Margaret would have been grateful for his name and protection, so much so that she would never condemn him or Jilly for their Indian blood. So much so that she would overlook Jilly's irregular birth.

Five-year-old Jilly was his life. Since she was motherless, it seemed sensible to find a solid woman who could be mistress to his plantation and care for his heir. He'd reasoned that an Englishwoman would be less likely to be prejudiced against Indians, and a yeoman's daughter would find her rise in fortune so unexpected that she would willingly trade any silly romantic notions for a secure life of companionship.

The Lady Elizabeth was no such woman. From the looks of her soft hands, she'd never done a day's work in her life. She already considered herself superior to him. What would she think of Jilly and his Indian mother?

He rubbed his hands on his pant legs and exhaled softly. Damn, but it had turned out all wrong! As appealing as the wench was, it was clear they'd never make a lasting marriage. Like fire and gunpowder, they were, unable to exchange three words without arguing.

Elizabeth leaned toward him and whispered. "If you'd been any prize, you would have found a wife in the colonies. You wouldn't have had to contract a marriage with an innocent maid who didn't know what she was getting."

Rage bubbled up inside him. The arrow-tongued female had a way of twisting everything to put him at fault. "I didn't ask for an innocent maid," he hissed. "I wanted an experienced woman, one who knew her way between the sheets. And from the looks of you, you've never been kissed let alone propositioned by a man."

"You're mad as a March hare," she replied. "All men want a virgin bride."

"Well, I don't. As far as I'm concerned, virgins are vastly overrated. And that's another reason why you won't do."

She pursed her lips. "Varlet. No gentleman would inquire as to a lady's past."

"Are you or aren't you?"

"I've had more lovers than your horse has legs," she retorted. "It's the fashion at court. No sophisticated person takes any note of such things." She fluttered her lashes and looked at him in a way that made him slide closer to the table to hide his rising interest.

He guessed she was lying to him. He'd been with enough experienced women to know fact from fancy. Of

course, most females professed innocence, rather than
the other way around.

If only she didn't have such a slender throat, a neck
made for a man's kisses. And a full bosom that promised
pleasures untold . . .

No! He'd not allow himself to become ensnared. This
Elizabeth was trouble, and the sooner he was rid of her
the better. "Elizabeth—"

"My friends call me Lissa."

"Lissa. There is no need for us to argue. Our marriage
was a mistake."

"Your fault as much as mine," she said sweetly, "but
now that we are wed in the eyes of church and man, we
must—"

"Put an end to this farce," he said firmly.

". . . make the best of our holy union."

"That is not possible."

"Naturally, I cannot force you to live with me as my
husband, but if you decide to send me away, you may
pay me a settlement."

He leaned over the table, coming within inches of her
face. Her expressive brown eyes never blinked. "I've
paid enough to you already."

She lowered her gaze and inclined her head prettily.
"I'm sorry you feel you've gotten the worst of our bargain. But I am here, and I am your legal wife. If you
wish to be rid of me, I warn you that it will cost you
dearly."

"Now, I see. Blackmail is your game. How much do
you want to turn your sweet backside around and get on
the *Provider*?" The barmaid gasped and pointed, and
Reece looked down to see that he'd destroyed the pewter
water goblet in his hands. He'd squeezed it so tightly
that it was twisted out of shape.

"You'll 'ave to pay fer that, Master Mackenzie," the
astonished girl said. "Comes dear, pewter does."

"Put it on my bill," he muttered. A scowl sent the
wench bustling away. Lissa was still watching him, un-
ruffled, not in the least daunted by his anger. He gave

her his fiercest glare, one that had sent Iroquois braves scrambling for the trees, and she had the audacity to smile at him. "I asked you a question," he said to her. "How much?"

She named a figure.

He leaped to his feet and swept the dishes off the table onto the floor. "Not in your lifetime!"

She shook a spoon and saucer off her skirt as nonchalantly as if they were wisps of cobwebs and stood to face him. "Now who is making a scene, husband?" she asked coolly. "If you won't pay, then take me to your home. For will you, nill you, I shall have my fair portion, or I shall remain here in Maryland as your devoted wife."

"Oh, I'll take you home," he shot back, trying to ignore the faint scent of violets that came from her gleaming dark hair. "But I promise you, woman, you'll rue the day you tried to get the best of Reece Mackenzie."

Lissa couldn't believe that only twenty-four hours had passed since she'd first laid eyes on her exasperating husband. Here she was, somewhere in a godforsaken forest, miles from Annapolis and any vestige of civilization. She was clinging to the stubby mane of a knifenecked mule and trying to maintain her balance while riding sideways on a man's saddle.

Mosquitoes buzzed around her head, and she had a welt on her cheek from a fly bite. Her hat hung down her back by a ribbon; she'd given up trying to wear it the fifth time it had been knocked off by a low branch.

Reece had secured lodgings for her at the Gilded Pigeon after their argument. Where he'd slept, she didn't know or care. She'd shared a narrow, hard bed with the innkeeper's wife, who snored. Then she'd been rudely shaken awake before the sun rose, offered breakfast, and been set on top of this horrible animal.

"We need to make an early start if we're going to reach home before dark," Reece had said all too cheerfully. She'd protested that she could only ride a sidesaddle. He'd replied that the stable had none to hire and she must make do. "A planter's wife must be tough," he'd said. "Of course, if you've changed your mind about the marriage and decided to return to England, then—"

"I'd rather ride the mule," she'd answered.

Now she wondered if she'd made the right decision. For all she knew, Reece Mackenzie might be crazy. She had put herself completely in his hands. Suppose he decided to be rid of her by abandoning her in the wilderness—or even murdering her?

He rode just ahead of her on a dun-colored gelding, leading the way through thicket and meadow, over streams and down game trails in the forest, hardly bothering to speak to her or even look back. How he knew where he was going was a mystery to her. Every tree looked just like every other tree!

"Are you certain we're not lost?" she'd asked him more than once.

"No, no, I don't think so," he'd replied, with just enough doubt in his voice to make her anxious.

Lissa's bottom hurt and she was sweating. She was wearing one of the gowns Reece had ordered made in England for his bride, a plain, sturdy garment of linsey-woolsey in olive green. She had on her corset, a linen shift, three layers of petticoats, a small whalebone hoop under the gown, woolen stockings, and stout leather boots. She also wore a close-fitting coat of darker green wool, riding gloves, and a buff linen stock tied around her neck.

It was only May. Lissa could never remember the sun feeling so hot at this time of year in England. If it was so warm at mid-morning, what would high noon be like? No one had warned her that Maryland was the tropics.

Most of her clothing was still in the hold of the *Provider*. Her silk gown, slippers, and under-things had been left at the Gilded Pigeon. Reece had assured her that those things would be brought to Wildcat Purchase by a servant.

"We need to travel light," he had said ominously. "In case we have to make a run for it."

"Run from what?" she'd asked.

"Hostiles."

She wasn't certain if he'd been referring to wild beasts or unfriendly Indians, but she hadn't given him the satisfaction of asking further questions.

The trees overhead were fully leafed out and alive with bird calls and the scampering of squirrels and chipmunks. Twice the mule had sent a rabbit scurrying for cover, its white tail fluffed. The air smelled of musty peat and honeysuckle and pine. From somewhere to Lissa's right came the *rat-ta-tat-tat* echo of a woodpecker. She broke the silence.

"If you wanted to murder me, why didn't you do it back in Annapolis where I could be assured of a decent burial?" she demanded.

Reece laughed, a husky rumble that touched something deep within Lissa despite her discontent. "What makes you think I'd want to kill you?" he called back over his shoulder. "Just because you tricked me? Just because you're trying to blackmail me out of support you've no right to?"

"A gentleman wouldn't keep bringing up those disputes."

"Most of the gentlemen I've known would have tied a brick to your neck and dropped you over the side of the *Provider*. You may thank your lucky stars that women are valued higher than that in Maryland. We don't murder our wives here, as much as we might wish to be rid of the annoying ones." He turned and grinned at her devilishly. "No, Lissa, you need not fear murder at my hands. Not even physical abuse. Remember, I'm part Nanticoke Indian, and Indians don't strike women or children. We consider it uncivilized."

"Being beaten wasn't my worry," she replied. "I'm a Rutledge. The last Rutledge woman who was mistreated by her husband saw him get drunk one night and tumble into his own well. A terrible accident, of course."

She sighed dramatically. ''There was talk that perhaps Great Aunt Jane had pushed him in. I suppose there always is gossip when a young, attractive woman is left a rich widow.''

''Lucky for me I don't drink.''

''Yes. Fortunate.''

When they stopped for nooning, Lissa sank onto the ground with a moan of relief. Her bottom was a mass of pins and needles, her back was stiff, and her teeth felt as though they had been jolted loose by the mule's stiff gait. She drank greedily from the water flask and made no complaint about the meager bits of cheese and bread Reece offered.

''Is Wildcat Purchase much farther?'' she asked.

''Oh, we've been on it for some time now.''

''Then the manor house is nearby.''

''You could say that.''

Getting back on the mule was harder than boarding the *Provider* in England had been—despite knowing then that she was turning her back on home and family, and that she might never see London again.

Reece took hold of her waist and swung her up into the saddle as easily as if she was a child. She knew that she was no featherweight and secretly wondered at the strength in those wide shoulders and muscular arms.

He stood alarmingly close to the mule, putting the reins in her hands. For an instant their eyes met, and Lissa was sure she saw a hint of admiration in his gaze. Then, quickly, the emotion was replaced with one of amusement.

She felt the blood rise in her cheeks and lowered her head. ''Thank you, husband,'' she murmured.

''You'll ride easier if you sit astride,'' he suggested.

''A lady does not ride astride, sir.''

''Suit yourself. It's your arse.''

Sometime in mid-afternoon, she twisted around and dropped her right leg over the saddle. She felt for the stirrup with the toe of her boot and sighed with satisfaction when she was able to take some of the weight off her buttocks. It felt odd to be riding in the men's fashion, but not so unpleasant as trying to balance on the slippery saddle sideways.

"I told you so," he mocked a few moments later.

She concentrated on counting the number of hairs in the white mule's mane and cursed Reece and his ancestry under her breath.

It was nearly dusk when Lissa caught sight of a human dwelling. At first, she thought it might be a charcoal-burner's hovel; she'd seen crude log structures something like this in the New Forest. "What's that?" she asked.

Reece turned his horse's head toward the ramshackle hut. As they drew closer, Lissa saw that the structure was abandoned. There was no glass in the windows, and the rough plank door hung crazily by one leather hinge. What had once been a wooden porch had surrendered to the woods. The rotted boards had caved in; the upright posts sagged. A brownish-black animal the size of a plump dog, and somewhat resembling a hedgehog with long needles all over its back, scurried down the slanting steps and vanished in the underbrush.

"What was that creature?" Lissa cried.

"Porcupine." Reece swung down from the saddle and led his horse toward a stream at the bottom of the slope.

"What are you doing?" she asked. "Why are we stopping here?"

He turned toward her and grinned. "Why, honey, I thought you'd guessed. This is your new home. This is the manor house of Wildcat Purchase."

3

Lissa stared at the broken-down structure for a moment, then swung her leg awkwardly back over the cantle and slid off the mule in a tangle of petticoats. Ignoring Reece's chuckle, she secured the mule to a tree by the reins and ventured cautiously onto the creaking porch.

The inside of the hovel was as disreputable as the outside. Dust and leaves littered the floor. The only furniture was an overturned bench. Cobwebs hung from the ceiling, and a trapped bird fluttered near the peak.

A floorboard cracked under Lissa's weight and she scrambled off the porch. She glanced at Reece and saw that he was watching her with an amused expression. "I don't know what haystack you think I crawled out of, sir," she said loudly, "but I'd sooner believe that you're the prince of England than this is your manor house. I don't find your joke funny in the least."

He nodded and pointed down the stream. "You mistook me, madame. That isn't my home. This is."

She walked around the corner of the hut and looked in the direction he was pointing. Through the trees, on the far side of the water, she could make out a somewhat larger dwelling with smoke coming from the chimney. "Oh," she said. Leaving the mule, she walked down to the edge of the stream to get a better view of what was not one, but two log structures.

"We abandoned this cabin when we built the new one over by the spring," he explained.

Her boots began to sink in the soft ground and she stepped back. "Is there a bridge?"

"Across this?" He chuckled. "A cat could walk through this little creek and not wet her paws. It's not deep." He glanced back at her mule. "Of course, you could ride over."

Lissa looked at the tall mule and weighed the pain and indignity of trying to get back in the saddle against simply wading across the water and getting her boots wet. "Could you help me?" she asked.

"My pleasure." Before she could protest, he dropped his own animal's reins, gathered her up in his arms, and was carrying her across the stream.

Her first instinct was to struggle. Immediately, he loosened his hold on her shoulder and she began to fall backwards toward the water. She gave a little shriek, threw her arms around his neck, and held on for dear life.

Reece stopped short and gazed down into Lissa's luminous brown eyes. She wasn't struggling now, but he had the strongest urge to hold her even tighter against him. What had begun as a prank had changed to something else.

He was suddenly aware of just how desirable this English wife of his was. Her eyes were large and intelligent, framed by dark, silky lashes; her perfect mouth—with its slightly fuller lower lip—was partially open, revealing her white, even teeth. And her rosy cheeks were infused with color. Lissa's breath was fresh, and the scent of her hair tantalized him until he wanted to bury his face in her shiny clean tresses.

She felt good in his arms, strongly muscled and soft in all the right places. No dainty child-woman, Lissa had a tall, lush frame. He'd always favored tall women, and he wondered what she'd look like without all the layers of gown and petticoats. He wondered what shape her breasts were . . . and if her nipples were as rosy pink as her lips and cheeks.

The erotic thoughts sent shock waves racing through him, and before he could stop himself, he'd lowered his head and brushed her lips with his.

The taste of her was his undoing . . .

Stopping the kiss after that was like trying to hold back the flow of a stream with a single rock. Her lips molded softly to his, as though they had been made for each other. She responded to his caress with pleasant surprise, then with an innocent ardor that made his loins grow hot and his head spin.

"Mother of God," he murmured into her moist, warm, mouth. He parted her lips with the tip of his tongue, and she sighed with delight. Tentatively, he explored the sweet interior, forgetting where they were and who she was. Forgetting everything but how good she felt and tasted and smelled.

She gasped and twisted in his arms. "I—" she began.

He stepped back to steady his balance, and his left foot slipped on the muddy creek bed. She cried out in alarm as they both went down into knee-deep cold water. Dumbly, he sat there, still holding her in his arms. He stared into her startled face, and she began to laugh.

Her peals of merriment echoed through the trees, and he found himself laughing with her. "By all that's holy," he sputtered, surveying her soaking skirts. "You've near drowned us both."

"*Me?*"

He tried to get to his feet, slipped again, and went completely under. She squirmed free and waded toward the far bank.

"My hero," she mocked. "My knight in shining armor." She pointed at him and dissolved into giggles. "It was worth getting wet to see you in such a state."

"As much as you weigh, I doubt if the mule would have had any more luck getting you across," he answered. There was no regaining his dignity. He shook his head and tried to squeeze some of the water out of his leather vest. "You, madam, are trouble," he said. But his mouth still tingled from the feel of her lips, and he could still taste her honey sweetness on his tongue.

She ignored him and walked up the incline toward the cabin. She was shivering in the cool air, but she made no protest.

As tough as an Indian squaw, he thought admiringly. Then reason returned, and a scowl crossed his face. A man could not be led about by his nether member, he admonished himself. Yes, the wench was attractive, but she was not for him. Their marriage had as much chance of surviving as the union of a trout and a porcupine.

What use was it for a man to have a brain if he didn't use it? Reece reasoned as he went back for his horse and the mule. He had lived through a turbulent childhood with parents who loved each other and their only son with a white-hot passion. But it hadn't been enough. His mother, Cholena, was Indian; his father, Alec, was Scots-Irish. They differed in everything from religion to opinions on child raising.

His father believed in strict obedience. Alec Mackenzie had suffered the taste of a rod often when he was a lad, and he expected to administer the same to his son. But when he'd attempted to curb Reece's natural mischief, he'd come up against the unyielding will of a wife who would not allow her child to be beaten.

Reece's father had never abused his spouse, but he'd expected the obedience that the Christian Bible urged a wife to give her husband. Cholena never accepted her husband's rule. She followed his wishes when they agreed with her own, and otherwise ignored them and went her own way.

Reece's Indian relatives never approved of Alec Mackenzie, and Tidewater society did not accept Cholena. In the end, despite their love, and twelve years of wedded life, the couple had separated.

Reece would not make the same mistake. His daughter, Jilly, had already lost one mother. She'd not lose another. He knew the pain of being torn between parents;

he'd spare Jilly that. He'd make a match with a woman who could be his companion, friend, and helpmate. And there was no chance that Lissa and he could ever have that kind of marriage.

She was a lady, born to a title, above him in station and wealth. She was accustomed to luxury, to efficient, soft-spoken servants, and to fancy court balls. Women of her class did not mother their own children; they left them to wet nurses and aging nannies. They did not saddle their own horses or trade with visiting Indians.

He could imagine Lissa's disgust at his mother's native customs—her scorn when she learned that Cholena could not read or write. He could foresee his English bride's disapproval of Jilly's unorthodox birth and upbringing.

No, he would not be swayed by physical desire for a beautiful woman, or even by the sound of her laughter. He would hold to his plan and force Lissa to renounce the marriage and return to England. And he would do it without agreeing to support her for the rest of her life.

Lissa folded her arms over her chest and shivered. It wasn't the cold or the drag of her wet skirts that made her teeth chatter or bubbles of excitement run up her spine. It was the memory of Reece's kiss . . . a kiss unlike any she'd ever known before.

And she was no stranger to a man's kisses. Although still a virgin, she had had her share of tease and tickle. But nothing like this . . .

She closed her eyes for a moment and tried to recapture the feel of his lips pressed against hers . . . of his strong arms around her. Not even the icy water could dampen her joy.

She opened her eyes and inhaled deeply, reveling in the scent and sight of the forest greenery, savoring the bite of cedar and pine in the air. Had she ever smelled anything so heavenly as she had in Reece's embrace?

He smelled of leather and horse and woods. It seemed right and natural, although she'd never known a man to give off just such a blend of scents. Reece seemed . . .

She struggled for just the right words, then realized she had none. Reece was Reece.

And he was her wedded husband.

Immodest thoughts played across her mind. What would it be like to awaken each morning beside Reece Mackenzie? To see his handsome face over her rumpled bedcovers? Sweet Mary! If the first one had been a hedgehog, this one was a black-maned lion.

She sighed and hurried toward the cabin. This husband was a keeper. She knew they were made for each other, even if he didn't. And it would be only a matter of time before she could bring him around to her way to thinking.

As Lissa reached the bottom step, the door opened. A tall, comely woman with huge dark eyes smiled at her.

"N'tschutti, welcome to this house," she said in softly accented English. She stepped back and motioned for Lissa to enter. "I be Cholena."

Forgetting her manners, Lissa stared at the woman in astonishment. She wore a man's linen shirt of scarlet, belted over a doeskin fringed skirt that ended just below her knees. Bare, tanned legs were clearly visible above soft, leather-beaded shoes. Around one slender wrist was a string of white shells, and she wore tiny silver bells in her ears. Her thick, black hair was braided into a single plait, which hung down her back much as Reece's queue did.

Lissa couldn't keep her gaze from dropping once more to the outlandish skirt. The garment clung to Cholena's hips, and when she walked, a slit up one side parted, proving that the woman wore no shift or petticoats. Lissa was shocked at this brazen display and wondered if Cholena might be a person of ill repute.

As Lissa raised her eyes to the woman's face again, she found an amused expression. Cholena was barely containing a chuckle. Lissa flushed as she realized that the stranger knew what she was thinking.

"I see you two have met," Reece said as he came in the door behind Lissa. *"Ili kleheleche, Onna."*

"*Ila kleheleche, Giis,*" Cholena replied in the same strange tongue.

Lissa looked to Reece for an explanation.

"This is Cholena," he said. "She cares for Jilly." He fixed Lissa with an inquiring gaze. "You did know that I have a five-year-old daughter?"

Lissa nodded. Nanny had told her that much. A daughter who would be his heir, her old nurse had said. "Is the child here?" she asked.

Reece repeated the question.

The woman shrugged. "She was, but you know Jilly." She glanced at Lissa and rattled off a string of words that Lissa couldn't understand. Reece replied, and then Cholena said something else.

Lissa stiffened at this display of bad manners. She was still standing here, dripping onto the floor and getting colder by the moment, while Reece chatted with a servant.

Lissa looked around the spotless room. The walls and roof were of peeled logs, the floor was planked. A brick fireplace dominated one wall, and beside it stood a large wool wheel and a three-legged stool. In the center of the room was a trencher table with wooden benches on either side. At the other end of the room a Welsh dresser and a painted chest flanked a small glass-paned window. Animal skins were tacked to the walls and woven baskets hung from the rafters. High above the fireplace mantel a shelf extended from the wall, and on the shelf crouched a huge stuffed animal with a cat face, little pointed ears, bared teeth, and a short, stubby tail.

Lissa shuddered and pointed toward the fierce creature. "What is it?" she demanded, interrupting the heated discussion.

"A wildcat," Reece replied. "The wildcat of Wildcat Purchase. Don't worry, it can't hurt you."

She scoffed. "I'm not a child, sir. I know a stuffed animal from a live one. My question is, why would you have such an odd thing in your house?"

"My father said it brought him luck."

"It certainly couldn't have been too lucky, or it wouldn't have ended up on your wall," Lissa answered.

Cholena chuckled. "Alec Mackenzie, Reece's father, did not harm the *pay shay ew*," she explained. "It once saved his life. He honored it and only brought the skin here when it died of old age."

Puzzled by this familiarity between Cholena and her master, Lissa went to the hearth and held out her hands to the fire. A spit held a roasting fowl over the coals, and Lissa licked her lips, suddenly realizing how hungry she was. "Ask her to find me dry clothing to put on," she said. "I'll catch my death if I stand here long in these wet things."

Another exchange in the foreign language followed. Then the woman went through an open doorway into another room and returned with a bundle slung over her shoulder.

"Do not let him get the best of you," she said to Lissa. "He be a man too fond of having his own way." With a nod, she flashed a bright smile at Reece and left the cabin.

"That is your daughter's nurse?" Lissa asked. Suspicions tumbled over one another in her mind. "Where is the child? And where are your other servants?"

"Jilly probably fled when she saw us coming. She's not partial to white women. She has spent most of her life with Cholena and has learned Indian ways."

"Her nurse is Indian?" He nodded and she went on. "Then I presume that was a native tongue you were speaking?"

"Delaware."

"But Cholena does know English?"

"Yes, of course."

"Then I will tell you that I found it quite rude of you to speak so that I could not follow what you were saying."

He nodded again. "I suppose it was."

"Who is she to you?"

"A friend."

"That's all?" She watched his eyes closely.

"It's all you need to know." He went into the next room and returned with a deerskin garment thrown over his arm. "I'll settle the animals in the barn. You can put this dress on. You needn't be afraid. There's no one here but the two of us."

She held up the shapeless fringed dress. "You want me to put this indecent garment on?" she demanded.

He shrugged. "That or nothing. Did you believe I'd have a wardrobe ready for you? There are blankets if you'd rather wrap yourself in one of those."

"Does this belong to *her*?"

"Cholena? I imagine so. It's too big to be Jilly's." He scowled. "The dress is clean, I assure you. Cholena bathes every day—even in winter."

"How very odd."

"Yes, isn't it," he replied sarcastically. "You'll find we have all sorts of odd customs in the colonies." He turned toward the door. "Suit yourself. If you'd rather stay in wet clothes than put on an Indian woman's dress, the loss is yours."

Reece closed the cabin door behind him and walked slowly down the steps. He knew his mother would be waiting for him in the stable, and he wasn't eager to feel the lash of her tongue.

"So!" she said in the Delaware tongue, when he led the animals into the barn, "this is how you show respect for the one who gave you life? You are ashamed to tell your English bride that I am your mother?"

Reece stiffened. He'd not introduced Cholena to Lissa as his mother because it would only complicate getting rid of Lissa. His mother had a way of taking situations into her own hands, regardless of what he wanted.

If he wasn't firm with her, she'd take a stand for or against the marriage. And if Cholena chose to take Lissa's side, there'd be hell to pay. "You know that's not true," he protested. "I've never been ashamed of you, *Onna*. I've already told her that my mother is Nanti-coke."

"Then why do you let her think that I'm a servant?"

"I never told her that. She reached that conclusion herself."

"So." Cholena sniffed and folded her arms over her chest. "My son has become an Englishman if he believes that allowing an untruth to go unchallenged is not as bad as telling the untruth."

"She's not my wife." He had to fight back a chuckle, realizing that he was basing his logical statement—that they weren't married—on Indian law and not English, when he'd contracted the agreement as an Englishman. Not only had he told Lissa that he was her husband—he was afraid that he'd also said to her that she wasn't his wife. He was so confused that the only thing he could do was to try anything to get Lissa to repudiate the marriage.

He sighed. It wasn't just the proxy marriage that he found confusing. All his life, he'd been torn between two sets of laws and beliefs. Usually, he found himself following his Scottish father's ways while inwardly thinking that his mother's Indian customs made more sense. Half-breed, he'd been called. And although Jilly was only one-quarter Indian, she would probably face the same conflict.

"By English law or ours?" his mother asked.

"What?" He realized that he'd been so deep in thought that he hadn't heard what she'd said.

"Are you saying that Lissa isn't your wife by English law, or by Nanticoke?"

He nodded, feeling more uncomfortable by the moment. He loved his mother dearly, but she had a way of seeing through him and making him feel ten years old. "By English law, we are married. But it is a marriage on paper only. Lissa isn't the woman I agreed to take as my wife. I asked for a farmer's daughter. She—"

Cholena laughed. "This English Lissa with the Indian eyes, her hands are white and soft. She has never known the soil. She carries herself with the pride of a Shawnee." She relaxed her stance. "I like her. She has promise."

"Don't start, *Onna*. I'm not keeping her. She's not right for me or for Jilly. She'd soon make our lives miserable." He busied himself with unsaddling his horse. "I only brought her here because she insisted on coming to my plantation."

"And she knows that you intend to send her back." Cholena removed the mule's bridle and slipped a halter over the animal's head.

"I won't have Jilly hurt," he replied, ignoring her question. His mother was no ignorant savage. Despite her lack of formal education, she was shrewd and quick thinking. Still, there were some aspects of English prejudice against Indians that she could never comprehend. Things he could not try to explain without hurting her . . .

"She is a beautiful woman, this Lissa."

Reece hung the saddle blanket over a railing. He didn't need his mother to tell him how beautiful Lissa was; he could damn well see that for himself. "Yes, she is," he said grudgingly, "but I can't let that—"

"Yes," his mother said. "I know about this logic. It is English thinking that makes a man choose a woman he does not know, because if he takes one that his heart bids, he may risk having that heart broken."

He turned back and took her hand. "I'm trying to do what's best for all of us," he said, lifting her fingers to his lips and kissing them. He loved his mother deeply; he always listened when she gave advice, but in the end—as always—he made his own decisions. "I'd not live with a woman who could not show you respect, or one who would look down on my daughter for what she is."

Cholena stepped closer and embraced him. "My son, my son! Always you take the difficult trail. What is Jilly but a precious child? A gift of the Great Spirit? She is bright and healthy. Any woman would be overjoyed to have such a daughter. As for me, I am what I am. Your wife, this woman or another, must take me as she sees me. I could not change for your father, whom I loved in ways beyond counting, and I cannot change now for whoever you call wife."

He released her and moved back. "I'm not asking you to change." He gazed into her loving eyes. "Let me handle this as I see best. You and Jilly are what matter most."

"And you, my son? What of your own happiness? Would you not be happier with a wife you could love?"

"I will love her, whoever she is. I will care for her and protect her. I will put her interests ahead of mine, and I will—"

His mother shook her head. "I do not mean that kind of love." She touched her breast. "What I felt for your father was—"

"It wasn't enough," he protested. "You couldn't live together." Memories of their heated arguments swept over him. He could almost hear his father saying, *"You are my wife. You have to do as I say, woman."*

"No. We could not." She looked at him intently. "But we never stopped loving. Never. I never took another husband, and he never took another wife."

"I don't want to experience that pain."

"Pain is part of life."

He shook his head. "You won't change my mind. Lissa belongs in England. She doesn't belong here in Maryland as the wife of a half-breed tobacco planter."

"Perhaps you should ask her that."

"Onna." Damn, but his mother was as stubborn as a snapping turtle. When her mind fixed on something, it was nearly impossible to budge her. "Please. All I'm asking is two days. Just go and take Jilly. Visit Uncle Comes Running, or go to Little Badger's baby daughter's name feast in Delaware Turtle Village. Two days, and I'll have Lissa back on the ship for England."

"Two days?" She raised an eyebrow wryly. "So. You are very like your father. Hard-headed, too logical for your own good. But the Great Spirit made most men like this. Why, I do not know." She nodded. "Yes, I will give you a week, my son. But if you have not settled this matter of your wife who is not your wife, I will think it my duty to welcome her to our family and to learn for myself if she will be a bad mother to Jilly.''

"Agreed.'' Willingly, he helped her ready her own mount and Jilly's pony. He held her mare's head while she put a moccasined foot in the stirrup and swung lightly into the saddle. "*Onna*, where is your pistol? You know I don't like you to ride about unarmed.''

"Tuh!'' She chuckled. "What harm can come to me on Wildcat Purchase or on Delaware hunting ground? You grow soft, you young ones. When I was your age, there was danger from Iroquois war parties and English soldiers. They used to shoot us for sport.''

"Take my pistol.'' He removed it from his saddlebag and handed it to her. "You won't have any problem finding Jilly?''

"Me?'' A giggle sounded from the rafters overhead.

Reece threw up his arms to catch the child as she jumped down to him.

"*Nukuaa!*'' she exclaimed.

"English, Jilly,'' he reminded her, squeezing the wriggling child against his chest. God, how he loved her. She was the light of his life, and as wild as any Iroquois brave.

"Papa.'' She giggled again. "You didn't see me. I saw you, and you didn't see me.'' She squinted her brown eyes to slits and made claws of her hands. "What if I was an enemy? I could scalp you!''

He looked into the small round face and melted. Jilly was a natural beauty, an imp of a fairy child with wheat-colored hair and huge dark eyes. "Not if you were here to protect me, little warrior.'' He didn't have the heart to chide her for not wearing a skirt. Instead, she was clad in a fringed yellow vest and boys' doeskin breeches that came to just below her knee. "Your grandmother is taking you with her to the village. Will you shame her by dressing like a bound boy?''

"Oh, *Nukuaa!*'' She giggled again.

Reece kissed the top of her head, tugged one pigtail playfully, and sat her on her pony. "Mind your grandmother, and stay out of trouble.''

"Will you send away the English lady, Papa?"

"Do you want me to?"

"*Kehella kella*! Yes. I don't want a new mother."

"Well, what little girls want and what they get is not always the same," he replied. "That is for your Papa to decide."

"Send her away," Jilly repeated. "Or . . . or . . ." Her long eyelashes fluttered in the solemn face. "Or I'll creep into her room at night and take her scalp."

"Enough of that, my Jilly," Reece's mother said. "Come, we must ride if we are to arrive at the village in time for the evening meal and the stories." Cholena smiled at Reece and held up a finger. "One week."

"Yes, mother."

He watched as they rode down the narrow trail, then he turned back to the house to get out of his wet clothes. He wasn't sure what he would say to Lissa, but he'd think of something. Some way, somehow, she'd have to be on her way back to Annapolis first thing in the morning.

4

LISSA had watched with mixed emotions as Reece followed the Indian serving woman out of the dwelling. She still wasn't certain if he was telling the truth about this being his manor house, and she was uneasy about Cholena. Was Reece deceiving her, or was she being overly suspicious?

England and her past life seemed very far away. Even

though she knew it had been only a few days since she'd first laid eyes on Reece in Annapolis harbor, she felt as though it had been months. Everything here in the colony was larger, more colorful, and highly intense—so much so that it was hard for her to separate what was real from what she imagined.

Reece's kiss had been real.

She closed her eyes for an instant, letting the rough cabin recede from her thoughts as she tried to relive the magic of that first kiss. When Reece had held her close to him, when their lips had touched, she'd known that she was experiencing something that came once in a lifetime. It was a feeling that she wanted desperately to hold on to. "I want him," she whispered. "I do."

But he didn't want her. Or at least he said he didn't . . . And he intended to send her back unless she could change his mind.

Drops of fat from the roasting bird sizzled loudly as they dripped into the flames, and the room was filled with the rich scent of meat. Lissa's eyes snapped open as the wonderful smell snatched her from her romantic reverie to the reality of a rumbling stomach. She blinked twice and giggled. "A husband will do me no good tomorrow if I starve to death today," she said. Her gaze was drawn to the crispy, golden-brown fowl, and she licked her lips.

She was so hungry she could hardly resist stealing a leg. She didn't know if the bird was chicken or duck or some exotic wilderness creature, but she didn't care. She licked her fingers and reached out to break off a piece, but before she could manage the theft, she sneezed.

"Oh!" Her nose tickled and she turned away from the bird, realizing that she was still standing in wet clothing. If she didn't get dry soon, she'd be sick. Reluctantly, she left the warmth of the hearth, gathered up the dress Reece had brought her, and went into the second room.

This was evidently a bedchamber. Three double beds were built against the walls, all hardly more than raised boxes. This room had a fireplace too, but it was cold, the hearth swept clean. The center of the room was empty; there wasn't even a chair, but the floor was covered with rugs of animal pelts, and a curved-top wooden chest stood at the foot of each bed. A wide shelf near the hearth held a stack of bright-colored wool blankets.

The log walls of the room were covered with painted wooden masks, a bow and arrows, animal skins, baskets, and bundles containing God knows what. Dried corn, tobacco, and herbs hung from the ceiling. It was the most unusual room Lissa had ever seen, spotless and as strangely furnished as if it stood at the far corners of the earth.

Shivering, Lissa began the awkward task of undressing herself without the services of a maid. On the ship, she had made do with the part-time assistance of one of the minister's serving girls. Before leaving England, she had never dressed alone. In her father's house, she'd had a personal maid, two upstairs girls, a jill-of-all-work, a hairdresser, and several footmen just to assist her in her morning preparations.

This gown laced up the back, and the ties were wet, but finally, with the aid of several choice words, she was able to work the knot loose. She removed the green linsey-woolsey, her petticoats and hoop, and her boots and stockings. She left on her linen shift and her stays, and considered the deerskin dress.

Should she put it on? She rubbed the soft leather between her fingers. It was a lovely thing, but far too exotic for her, she decided. She folded the dress and lay it on a bed, then wrapped herself in a red blanket she took from the shelf. To her relief, the wool was clean and smelled of pine.

She nearly left her garments where they had fallen, but then realized that if Reece truly had no servants except Cholena, nothing would dry. She thought better of her action, retrieved her gown, petticoats, and stockings, and carried them back to the main room. "It certainly is an odd way to live," she murmured aloud.

In her home she had rarely been alone. There were

always servants standing around listening to conversations, staring, and intruding on one's privacy. Actually, she decided, she could learn to like the solitude. The realization that she could hum or whistle or even talk to herself without being considered as mad as May butter was intriguing.

Reece hadn't returned from stabling the animals, so Lissa dragged a bench to the hearth and arranged her things in front of the fire to dry. She was just lining up her boots when the door opened and Reece entered.

"You'd be more comfortable in the doeskin dress," he said, closing the door behind him.

"I'm not a native. I'll not dress like one, thank you."

"You are a contrary lady if I ever met one."

Lissa's heart thudded and began to beat faster. She'd tried not to think of him while he was out of sight. She'd concentrated on the physical motions of removing her wet things and getting warm. But now he was here, and he filled the small room with his overwhelming male presence.

Reece was as wet as she was, she realized. His damp leather garments gave off a tangy but not unpleasant smell. He was smiling as though he knew a secret jest, and he looked younger and more approachable than he had at the inn.

Swallowing back the lump in her throat, Lissa let herself dwell on the possibility of making a life with this man . . . of living here in the wilderness in this crude house. Of having him as a husband.

It was impossible. And yet . . . She offered him a faint smile, and his features lit with warmth.

"You must be hungry and tired," he said, coming toward her. "I don't suppose you know how to . . ." He shook his head. "Never mind. Give me a moment, and I'll see what Cholena has left for us to eat."

"Where is the child, your daughter?"

"She and Cholena have gone to the Delaware Indian village."

"I wanted to meet Gillian."

"Jilly. We call her Jilly." He frowned. "There's no need. It would only upset both of you. She's afraid of white women, and she can be quite a handful when she's crossed."

"What can you expect if her upbringing is left to her Indian nurse? What of the child's mother? Was she a native as well?"

"Jilly's mother was Irish. Her name was Nora, and she died several years ago."

"Nora was your first wife?"

"No. Nora was . . ." He searched for the right word. "A friend. She had a husband who deserted her. When Jilly was born, we thought it best if I took the child to raise."

"Jilly is your by-blow?"

"I have taken legal steps to give her my name and to make her my heir. Her irregularity of birth is my fault, not hers," Reece replied stiffly. "Nora died of a summer fever when Jilly was two, but she was never a vital part of my daughter's life. My mother has been the only mother Jilly's ever known. It was Mother who urged me to take a wife." Reece pulled off his vest and hung it on a peg.

Embarrassed, Lissa averted her eyes. Whether he was her husband or not, she was unaccustomed to men removing their clothes in her presence. Then the absurdity of it all struck her and she stifled a chuckle. If Reece was to be her husband in truth as well as in name, she'd have to see far more of him than a bare chest!

When she looked back at him, he was unlacing one of his soft deerskin shoes. His eyes were focused on the leather tie, and she could gaze at him without meeting his arrogant stare.

Lord, but he was beautiful! Reece's exposed chest and shoulders were lean and hard, muscular in all the right places, and tanned to a smooth copper hue. His sinewy arms gave her goose bumps as she remembered how effortlessly he'd swung her up to carry her across the stream.

He glanced up into her face and she started, hoping he couldn't read her brazen thoughts. He grinned at her and set his moccasins beside her boots on the brick hearth. She moved aside to let him pass, and his hard hand brushed hers accidentally.

Again, Lissa felt a jolt of lightning burn through her skin, and her knees went weak. Her chest felt tight, and she struggled for breath. Her mind struggled with her rebellious body for control. What in the name of all that was holy was wrong with her? She was blushing like a green country wench. Handsome men had never made her nervous or awkward before.

Vexed with her own foolishness, she spoke too sharply. "I . . . I hope you'll have the decency to go into the other room to remove your—"

"Aye, so I will," he teased her, not letting her finish. "There are plates in the Welsh dresser. Make yourself useful by setting the table."

Her eyes widened in surprise. "Me?"

"Who else?"

"In my father's house, there were servants to—"

His features darkened. "Aye, I'm certain there were. But here, our women are accustomed to honest labor."

"You have no maids or cooks at all?"

He scoffed. "Of course we have servants!" He shook his head in amazement. "We're not uncivilized in Maryland."

Lissa didn't miss the amused twinkle in his eyes. He was having fun at her expense, and she didn't care for it a bit. "Where then, sir? Where are these paragons?" she demanded, hands on her hips. "Perhaps they are polishing the silver in the orangery?"

Reece sighed patiently. "Pegleg is off somewhere in the bush. It's a full moon, and he always runs off on a full moon. He'll be back in a few days. He's not been right since the Mohawks sawed off his leg and ate it in front of him."

Lissa covered her mouth with her hand. "Mother of God! You're not serious?"

"A Mohawk is the most serious thing God ever created," he answered in deadly earnestness. "My mother's people say the name means man-eater. They're a scourge, for certain." He took a few steps closer to her. "If you're still here when Pegleg returns, don't raise your voice around him. The poor man's nerves are shot."

"And what position does this Peg person serve in your household?" she asked suspiciously.

"Pegleg is our cook. Not a bad cook either if you like muskrat stew. Pegleg favors muskrat, and he serves it often."

"Muskrat?" She wrinkled her nose.

"Aye, it's what we're having tonight." He pointed to the spit. "The plantation is overrun with muskrats. They burrow under the house and fall down the chimney. Eating them doesn't put a dent in the population, but—"

"I don't believe a word of it," she replied. "You, sir, are a liar." She gestured to the bird. "That's chicken or duck, not rat."

"Not a rat in the true sense of the word, certainly," he said. "Nay, lass. A muskrat is more of a swamp animal. They can't really fly, but they use their wings to glide from hummock to hummock—something like a giant bat." He came closer, so close that Lissa could see the slight muscle twitch in his upper lip.

"I'm no simpleton," she said. "And muskrat or not, I intend to eat before I starve to death."

"The twins help around the kitchen, but they are off crabbing. We have long winters here in Maryland and when the horseshoe crabs come upriver, the women net them and salt them down for winter. They'll bring a wagon load back to the house for jelly. Hedvig makes a horseshoe-crab pie that will match anything you've ever eaten at a lord's table."

"I see," she said. "Hedvig and . . . I take it Hedvig is one of the twins?"

"Hedvig and Hulda. Good girls, both of them, even if they don't speak much English. They're indentured servants from Sweden. Big girls, and strong."

"Housemaids?"

"After a fashion. Hedvig tends the goats and makes cheese. You do know how to make cheese, don't you? We eat a lot of goat cheese here."

"No, sir. Cheese making was not considered a ladylike art in my father's household."

Reece frowned. "Can you at least make decent jellied eels?"

"I'm afraid not."

"Can you dry fish or shear sheep?"

"No."

"Shoe a horse?"

"I'm not a blacksmith."

"Can you set broken bones?"

"Nor a barber," she retorted hotly. "The trouble with you, Reece Mackenzie, is that you don't want a wife, you want a slave."

"Margaret could do those things. If Margaret had come as we agreed, there'd be no problem. As it is . . ." He shrugged. "You can see that we're completely unsuited to each other."

"Break your word, then," she taunted him. "Sunder your holy marriage vows."

"Not even the church recognizes a marriage that hasn't been consummated," he said. "And I have no intention of sleeping with you."

Anger boiled up inside Lissa and she balled her hands into tight fists, all the while keeping her features from revealing her true feelings. Instead, she nodded meekly. "I cannot force you to behave like a husband," she murmured between clenched teeth.

"Good. Then we are agreed," he replied smoothly. "I'll take you back to the ship in the morning." He started toward the doorway between the two rooms, then paused and glanced back at her. "Put the muskrat on the table while I change into dry breeches," he said. "There's something cooking in the Dutch oven, and Cholena usually keeps fresh Indian fry bread in the cupboard."

She stared after his retreating back in astonishment. What arrogance to expect her to wait on him hand and foot while he behaved like a royal arse! Grumbling, she went to the cupboard and found wooden platters, spoons, forks, and eating knives. The only bread she saw consisted of flat cakes heaped in a woven basket. She put the basket and a small crockery container of honey on the table, with the plates and pewterware, then went to the fireplace.

Using a corner of the blanket to protect her hands from the heat, Lissa removed the iron spit with the meat. Holding one end of the heavy rod, she walked back toward the table. She was nearly there when she trod on a corner of the blanket she was wearing and stumbled. The bird slipped off the spit and rolled across the cabin floor.

Mortified, she dropped the iron and ran after the roast. She snatched it up, only to drop it again when the crispy skin burned her fingers. "Ouch!" she cried. She popped a smarting finger into her mouth, then retrieved the spit and tried to stab the bird with it. To her horror, the supper slid under the table. Quickly, she got down on her knees and jabbed at the fowl with the pointed rod.

"What are you doing?" Reece roared.

Lissa crawled out from under the table, minus her blanket, with the bird firmly skewered on the spit. "Serving the evening meal, sir," she snapped sarcastically.

"What have you done to my muskrat?" he demanded. "And why are you serving supper in your undergarments?"

Lissa glanced down at her low-necked shift and partially unlaced bodice and uttered a strangled squeak of shame. She snatched up the blanket and wrapped it around her with as much dignity as she could muster.

"You don't expect me to eat that, do you?" Reece asked sternly, pointing at the battered bird. "I've ridden all day. I'm hungry. What am I supposed to eat?" Each word was louder than the one before, until he was bellowing like an enraged bull.

Lissa swallowed the lump in her throat. "No, of course not," she croaked. "I'll . . . I'll just step outside and fetch the other one." Holding the blanket around her like a cloak, and carrying the bird on the spit in the other, she stalked out the door and down to the stream.

"Damn him," she muttered. "Damn him!" Removing the fowl from the spit, she washed it thoroughly in the stream and put it back on the rod. "You'll pay for this, Reece Mackenzie," she swore. "I promise, you'll pay for this."

Reece contained his pent-up laughter until she was far enough from the cabin to be out of hearing, then he exploded with mirth. The sight of Lissa's shapely damp bottom coming out from under the table was the funniest thing he'd seen in months. And the most sensual . . .

Waves of desire swept over him, drowning the amusement and turning his thoughts to what delights might lie under that thin linen shift. Her bodice ribbons had come untied, and two very attractive breasts had glowed rosy-pink in the fading twilight.

She was his wife. He had every right to lie with her. And she was willing. He could read it in her eyes.

"Damn me for seven kinds of a fool," he murmured under his breath. "I can't let a pretty ankle force a decision that could make me unhappy for the rest of my life. I can't ruin Jilly's future for the sake of a woman's sweet bottom."

But lady or not, Lissa had spunk. He had to give her that. "I'll get the other one," she'd said, knowing full well that they both knew that there was only one spitted grouse.

A sense of humor didn't make her a fit wife either. He tried not to think of his mother's saying: "Laughter is the oil of the gods. It greases the movement of all living things. Without laughter, life moves awkwardly."

He exhaled loudly. He'd not be much of a man if he couldn't hold out against this Englishwoman's wiles for one night. Tomorrow, he'd return her to the ship, give her passage home, and bid her farewell. He was doing her a favor—saving her from a life of misery in the colonies.

He heard Lissa's step on the porch. Quickly, he went to the fireplace, scraped away the coals, and retrieved the Dutch oven. He lifted the lid and sniffed. Rabbit stew. Carefully, he carried the bubbling contents to the table. He pretended not to notice as Lissa crossed the room and dropped a dripping bird, minus one wing, on a large wooden platter.

"It's about time," he complained. "I—" Then, he made the mistake of glancing into her tear-filled eyes. "Lissa . . ." Remorse clouded his reason, and he took hold of her arms. "Don't cry," he said. Gently, he reached up and brushed a tear from her cheek . . . a cheek as soft as a newborn fawn. "It's all right, Lissa."

She lowered her head against the hollow of his shoulder and began to weep softly. "I tried to . . ." she whispered. "I wanted . . ."

"Shhh," he soothed. "It's all right, lass." He tilted her chin up and kissed her quivering mouth.

And lost the battle.

A feeling of possessiveness welled up in him as his slow, tender caress deepened and gained in intensity. Her lips were as firm and sweet as ripe cherries. They tantalized him and set his mind spinning.

He wanted to touch her . . . to taste her . . . to make her completely his.

She molded against him, soft and warm and yielding. Her lips were a trap that lured him on, daring him to cup a rounded breast. She moaned deep in her throat, and he filled her mouth with his tongue.

Before he could stop himself, his fingers had slipped through her open bodice to find a silken nipple. "Lissa," he groaned. "Sweet Lissa."

She moved closer still, wrapping her arms around his neck and kissing him as fervently as he was kissing her. She shuddered with pleasure as he teased her nipple to a hard, red bud, then lowered his head to take it between his lips and suck gently.

"Oh . . . oh . . ."

Her tiny whimpers fanned the coals of his desire, and he felt a growing ache in his loins. He kissed one perfect nipple and then the other as she arched her neck and ran her fingers through his hair.

She sighed contentedly and gazed up at him through thick, dark lashes. Her eyes were as brown as any Indian maid's and heavy-lidded with passion.

He wanted her, and she was his wife. He could have her. She was his for the taking . . .

"Lass . . . lass," he murmured, pulling at the ribbons of her bodice. He wanted to bury his face between her breasts, to fill his head with her intoxicating woman scent. He slid one hand down her midriff and over her flat belly to feel the warm nest between her thighs.

She gasped, and he kissed her again on the mouth, lingering at her lower lip and brushing the tip of his tongue against hers. His hand moved lower and found the hem of her shift. He traced the curve of her leg and stroked her inner thigh until she trembled under his touch.

Her hands were on his chest, her fingers making small circles on his skin. He sought her breast with his mouth once more, and the salty-sweet taste of her skin, the feel of her nipple between his lips and against his tongue, drove him wild with desire.

She moaned, and he touched her damp folds. "Oh," she cried. "Oh."

His shaft was tight and hard, swollen almost to the point of painfulness. He couldn't help catching her hand and bringing it down to clasp his rigidity.

"Husband," she cried.

He heard the familiarity, and it struck a false note, but he was too engaged in his task to pay it full heed.

He laved her nipple with his tongue and slipped a finger deeper into the dewy petals of her flower.

"Oh, husband," she repeated.

The awful truth of what she was saying struck home at the same instant his searching fingers felt a tightness that no experienced woman should possess. He stopped short. "What?" He withdrew his hand as though he had touched a red-hot branding iron. "What?" Suddenly Lissa's address, the shock of what he was doing, hit him. "What trickery is this?" He pushed her to arm's length and looked into her stunned face. "You told me you were not a virgin."

She gasped for breath and covered her face with her hands. "A virgin . . ." she stammered. "I am . . . I mean . . . I am? That's impossible."

"What kind of man would do what we . . ." She blushed crimson. "What we were, and stop before . . . Just because you think I'm not—"

"You tricked me, woman."

"I? *I* tricked you?" she cried, pulling down her shift, trying to lace her bodice, and scrambling for the blanket all at the same time. "I am innocent. I was only submitting to the duties of a wife to her husband."

"You wanted me to consummate this marriage so that I couldn't be rid of you!"

"I didn't ask for your attentions, sir. The blame is yours."

Reece drew back, shaken by his still-throbbing need. She was right. By all that was holy, she was right. The blame was his. No matter what Lissa had said about having lovers, she was an innocent woman. And he had come very close to taking her maidenhood without being prepared to become her husband in truth.

He shook his head, ashamed. He'd let his emotions rule his head as he'd sworn never to do. He'd nearly made a life commitment on the basis of his desire for her body.

He'd wanted her that badly.

He still wanted her.

And he knew if he didn't put distance between them tonight, he'd weaken. He'd make love to her. And if he did, they would be husband and wife, and he would be committed to her for the rest of his life.

"Forgive me," he said gruffly. "The fault was mine."

He looked into her haunting brown eyes and felt the air sizzle between them. "You are a desirable woman," he admitted. "I find you very beautiful."

She waited, vulnerable, lips slightly parted, breath still coming in tiny, quick gasps.

"It's better if you remain alone here tonight," he said. "If I stay . . ."

"You wouldn't leave me alone?"

She sounded like a frightened child, and pain knifed through his gut. He wanted to take her in his arms again and kiss away that helpless expression. He wanted to . . .

"Aye," he said firmly. "You should be safe enough. We've had no hostiles on Wildcat Purchase for weeks." An understatement. There'd been no trouble here for three years, but she didn't need to know that. It was better if she lay awake listening for noises in the night.

Lissa's eyes widened. Her mouth firmed into a thin line.

She was scared, but she didn't say so. The invisible knife twisted inside him, and he felt sick. He'd never been so cruel to a woman. But, he reasoned, he was doing it for all the right reasons. Tomorrow, he'd take her back to Annapolis. He'd give her more money than she was entitled to, and they'd both pick up their separate lives.

"Will I . . ." Her voice cracked and she began again. "Will I be in danger from animals?"

"Keep the fire going," he said, "and the door bolted. As long as you don't go outside, you shouldn't be bothered by the bears."

"That's a comforting thought."

"Aye." He gathered up his musket and powder bag. "I'll be back for you in the morning." He started for the door and glanced back. "You'll thank me for this when you're safe in England," he said. "We really wouldn't suit each other as man and wife. You deserve better."

His words echoed in his ear as he slammed the door

and started toward the barn. *You deserve better . . . deserve better . . . deserve better.* The truth of it was . . . she did. At this moment, he felt like the lowest cad. Resolutely, he kept walking.

5

L ISSA picked up the grouse and threw it at the closing door. "Damn you to a fiery hell, Reece Mackenzie!" she shouted after him. The bird bounced off the plank door and disintegrated into a dozen pieces. One wing stuck to the wall, a leg flew off over a bench, and shreds of dripping meat scattered across the floor. "Go off and sleep in a tree for all I care," she continued hotly. "I hope the bears eat you!"

As an afterthought, she slammed the iron bolt in place, locking the door. "Crazy colonial," she muttered.

Her hands were trembling; her breathing was erratic, and her insides felt as if she'd been swallowing live frogs. She wanted to curse and weep at the same time . . . she wanted Reece to keep on making love to her.

No man had ever made her feel this way . . . She hadn't even guessed that she had such emotions locked inside her. She'd heard that there was pleasure to be found in a man's embrace—else why would women seek sexual liaisons outside the bonds of marriage? But she'd never dreamed it would be like this . . .

Her face and throat grew hot as she remembered the intimacy of Reece's touch . . . the intensity of his kisses. Heaven help her! She had never been so close to losing her maidenhead before. A few minutes more and she would have known what it was like to be joined in body and spirit to a man.

And he was a man. For all his stubborn, exasperating mannerisms, Reece was all man.

"Damn you!" she cried again. They'd come so very close. Now she felt a sense of loss. A single tear trickled down her cheek, and she dashed it away. "I'd gladly trade all that England has to offer for a lifetime in Reece's arms."

Another tear fell. Lissa blinked to clear her eyes. She'd never been a simpering goose, and she wasn't about to begin now.

"Spilt milk was never retrieved by wailing over it," she murmured. Besides, Reece wasn't lost yet. What could he do if she simply refused to go back to Annapolis? As long as she stayed in America and didn't sign any annulment papers, she was his legal wife. And given a little time, anything was possible.

She sniffed and wiped her nose. Her stomach rumbled and she remembered how hungry she was. She returned to the table and dipped a spoon into the Dutch oven and tasted the stew. All it needed was a little salt. She dished out a generous helping and began to eat.

Later, when she had devoured the rabbit stew and eaten two pieces of fry bread, she rummaged in the Welsh cupboard and found a tin of tea leaves. She made herself two cups before the fire grew so low that the light in the room faded.

Since there was no more wood in the house, there was nothing to do but go to bed. She pushed the table in front of the door and stacked plates and cups on top so that they'd fall and make a racket if anyone or anything tried to come in. Then she went into the sleeping chamber.

Her shift and stays were still damp, too wet to sleep in, so she removed them and hung them on pegs on the wall. She unfolded the fringed skin dress Reece had given her earlier and slipped it over her head. To her surprise, it was as soft as silk. What had looked shapeless before she'd put it on was transformed.

"Her royal highness, the Princess Pocahontas," Lissa proclaimed into the empty room. She spun around, enjoying the tickle of the leather fringe against her bare skin. "Mistress Mackenzie," she corrected herself, "lady of Wildcat Purchase." Still giggling, she crawled into bed and wiggled under the covers.

She closed her eyes and tried not to listen to the scrape of tree branches against the roof. Outside, frogs peeped and crickets chirped. Something rustled under floorboards, and Lissa hoped it wasn't a hungry muskrat. An owl hooted, and something thudded softly on the roof.

Clutching the blanket to her chest, she sat bolt upright. What if that was a bear? She strained her ears to hear, then exhaled in exasperation. What if it was Reece trying to frighten her?

"I don't care what it is," she whispered. "The door's bolted and the windows are too small for anything big to get in. He's the one sleeping in the woods."

Determined to get a good night's rest, she closed her eyes again, lay down, and pulled the covers over her head. Gradually she drifted off into a fitful sleep.

Minutes or hours later Lissa was disturbed by what she imagined was a rattling at the door. She opened her eyes and listened. Moonlight streamed through a tiny glass-paned window and pooled like liquid gold on the wide plank floor. All was quiet; even the owl's hoot was absent. She could hear nothing but the rise and fall of her own breathing.

She knew she should call a chambermaid to rise and investigate the noise, but she was so tired that her eyes kept shutting. Exhausted by the day's events, she sighed and snuggled down in the warm blankets.

Thunder rumbled through her dreams, but it was too far away . . . too faint to pull her from her stupor.

The next time she awoke, the thunder was louder. A flash of lightning illuminated a room that was choked with smoke. She gasped for air and tried to remember where she was. A fit of coughing seized her, and she threw back the covers and crawled out of bed. Instantly, her eyes began to stream tears. Trying to get her bearings, she stumbled toward what she thought was the door to the main room, tripped, and fell face down on the floor.

To her intense relief, the air was clearer there. She was still coughing, but at least she was able to breathe. On hands and knees, she crawled into the kitchen, then screamed as she realized one wall of the house was on fire. Yellow and red tongues of flame danced along the cupboard wall and turned the room an unearthly orange. Thick gray smoke billowed from the seams of the logs and formed a false ceiling only inches over her head.

Lissa clenched her eyes shut and kept moving toward the outside door. The floorboards were scorching hot against her hands and knees, but she ignored the pain, knowing that her only chance of survival lay outside the barred door. When her head struck the base of the table, she thought for one instant that she'd become confused and forgotten where the door was, but then she remembered that she'd moved the table in front of the entrance-way to keep out wild animals.

She felt her way up the table and wrestled blindly with the heavy piece of furniture. As it toppled over with a crash, a shrieking shout came from outside. But she was past knowing if her mind was playing tricks on her—her only thought was getting away from the fire. For long, choking seconds she fought with the iron bolt before it slid back. She flung open the door and staggered out into the night.

Lissa's eyes were stinging with smoke, her lungs filled with it. Coughing and gasping for air, she ran from the porch, only to collide violently with hard, human flesh. "Reece!" she cried, then realized her mistake as a musty scent filled her head. She stared into the face of a hideously painted savage.

Another scream burst from her throat and she threw up her arms to protect herself. Unfamiliar hands pawed at her, but she twisted away and, yelling like a banshee, hurled herself toward the woods.

Thunder rolled overhead, and lightning flashed as another apparition, brandishing a stone club, loomed up before her out of the billowing smoke. She dodged him and caught sight of a leering giant coming from the shadows with a feathered hatchet in one hand and a knife in the other.

"Mother of God, I must be dreaming," she babbled.

The giant was a head taller than Reece with shoulders as wide as a longbow and tattooed hands as large as buckets. His bulbous head was shaved along both sides, leaving a ridge of stiff hair down the center. His face was divided in two at the nostrils; the top half was painted yellow, the bottom blue. A bone was thrust through his broad nose, and animal skulls dangled from his elongated earlobes. Worse, the man was naked except for a narrow scrap of leather around his loins, and his copper skin was oiled so that it glistened in the light of the burning cabin.

Lissa backed up until she felt the rough bark of a tree behind her. She shook her head, trying to make sense of what was happening.

The three Indians—no, she realized there were four— formed a semicircle around her. They were shouting and jeering in an incomprehensible tongue. Howling like a demon, the obscene giant pointed at her and waved his barbaric weapon. The fourth savage, little more than an overgrown child, pointed a musket at her head and mimicked the sound of a gunshot. When the others laughed at the youth's cruel jest, he hopped up and down on one foot and cawed like a crow.

"Bedlam," Lissa muttered under her breath. She wished for once in her life that she was a swooning woman. She shut her eyes, thinking that if it was a nightmare, she'd wake in her own bed. But the stench of burning wood and the shriek of her tormenters forced her to look again after a half-dozen thudding heartbeats. She took a deep breath and screamed as loud as she could. "Reece!"

One of the Indians, a light-skinned, big-nosed man wearing what appeared to be a bird's nest on his head, ran at her and struck her across the face. "No talk!" he shouted. "Make talk, we kill!"

Lissa staggered back against the tree in shock and put her hand to her face, then drew it away and stared at the blood. She was too stunned to feel pain, only a rising fury. How dare these bullies treat her so? In her entire adult life, no one had ever subjected her to physical abuse!

"You maggot-brained Sodomite!" She glared at her attacker fiercely, then drew back her arm and punched him square in the mouth. The blow caught him unawares and split his lip. Blood flew, to Lissa's delight. As he grabbed his injured mouth, she lowered her head and slammed into his belly with all her might.

When he went down, she went with him, but she came up faster. She scrambled to her feet and ran for the woods, but before she'd gone three feet, the boy with the gun grabbed her by the hair and yanked her off her feet. She landed on her backside hard, and he kicked her in the hip. She twisted around and sunk her teeth into his bare leg. When he tried to hit her with the musket stock, she rolled over and seized the gun with both hands, wrestling him for it.

The man with the bloody lip and the bird's nest in his hair dropped down on his knees beside her and lifted a knife over her chest. Lissa's breath caught in her throat, and she froze, staring in horror as the naked blade flashed down toward her.

Somewhere nearby a musket roared. The Indian who was crouched over her swayed as a red flower blossomed in the center of his chest. Blood sprayed over her. She screamed again as he toppled forward, pinning her to the earth.

There was a flash of light and an explosion as the youth's musket fired. Lissa freed herself from the arms of the dead man, scrambled to her feet, and ran for cover, only to trip over another body not six feet away. The painted savage, the one she had first run into when she'd fled the house, lay sprawled on his back with the handle of a knife protruding from his throat.

The giant let out a horrifying whoop and rushed, axe in hand, toward a shadowy figure under the trees. The big Indian's teeth were bared, his face contorted in a mask of twisted rage. Each mighty stride carried him closer to the stranger, as the boy struggled to reload his flintlock.

The newcomer met the giant's onslaught with a chilling war cry of his own, charging out of the darkness, swinging his musket like a club. In the glow of the blazing cabin, Lissa recognized Reece and shouted his name.

The boy jammed his ramrod down the barrel' of his weapon and raised the musket to take aim at Reece.

"No!" Lissa screamed. Without thinking, she threw herself at the youth. The boom of the musket was drowned in the deafening crash of thunder, but she didn't let that keep her from climbing onto the Indian's chest and pounding him as hard as she could with her fists.

When she looked up, Reece and the giant were crouched and circling each other like two angry dogs. The giant lunged toward Reece, cutting a swath through the air with his terrible hatchet. Reece ducked aside, and when the Indian hurled past, Reece thrust his musket stock between the man's legs. The giant crashed to the ground, and Reece leaped on top of him. Lissa saw the gleam of a knife blade, then the boy struck her on the chin and stars skyrocketed through her head.

When she opened her eyes again, she was cradled in Reece's arms. "Lissa. Lissa, are ye all right?" he asked huskily. His face was bruised and streaked with dirt. Beads of sweat stood out on his forehead, and he was breathing hard.

"Reece?" Her face felt as though she'd been kicked in the head by a horse, and she tasted blood in her mouth. "What . . ."

"Shhh," he soothed. "Dinna try to talk. It's all right.

They'll nay hurt ye. None will hurt ye now.'' His deep voice was near to breaking with emotion and heavy with the Scot's burr.

"What happened? I thought..." She sighed and closed her eyes, laying her head against his chest, feeling so safe that she never wanted to leave his embrace. Drops of something wet were falling on her face, and she had the strangest notion that he was crying. "Reece?"

"It's all right. I'm here," he repeated, rocking her against him and showering her face with kisses. He was holding her so tightly that it was hard for her to breathe.

Reluctantly, she put her hands on his shoulders and pushed far enough away to see that Reece had blood on his chest. "You're bleeding!" she cried.

"No, 'tis not my blood. It's the Mohawk's."

She twisted around, suddenly remembering the boy. "There's a second man," she insisted. "He has a gun."

"You mean the one who hit you? He won't be back. I put a knife in the big brave. He's losing a lot of blood. The boy will have his hands full getting him back to Mohawk country alive." Reece's face hardened, and his black eyes glowed like the fires of hell. "Did they hurt you?" he asked her hoarsely. "If they did, I'll go after them and—"

She looked down at her dirty bare feet and torn dress, realizing that he must think she had been sexually assaulted by the marauders. "No. No, I'm fine," she lied. She rubbed her aching jaw and tentatively touched her nose. It was sore, but no bones seemed to be broken, and her nosebleed had stopped. "Let me up." Water was still dripping on her face, and she realized it was raining.

"I'm sorry. It was my fault you were here alone when they came," he said. "I never should have left you." He released her, steadying her as she stood up.

She touched his bare chest, reassuring herself that his flesh was whole, and that the bloodstains were indeed from the Indian and not from some terrible wound. "You're not hurt?" she asked.

"Nothing that a few weeks' time and a bath won't cure." He brushed a lock of hair from her face and stared into her eyes as though he thought she was made of precious stones and might vanish at any second.

Lissa took a deep breath and glanced back at the house. The flames had reached the roof, casting an orange glow over the clearing. Sparks hissed and danced in the air, and the heat from the fire was hot on her cheeks. "Shouldn't we throw water on it?"

He shook his head. "The rain will put it out. Can you walk?" When she nodded, he led her toward the stable. "This wasn't supposed to happen," he said. "We haven't had a raiding party here for years."

Lissa was trembling and her teeth were chattering. The rain was cold against her skin, but her real chill came from within. As they entered the barn, they nearly stumbled over the body of her riding mule. Lissa let out a cry and turned back to Reece, burying her face in his chest.

"I'm sorry. I didn't know they'd killed the mule," he apologized. "Wait here." He moved off into the shadows, stepping carefully over the stiffening legs of the animal, then returned to drape a blanket around her shoulders. "My horse is in the woods, a few hundred yards from here. Can you walk that far?"

"Anywhere, away from this," she murmured.

They stopped by the stream, and Reece cut off a corner of the blanket, dipped it in the water, and used it to clean her face and hands. Then he washed himself. "You saved my life back there," he said, after a long silence. "When you kept that young brave from putting a musket ball into me."

She didn't answer. Standing in the falling rain, she concentrated on the sounds that the drops of water made as they pattered against the leaves, on the rich smell of musty earth and wet grass. What had happened was too ugly to dwell on. It was past and done, and she wanted to put it behind her. Hesitantly, she placed her hand into his and squeezed.

"I was coming back, for what it's worth now," he said. "I've never considered myself a coward, Lissa, but I was afraid to spend the night in the cabin with you."

She waited, content to have him beside her, as tall and steady as an oak . . . proof that the nightmare was over.

"I knew if I made love to you I couldn't send you away," he continued huskily. "I thought you were the wrong woman for this country, but I was wrong."

"Maybe you were right."

"I wouldn't have left you in danger, I swear it. I thought a night alone in the cabin would scare you back to Annapolis and out of my life." He raised her hand to his lips and kissed her scraped knuckles. "You're the bravest woman I've ever known," he said. "You had those Mohawks on the run before I got there."

"They were Mohawks? Really?" she asked, remembering his story about the cook, Pegleg, and his capture by Mohawks.

"A war party, or what was left of one. Likely, they went south along the mountain trail to raid the Indian tribes in the Carolinas. They usually travel in groups of ten to twenty—four's too small for a war party. They must have had bad luck and didn't want to go home empty-handed."

"Would they have killed me?"

He shook his head. "I don't know. Maybe. Maybe not. You can't tell about Indians. I'm half-blood myself, and I never stop being surprised by what they do. But Mohawks are bad business. I'm taking you home, and then I'm riding to Delaware Village to be certain these warriors weren't part of a larger raid. I'm worried about Mother and Jilly."

"Home? Where's home?"

"You'll see," he said. Then he picked her up in his arms again and began to carry her as easily as if she weighed no more that a ten-year-old child.

"I told you," she protested. "I can walk."

"Not in the woods in your bare feet. I've put ye

through enough. I can spare you this, at least.''

It was dark, so dark Lissa couldn't see her hand in front of her face. Rain was falling in sheets. But Reece kept walking steadily. He didn't slip, and he didn't stumble. And when he put his feet down, he didn't make a sound.

The horse whinnied and Lissa jumped, frightened by the noise in a rain-whipped world. "It's all right," Reece assured her. He spoke softly to the animal, then lifted Lissa up into the saddle. Without using the stirrups, he vaulted up behind her and turned the animal's head. "It won't be long," he promised. "We'll get you dry and into a real bed."

"But where? How?"

"You'll see, soon enough."

How long they rode, Lissa couldn't be certain. Once, she thought she dozed. Then she heard hounds barking, and she saw a lantern swaying in the distance. As they got closer, a man's voice called out to them.

"Who goes there?"

"It's me," Reece answered. "Any trouble here tonight?"

"Nope."

By the lantern light she saw a black man wearing a wide-brimmed hat and cloak. He was tall and broad and was carrying a musket.

"Samuel, this is my wife, Mistress Elizabeth. Elizabeth, meet Samuel Ajani. He works for me part of the year. He's the best blacksmith west of the Chesapeake."

Samuel lifted the lantern so that the light shone into their faces. "You've had trouble, I'd say."

"Hostiles. Four Mohawks attacked my mother's cabin and set it afire."

"Should I call out the men?"

Reece nodded. "Best you do so. Send riders to warn the neighboring plantations. Tell John to take the same precautions we did when those pirates landed along the river. I think it was an isolated war party, but I'm riding out to Delaware Village to be certain my family is all right, and to put our people on alert.

"Samuel's a second-generation freeman, not a slave," Reece explained as they rode on toward the house. "He owns a forge near Annapolis. John is my lumbering-crew foreman. He used to be a bosun; he's as tough as they come. You'll be safe here while I go to warn my mother's village."

More men and dogs ran out. Reece paused for a moment to pass the news to them, then they rode on down a dirt path, through a farmyard with several large barns and outbuildings, and up a crushed oyster shell drive to an imposing brick manor house.

"This is your home?" Lissa asked, staring up at the two-story dwelling. It was not so large as her father's country place by half, but even in the rain she could see that the house was fit for a gentleman of wealth and position. "This is Wildcat Purchase?"

Reece reined in his horse near the front door, dismounted, and lifted her down. "Yes," he admitted. "This is my home—and yours, if you'll have it so." He pulled her against him and kissed her hard. "I wronged you, Lissa," he said. "I tricked you, and I put you in danger. But if you'll forgive me, I promise I'll be a good husband to you."

She stiffened and struggled free. "You lied to me!" she exclaimed, furious. "You deceived me, and now you expect me to—"

"For God's sake, woman, if you're going to argue with me, at least let's do it in the house. It's pouring rain out here."

A serving girl opened the door and sank into a curtsy as Lissa flounced into the wide entrance hall, barefooted, as wet as a drowned hen, and nearly as angry with Reece as she'd been with the Mohawks. "You're the one who said I wasn't your wife!" she accused. "I trusted you. I thought you were a man of your word. I thought—*ah . . . ah-choo!*" She wiped her nose and promptly sneezed again, louder than before. "I wouldn't marry you, sir," she cried, "if I had to take the veil and spend the rest of my days in a convent."

"Hedvig," Reece said to the maid, "take your mistress upstairs to the west chamber. See that she has a hot bath and is tucked into bed."

The sturdy, yellow-haired woman nodded. "Ya, Master Reece. I vill," she said. Her accent was so strong that Lissa could barely understand what she was saying.

Reece turned back to Lissa. "We'll talk about this tomorrow, when you're more yourself."

"Talk until your face turns blue," she said. "I won't have you. I'll be on that ship when it sails for England. I swear I will."

"You're mine," he replied, raising his voice. "I risked my scalp to take you from those Mohawks, and that makes you mine. You'll go nowhere."

"In a pig's eye!" she flung back at him.

"Go with Hedvig," he ordered. "We'll talk about this in the morning—in private."

"In the morning I'm going home to England," she insisted. "And you, and all the Indians in Maryland, can't keep me here." She began to shiver and clenched her teeth together to keep them from chattering. Water was dripping off the fringes of the ruined doeskin gown and pooling on the polished wood flooring.

"Go to bed, woman!"

Lissa looked around at the elegant mahogany furniture, the tall case clock on the landing, and the old family portraits, and remembered the rustic hut Reece had tried to pass off as his home. She was so mad that she wanted to grab a porcelain vase off the lovely Irish hunt table along the wall and smash it over his head. "I won't be ordered about by . . . by a . . . by a puffed up, arrogant, lying colonial!" she spat.

"And who lied to whom first?" he demanded. "Who deceived whom?"

"It doesn't matter," she said, trying to hold back tears of frustration. "It doesn't matter who lied to whom first. What matters is that you were right from the start. We aren't suited to each other, and the sooner I return to England, the happier we'll both be.'' She turned and dashed up the wide staircase.

''I warn you,'' Reece called after her. ''I'm not letting you go.''

''Try and stop me!'' she flung back. ''Just you try and stop me.'' Back ramrod straight and chin high, she marched up the stairs, not sparing Reece a glance over her shoulder when she heard him swear a foul oath, not even when she heard the front door slam behind him.

6

A warm breeze drifted through the open window. Outside in a tall poplar, birds twittered and fluttered from leafy branch to branch. Lissa turned over in the curtained poster bed and pushed back the crisp linen sheets.

What time is it? she wondered. It must be early dawn, judging by the dim light, but she felt much more rested than she should have after only a few hours' sleep. She yawned and rubbed her face, then slid off the high bed and went to the open window. She was wearing one of Reece's white shirts, the only article of clothing Hedvig had been able to find for her to sleep in.

Lissa chuckled as she remembered the maid's reaction when she'd asked for a sleeping gown.

''Vat you need dress for sleep? Is English custom?'' She'd shaken her head in disapproval. ''Such a vaste. Be dere someting vong vit your bare skin?''

Insistence on Lissa's part had produced a hot bath, soap, towels, and Reece's shirt. She had bathed, washed her hair, and climbed between the sheets more dead than alive.

This morning, the events of the night before came rushing back in vivid detail. First had come the attack by Indians, then Reece's courageous rescue, and then their terrible fight. Lissa nibbled her lower lip. Had she really told him that she wouldn't have him as a husband? Had she been so foolish as to declare she was going back to England?

Sweet Mary, Mother of God, would her shrewish tongue never cease getting her in trouble? She sighed and swallowed the lump in her throat as she leaned on the windowsill and stared out at the rich green fields and orchards.

She'd wanted a wealthy colonial husband, a man young enough to make her blood sing and her heart skip at the sight of him. Reece Mackenzie was all that and more. He'd taken on four savage Indian warriors—risked his life—to save her. And she had condemned him for being a man of property, for trying to trick her after she'd tricked him.

Certainly she was angry with him for making her look foolish. But it was a small sin, not one for which a sensible woman would give up the best man she'd ever met. Why hadn't she accepted his apology, fallen into his arms, and let him carry her up to bed?

Lissa turned from the window to see Hedvig standing just inside the bedchamber door with a heavy tray of dishes in her hands. "Is that breakfast?" Lissa asked. "What time is it?" Steam rose from a teapot, and she caught a delicious whiff of what could only be country sausage and eggs.

Lissa's eyes widened in surprise as an identical copy of the Swedish maid, her arms filled with clothing, appeared in the doorway. "Two of you?" she said, then remembered Reece had said there were twin bondwomen. Four round, pale blue eyes stared at her.

"I be Hulda," the second girl said. "And you be da new mistress."

"Yes, yes, I am," Lissa said, recovering her dignity. She motioned to a small gateleg table. "Put the tray there."

"Master Reece says you vill not stay," Hedvig said. "Is goot. A lady such as you—"

"English lady," Hulda put in.

"English lady vould not be happy here in da big voods."

"In da vilderness," Hulda corrected.

"Vit bears and vild animals," Hedvig finished solemnly. She nodded at her sister, and Hulda nodded back.

Lissa barely concealed a giggle at the droll picture they made, before remembering her position and responsibility in the household. If she stayed at Wildcat Purchase, these two would require a good deal of attention to turn them into proper English servants.

The sisters were hardly more than out of their teens, tall and broad-shouldered, with flaxen hair twisted in identical knots at the back of their heads. They were pretty, in a country way, with skin as pale as milk and identical moles at the corner of their mouths. Both girls wore blue homespun gowns and white aprons, and each had an undersized mobcap pinned to the back of her head.

"Herr Reece says to bring you tray. Since you sleep all day, he says tell cook to make breakfast in the evening, but . . ." Hedvig trailed off, the curve of her lips saying plainly what she thought of a mistress so lazy she would lie in bed all day.

"Supper? Then it's evening, not morning?" Lissa said, glancing out the window at the fading light. God in heaven! Had she slept all day?

"Ja. The clock on da stair, she make eight o'clock." Hulda cast a disapproving gaze at Reece's shirt, which came only to Lissa's knees. "Here be clothes for you. Herr Reece—from a neighbor he borrows."

"From the ship your things do not yet come," her

sister added. "Maybe no need to come at all."

"Ya. Not at all," Hulda agreed.

"Are the two of you from Sweden?" Lissa asked, unable to contain her curiosity. "How did you get to Maryland?"

"Ve come by ox cart," the nearest one replied.

"From New Sveden on the Delaware," added the farthest.

"Ja, New Sveden on the Delaware."

"For da cow," Hulda explained.

"Cow?" Lissa asked, puzzled.

"Three years vork to earn cow and hard silver, so ve can find husband."

"I see," Lissa said. The sisters stared at her with identical expressions. "Is the child, Jilly, here at the house? And Master Mackenzie's mother, Cholena?" That Cholena was Reece's mother was a wild guess. A guess that paid off when Hedvig shook her head, and Hulda repeated the motion.

"No. They do not come. Miss Cholena and Miss Jilly stay in da skraeling village."

"Better Jilly stay away. She is too vild for English lady," Hulda agreed.

"Vant us help you dress?" Hedvig asked.

"No. I will not be leaving my room this evening. You may tell the master that I am not to be disturbed." She affected her most imperious air. "And from now on, I am to be addressed as Lady Elizabeth. Do you understand?"

"Ja. Ve speak good English."

"Ja. You vish to be lady." The two left without a proper curtsy, closing the door none-too-gently behind them.

Lissa sighed and turned to her supper. She was ravenously hungry—she always seemed to be hungry since coming to Maryland. And by staying in her room this evening, she reasoned she would have more time to think of a plan whereby she could remain on Wildcat Purchase and not seem to back down on her decision to leave.

The tray was covered with assorted dishes, and she began to uncover them one after another with the curiosity of a child. Under the pewter covers were a bowl of ripe strawberries with clotted cream, a saucer of golden-brown scones, scrambled eggs, sausage, oysters on the half-shell, asparagus, and an apple tart.

And under the last lid, she found a sprig of apple blossoms with a blue silk ribbon tied to the stem. On the ribbon were three words, written boldly in a masculine hand. "Forgive me—Reece."

Lissa nibbled at the wonderful food and tried to think of what to say to Reece to make up for last night's temper tantrum. When she had eaten all she could comfortably hold, she pulled the bell cord by the door and summoned the twins.

"I will dress and go downstairs," she announced. "Hulda, I require you to help me with my hair and gown. Hedvig, please go to your master and ask him to meet me . . . in the great hall in half an hour."

The borrowed garments, the hoops and rose taffeta gown, were more than adequate. Hulda's knowledge of hairdressing was pitiful; in the end, Lissa instructed her to simply brush out her dark locks and secure them at the nape of her neck with a silk ribbon. Then, gathering all her courage, Lissa went down the stairs to face her husband.

The gentleman waiting for her in the formal parlor shocked her speechless. Reece Mackenzie was not the man she had believed him to be.

The buckskins were gone, and in their place Reece had donned a cobalt-blue waistcoat and coat with jeweled buttons and wide embroidered cuffs, over buff velvet breeches that fit him without a wrinkle. Fashionably clocked stockings ran down shapely male calves to silver-buckled shoes of the finest kid leather. At his throat was a cascade of Irish lace. The earring was gone from his ear, and his thick, dark mane of hair was decently groomed and twisted into an elegant queue and fastened with a wide ribbon of buff silk.

He had shaved so recently that his cheeks were still damp, and Lissa caught a whiff of French soap in the air. The firm hand that he extended in welcome was clean and well-manicured, free of dirt and blood. It was a courtier's hand . . . a stranger's. "Madam," he said, "you wanted to speak to me?" He raised her fingers to his lips in a graceful manner that would have made ladies' hearts flutter.

"Yes . . . yes, I did," she stammered. Suddenly her tongue seemed too large for her mouth. She had come downstairs prepared to deal with a colonial rustic and now faced a sophisticated patrician. "I thought it best we confront our . . . our dilemma." He led her to a settee that would accommodate her wide hoops, then took a chair nearby. "What of Jilly?" she asked, remembering the child and the danger they'd faced last night. "I thought you'd bring her here."

Reece's jet-black eyes softened at the mention of his daughter. "She's safe. We're all safe. The Mohawks who escaped were surprised by a Delaware hunting party. There is bad blood between the tribes. I sent a burial party this morning for the ones I killed; the remaining two are dead as well. They will carry no tales to Iroquois longhouses." He smiled. "I thought it best if Jilly remained at the village until after you returned to Annapolis."

Lissa's heart felt as though it were made of lead. "Return? But last night you said—"

"That I would keep you here?" He sighed. "I have a damnable temper, Lissa. You're right, of course. I let sentiment overcome reason. I can't keep you here against your will, just because I—"

"You don't want me?" Suddenly, she found she preferred the forthright woodsman to this cool gentleman. "I thought . . ." She gripped the flowered settee until her fingernails dug into the fragile fabric, and she looked away, trying to regain her lost composure. Tears welled up in her eyes. How could Reece have changed his mind in a single day? She steeled herself and looked back. "I was overwrought, perhaps hasty. My own temper is—''

She thought she saw a hint of amusement flicker in Reece's gaze, but then it was gone as if it had never been.

''I could not expect you to forgive me,'' he said. ''Naturally, I will bear the expense of your return to England and provide you with—''

''A great deal of expense,'' she said quickly, ''for which I should feel responsible. Cannot we apply . . .'' What was his word? ''Reason!'' She smiled at him with all the charm and coquetry she could muster. ''It would seem reasonable that since neither of us is repelled by the other, that we should attempt a—''

''A trial marriage,'' he finished. ''Quite rational.'' His eyes narrowed. ''Naturally, this trial marriage would be in name only . . . without consummation. That way, if we do not suit, an annulment would be much easier to obtain.''

''Naturally,'' she said in dismay. A marriage to this man without sex was definitely not what she wanted, but there was no way she could tell him so. Beads of perspiration gathered in the hollow between her breasts; there was no fire on the hearth, yet the room was suddenly too warm. ''Six months,'' she ventured. ''We could try for six months.''

He took a long time to answer. ''Too much of an imposition,'' he replied. ''And you would miss the sailing season. A winter voyage is too dangerous to consider. Six weeks.'' His heathen Indian eyes surveyed her with inscrutable challenge.

''I would keep to my bed and you to yours?''

''Precisely.''

''You speak much like a barrister, sir,'' she said, stalling for time. Six months would be better; it would give her more time to win him over, but even six weeks was preferable to being packed off to Annapolis in the morning.

''I spent three years at the Inns of Court, studying the law in England,'' he explained. ''My father comes of good family, although he cannot claim nobility as you can.''

''You studied in England?'' She stared at him in surprise, wondering if this was the truth or another tall tale and realizing that she didn't care.

''I'm afraid I paid more attention to gaming and horse racing than to my books. I'm a planter, Lissa, plain and simple. I like Tidewater dirt on my hands, and I'm not ashamed of my Indian heritage. If ye take me as husband,'' he said, slipping into less formal speech and the soft colonial accent that had so intrigued her, ''ye must realize that I willna' change.'' He glanced down at his elegantly tailored clothing. ''Outside, I may look English, but here . . .'' He tapped his waistcoat over his heart. ''Inside I am still a half-breed.''

She looked down at the toes of her slippers, peeking out from beneath her skirts. Her heart was racing, and she felt not a little dizzy. She swallowed and glanced up at him through a veil of lashes. ''I should like to try to see if we are suited,'' she said meekly.

If she had to play a part to win him, then she would do it. Still, she couldn't keep her eyes off him. He wore the stylish coat and tight breeches with a nonchalance that would have been the envy of any London gallant. How could she ever have been so foolish as to think Reece a colonial bumpkin?

''Very well, madam, we shall try for six weeks,'' he agreed, resuming his gentleman's air. He rose and came to her side, dropping gracefully to one knee and taking her trembling hand in his. ''Will you grant me the honor of becoming my wife?'' His brushed her fingers with a feather-light kiss.

It was a silly gesture of romantic playacting, yet Lissa was acutely aware of the corded muscle beneath Reece's satin and lace. Whatever game he played, he played to win, and she would not back down. Her stomach knotted. She felt as frightened and excited as she had the first time she'd taken a horse over a high stone wall.

''For six weeks,'' she murmured. His breath was warm

on her hand, and the pressure of his grip sent ripples of sensation racing up her arm. "Perhaps a kiss of peace between us?" she dared.

His answer was to pull her to her feet and crush her against him. His lips pressed hers in what she supposed would be a cool sealing of the bargain. Instead, lightning leaped between them.

Not so much a kiss as a searing flame of temptation, Reece's heated caress left her breathless and wanting more. She stared at him, mouth bruised and aching, head full of the virile man-scent of him, wondering if she dared to—

"Perhaps you would care to walk with me in the garden," he said provocatively, tucking his arm in the crook of hers. "The river is beautiful in the evening." His dark eyes glittered in the flickering candlelight, and Lissa felt giddy with the curious fluttering in the pit of her stomach.

"Yes, thank you," she stammered. "I would . . . would like that."

She clung to his arm as he led her out into the entrance hall, through the back of the house, and down a set of outside steps to a crushed oyster-shell walk. "We have no hope of resolving things between us if you can't accept Jilly with an open heart," Reece confided. "She was born out of wedlock, but she is my legal heir, and she's the dearest thing in the world to me."

Lissa looked up into his moonlit face. "I had a stepmother," she answered. "I know the pain of being a hindrance in my father's house. I could never do that to a child."

He exhaled softly. "Jilly will be difficult. I've let her run wild, and she won't take to you easily." He stopped. "I won't have her whipped. No matter what she does, you are never to strike her, or to permit the servants to do so. Among the Nanticoke and Delaware, only the lowest sort of person would hit a child."

"I abhor violence against children. But how can you expect Jilly to learn proper behavior if you refuse to permit any of the household to discipline her? An unruly child is like an unschooled horse; neither will come to much.''

Reece's lips compressed tightly. ''I didn't say I didn't discipline her or wouldn't allow you to. I just want it clear that she's not to be abused physically.''

''Do I seem to you the type of woman who would take pleasure in hurting a motherless child?''

He shook his head. ''No. No, Lissa, you don't. But I'd be less than honest with you if I didn't—''

''I've never been a mother,'' she interrupted. ''I'm not accustomed to small children. But you must believe that I would be fair with Jilly. I hope to be her friend.''

''She needs a mother.''

''Small steps, husband.'' The word rolled off her tongue before she could stop it. ''First friendship, then guidance, and then, if she desires it, I could try to be her mother. Will Cholena feel threatened?''

He didn't flinch. ''You know she's my mother.''

''I guessed. Why did you try to hide her identity from me? Are you ashamed of her?''

''Of Mother? God, no! The cabin is hers, you know. I just wanted to get her away so that you and I could work things out. I suppose I was afraid that she'd take a liking to you and insist I keep you. She's as stubborn as a Newgate judge once she makes up her mind about something. She gave me a week. One week, and then she would make herself known and welcome you to the family.'' He chuckled. ''My guess is that if you are good to Jilly and do not make my life a total hell, Mother will like you well enough.''

''But if the cabin is her home . . . Now that the fire destroyed it, where will—''

''She can stay here or with her family at the village while I have her house rebuilt. I've wanted to provide her with a larger home for years, but she's always been happy with it as it was.''

The path curved across a close-cropped lawn, around a boxwood hedge, and into a small orchard. Lissa inhaled deeply of the sweet smell of apple blossoms and remembered the bloom on her supper tray. "Thank you for my bouquet," she murmured. He squeezed her arm in reply.

Darkness had fallen like a velvet cloak over Wildcat Purchase. Overhead, a sprinkling of stars winked on, and a full moon was rising over the treetops. Lissa stared up at the sweep of heaven. "The sky never seemed so big at home," she said.

For a long time, she heard nothing but the crunch of oyster shells under their feet and the faint rustle of wind through the branches.

"I missed the clear skies at night when I was in England," Reece said. "In winter, in London, the air is so thick with the smoke from coal and wood fires that you can hardly see the moon, let alone the stars."

Just ahead was an opening in the orchard with a grassy clearing, and beyond that the river. The path had ended, and they wandered on with a thick carpet of grass beneath their feet.

"I didn't know you were so close to the water here," she said, breaking the silence. The sounds of the river were soothing, the lap of waves and the croak of frogs. The scene reminded her of her grandmother's house on the lake in Wales. She'd visited there only once, when she was very small, but she'd cherished the memories of that precious summer when she'd laughed and run rampant with her Welsh cousins.

"The bay isn't far away, but without the river we'd be lost. It's deep enough for oceangoing ships to anchor here. We get our supplies by water, and we send out our tobacco, lumber, and wheat. Half of the food we eat comes from the bay or the river—fish, clams, oysters, ducks, and geese."

"Horseshoe crabs too?"

Reece couldn't quite conceal a chuckle. "Yes," he replied in a strangled tone. "Horseshoe crabs as well." He brushed a flurry of apple blossoms from her hair. "I like your hair this way," he said.

"I've no hat," she apologized. "I'm too old to run about—"

"I like it," he repeated. He cupped her chin in his palm and tilted her face so that she looked directly into his eyes. "I like you, Lissa . . . very much." He traced her upper lip with his finger and her pulse quickened. "It's a good life here," he said huskily. "Very different from what you've known in England, but a good life just the same."

Moonlight turned the surface of the river into a cascade of diamonds, glittering all the brighter because of the soft black shadows on the far bank. She could feel the gentle breeze on her cheeks, a warm, fresh wind that brought the clean smell of woods and saltwater. It seemed an enchanted spot, and Lissa had never felt so alive or so much at home.

"My mother is Nanticoke," Reece said, "but she has always lived among the Delaware Indians. They are an ancient people, primitive and superstitious, but wise and kind-hearted. Family is everything with the Indians. Try not to judge her too harshly until you've come to understand her ways."

"Will you please stop talking and kiss me?"

He laughed. "Your wish, madam, is my command."

This time, when she came into his arms, their kiss was mutual. Somehow, she knew just how to turn her head and fit her lips to his. Tender and tentative, it was as sweet a kiss as any young maid's dream.

Lissa sighed with contentment. Reece was strong and solid, as gentle as he was caring. She could not let this man go . . . not now, not ever. Happiness unfolded in her heart like a flower petal opening to the morning sun. *I love you,* she cried silently.

It wasn't the time to speak of her love to Reece—not yet—but neither could she deny the truth to herself. No matter what she had to do, she would make this man her husband and her lover, and she would never leave him . . . not so long as she drew breath.

She stood in the circle of his arms and raised herself on tiptoe, moistened her lips with the tip of her tongue, and waited.

He chuckled softly and kissed her again. This time, their caress deepened, and she clung to him as a fierce wind of longing swept over her. Her knees went weak, and she began to tremble.

He kissed her hair and eyelids, and whispered sweet nothings into her ear. She sighed deeply, letting the fairy wind carry her up and away to a place where she didn't have to think . . . to a place where there was only Reece and the silken touch of his hands and the magic of his lips on hers.

Then, without her realizing how it happened, they were no longer standing, but lying in the grass together. Reece's coat was off and he was kissing her as she had never been kissed before. His tongue filled her mouth, teasing, tasting, playing along the ridges of her teeth, stroking the contours of her lips. His hands moved over her bodice, so hot that they burned her skin through her clothing.

"Reece, Reece," she murmured breathlessly, when he kissed her throat and ran his tongue lightly over her swelling bosom. Spirals of joy coursed through her veins, and she found herself laughing and crying at the same time. "Oh, Reece."

"Sweet Lissa." He strained against her, moaning when she molded her body against him, when her fingertips caressed his throat and traced his brows.

She closed her eyes and arched her neck, twining her fingers in his hair as his kisses grew longer and more demanding. Her breasts throbbed; she could feel the ache of her swollen nipples against the linen lining of her stays. Catching his hand, she brought it to her right breast. "I want you to touch me," she whispered.

"I want to," he answered. "I want to see you and kiss you." He kissed her again, all the while loosening the ties at the back of her gown so that he could slip the bodice down and undo her stays.

She sighed as his mouth found her nipple and closed moist and warm around it. "Ohhh," she cried. The gentle tugging of his lips, the pressure of his tongue against her skin, brought an incandescent pulsing to her loins. Her breath came in ragged gasps as she offered him first one love-swollen nipple and then the other. "I never knew anything could feel so good," she whispered. "I love it when you kiss my breasts and suck them."

"I wanted to do this the first time I laid eyes on you. You have such beautiful breasts, Lissa." He fumbled beneath her skirts and touched the bare skin above her left knee. "Let me touch you," he said. "Just feel you . . . nothing else."

"Ohhh," she whimpered.

"Does this feel good?"

"Yes . . . yes."

"And this?"

"Oh, yes . . ."

"Now do the same for me," he urged, taking her hand in his and guiding her to the source of his rising desire.

Hesitantly, with trembling fingers, she touched the swollen length of his sex through the taut velvet. Reece groaned with pleasure, and the sound made her bold. Laughing, she pushed him back against the grass and pressed her lips to the warm cloth.

"Ahhh," he sighed. "No . . . don't stop."

Lightly, tantalizingly, she continued her brazen exploration, running her fingers along the top of his breeches and sliding a hand inside to cup his impassioned tumescence.

He moaned as she guided her hand through the folds of velvet and down the length of his member. Startled by the size and heat of him, she drew back her hand and stared into his eyes.

"I want to love you," he whispered. "Here and now."

She hesitated, and he pulled her into his arms again and began to kiss her fears away.

"I won't hurt you," he said. "I'd never hurt you, Lissa."

The taste and scent of him were overwhelming. Her heart was thudding wildly, and she could feel the damp need between her legs. She wanted him as much as he wanted her . . . And yet . . .

A warning voice whispered from the farthest corner of her mind. Reason . . . reason . . . reason . . .

Lissa pushed away from Reece. It was impossible to think while he was kissing and touching her, making her feel like no man had ever made her feel. "We can't," she protested weakly. "Not like this. We can't."

"What do you mean, we can't?" He made no attempt to hold her, but his voice was raspy with puzzlement. "We are wed, Lissa, wed in the eyes of church and community. Why can't we?"

"Because . . . because . . ." She got to her feet and stepped back so that his face was hidden in shadow. "If we did this . . ." She shook her head. The words were so hard to say, and she wanted desperately to get them right. "If we lie together here, we will make a marriage," she whispered.

"And I'll keep my vows," he promised. "I'll not send you away or leave you."

"I know you would, Reece." She took a deep breath and forced herself to say the words that rose in her heart. "But I would never know if you'd taken me out of love or out of lust. I want you as my husband, but I never want the day to come when you look back on this night and feel I tricked you." She held out a trembling hand. "Do you understand? I want you to want me . . . but only if you have come to the decision with a clear mind."

"You're certain?" he demanded hoarsely. "This is what you want?"

"Yes. I want this to be right and sure, for us, for Jilly, and for the children I hope to give you in the future. I love you, Reece, but I can't do this." Her composure faltered, and she turned away with tear-filled eyes and ran back toward the house.

She heard the sound of his running footfalls behind her and tried to outdistance him, but he caught her before she reached the oyster-shell path. He seized her shoulders and swung her around, trapping her in his arms. She didn't struggle; she was past fighting him. She stood still, breathless, heart pounding, waiting for him to make the first move.

"Lissa." His deep voice was tender. "Don't cry, Lissa." He cradled her against his chest and stroked her tangled hair. "Did I hear right? Did you say you love me?"

She nodded, her throat too constricted with emotion to speak.

"Then we have no problem. No problem at all."

Her shoulders quivered and she tried to explain, but all that came out was a single word. "Reason."

"Aye, lass. A man should be logical in all that he does—but some things are too important to be reasoned out. You've taught me that. There are some decisions that a man must make with his heart."

"I don't understand," she whispered into his tear-dampened shirt.

"What is it that ye dinna ken?" he teased. "You love me, and I love you."

"But we've known each other only a few days."

"True enough. So I think we should take careful measures to make certain ours is a marriage that our children will be proud of."

The terrible tightness in her chest drained away, and she stared up at him in joyful hope. "You love me?"

"I've said it, haven't I?" He raised her face and kissed her gently on the lips. "We'll have a second ceremony in three days," he said. "We'll invite half the colony, and then no one can say we're not properly wed."

"Three days? How could we be ready for a wedding in three days? What of your mother? Of Jilly?"

He laughed. "You're right, of course. Preparing for a hundred guests or more will take time. Four days."

"But—"

"This is your last chance, woman! Accept my offer of honorable marriage in four days, or I swear, I'll carry you back to the riverbank and ravish you here and now. What shall it be?"

"I don't know what to say," she protested.

"Say 'yes, Reece.'"

"Yes, Reece." And then his lips were on hers again, and all her fears and doubts were swept away in his deep laughter and warm embrace.

7

Two days had passed since the night Lissa and Reece had agreed to hold a second marriage ceremony. In that time, Reece had made no further attempt to make love to her; instead, he had played the romantic courtier, taking her sailing on the river, riding over his vast acreage on horseback with her beside him, and introducing her to his many servants and field-workers.

Wildcat Purchase was more than just a farm; it was a plantation as large as some counties in England and contained its own small village. There were tobacco barns, horse barns, a dairy stable, poultry and sheep houses, a forge, a weaving shed, a leather shop, a lumber mill, and a carpentry workshop. Cabins for the bond servants and slaves stood beyond the smokehouse and bake ovens. Two sloops and an oceangoing brigantine were anchored at the river dock near a tiny shipbuilding yard and warehouse. At the far end of the orchard was a dovecote, and a kennel where Reece's prize foxhounds were kept in better quarters than some of Lissa's father's tenants.

In the evening, the two lovers retreated to Reece's library, where they dined in private and played backgammon and piquet until the hall case clock struck midnight. Reece regularly beat her at backgammon, and she trounced him at piquet. Lissa found, to her delight, that despite his mock howls of protest, Reece was as good-natured a loser as he was a winner, and best of all, he possessed an outrageous sense of humor.

The one thing that troubled her was that she had not yet met Jilly or confronted his mother with their coming nuptials. "Surely, it will make it difficult for the child to come home and—"

"I sent a messenger to Mother, telling them both that I would come for them the evening before the ceremony," Reece replied, as he escorted her to her bedchamber door.

"But I think—"

He silenced her with a tender kiss. "No," he said, stepping back from temptation. "As much as I'd like to, I'm not coming in. We'll save that for our wedding night." He grinned at her with the slightly crooked smile that always set her pulse racing. "Leave Mother and Jilly to me. You'll have your hands full with the two of them afterwards. There's no need to complicate matters now." He kissed her one last time. "Sleep late in the morning. I have to ride to Annapolis and make some final arrangements for the wedding. Don't worry about preparations for the guests. I told the cook . . ." Reece paused and grinned again. "You met Pegleg earlier."

Lissa sniffed. She had, indeed, met Pegleg, a stout, dignified man with red cheeks and a bald head. And although he did have only one leg, she doubted Reece's wild tale about the Indians eating his missing limb.

"I told Pegleg to prepare enough food for two hundred people," Reece continued. "He'll double that, no matter what I say. You're not to worry about anything. He's quite capable."

Lissa put her hand on the doorknob and looked at Reece expectantly. She didn't want to go to bed alone. She wanted to invite him into her chamber—to become his wife in fact as well as in name. She couldn't keep her eyes off him. Somehow, this man whom she'd known only a few days had become the center of her world. She wanted to touch him . . . to inhale his special scent . . . to make herself drunk on his kisses. But instinctively, she knew that this agreement to remain apart until the wedding ceremony was one she had to keep. "Good night," she murmured softly. "I love you."

"And I love you." He kissed her again.

His lean fingers lingered on her cheek, making her blood race. For an instant, she thought he would weaken, but then he winked at her, turned, and went down the hall to his own room.

Frustrated at their parting, Lissa closed the door and undressed by the light of a single candle. Then she put on Reece's shirt, brushed out her long hair, and plaited it into a thick untidy braid before climbing into bed. Once there, she tossed and turned until the candle sputtered out. Finally, she fell asleep sometime after two.

Daylight was streaming through her open window when she opened her eyes, but she was still sleepy. Remembering that Reece was away, she ignored the loud crowing of a rooster and turned over to go back to sleep. She was just drifting off when something tugged at her hair. "Ouch," she murmured. She rubbed the back of her head and sat bolt upright, eyes wide and mouth open in surprise.

Standing just out of arm's reach was a small, angry boy in ragged breeches and vest, his face smeared with black and yellow paint, holding a pair of scissors and a long dark braid of hair in his hands.

"What the—" Lissa began. She broke off in astonishment, realizing that the pointed little chin and the huge brown eyes in the shock of wheat-colored hair were much too delicate for a boy. "Jilly?"

"Go away! We don't want you here!" the child shouted. She waved the braid at Lissa. "I said I would take your scalp, Englishwoman. I did. Go home and leave my father alone."

"You cut off my hair!" Lissa stammered in disbelief.

"I will hang it from my lodge pole. I don't want a mother. I don't want you. Go away."

Lissa felt the back of her head. Her hair ended in a jagged line at the base of her neck and something else . . . Her left earring was missing. Frantically, she reached for the right one. It was still in place. "Did you steal my earring as well?" she demanded.

A deep red flush washed over Jilly's face. "No! I'm no stealer. There's your dumb earring." She pointed to the floor beside the bed. "Go away," she repeated. "We don't want a new mother."

Lissa retrieved her emerald earring and fastened it in her ear. "How did you get in here? And how dare you cut off my hair! That was very, very naughty." The audaciousness of the act shocked her. She didn't know whether she wanted to spank the child or laugh.

Unbidden, the memory of her stepmother's stern face came to mind. Once, furious at something her father's wife had done, Lissa had put a rotten egg in each of the lady's best dancing slippers. When her stepmother had slid her stocking feet into the shoes, both eggs had exploded. The woman had nearly had a stroke. Lissa had been accused of the crime and punished for it, but she'd not had the nerve to admit she'd done the deed. And as angry as Lissa was at Jilly for cutting her hair, a small part of her admired the child's spunk.

"Am not naughty." Jilly pursed her lips in a thin line and glared back. "I am a great warrior. You are—"

"I am your father's wife."

"Are not!"

"Does your grandmother know where you are?"

Guilt flashed across the child's face.

"Your father will be very angry with you."

"Go away," Jilly said in a subdued voice. "I want you to go away."

Lissa crouched down so that she didn't tower over the little girl. She desperately wanted to like her stepchild, and she wanted Jilly to like her. "I'm not going away, Jilly. I love your father, and I want to love you."

"I hate you."

"How can you hate me when you don't know me?" Lissa reasoned. "You love your father, don't you?" Jilly nodded. "And you love your grandmother," Lissa continued softly.

"Don't want a new mother."

"When I was a little girl, my Papa married again. I had to learn to get along with a new mother."

"Was she mean to you?"

"Yes, she was. And I decided that if I ever had a little girl, I'd try never to be mean to her."

Jilly's dark eyes narrowed suspiciously, and for a moment, Lissa saw a miniature Reece standing before her. "Want you to go away," she repeated, then turned and dashed to the open window.

"Wait," Lissa cried. "Don't—"

Jilly hopped up on the windowsill, spun around, and lowered herself over the edge with Lissa's braid clenched triumphantly in her teeth.

"Jilly!" Lissa ran to the window, afraid that the child had fallen, only to see her nimbly scrambling down a poplar tree. She dropped the last few feet, rolled, scrambled up, and vaulted onto the back of a fat brown pony.

Lissa opened her mouth to shout "wait until I tell your father," but the words never came. She realized with a start it was the same threat she'd heard her stepmother utter a thousand times in her own childhood.

No, she decided. Her battle with Jilly would have to be fought and won without Reece's assistance. She'd not drag him into the middle of their combat as her father had so often been. "Jilly . . . Jilly," she whispered. And then she thought again of the rotten eggs in her stepmother's shoes, and the corners of her mouth turned up in a faint smile.

Lissa's wedding day dawned with a threat of rain, but by mid-morning, the sun had broken through the clouds and preparations for the celebration were in full swing. The minister had arrived, servants were setting up tables in the garden to hold the food, and Lissa had chosen a leaf-green satin gown to wear from those she had brought with her from England. The green, although unfashionable, would go wonderfully with the Rutledge emerald earrings.

Reece had arrived home so late the evening before from the Indian village, where he'd gone to get his mother and daughter, that Lissa hadn't seen any of them except Jilly, and she hadn't had to explain her shorn locks. Today, custom kept bride and bridegroom apart until the ceremony. Lissa remained in her room, trying not to become despondent over her ugly hair, and wondering what Reece and their guests would think when they saw her.

Impatiently, she paced her bedchamber, feeling much as she imagined a caged bird must feel. Everyone in the house seemed to have something to do but her. Below, in the great hall, musicians were tuning their instruments. The cooks and assistants were busy not only in the summer kitchen but also outside, where whole pigs and a steer were roasting over open pits. Hulda and Hedvig were rushing to and fro, welcoming guests from the neighboring plantations and from as far away as Chestertown and the Eastern shore.

"Everyone like vedding," Hulda had said, when she'd brought up Lissa's breakfast tray. "Dance, eat, race horses, gamble. Stay three . . . four days."

"Three or four days?" Lissa echoed.

"Ja. Maybe more. All vant to see vat kind of lady Herr Reece get from England."

Lissa wasn't certain what she'd say to total strangers for four days, and she wasn't looking forward to being the entertainment for Annapolis society. Dogs barked outside, and she looked out the window to see what was happening.

"Lis-sa."

She spun around to see Reece's mother standing just inside the bedchamber. She had come in so quietly that Lissa hadn't heard the door open or close.

"Welcome to the family, Lis-sa," Cholena said. She was dressed in an old-fashioned English-style gown of flowered silk. "My son says you are satisfied with each other."

"I love him," Lissa answered. She put her hand to her hair self-consciously. "You must think I look—"

Cholena shook her head and frowned. "Jilly told me what she did. I have a great anger with her. She brings shame on our house." She reached into the bundle she carried and produced Lissa's braid. "I tell her she must give back your hair, and she must make apology for what she has done."

Lissa nodded. "That would help."

"Jilly is much like her father. Sometimes they do not know what is best for them. If you are patient with her, you will learn that she is a child with great heart and much courage."

"I've seen the bravery," Lissa replied. "As for heart . . ."

Cholena smiled. "My son loves her. If you would have his gratitude, then you must be the mother to her that I cannot be. You must teach her to be English."

"I'll try."

"Good." Reece's mother walked over to Lissa and looked at her ravaged hair. "Among my people are some women who must add hair to their own. Perhaps we can do this for you, Lis-sa. You did not tell on Jilly."

"No, but Reece will have to know sometime. It's not something I can hide."

"But we can hide it from those who come to stare at the new wife, can we not?" Cholena's dark eyes sparkled with mischief. "If we make a crown of the cut hair, we can pin it to the back of your head, yes?"

Lissa sighed with relief. "Yes. Thank you! I can deal with Reece. It was the guests I didn't want laughing at me. You've saved my life."

Cholena held out the bundle. "I bring you something else, for luck." Her inscrutable gaze met Lissa's. "A bride must have a wedding dress. Long ago, I make it for my son's bride. It smells a little of smoke, but the fire at my lodge did not harm the doeskin.''

Hesitantly, Lissa took the garment and unwrapped it. It was an Indian-style dress of white leather, all fringes and beads, with a row of animal teeth around the modest neckline. ''I—I don't know what to say,'' she stammered. The gown was butter-soft; the leaf design breathtaking. Underneath the dress was a matching pair of intricately beaded, knee-high leather moccasins. ''It's . . . it's beautiful.''

Lissa looked down at the gown in confusion. Surely, Reece's mother didn't expect her to wear an Indian costume to her wedding? What would the guests think? She'd be an object of scorn—of ridicule.

Her panic was brought up short by a mind's-eye image of her stepmother's disapproving face. Both her proper father and her stern stepmother would be horrified at the thought of Lissa appearing in public in such barbaric attire.

But my priorities are different, she thought with a sudden burst of joy. This was a new country and a new beginning for her. What did it matter what Reece's neighbors thought? If she could please her new mother-in-law by accepting her gracious gift, why shouldn't she wear the exquisite Nanticoke gown that had been sewn with so much love and skill?

She raised a corner of the skirt and rubbed the pliant leather against her lips. ''How did you get it so soft?'' she asked. ''I never—''

''You do not want to wear an Indian dress,'' Cholena said flatly.

''Oh, but I do.'' Lissa smiled and held the dress up against her. ''I would be honored to wear your dress.'' To hell with Maryland society, she thought. I'm a Rutledge, an earl's daughter. I can damn well wear what I like to my own wedding. ''I certainly will wear it,'' she said to Cholena. ''Thank you. Who knows, perhaps next year every bride in Annapolis will be crying for a gown like this?''

The older woman nodded solemnly, but her eyes glowed with gratitude. "I think we will be friends, Lissa," she said. "I think I am proud my son chose you."

"He didn't choose me," Lissa corrected, stifling a giggle. "I chose him."

"Or the gods chose for you both," Cholena said. "I—"

Suddenly, there was loud rapping on the door. "Fru Reece! Fru Reece!" The door flew open. "Fru Reece! Come quick. Jilly has—she bring—"

Lissa pushed past the maid and ran to the head of the staircase with Cholena right on her heels. The entrance door to the hall stood ajar, and Reece's daughter was dragging a reluctant pony up the bottom step.

"Jilly! What on earth?" Lissa cried. "Why are you bringing a horse up the stairs?"

Jilly's lower lip quivered. She was dressed in a stylish ankle-length wide-hooped sacque gown of robin's-egg-blue silk with deep laced cuffs and a dainty white-lace cap. The impish face that had been streaked with paint the last time Lissa had seen it was scrubbed clean. But under the gown, in place of kid slippers, Jilly still wore her fringed moccasins.

Her grandmother said something in the Indian tongue, and Jilly nodded. The child looked up at Lissa. "I'm sorry," she said. She gave the pony's bridle a sharp tug.

"The horse can't come in the house," Lissa said.

"But it's a present. For you."

"I can't—" Lissa began, but Cholena leaned close and whispered in her ear.

"You must accept Jilly's gift. If you do not, you dishonor her. It is her way of making up for scalping you."

"I can't thank you enough," Lissa said. "He's a wonderful gift, but he'd be happier outside." She turned to Hedvig. "Take the animal to the barn." Then she smiled at Jilly. "You come up. Let Hedvig take care of my horse, and you come upstairs."

Ignoring the stares of guests and servants in the lower

hall, Lissa returned to her chamber with Cholena and Jilly. When they were safely inside, Lissa closed the door and crouched down to Jilly's level. "That was a grand present," she said, "but you didn't have to give me—"

"I shamed the family," Jilly answered contritely. "I had to give you the best thing I had to make up for it." She wiped away a tear, smearing dirt across her face in the process. "Besides, Tuck is a pony, not a horse."

"I see." Lissa nibbled her lower lip. "Do you always give away the best thing you have when you give a gift?"

Cholena nodded. "It is the Indian way."

"I'm afraid I have a lot to learn about Indians. You'll have to help me, Jilly. I'm not sure, but . . . do I . . ."

Cholena motioned toward Jilly without letting the child see her.

"I give you a gift in return?" Lissa asked.

Jilly nodded. "An' . . . an' I hav' to take it, even if . . . if I still wish you'd go away."

Lissa laughed. "You know what I like best about you, little Mistress Wildcat?"

The child shook her head.

"You're absolutely honest." Still chuckling, Lissa removed first one of her emerald earrings, and then the other, and handed them to Jilly. "These are for you. They are very old. They came from my great-great-great grandmother. Would you like to wear them to the wedding?"

Jilly nodded, then hopped impatiently first on one foot and then the other while her grandmother fastened the emeralds in her ears.

"They're a little big for you," Lissa said, "but I think you'll grow into them."

"You can wear my shells," Jilly said. "I'm not giving them to you, but you can wear them today. One present is enough for you."

Lissa laughed again. "I think one present is all I can afford today."

Someone knocked at the door again. "Lady! Lady! Herr Reece says is time for vedding!"

"I'll be there," Lissa answered. "I'll be there." She glanced at Jilly. "If you'll help me get ready."

"Do I hav' to?"

"No," Cholena said with a chuckle. "But it would please your father. It is the Indian thing to do."

Jilly sighed. "All right. But I still wish she'd go away."

Cholena caught Lissa's eye. "I don't think there's much chance of that happening."

"No," Lissa agreed. "Not a chance."

Minutes later, Jilly wiggled through the crowd and spied her father by the door that led to the garden. Dodging stout Mistress Isabel Hood from Hood's Folly on the Choptank, and dashing past the Widow Wright and her cheek pinching and cries of "sweet little darling," Jilly bounced off Reece's knee and grabbed his hand.

"I've got to talk to you, *Nukuaa,*" the child exclaimed in a mixture of Delaware and English.

Reece crouched down in front of her. "Jilly, what's wrong?"

"*Nukuaa! Nukuaa!* Listen!"

"English, child, speak English," he reminded her. Then he remembered the minister. "If you'll excuse me, Reverend, I think my daughter needs me."

"Is there some delay with the ceremony?" the cleric asked.

"Mistress Hood," Reece called. "Could you see to—"

"Of course," Mistress Hood replied, swaying toward them in her wide yellow gown. "Dear Reverend. I've been wanting to ask you . . ."

"Papa, I—"

Reece tucked Jilly under his arm and carried her to a secluded spot in the garden. He sat down on a weathered cedar bench and pulled her, skirts and all, onto his lap. "Now, what's wrong, baby?"

"Not a baby," she protested.

"Nay," he said. "You're not. What's wrong?"

"Don't want a new mother. Don't want her."

Reece sighed and kissed the crown of Jilly's wheat-colored head. "I want her, Jilly."

"Don't you love me?"

"Baby, baby." He lifted the small chin with one finger and stared into her huge dark eyes. "It's a hard thing for ye, I ken. But ye must try to understand. Love isn't something that runs dry like a shallow well. It's more like the Chesapeake—it's big and wide and runs on forever. I've got enough for you, and *Onna*, and Lissa."

Jilly pouted. "Don't like her."

Reece chuckled. "I didn't like her either, not until I got to know her. Now . . ." He hugged Jilly tightly. "Now I can't imagine living without her."

"We don't need her, Papa."

"Oh, but we do, lassie. We need Lissa powerful badly. There's been something missing here at Wildcat for a long time." And it was true, he realized. There were times when the heart made more sense than the head, even to a man of reason. Lissa filled an emptiness he hadn't known was there. She made him feel whole and strong, powerful enough to face any challenge—even the one of helping Jilly adjust to a new mother.

"Don't want you to marry her."

"Sometimes, pumpkin, big people do things that little ones don't understand. But Papa always loves you, and he always tries to do what's right for you. Remember when ye were sick last winter and I made you take that bad-tasting medicine?"

She nodded, grimacing.

"But it made you better, didn't it?"

Jilly sighed and nodded.

"Well, Lissa is a special kind of medicine that I think will make us all happier than we've been. She'll teach you what ye need to know to be an English lady."

Jilly's bottom lip went out. "Don't want to be an English lady. Want to be a warrior."

Reece laughed. "You'll have to decide that when you're big, but for now, ye must treat Lissa with respect. She'll need a lot of help too. Wildcat is new to her. There are lots of things ye can teach her."

"Me?"

"Aye, lassie." He kissed her hair again. "As ye can teach your father." He sat her on her feet. "I'll never stop loving ye, Jilly. I promise ye that. I love Lissa with all my heart, but you came first, and you'll always have that place."

"I'm first?" A hint of a dimple flashed.

"My firstborn, and the heiress of Wildcat Purchase," he assured her.

"Reece! Reece!" a man's voice called. "It's time."

Taking his daughter's hand, Reece rose and walked quickly back toward the house. "She's waiting for us," he said to Jilly. "Lissa's waiting." And suddenly his mouth was dry and his pulse was racing as fast as it had the time he'd faced the big Iroquois.

I dinna ken what I've done to deserve ye, woman, he thought as his eyes scanned the crowd to find Lissa. But I can tell ye one thing, now that I've got ye—I'll hold ye close and treat ye like the great lady ye are. And then he saw her and he couldn't hold back the smile of joy that broke over his face.

8

THE tall case clock was striking ten at night as Reece seized Lissa's hand and pulled her through the low door under the grand staircase that led to the cellar. "Shhh," he whispered. "Come with me."

"What about the guests?" she protested, following him down the narrow wooden staircase to the dimly lighted, dirt-floored room below.

He pulled her into his arms as closely as her wide hoops would allow and covered her face with kisses. "What of the guests? They sound like they're having a good time, don't they?"

Strains of a lively country reel and the tap and thumps of dancing feet seeped through the thick floors above. Lissa giggled and let herself be pulled into another deep kiss.

"I've shared ye with them long enough," Reece said. "Now I want you all to myself." He kissed the top of her shoulder and nibbled his way down the daring neckline of her green gown to the hollow between her breasts.

Lissa shivered with excitement and closed her eyes. The hours since the simple ceremony in the garden had flown by, filled with unfamiliar faces, laughter, and dancing. Vaguely, she'd been aware of eating something, and of dancing the first dance of the evening with Reece. Since then, she had been passed from man to man, with much teasing and well-wishes, until she was certain she had danced with every male in the Maryland colony from eight to eighty at least twice.

"They won't go home for days," Reece whispered. "Not until they've worn out their dancing shoes, lost every shilling in their pockets on horse racing, and eaten every scrap of food on Wildcat Purchase." He kissed the back of her neck. "I want you to let down this hair and—"

Lissa moved playfully out of his reach. "It's a wonder they didn't all leave when they first saw me."

"Aye." He chuckled. "Knowing Mother, I'm not sure if she wanted you to wear the doeskin dress for luck or to test you." He caught her right hand and planted a warm kiss on the inside of her wrist, then kissed his way slowly up to the inside of her elbow. "You made a fetching Indian maid in any case."

"You aren't angry with me for shocking them?"

"Better them than mother. She holds a grudge longer. Just remember, these good people are the same ones who wouldn't let me court their daughters because of my Nanticoke blood."

Lissa felt giddy with relief. If Cholena had been testing her, then she assumed she'd passed. After the wedding ceremony, she'd left Reece and her guests long enough to return to her room and dress in the lovely green gown with its apple-green petticoat and matching satin slippers. With a modest lace cap over her pinned-up hair, she'd looked the model of decorum. Jilly had even loaned her the Rutledge emeralds to set off the dress.

"I especially liked your pretty speech about honoring my mother's heritage," he murmured, as he expertly untied the lacing at the back of her gown.

"Reece," she hissed. "Not here. I'll never be able to—"

"No," he agreed, "not here." Taking her hand again, he led the way out of the small chamber, through a center hall past the wine and vinegar kegs, and up a flight of brick steps. The outside cellar-way door opened onto a covered passageway. "Shhh," he warned.

Torches and a bonfire lit the yard where servants and lesser folk gathered for their own dancing and wedding feast. The laughing and clapping was so loud that Lissa could have shouted and no one would have paid any attention. Dogs and children ran in and out among the crowd, the children dancing with each other and adults, the dogs barking and stealing food from the overloaded tables. Fiddlers and other musicians played loudly from atop a farm wagon, while two slaves and an Indian added to the din with drums.

"This isn't a wedding—this is a circus," Lissa said to Reece.

"Wait until tomorrow night. They're just getting warmed up. Marylanders work hard, lass, but they know how to have a good time."

Keeping to the shadows, the two hurried around a well house, though the dairy, and past the smokehouse to a large barn at the edge of the farmyard. Holding Lissa's hand tightly, Reece moved to the far side of the building, away from the light and celebration, and opened a door. "In here," he ordered.

The interior of the barn lay in total darkness. "I can't see," Lissa said.

"You don't need to see," he replied. "I know where we're going." He pulled her against him and kissed her. "Trust me." Then he began walking, pulling her after him.

"My nurse warned me against trusting men," she teased. Her heart was racing. The darkness and Reece's nearness made her insides fluttery and her knees weak. The air was thick with the scents of hay and animals and grain—warm, secure smells that filled her with contentment. "Where are you taking me?" she demanded, but she knew it didn't matter. Tonight, she would have followed Reece Mackenzie to hell and back.

"Have I told you that I love you?" he asked huskily.

"Not in the last ten minutes."

"Well, I do. Here," he stopped. "Climb up this ladder."

"In my gown?"

"Hmmm. I suppose that is a problem, but I think I can figure something." He spun her around and began to undo her laces.

"Reece!"

"Quiet, woman. Can't ye see this is serious work?"

Amid much laughing and not a few kisses, he got her out of her gown, several petticoats, and her hoops. She climbed to the hayloft with him behind her to catch her if she fell. "I won't fall," she insisted.

"Aye," he answered with a suggestive chuckle, "but if ye did, I'd be in such an interesting position."

As she stepped away from the ladder opening, Lissa blinked to adjust her vision. Moonlight streamed through an open loft window, illuminating a blanket spread on a mound of hay. "And how did you know this would be here?" she asked.

" 'Tis part of my cunning, madam," he teased. "Did we wait for the wedding guests to give us privacy, we'd not have been alone until Wednesday." He threw off his waistcoat and pulled his shirt over his head. "I've waited a long time to be with you like this, Lissa."

Suddenly she was shy. She turned away from him, shivering with apprehension, and removed her lace cap and the pins that held her braid in place. Only a woman listening as intently as she was would have heard Reece's gasp of astonishment.

She turned to face him, pretending courage when her knees were knocking and her heart was in her throat. "You don't like it?" she asked, running her fingers through her close-shorn hair.

"What in the name of all that's holy ha' ye—"

Lissa wanted to laugh and weep at the same time. Already she was beginning to learn her new husband's ways. She could tell how upset he was by the intensity of his Scot's burr. "It is a custom," she lied glibly. "In my family, a new bride always cuts her hair for her wedding. It's a symbol of . . . of . . ." She hesitated, scrambling wildly for some excuse for such a stupid act.

"Of modesty and a lack of foolish pride," she finished quickly.

"The women in your family clip their hair as close as spring sheep to show modesty?" he said in a disbelieving tone. "Why do I think there is more to this than ye are telling?"

She lifted her chin and forced her voice not to waver. "It's all you'll ever hear from me," she answered. "Torture won't make me talk."

"Nay," he said. "I can see that."

"It will grow again."

"Aye." He chuckled.

"Do you hate me this way?"

"Nay."

His voice was a deep, warm caress and she shivered. "I'd rather be here with you tonight than anywhere else in the world," she said.

"Ah, lass," he murmured. He touched her bare shoulder, a whisper-soft touch that drew her to him as surely as parched soil draws morning dew. His eyes rose to stare into hers . . . twin onyx stars, glowing with an inner heat.

She sighed and stared up at him as he slipped strong arms around her, not imprisoning her but holding her as though she were made of priceless crystal. His clean, honest smell . . . all pine boughs, leather, and tobacco . . . intoxicated her with every breath she took. Her eyes clouded with tears of happiness.

"I'd never harm ye, Lissa," he promised. His mouth covered hers, tender and beseeching. And when she met his kiss with trembling anticipation, his breathing quickened and she felt his muscles tense. "Oh, Lissa," he rasped huskily. "God in heaven, but ye are a gift, woman. I love you more than my own eyes."

His next kiss seared her mouth with pent-up passion, and she parted her lips, accepting his deep caress, reveling in the intimacy of his warm, wet tongue.

"Lissa . . . Lissa," he whispered as he gathered her up and carried her toward the place he had prepared for their wedding-night tryst. She clung to him, wrapping her arms around his neck and pressing her face against his hard, superbly muscled chest. "You are so beautiful," he said.

Reece's skin beneath her cheek was smooth, almost hairless . . . silk-soft over solid hickory. His sinewy arms were as hard as bronze . . . muscles as taut as bowstrings, lean hands as strong as they were gentle.

His rich, full-toned voice with its curious blend of Scottish and colonial accents flowed over her and swelled her heart with happiness. All her life, she had wanted to hear a man tell her she was beautiful and mean it . . . now her wish was coming true. "I'm too tall," she murmured.

"Nay, wench. You're perfect. See how well ye fit in my arms." He chuckled. "Who wants a woman who will blow this way and that in every puff of wind?" he said, laying her down on the soft, sweet-smelling cushion of hay.

"I am too dark," she protested, when he paused to make short work of his own remaining garments.

For a moment, he stood over her in the moonlight, magnificent and male, and Lissa's mouth went dry as her eyes were drawn to his rigid, love-swollen member.

"My skin is too sallow for beauty," she managed, trying to cover her sudden apprehension with words.

"You look like an Indian princess," he replied, kneeling beside her and loosening another layer of her petticoats. He kissed the tip of her nose, took hold of the hem of her shift, and pulled it over her head. "With eyes like ripe blackberries and breasts a man can rest his weary head on." He nibbled at her throat as he began to undo her stays. "I love your long legs, and your bottom, and the—"

"Do you really love my bottom?" Her breath quickened as he trailed a chain of moist kisses to her ear.

"Aye." He slid a hand possessively over her hip and fondled one rounded cheek. " 'Twill keep me warm on cold nights." They kissed again . . . an intense exchange of promise and yearning. His hands were doing wonderful things to her body, causing a growing agitation in her loins.

She uttered a small cry as her stays came away and she trembled, naked before him.

"Beautiful," he murmured, cupping a full breast in the palm of his hand.

"Ohhh." She closed her eyes as tremors of sweet sensation rippled through her belly. "Ohh." He flicked her bare nipple with the tip of his tongue and she moaned, deep in her throat, unable to hold back her sounds of ecstasy. "That feels good," she said. "So good."

His lips were warm on her nipple, and she felt it harden as he drew it into his mouth and suckled. Gently at first, and then harder . . . tugging . . . drawing . . . The delicious feelings intensified until she arched against him, offering first one breast to be pleasured and then the other.

"I want to please you, Lissa," he said. "What we do here may cause you hurt the first time, but only a little, and I promise, it will never hurt again."

She knew that a woman suffered when her maidenhood was breeched, but she was past fear of the pain. He was her husband, and it was right and good that he should teach her the ways of love. This time there would be no stopping . . . this time he would fill her with his passion. He would make her part of him in a way that could never be forgotten so long as the two of them lived.

"Sweet Lissa," he groaned. "What did I ever do to deserve a woman like you?"

She stroked his shoulders and chest, kissing him, savoring the salt taste of his skin, nipping at him with gentle love bites. He was so big . . . so hard . . . yet, so tender. "I love you, Reece," she whispered. Her searching fingers untied the ribbon at the back of his head, and his long hair fell like a dark, silken curtain over her face.

Restlessly, she moved under him . . . wanting more . . . knowing but not knowing . . . She felt as though she was being carried by a strong current closer and closer to a roaring waterfall, but she was powerless to save herself.

She didn't want to be saved. She wanted to be caught up in the force of the turbulent river, to be part of it.

His hands caressed her trembling flesh, stroking, rubbing. His wet tongue laved her nipples until they ached with wanting. His fingers tangled in the moist curls above her thighs and delved into her most intimate folds. She thrust her hips up to meet the sweet probing, all modesty forgotten, driven by a primeval urge.

"Lissa, Lissa." He groaned again as she parted her legs and pulled him down against her.

His throbbing rod pressed against her sweat-sheened flesh, and she thrilled at his weight and nearness. She tossed her head from side to side in abandon as the fire in the pit of her belly whipped higher and higher.

He took her nipple between his lips and suckled hard and deep, and she lost all control, writhing against his heat and length, yearning to be consumed by the conflagration.

"I can wait no longer," he said.

Lissa's eyes flew open as he pressed into her. She felt him go taut, and then he drove deep inside her in one powerful thrust. She gasped at the brief burning sensation and at the overwhelming sense of fullness. He was so big. Surely, he would tear her asunder. Surely, she could not . . .

But the moment of discomfort passed as Reece kissed her swollen mouth and her throat and whispered words of love in her ear. Then he began to move again, slowly at first, and then faster. And she found herself caught up in the rhythm and heat of his passion. Again, she found herself arching against him, meeting his plunging virility with her own eager desire.

Then without warning, she heard Reece groan with joyous release, and she felt a hot pulse of liquid deep inside. Once more he thrust and suddenly Lissa's world exploded in a burst of falling stars and apple blossoms. She drifted on an invisible cloud of sparkling mist, round and round in slow motion, losing all sense of time and place until she came to rest in Reece's strong arms.

"I love you," he whispered. "I'll always love you."

"Mmmm," she sighed, unwilling to let the magic go, unwilling to return to earth.

"That wasn't so bad, was it?" he teased.

"Mmmm." She snuggled against him.

"Next time it will be better," he promised.

She opened her eyes and looked up at him in the moonlight. "Better than that?"

"Aye, woman. 'Tis a thing between man and wife that gains with practice."

"And will we have to practice a great deal?"

"Until you are ninety and nine, and begging for rest."

"Good," she replied with a sigh. "For there is no one in all the world that I'd rather share such lessons with than the master of Wildcat Purchase."

And they laughed and kissed and dozed in each other's arms before waking again to practice their love, until the first mockingbird trilled the coming of dawn over the treetops. Then Reece and Lissa dressed reluctantly and left the barn.

They were halfway to the house when a small form clad only in boy's breeches shot out from behind the dairy and catapulted into Reece's knees. "Papa!" came the muffled cry. "Papa!"

"Jilly." He laughed and lifted her up onto his shoulders. "What are ye doing out of bed so early?"

"It's not early, Papa. It's not." She glanced at Lissa warily. "Is it?"

Lissa made an obvious show of considering Jilly's question. "No, I don't think it is so early," she said solemnly, then laughed and reached up and tickled the child's bare belly. "Not for the young mistress of Wildcat Purchase."

Jilly looked at Lissa's hair and giggled.

Lissa raised a finger to her lips. "Shhh."

"And are the two of ye conspiring behind my back?" Reece demanded of his wife.

The twinkle in his eyes belied the stern tone of his voice, and Lissa laughed again. "We'd never do that," she answered meekly. "Would we, Jilly?"

"Nay," the child replied in her best imitation of her father's accent. "We'd nev'r do that."

"Ye'd better not," Reece said, winking at Lissa. He steadied Jilly with one hand and took hold of Lissa's hand with the other. "If it's not early, then it's late for breakfast. I could eat a pony."

"Not *my* pony," Lissa retorted, and winked at Jilly. Their laughter mingled with Reece's as the three of them walked together to start the first bright morning of a lifetime of tomorrows.

Judith E. French

When Avon Books asked me to contribute to their bridal collection, I was delighted. I am a romantic at heart, and I believe in strong marriages full of love, tenderness, and always—passion. After all, doesn't a family begin with the union of two people who care more for each other than anyone else in the world?

I was married at seventeen to my childhood sweetheart, and we have managed to sustain that magical essence that we call love for thirty-three years, four children, and ten grandchildren. It was easy to remain steadfast in the happy times, not so easy when trouble invaded our lives. But I am one of the lucky ones; I was the child of strong, loving parents, and four wonderful grandparents. They are absolute proof that unselfish caring and devotion to marriage can withstand anything the world can throw at a couple.

I would like to dedicate this story to every bride and to every woman who has ever wished a bride good fortune. Without courageous women like you, there would be no romance and no hope for a bright, shining tomorrow.

Store-bought Woman

Linda Lael Miller

Onion Creek, Washington Territory
April 1872

BESS Campbell felt a big hand come to rest on her shoulder, noting the gentleness of the touch even in her sleep. For one blissful moment, she thought she was still home in Philadelphia; that Papa, or perhaps her brother, Simon, was waking her so that they could go out for an early-morning horseback ride.

"Wake up," an unfamiliar voice commanded.

Bess, who had been curled up on a pile of empty seed sacks in a corner of the Onion Creek General Store, for want of a better place to sleep, opened one dark blue eye to see a bearded wild-man grinning down at her. She gave a small, involuntary squeal of alarm.

"You Miss Elizabeth Ann Campbell?" the giant inquired. He was obviously a frontiersman, roughly clad in a homespun shirt, woolen trousers, and suspenders.

Bess, who was fully clothed and had slept the night through clutching her valise and handbag to her bosom, sat bolt upright on her improvised bed. "I might be," she answered, smoothing her tangled blonde hair. "Who are you?" He *wasn't* John Tate, the man she'd come all this way to marry, that much she knew.

It was still dark outside, and the little store was lit by a single lantern set on top of a pickle barrel. Mr. Sickles, the proprietor, stood nearby scowling, clearly unhappy

213

that he'd been rousted from his bed at such an hour.

The wild-man chuckled, regarding Bess through pale brown eyes that seemed to dance with humor and mischief. "Well, ma'am," he answered, showing unusually straight white teeth when he spoke, "I reckon I'm not the gent you're expecting, but in the circumstances, I'm afraid I'll have to do for a bridegroom."

Bess stiffened, felt a shiver weave itself from one end of her spine to the other. She had not expected her flight to the Golden West to be as fraught with danger and discomfort as it had been, and she was not only exhausted, but disillusioned as well. Now, this disreputable person was crouched beside her bed, apparently confident of his acceptability as a husband.

"I beg your pardon," she managed to sputter, grappling for her handbag and nearly ripping it open when the strings became tangled. "I'm promised to one John Tate," she went on, plundering for the crumpled, much-read and much-regretted marriage contract that had brought her to this place even God had forgotten. She held out the document. "See for yourself."

The man was looking at her hands, his expression curious and thoughtful. "Do you always sleep in gloves?" he asked.

Bess blushed crimson, and her temper surged to life. "Don't trouble yourself wondering, sir. It is certainly none of your business what I wear when I sleep!"

The whiskey-gold eyes laughed at her and he ignored the marriage contract until Bess finally lowered it, with a shaking hand, to her lap. "I reckon it is my concern, ma'am, since I'm going to be your husband."

Bess had at last gathered enough aplomb to stand, albeit tremulously, shake out her rumpled skirts, and tug at the hem of her trim velvet traveling jacket. "I have already told you," she said coldly, "that I am pledged to Mr. John Tate. Are you deaf, sir?"

He stood, offered her a huge, but as far as she could see in the dim lantern light, *clean* hand. "Yes, ma'am, you were to be my brother's wife," he said patiently.

"Trouble is, John has gone north, looking for gold, and it falls to me to fulfil his obligations. Which include marrying you."

Bess paid no more attention to his hand than he had paid to the marriage contract. She tugged at her jacket again, even though she knew it was already about as straight as it could get, and held her chin high. More than anything, though, she wanted to crumple herself up into a little ball on those rough feed sacks and weep until the very angels in heaven wept with her in sheer sympathy.

"Well, then, Mr.—Tate, I assume?—allow me to absolve you of at least one of those obligations. I would not think, you see, of joining myself to a stranger in holy matrimony."

For a moment, Mr. Tate looked disappointed, but he recovered quickly and grinned again. The expression gave him the look of a mischievous choirboy, so incongruous with the rest of his person. " 'Course you would," he argued. "You were going to take up with John, and he was a stranger to you—I know that for a fact, 'cause he told me so before he went off chasing rainbows. And you can call me Will from here on out, because I don't hold with silly eastern manners."

Bess bristled again, and she felt color warming her cheeks, which were no doubt less than clean, even though she'd splashed her face and neck carefully at the stream the night before. "That was different," she said. "I met Mr. Tate, and found him personally acceptable." She blushed once more, realizing too late that she had been tactless.

Will Tate arched one golden eyebrow, and his grin wobbled slightly, then held. He gave a great, philosophical sigh, finally remembered that he was still wearing his hat, inside and in the presence of a lady, no less, and quickly snatched the battered thing off his head.

He had more hair than a crazy man Bess had seen once as part of a circus sideshow. She'd pitied that poor fellow to the depths of her soul, but Mr. Will Tate didn't need anyone to sorrow for him. He was big, a full head taller than Bess, and his shoulders were so wide he'd have to turn himself sideways just to get through an ordinary doorway. He was plainly strong, of temperament as well as body, and he exuded some kind of primitive heat that seemed to come from the core of his being.

"I know I'm not as fair of appearance as my brother," he said, holding the disreputable hat close to his bosom, which looked to Bess as though it would be harder than tamarack, were she brazen enough to touch him. "But I'm a good bargain, Miss Elizabeth. I don't drink, nor cuss more than the average man, and I firmly believe in bath-taking and churchgoing. Fact is, I've been known to break the ice on Onion Creek in the winter time, just so I can get myself some washing water to carry up to the cabin and warm by the fire. And I swear by my own mama's grave that I'd never lay a hand on you in anger."

Bess knew an unwelcome warmth, deep inside, and she fought it. Agreeing to marry John Tate had been rash enough, the act of an impetuous and, all right, *desperate* woman, but this brother of his was another matter entirely. To Bess, he looked fierce and primitive and, besides, all of a sudden she was feeling things and getting ideas that were distinctly un-Christian.

She retreated a step and took refuge in righteous indignation. "I must say it was incredibly rude of your brother to summon me all the way out here to this—this place, and leave me stranded!"

Will smiled, and Bess felt another wrench, for it was even more dazzling than the grin she'd seen before. "But he didn't leave you stranded, Miss Elizabeth," he reasoned patiently, as though speaking to a terrified cow up to its udder in sticky mud. "John knew I'd take up the slack. It's always been that way between him and me."

Bess turned away, arms folded, blue eyes blurred with scalding tears. "Stop calling me 'Miss Elizabeth,'" she said fretfully. "No one has ever called me anything but Bess."

"Bess," he said quietly, and even that was somehow

sensual, the way he murmured the name, and seemed to taste and then savor it.

Bess tried to brush away the moisture brimming in her lashes with a surreptitious motion of one hand, but Will took a gentle hold on her other elbow and turned her to face him.

"There now," he said, with a gruff tenderness that made Bess feel a little safer in that foreign and hostile place. "No need for weeping and carrying on. You didn't plan on marrying me, and I certainly didn't plan on hitching up to you, but here we are and we might just as well make the best of things. Fact is, I could use a wife for company of a lonely evening, as well as a helping hand around the farm."

Bess was amazed, not only by his blithe audacity, but by the fact that he could speak so lightly of such a holy institution as matrimony. "You'll just have to look elsewhere," she said, even though a bold and erstwhile unknown part of herself wanted to go home with Will Tate. "I'm returning to Philadelphia."

But even as Bess said the words, she knew she couldn't go back and face the shame and the gossip that awaited her there, and Will was evidently perceptive enough to see the realization in her eyes.

"You have the money and the strength for a trip like that?" he asked. "And once you got back there, you'd just have to handle whatever it is you're running away from."

"I'm not running . . ."

Will held up one hand. "Don't go lying to me, Bess. That's an unseemly trait in a woman, and I'm no more partial to it than I am to stealing and fornicating."

Bess's face went hot again. No gentleman in Philadelphia would have used such a scandalous word, except for the preacher, of course, and he'd have put it in a biblical context.

At last, the storekeeper, whose very existence Bess had forgotten, put in his two cents' worth. "You two better work this out somewheres else. I ain't done sleepin', and I don't care to listen to your damnable yammerin'!''

It was plain Bess could not depend upon this wretched man for help in a time of crisis, and since the town of Onion Creek consisted of two other buildings, a livery stable and a saloon, there was probably no one else to turn to, either.

"You have the advantage, Mr. Tate," she said bravely, bending to gather up her handbag and her small leather valise. "I was counting on your brother to be here, and I am friendless. I have almost no money, and I haven't had anything to eat since yesterday, when I arrived in Spokane by railway. I must depend, I'm afraid, on your kindness and honor."

Another grin lit Will's face, and Bess wondered fleetingly if he might not be very handsome, if only he were shorn of that awful beard and all that hair. When he turned his attention to Mr. Sickles, however, his features hardened, and Bess realized that Will Tate was not so lighthearted as she'd thought.

"Seems like you could have spared a lady a piece of bread and some dried meat, you tight-fisted old geezer," he said grimly. "And some would have given up their own bed, rather than see a female traveler lay herself down on a lot of old burlap."

Bess shuddered at the idea of sleeping on the storekeeper's bed; she was grateful that he hadn't offered that particular courtesy. Putting one gloved hand on Will's arm, which felt like living stone beneath the coarse cloth of his sleeve, she said, "Don't stir up trouble, Will. I'm not about to perish of starvation, and I slept rather well, as it happens." No need to add, she thought, that she'd wept with homesickness and regret, and cursed her own hasty nature.

"I ain't in the charity business, Tate," the greasy man said.

Still glowering at the storekeeper, Will pried a coin from his trouser pocket, tossed it across the cramped, dusty little shop. After that, he lifted the lid from a barrel, appropriated a small chunk of yellow cheese and held it out to Bess. "Here," he said. "This'll hold you till we get to my place, where there's beans and fatback and the like. It isn't far."

Bess took the cheese and gobbled it in a few bites, figuring she'd work out what "fatback" was later on. In the meantime, Will reached for the handle of her valise.

"You got anything else?"

Sickles snorted at that. "Ain't you got eyes, Will Tate?" He jabbed a thumb toward one of the walls. "My lean-to out there is half-filled with trunks and boxes and geegaws. Looks to me like it'll take half a day just to load it all."

Bess simmered. All the way across country, railroad men had given her grief about her belongings, and the freight driver who'd brought her here from Spokane had charged her double and told her she was lucky he'd just emptied his wagon at the train station.

"I couldn't just go off and leave everything I own," she protested.

Will gave her a look of resignation, and somehow that stung more than condemnation would have done. "Come along, Bess," he said, gesturing for her to precede him into the chill pre-dawn air. "I've got a farm to run, and I sure as hell can't afford to dillydally around here all day."

Feeling chagrined, Bess stepped outside. The air was indeed crisp, and she heard the rustling whisper of the creek passing by on its way to the low country. She gathered her skirts close and allowed Will to hoist her up onto the wagon seat, a task he managed easily.

"You do understand," she said, smoothing her skirts over her thighs, "that this doesn't mean I'm agreeing to your proposal of marriage."

Will had already turned away to assess the amount of luggage stacked inside the storekeeper's lean-to. He whistled an exclamation and muttered something that sounded like a swear word.

"I thought you said you didn't curse," Bess challenged, feeling stronger now, because of the cheese, and slightly braver.

"I said I didn't do it *much*," Will responded, hoisting the heaviest of her trunks and thrusting it unceremoniously into the back of his weathered wagon.

The whole vehicle shook, and the two horses harnessed to it nickered and shifted uneasily.

The storekeeper's uncharitable prediction notwithstanding, Will managed to load everything inside of fifteen minutes. The sun was just creeping over the mountaintops when he climbed up beside her and took the reins in hand.

"I'm quite sure this isn't proper," Bess said, sensing that he was about to join the ranks of her critics and make some snide comment about her tucking half the city of Philadelphia into her trunks and hauling it right along with her. "My going to your house and all, I mean."

Will released the brake lever with a practiced motion of one foot and made a clicking sound with his tongue to prompt the horses into motion. "No, ma'am, I reckon it isn't, but it appears to me that we don't have much choice for the time being. Ole Harlan Kipps will be passing through any day now. He's the circuit preacher, and we'll get him to say the words over us."

Bess drew in a deep breath, and it restored her as much as the bite of cheese had earlier. She would think about the prospect of marriage later; for now, she had more immediate concerns. "How do I know you won't take shameful advantage of me, now that we're alone?"

Of all the responses Will could have given, laughter was the one Bess would least appreciate. And laughter was what she got.

"Now's a fine time to start worrying about that," he said, when he'd composed himself a little, his hands idle and easy as he held the reins. "You just spent the best part of a night under the roof of the meanest sinner the Lord ever despaired over. You're a whole hell of a lot safer with me than you were with ole Purvis Sickles, I can tell you that.''

Bess was nearly undone by this news, but she did her best to hide the fact and stared straight ahead, as if unmoved. ''You swear considerably more than you claimed to when we first discussed marriage,'' she said primly.

Will laughed again, but he offered no statement in his own defense. He simply settled down, humming to himself, and concentrated on driving the team and wagon over the rutted, muddy strip of dirt posing as a road.

The territory surrounding the community of Onion Creek was a peculiar combination of flat land and timbered hills. Bess took a certain grudging solace in its beauty as the rising sun revealed a clearing of flowing green grass sprinkled with wildflowers, a rugged, rocky hillside too sheer to climb, and trees so tall and so broad that they'd probably already been thriving when the pilgrims stepped off the *Mayflower*.

''Why didn't you go north to look for gold, like your brother did?'' she asked, just to make conversation, when the silence had gone on too long and she started to feel lonely.

Will swept off his hat, as if in exasperation, then put it back on again in a motion just as brisk. ''This is fine country right here,'' he said. ''It has everything a man could ask for—timber, good soil, and lots of elbowroom. Why anybody would want to turn their back on these good hills for a place where it's dark for six months of the year and the rivers freeze right down to the silt on the bottom is beyond me.''

Bess looked at Will out of the corner of her eye, and her mood was thoughtful. He didn't have his brother's good looks, not that she could tell, anyway, but he was a man to stand fast and fight for what he wanted.

Which meant he was made of sturdier stuff than she was.

''Just what happened back there in the East that made you hightail it out to the far side of beyond, anyhow?'' Will asked, showing that dratted intuition of his again.

"That was certainly a blunt question."

"Out here, we don't take the time to embroider our words and deck them out in fancy trim," he answered. "We just say what we mean, for the most part. It saves time."

Bess sighed. Sooner or later she'd have to confess anyway, so she might as well get it over with. "I was supposed to be married to a man named Jackson Reese," she said, sitting up very straight and not looking at Will. "It was the social event of the Christmas season. My wedding dress had real pearls stitched to the skirt—Mama had it made up in New York and we took the train there three times for fittings." Bess paused, for what she was saying was mortally hard to get out. "I guess none of that matters, about the dress and all, I mean. The point is, Jackson and my sister Molly ran away together, the morning of the wedding."

To Bess's abject surprise and mortification, Will pulled the wagon over to the side of the road and stopped the team with a forceful "Whoa!"

Bess trembled on that hard, cold wagon seat, wondering why Will had stopped their progress all of a sudden. Maybe he'd decided to put her out, bag and baggage. Maybe he'd decided he didn't want her, just as Jackson had.

"That man must have been the king of all fools," he said quietly, putting one strong arm around Bess's waist and squeezing her against him once.

She wasn't frightened or insulted, for she knew the embrace was meant as a gesture of comfort, not familiarity.

Will cupped her chin in one hand and made her look up at him. "You remember this, Bess Campbell. What happened back there was their shame, your sister's and that bastard she took up with, not yours. If you're wise, you'll put it behind you and get on with making a place for yourself right here."

Bess finally nodded, not trusting herself to speak, and, mercifully, Will let go of her chin, took up the reins,

and whistled to the team. Soon, they were jolting along
the road again, and Bess remembered how tired she was.
She yawned, leaned her head lightly against Will's shoulder, and drifted off to sleep.

He awakened her by drawing back on the reins sometime later, and yelling "Whoa!" again.

She started and looked around her, blinking. The sun
was higher now, spilling dazzling spring light over the
countryside.

Bess squinted and made out a small cabin made of
logs, just like the ones she'd seen in picture books. Someone—surely it had been Will—had planted a sizable garden next to the house. On the other side was a clothesline
with a faded quilt pegged to it.

Chickens squawked and fluttered in the dooryard, and
a big yellow dog came bounding from the direction of
the barn, which was much bigger than the house, with
the mournful cries of several cows following after him.

Will had climbed down and walked around the back
of the wagon to reach up for Bess, but he laughed when
the dog hurled itself against him in glee.

"Does that creature bite?" Bess wanted to know. She
had no particular fear of dogs, but common sense told
her to be wary of any beast that weighed more than she
did.

"Calvin?" Will marveled, favoring her with yet another of those soul-wrenching grins. "No, ma'am, Calvin doesn't bite anybody but outlaws, tax men, and
peddlers—do you, boy?"

Bess indulged in a little mild annoyance that Will was
paying more attention to the dog than to her, then moved
to help herself down from the wagon, since Will was too
busy greeting the dog to offer a hand.

She started to descend, her back to Will, but her foot
slipped. Suddenly, she felt Will's hands grasp her full
hips, then slide slowly up to her waist.

Bess was mortified, not only by the intimacy of the
contact, but by her own reaction to it. Why, she felt as

though she'd stuffed herself with Chinese rockets, and now they were all going off at once.

One side of his mouth crooked upward in a half-smile, as if he'd read her thoughts, and she would have sworn it was on purpose that he let her slide along the length of his torso until she touched the ground.

He looked down into her eyes for the longest time, his hands lingering on her waist, and she found herself imagining what he'd look like with a trim haircut and a shave. The face in her thoughts made her heart thump with excitement.

Finally, Will stepped away and began unloading her baggage. Bess hurried away, 'round the back of the cabin, and found the privy.

When she was through, she came back to the front of the house again and, seeing no sign of Will, ventured to the open doorway.

He was stacking her things in the middle of the cabin's single room, a grim expression in his eyes. The trunks and cases made a convenient wall, it seemed to Bess.

She would sleep on the neatly made bed, with its polished brass frame and clean spread, and Will could take his rest on the bear rug at the other end of the cabin, in front of the fireplace. Yes, that seemed like an acceptable arrangement, at least until she decided whether to go or stay, and she said so.

Will looked at her incredulously, straightening his powerful back until he seemed to loom like the Grim Reaper.

"I beg your pardon?" he said, in a low but nevertheless dangerous voice. "Are you asking me to give up my bed?"

Bess remained in the doorway, thinking she might have to turn and flee at any time, and spoke with stalwart conviction. "It's no more than you expected that storekeeper to do. In fact, you berated him roundly for the oversight, if memory serves me correctly."

For a moment, Will was silent, ominously still. Then, remarkably, he slapped his sides and smiled. "The colonists had a custom they called bundling,'' he said. ''We'll just practice that until Harlan gets here and makes it legal.''

Bess refrained from pointing out that she had not agreed to marriage. She depended upon this man's hospitality and was wont to offend him. ''Bundling?'' she echoed, in a squeaky and uncertain voice.

''Yes, bundling,'' Will answered, trying to make a sensible order of the baggage. ''Stop dawdling in the doorway like you mean to bolt and run. There's beans and fatback on the stove, and there should be some coffee, too, unless some Indian came through and made himself to home while I was gone.''

Bess swallowed, sought and found the stove with a tentative glance, and started toward it. She did not ask about bad-mannered Indians; she was still chewing on that other word he'd used, the one that concerned sleeping arrangements and sounded disturbingly cozy.

''What is bundling?'' she insisted, lifting the lid off a pot of warm beans and bacon and nearly swooning under the wave of hunger that swept over her.

She'd found a bowl and ladled in some of the fragrant soup before Will answered and, when he did, she started because he was right behind her.

''It's simple.'' He spoke quietly, reasonably, and yet there was an undercurrent of energy in his voice, too. Something elemental and manly, and better left alone. ''In colonial days, when a man traveled a long way to call on his sweetheart, through perilous country and sorry weather, it wasn't a kindness to ask him to turn right around and ride home when the visit was through. So the girl's father would put a board down the middle of her bed for a barrier, and both the young lady and her suitor would be bundled up in quilts, tight as those Egyptian mummies you read about. That way, the two of them could lie there and talk the night through if they wanted to, but there was no question of fornication because they couldn't get themselves unwrapped without help.''

There it was again, that impolite word. *Fornication,*

she repeated silently to herself, in order to fortify herself against future shock.

Bess's hands trembled a little, as much from nerves as hunger, as she set her bowl on the table, which had been hewn from simple pine boards, and sat down on an upturned crate to eat. "It won't work, Mr. Tate," she said moderately, not daring to meet those mischievous eyes of his, or risk one of his knee-melting grins. "And I would think you'd have the sense to see it. Only one of us could be bundled, since there would be no one to wrap up the other."

She felt his amusement, then heard it in his voice.

"Well, then, I guess we'll just have to content ourselves with a board down the middle of the bed, Bess-my-love, because I'm not about to sleep on the floor."

Bess, who had been fairly gobbling up the succulent bean and bacon soup, at last dared to raise her eyes to meet Will's. "Fine. Then *I'll* sleep on the bear rug. Just don't present yourself as more of a gentleman than that dreadful storekeeper in the future, Mr. Tate, because you are no better."

She thought Will reddened a little, though it was hard to tell because of his bushy beard. "No lady will sleep on the floor under my roof," he said forcefully, "and that's final."

Bess decided it was futile to discuss the topic further, and so she shrugged. When nightfall came, she would simply sit up by the fire. Unless he was the worst kind of scoundrel, he would not force her to lie on the same mattress with him.

If he tried, she would just have to take her chances with the wild Indians beyond the cabin walls.

So it was that Bess tucked into the first warm meal she'd had in a day and a half of traveling. Will said he had chores to take care of, pointed out the woodpile, the washtub, and a precious bar of yellow soap, and went off to the fields.

Bess was weary to the core of her soul, and she yearned for a warm bath, but it was a while before she could bring herself to take the chance of stripping naked in a strange man's house. She built up the fire, though, and hauled water from the creek that flowed behind the cabin to heat on the stove. That done, she arranged her suitcases into a wall-like structure around the tub and finally sank, blissful and bare-skinned, into the water.

Will waited as long as he could, but when the sun was high, and hunger from a morning of plowing stony ground gnawed at his belly, he went inside the cabin.

There was no sign of Bess, who might have been a Christmas angel gone astray, with those eyes the color of cornflowers and that pretty pale hair. For a moment he thought she'd taken to the hills, and the disappointment nearly stopped his heart. Then he heard the softest of sounds—a delicate snore.

He approached the wall she'd made with her bags and peered over it, holding his breath.

There she sat, in the washtub, cross-legged and bare as a statue, sound asleep. The sight moved something deep inside Will's being, something rusted-over and cold, like a key turning in a lock.

2

JUST looking at her sleeping there in the washtub, her blonde hair all a-tumble and her sleek arms folded across her breasts, filled Will Tate with a hunger that was rooted in his very soul. It wasn't just that he wanted to bed Bess, though he definitely did, and the sooner the better—no, this yearning was something more.

He longed to hear her laugh and sing, and call him in for supper. He imagined looking across the table of an evening and seeing her there, smiling at him, the lantern light catching in her soft hair and flickering in her eyes. He savored the thought of her bringing him water in the fields and rubbing liniment into his back when his muscles got sore . . .

She opened her cornflower eyes and blinked, as if stunned to see him there. Then, with a frosty manner, she reached for a towel—a fancy one that Will didn't recognize—and covered herself.

"We are not married yet, Mr. Tate," Bess said, in a tone that could only be called saucy. "In fact, I have serious doubts that we ever will be, and I will be most grateful if you do not lurk about and spy upon me while I am attending to private matters."

Will was both annoyed and amused, and he marveled to himself that he'd gotten by without a woman's company for so long. Even though Bess was being distinctly testy, her very presence in that lonely place was a sweet wonder.

He turned his back, but only after pausing a few seconds to let her know he wasn't going to jump every time she said grasshopper. Will had no desire to bully his bride, but neither would he let himself be henpecked.

"It's high time you had the noonday meal on the table," he said, glad she couldn't see his smile. "A man's got to eat, you know."

She sighed, and he heard soft rustling sounds as she dressed. The thought of her bare, clean skin, and the smooth, frilly things brushing against it made Will ache with sudden, blinding need—and that was further reason to be glad he'd turned away from her.

"I suppose you think I can't cook," Bess said, and he heard her bustling around amidst her trunks and boxes and satchels, opening this one, shutting that one. "You're probably telling yourself that I've been indulged all my life, and that I've never had to do a lick of work. Well, that's all you know, Mr. Tate—er, William. Our cook was called away last summer, because her sister had the grippe, and I took over Minerva's duties and fulfilled them so well that Papa and Simon swore they didn't know how they'd live without my biscuits.''

Will tensed, though it was silly, since this Simon fellow was obviously two thousand miles away and thus in no position to offer significant competition for Bess's affections. ''Simon?'' he asked, making his way to the wash table, which was next to the cabin door. He stripped off his shirt and started to rinse the field dirt from his face and upper body, mostly to give himself something to do.

What he hadn't counted on was being able to see Bess clearly in the cracked shaving mirror affixed to the wall above the washbasin.

He forgot the mysterious Simon, for the moment.

Sweet Lord in heaven but she was a pretty thing; it fair brought Will's heart right up into his throat just to look at her. She was wearing a shirtwaist and black skirt, clothes too fancy and impractical for the wilderness, and Will thought he'd never in all his life gazed upon a fairer sight.

Bess caught him looking and frowned, and he quickly shifted his eyes to his own reflection in the murky mirror before him. He was amazed to see a wild-haired, bushy-bearded hermit staring back at him. He couldn't remember the last time he'd really taken note of himself, beyond bathing regularly in the creek and keeping his clothes as clean as he could, and the sight came as a profound shock.

Hell, Will thought, snatching a clean shirt from a peg next to the wash table, it was a miracle Miss Bess Campbell hadn't taken one glance at him and lit out for the tall timber.

Will turned, buttoning his shirt as he did so, and indicated her belongings with a nod of his head. ''You wouldn't happen to have a good pair of scissors in there somewhere, would you?''

She smiled, brushing her pale gold hair and blithely interrupting Will's heartbeat again by lifting her arms to wind it into a plump bun at her nape. When she did that, her fine breasts jutted beneath her blouse and tempted Will so sorely that he had to turn away from her again.

"If it's a haircut you're wanting," she said to his back, "I'll be happy to oblige. It'll take me a while to find my sewing kit, I imagine." She was humming, clattering pans about on the top of the old, rusted-out cookstove Will's mother and father had brought all the way across the plains from Illinois, back in the early days.

He felt it was safe to look at her once more.

Bess was building up the fire and then peeping inside bins and barrels and sacks.

Miraculously, she soon had cornbread baking in the oven and canned sausage sizzling in a skillet.

Will watched her in wonderment. He'd known plenty of women in his time and had even been intimate with a few of them, though he truly didn't hold with fornication, but there was something different about Bess Campbell, something that just plain fascinated him.

For the first time in his memory, Will blessed his no-account dreamer of a brother for running off to chase yet another moonbeam. If John had stayed, after all, then Bess would have been *his* woman, and he, Will, would likely have spent the rest of his life lusting in his heart. And a few other places, too.

Make yourself useful, he chided himself.

He moved between the trunks, hoisted the tubful of bathwater—it was heavy, even for him—and headed for the dooryard. Once he'd flung the contents into the dirt, scaring the chickens out of three years' growth in the process, he returned to the cabin.

Will felt shy, all of a sudden, like an unexpected guest being cheerfully tolerated. Which was an odd thing, considering that he'd built the place with his own two hands and put down roots as deep as any of the tall Douglas firs growing on the hillsides.

"Where are we going to put all this stuff?" he asked, perhaps a touch too sharply, because he was feeling nervous. He meant the trunks and valises, of course—he'd never known a woman who owned so many things.

"We'll just leave it right where it is for the time being," Bess said pointedly, putting blue-enameled plates and mugs on the table with as much flourish as if she'd lived in that cabin from the day the walls were chinked against the cold mountain winds. "It'll serve admirably as a wall."

Will didn't want any walls between this woman and himself, but of course it was too early to say anything of the sort. "Did you make fresh coffee?" he asked.

Bess gave him a pert look that said he had sorry manners, and he probably did, compared to the men she'd known in Philadelphia.

"Who's Simon?" he inquired brusquely, remembering at last. He was glad of his beard, at least during those difficult moments, because it hid the heat burning in his face. Or so he hoped.

She lifted one side of her full, soft-looking mouth in a coy little smile. She took her sweet time getting the words out. "Simon is my brother."

The relief Will felt when she'd finally answered his question was out of all proportion to good sense—he drew back one of the crates next to the table and sat down heavily, for all of a sudden his knees had turned soft as bread dough. What the Sam Hill was happening to him, anyhow?

His brother had been right, Will decided, during that last, loud argument they'd had, just before John had headed north. He *had* been alone too long.

Bess gave him a look that fairly scorched his hide. "A gentleman never sits," she said tartly, "until any ladies present have been seated."

Will blushed again, under his dense beard, and his embarrassment stung. That made him angry.

He turned over his own crate, so abruptly did he rise, and stormed around the table to attend her royal highness. Once she was perched on the upended wooden box marked "Purity Salt," Will executed a slight bow.

Bess ignored him and began to serve herself rather generously from the plate of hot cornbread, the leftover beans, and the fried sausage. Will figured he could sit down, or he could starve, and it wouldn't concern her much either way.

He ate heartily, because he was ravenous and because he needed something to distract his attention from the beautiful creature sitting across from him. Why hadn't he noticed, back at Sickles's store, when Bess was curled up on those feed sacks, all dirty and rumpled, that she was like one of those fairy-tale princesses his mother used to talk about?

Well, she was *pretty much* like them, anyway. She was a trifle meaner than any he remembered from the stories, and as briefly as he'd known Bess, Will had already worked out that she wasn't the sort to lie around for a hundred years waiting for any man, prince or otherwise, to awaken her with a kiss.

No, sir. Bess Campbell was more the type to go out and find her own prince, knock him off his horse, and hog-tie him.

Will studied her through the thick lashes that had brought him so much teasing and grief when he was still a schoolboy, and smiled to himself.

After the meal was through, Bess made no attempt to start clearing away, and Will reasoned that she was leaving that task for later, when they'd had a sociable cup of coffee together. Lord knew, she'd said nary a word while they were eating, but that probably had something to do with eastern etiquette.

"John left a letter for you," he said, recollecting aloud. The words were out before he had a chance to assess them and, looking at Bess's sour expression, he wished he'd kept his mouth shut.

Since it was too late for that, he got up and went to

the pine trunk at the foot of his bed. His clothes and personal possessions were stored in that chest, things like his parents' marriage picture and the small, well-worn Bible his mother had carried across the country in the pocket of her apron.

John's letter had worked its way down amongst things a bit, since he'd been gone for some weeks now, and it took a while to find it.

Will carried the sealed envelope over to Bess and set it down in front of her, where her plate had been before she'd pushed it aside.

She looked at that letter as if it might sprout legs like a bullfrog's and jump at her. Then, with shaky hands, she picked up the envelope and carefully tore it open . . .

Bess wished Will wasn't standing there, watching her as she opened his brother's letter, but since she had her clothes on, she couldn't very well tell him to get out of his own cabin.

She bit her lip as she unfolded the single thick page inside.

Bess certainly hadn't loved John Tate—for mercy's sake, she hadn't even *known* him, really—but he was the second man in her life to ask for her hand in marriage and then abandon her, and that lent his words a certain bitter importance.

"My Dear Elizabeth," he had written, in a precise, formal, and very unfamiliar hand. "I apologize most sincerely for having to leave you before we stood up in front of a preacher, but I guess I wouldn't be much use to you even if I had stayed. I'd just be thinking about Alaska all the time, and the gold that lies at the bottom of those rivers and streams, and a pretty woman like you deserves better than me.

"Now, my brother Will here is a steady sort, and he's even fairly handsome under all that hair, and I know I can count on him to look after you. You could do worse than taking him for a husband, dear—by marrying me, for instance. Will is a good man, not fond of whiskey or wagering, and he doesn't even swear overmuch.

"The first thing I'm going to do, once I get settled, is send you a bank draft for as much money as I can piece together. That way, you'll have a choice—you can stay with Will and stake a claim to the three-hundred-twenty acres you're entitled to under the law, and have the wherewithal to make it productive, or you can go elsewhere and start new.

"Whatever you decide, lovely Elizabeth, I wish you well, and hope you will harbor some forgiveness in your heart for your errant friend, John Tate."

Bess closed the letter once she'd read it twice in an effort to make sense of it, and tucked it back into its envelope. Then she stood, without looking at Will, and started clearing the table.

"You'd best get back to the fields, William Tate," she said briskly. "You're burning daylight."

Will started to speak, stopped himself, then turned and left the cabin, letting the door gape open behind him. The big yellow dog came slinking over the threshold and threw itself down on the cold hearth to lie panting and watching Bess as she heated water for dishwashing.

While she worked, she thought about John Tate's words, and wondered for the thousandth time if there was something lacking in her, some trait that made a man want to stay with a woman.

Whatever that gift was, Bess thought sadly, her mother certainly had it. Her parents had been happily married for thirty-seven years.

For a moment, Bess missed her mother and father so much that she wasn't sure she could endure being apart from them. She lowered her head over the dishpan and sniffled, struggling to get control of herself before Will returned for some reason and caught her crying.

Laurel and Preston Campbell had been devastated when Bess announced that she was leaving forever, and Simon and his pretty wife, Jillie, had pleaded with her to stay. She'd get over Molly's betrayal someday, they'd said, and even forgive her flighty younger sister, and when that happened she would be free to fall in love with the right man.

Bess made a contemptuous sound, causing the panting dog to lift its head from its paws and study her for a moment.

"I'm never going to love any man again," she told the canine, "and I'm never going to trust another woman, either."

She saw the long shadow fall across the rough-hewn wooden floor before she heard the gruff voice.

"That's too bad," Will commented. "It's hard for anybody to make their way in this world if they don't let themselves believe in other people."

Bess brushed her cheek against one hunched shoulder before starting toward the door with the basin of dishwater. Will had the choice of stepping aside or getting run over, and in the end, he stepped aside.

All the same, he persisted, following her into the yard, standing in her path when she'd emptied the dishwater and turned to go back to the cabin.

She felt an incomprehensible urge to thrust herself into his strong arms, to let him hold and comfort her, and she resisted it with all her might.

To surrender, even if only long enough to cry on Will's broad and inviting shoulder, would be to trust, and she knew what pain that could bring, so she retreated a step and raised her chin a notch.

"I guess this farm must run itself," she said. "You seem to have all sorts of free time, Mr. Tate."

Will folded his arms and even through his beard she saw his jaw tense and then relax again. "I don't need you to tell me how to take care of this place, Bess—I've managed just fine without your advice all this while."

She plucked up her skirts in one hand and attempted to go around him, but he simply barred her way again. The urge to brain Will Tate with the empty dishpan was almost beyond her powers of restraint.

"What do you want?" she snapped.

"We're going to be husband and wife, you and I,"

Will declared, towering over her like one of the indomitable western mountains that seemed to fill that untamed territory. "We won't start off by hiding our feelings from each other."

Bess drew a deep breath and let it out slowly. She was exhausted from her journey, especially the last part, which had been made in a freight wagon, and every muscle in her body ached from the ordeal. But no part of her was sorer than her heart.

"I'll remind you again," she said, when she had brought her temper under control. "Our marriage is by no means a certainty. Furthermore, I will not be dictated to, one way or the other. My feelings are my own and if I want to hide them, I damn well will!"

Will stared at her in amazement for a moment, and she thought she saw something like admiration in his eyes, too, though she figured she'd probably imagined that part. "You're not like any other woman I've ever had the lame luck to run across," he said, and Bess couldn't tell for sure whether she was being complimented or insulted. His next words removed all doubt. "It's better to live in the desert and eat grasshoppers than get yourself tied up with a contentious female, according to the Good Book. Knowing you, even for this short time, has increased my appreciation for Scripture."

Bess threw the dishpan down and it clunked against a rock and bounced into the sweet, fragrant grass beside the footpath. "If you want to go and live in a desert, Will Tate," she hissed, "then you just feel free!"

Will bent, retrieved the basin, and handed it to Bess. "You're wrong to damn all men for what one polecat did to you," he said, with a quiet reason that made her ashamed of her outburst. "You'd best get rid of all that hate before it eats you up from the inside."

With that, he turned and walked away.

Bess watched Will as he went back to the field, shouldered the reins of the harness, and shouted an order to the horse. Gripping the weathered handles, he guided the plow forward, making a straight, clean furrow in the rich dirt.

Back inside the cabin, Bess sank down on the edge of Will's featherbed, feeling overwhelmed. Their exchange had confused and upset her, and yet it had stirred in her an odd, quiet elation as well.

She stretched out on the soft mattress with a sigh, not even bothering to unbutton her shoes and put them aside. She only meant to close her eyes for a while, and try to decide what to do.

Bess turned onto her side and yawned as she settled in deep. Will Tate, she concluded, was no prize, and at times he had the temperament of a bear with a burr stuck to its tongue, but at least he was straightforward. There could be little doubt of his beliefs, for he aired them readily, and he seemed decent and honorable, too.

She squirmed comfortably, noticing that the old quilt beneath her smelled pleasantly of sunshine and of Will's own distinct scent. Yes, Will was a gentleman, for all his frightening appearance; if he hadn't been, he probably would have flung her down somewhere and had his way with her by now.

Bess shivered. There were plenty of men who would do just such a despicable thing, especially in an isolated place like this, where there probably wasn't another human soul for miles.

For the second time in one day, Will entered his cabin and found Bess Campbell sleeping. He was both amused and exasperated—it seemed to him that the Lord was placing undue temptation in his way. First, he'd seen her naked, and now there she was, fully clothed, but stretched out on his bed, arms spread wide in unconscious abandon.

Will swallowed and let himself imagine, for a moment, what it would be like when he and Bess were married. *If* she agreed to become his wife.

Just thinking about the lush, delicious curves hidden beneath those costly clothes of hers made Will's blood turn hot, and his manhood was as hard as a chunk of seasoned firewood.

"God in heaven," he muttered, but he wasn't sure whether he was praying or taking the Lord's name in vain. He wondered if he shouldn't just go straight out to the creek and throw himself in; maybe that would calm him down a little.

Bess stirred and made a soft, whimpering sound, and Will thought he'd die of wanting her. He stood there, enduring, for a long time. Then, slowly, he turned away, grabbed up a couple of buckets, and headed for the creek.

He couldn't quite bring himself to jump in—that water came from melting snow high in the mountains, and it was colder than a politician's heart. Why, on Saturday, when he'd taken his last bath, he'd been numb for an hour afterwards, and it had been about that long before his teeth stopped chattering.

Will filled both buckets and returned to the cabin, making as little noise as possible as he built up the fire and poured the fresh water into the reservoir on the side of the stove to heat. He made three more trips to the creek before he was satisfied that there would be enough for a real, civilized bath.

Bess slept, snoring a little, while Will moved quietly about the cabin. He took clean trousers and a shirt from his trunk, along with a hairbrush he hadn't troubled himself to use in some time.

When the water was hot enough to suit him, Will patiently filled the tin washtub Bess had used that morning and carried it outside and around to the rear of the cabin. The dog and half the chickens gathered in the tall grass to watch with interest while he stripped to the skin, stepped into the tub, and scrubbed from head to foot. He wished he could barber himself, too, but he didn't own a pair of scissors and he wasn't about to go ferreting through Bess's things looking for hers.

The chickens soon wandered off, bored, but Calvin lingered, whimpering low in his throat. Will guessed the animal knew somehow that his owner was smitten with a difficult woman and was sympathetic.

Will didn't own a towel, so after his bath he let the late afternoon sunlight dry his skin. He had just pulled on his trousers, and was reaching for his shirt, when all of a sudden Bess came around the side of the cabin, headed toward the privy.

She started when she saw him, and laid one hand to her breast, and Will was so embarrassed he thought he'd never be able to face her again. It made no difference whatsoever that he had his britches on, or that she'd seen him earlier in the day without his shirt.

He blushed like a virgin.

Bess's eyes widened, then she burst out laughing. "If you could see your face!" she cried, in delight. Then she proceeded to the privy, humming to herself.

Will said a prayer of thanks that she hadn't caught him in the altogether, emptied the washtub, and carried it to the stream to be rinsed out. When he returned to the cabin, having taken his time in an effort to regain his dignity, he paused in the dooryard, stopped in his boot-prints by the sound coming from inside.

Bess was singing—it was some silly little ditty about a girl giving her heart to a seagoing man—but it might have been the joyous carolling of an angel, the way it affected Will. The sound touched his spirit in a place so deep that tears burned his eyes.

He stood outside in the gathering twilight, holding the washtub in one hand and wishing with all his heart that he could step over the threshold of that cabin a suave and dapper man, like his brother. Oh, he'd attracted more than his share of the girls as a boy, Will had, but this was different. He was grown up now, big as a mountain and looking as though he'd never been barbered in his life.

God only knew how long he would have stood there, alternating between misery and foolish elation, if Bess hadn't come to the doorway and given him a curious look.

"Are you rooted to that footpath, William Tate?" she asked, in her crisp way. "Supper's about ready, and after that I'm going to take my scissors to that mane of yours. You do own a straight razor, I presume?"

Will felt more foolish than ever, and that was saying something, considering all he'd been through in the space of a day. It was downright consternating, the upheaval one female could cause in such a short time.

"What's for supper?" he countered, after an awkward clearing of the throat. He occupied himself with the process of hanging the tub on its peg on the outside wall of the cabin while awaiting her response.

"I made an oven-dish of the beans, and boiled up some turnips and carrots," she answered, lingering in the doorway until Will approached. "Fried chicken and mashed potatoes would have been good, but I don't believe I have the courage to catch one of those poor stupid creatures and chop off its head."

Having made this pronouncement, Bess turned and went back into the house, while Will reflected that to his way of thinking, she had the courage to do most *anything*. Hadn't she traveled most of the way across a continent, all by herself?

Supper was delicious—even though the food was necessarily simple, Bess had a knack for making everything taste good.

While he ate, Will came to the startling conclusion that he was happy. Until then, he hadn't known he wasn't, hadn't fully credited how lonely he'd been since leaving town life behind to prove up on a homestead.

After the meal, Bess cleared the table, then got out her scissors and ordered Will to pull one of the crates over by the fire. There was a lantern burning on the hardwood mantel, and she needed to see clearly.

Will sat blissfully, an old flour sack tied around his neck for a barber's cape, while Bess snipped away. There was a small fire crackling on the hearth of the plain stone fireplace, and every once in a while she threw a handful of hair onto the logs to sizzle and shrink up to nothing.

When Bess was evidently satisfied that she'd shorn him properly, she started right in whacking off his beard. Will, having drifted into a half-sleep, jumped and started to bolt.

Bess laid a hand on his shoulder. "You just sit tight," she commanded. "You're going to look a lot better after this."

Will felt vulnerable in a new way; he was needing her company and her voice and her cooking too much. The realization made him peevish, coming on the heels of so many other realizations the way it did. "Just don't come at me with the straight razor," he grumbled. "I'm real choosey about who shaves me."

"That is evident, Mr. Tate," she said, removing the flour sack and going toward the door with it.

While she was outside, shaking out the improvised cape, Will went to the cracked mirror and peered warily at his reflection. His hair wasn't overly short, for it still touched his collar in back, and there was no arguing the fact that he looked better.

He stropped his razor, got out his shaving brush and soap, and filled a basin with hot water from the reservoir. Sometime during that process, Bess came back inside, found the broom, and began to sweep.

Will shaved, managing to cut himself a couple of times, but as he uncovered more and more of his old-time face, his grin got progressively broader.

When he turned around to face Bess, she dropped the skillet she was drying, and it made a considerable clatter on the splintery floor.

3

WHILE Bess had suspected that Will Tate might be a fine-looking man underneath his neglected hair and beard, nothing had prepared her for the way he actually looked.

He had a strong, square jaw, not the weak kind that some men hide beneath a beard, and a deep dimple in his chin. His dancing hazel eyes were full of laughter and mischief, and he was plainly much younger than she'd ever have guessed.

Embarrassed, Bess bent to pick up the skillet she'd dropped when Will had turned away from the mirror and confronted her with his clean-shaven and barbered self. It was curious, she thought, how her heart was pounding and those secret places inside her, places she hadn't really considered before, suddenly felt all achy and warm.

She straightened with dignity, pressing the skillet to her bosom like a shield with one hand and clasping the flour-sack dish towel in the other. Perhaps if she waved that towel, like a flag of surrender . . .

"Am I presentable?" Will asked. The question was guileless rather than artful; he really didn't know that he was breathtakingly handsome.

"Very," Bess allowed, though grudgingly, and the word came hoarse from her throat.

Will seemed gratified, and crossed the room to bank the fire. "You'll want to start your sitting up long about now," he said, without looking at her. "Fact is, it's been a long day for me, and I'm ready to bed down.''

Bess felt her face heat, and she was grateful that Will's attention was otherwise occupied. She glanced wistfully toward the bed, which she knew to be comfortable, and swallowed. Even though she'd fallen asleep that morning in the bathtub, and napped in the afternoon, she was still exhausted. The journey out from Pennsylvania to the Washington Territory had taken a lot more out of her than she'd ever dreamed it would.

She cleared her throat again. ''You were talking about something called bundling before—exactly what does that entail?''

Will turned from the fire, casting a giant shadow on the cabin wall. Bess thought she saw the brief white flash of a grin, but she couldn't say for sure because he still wasn't looking at her. ''You'd lie on one side of the bed and I'd lie on the other,'' he said, and he sounded as reasonable as could be.

''And what would be between us?'' she pressed.

''We could put some of your baggage down the middle of the mattress, I guess, but there's really no call for that. I'm giving you my word that I won't touch you until we're married, and I've never gone back on a promise in my life. No point in starting now.''

Bess believed him and, at the same time, she told herself she was crazy. Her own sister-in-law, Simon's wife, Jillie, had told her in all sincerity that men couldn't resist a woman who was lying down. They just had to jump on her, she'd said, though if a lady was fortunate, she'd enjoy it.

''I'm sure my reputation would be completely destroyed,'' she mused aloud.

Will turned down the single kerosene lantern on the table and the cabin was cast slowly into a sleepy darkness, broken only by the light of the dying fire. His chuckle was a distinctly masculine sound, and it both troubled and thrilled Bess. ''There's nobody around here that would care much, one way or the other, about your 'reputation.' Besides, I reckon you probably lost that long ago, when you offered yourself as a mail-order bride and struck out for the romantic West.''

Bess might have been stung by his assessment of her situation earlier, but supper and the peaceful task of trimming Will's hair had mellowed her temperament. She thought of the downtrodden Indians she'd seen after crossing the Mississippi River, the ugly weathered buildings marring the landscape, the multitudes of dead buffalo alongside the railroad tracks, slaughtered for sport, and Mr. Sickles, the filthy proprietor of a vermin-infested store.

"I would not call the West romantic," she said. She was still standing near the table, like Joan of Arc about to be tied to the stake. "But it's big, at least, with plenty of room for all kinds of people."

If Will thought it strange that she was chattering away in the darkness, he didn't give any indication. No, he just went to the bed, sat down on its edge, and kicked off his boots.

Bess looked away when he pushed his suspenders down off his shoulders and proceeded to unbutton his shirt.

"This is the last time I'm going to tell you, Bess," he said. "You're safe here. You can lie down and rest your bones without fearing that I'll take advantage of you."

Bess let out her breath in a long and somewhat forlorn sigh, then went to her mountain of baggage and opened a valise. From it she took her primmest flannel nightgown, her toothbrush, and a small tin of polishing powder.

"Very well," she said, as though granting him some great favor. "Now, if you would just get up and escort me to the privy."

The bedsprings creaked as Will stretched out his large, powerful frame to sleep. "Take the lantern and the dog," he said. "You're not likely to meet anything bigger than a field mouse out there, anyway."

Bess glanced warily at the canine and wondered if she

could get through the night without relieving herself. The answer was no, and she was terrified to venture out of the cabin, but she was also too proud to beg Will to walk with her.

"You'll come for me if I scream?" she inquired.

Will yawned expansively. "On winged feet," he answered.

Bess put her nightgown and toothbrush on the table, along with the polishing powder, and took up the lantern instead. She struck a match to the stone face of the fireplace and lit the wick, then bravely headed for the door. The dog raised itself from its resting place, a patch of moonlight under the window, and followed her.

"You're more of a gentleman than your master," she told the animal, making no effort to keep her voice down as she raised the heavy crossbar on the door.

Beyond the walls of the cabin, the world was dark and large, full of looming shadows and curious sounds a city girl has no way of recognizing. Calling upon all her fortitude of spirit, Bess marched around the chinked log walls and headed for the outhouse.

She was on her way back, and congratulating herself on her stalwart nature, when she noticed that the dog had vanished. In the next instant, the chickens started squawking and there was cursing and crashing about inside the cabin as Will jumped up from his bed.

Bess saw a shadow rushing toward her and she stood there in the middle of the outhouse path, too terrified to move. A savage in ragged clothes stood before her, just for a moment, a fluttering, complaining chicken in each hand, and then bolted into the darkness.

The thief had already disappeared into the birch, fir, and pine trees behind the cabin when Will finally appeared, wearing only his trousers and carrying a rifle in one hand.

By some miracle, Bess found her voice. "You're too late," she said acidly. "Of course, if you'd seen fit to escort me, like a gentleman should, you would have encountered the Indian yourself."

Will cursed, scanning the tree line in the dim light of the moon. Then he took Bess's elbow in one hand and propelled her toward the cabin. "It's clear enough that he wanted the chickens, whoever he was, and not a yellow-haired white woman with a sharp tongue."

His words brought to mind every horrible story about captivity among the savages Bess had ever read or heard, and she started trembling so badly that Will had to let her arm go and take the lantern before she dropped it. "You needn't be flippant about this," she said, stumbling along beside him. "Furthermore, I believe I would do for a captive as well as the next woman."

Calvin began to bark in the distance, but Bess imagined it was all show. That mutt wanted them to think he'd chased the intruder off, though in truth he'd probably bolted into the timber at the first sign of trouble and cowered there until it was past.

They had reached the cabin door, God be thanked, and Will stepped back to let Bess go in before him. "The Indians around these parts are having enough trouble feeding themselves—they're not likely to be taking on slaves."

Bess shuddered, dizzy with relief at being safe inside the cabin, with Will there to protect her. "But why?" she asked. "I thought Indians were such legendary hunters."

Will latched the door, put the lantern back in the middle of the table, and hung the rifle above the fireplace before answering. "Last winter was especially hard, so there isn't much game this year. Also, they've had some trouble with a tribe from the north—the strangers come down from Canada every now and then and steal all their horses and women."

Bess went to Will's bed without hesitation, and without removing her clothes; not even for the sake of personal honor would she have willingly strayed more than a few feet from the safety of his side. "Women?" she echoed, in a flimsy voice.

Will chuckled, as calm as if he handled an Indian raid

every night of the week. "*Indian* women," he stressed. "Both tribes think 'Boston' females are too troublesome, even in prosperous times."

She sat on the edge of the mattress, on the side closest to the wall, and had the devil's own time unbuttoning her shoes because her fingers were trembling so much. "Wait until I write Mama and Papa and Jillie and Simon about *this* night," she said, painfully aware that Will had bedded down again, and probably had taken off his trousers before doing so.

What if she rolled over in the night, sheerly by accident, of course, and touched him?

He sighed again, the deep, lusty sigh of a strong man made weary by a hard day's work, and replied, "Just don't make one damn Indian into a full-scale massacre and scare the folks back home white-headed."

With that, he drifted off, leaving Bess to slide gingerly under the covers, fully dressed except for her shoes and the corset she'd removed that morning, on the occasion of her bath. It seemed that the cabin walls grew thinner with each passing moment, while the night-sounds got louder.

In her vivid imagination, Bess pictured Indians in loincloths, with glistening coppery skin, gathering around a blazing fire and making plans for war . . .

She awoke to the sound of a skillet clanging against the metal surface of the stove top, amazed and more than a little relieved to find the cabin full of daylight.

The master of the house cracked several eggs into a pan and then turned his head to grin at Bess over one shoulder. She felt a lurch, seeing this new, clean-shaven Will, and her heart set itself to hammering again.

"Mornin'," he said companionably.

The door of the cabin was open to the fresh air and sunlight, and the good-for-nothing dog was back from its cowardly night wanderings, lying in comfort on the hearth.

"Good morning," Bess replied, trying to find the right balance between civility and improper friendliness. She'd never seen a man cook before, and it was hard not to stare—for more reasons than one.

Will poured a cup of coffee and set it on the table, and its scent wafted across the cabin to tease Bess. He tossed her another of his dangerous grins, and she made her way around the end of the bed and past her baggage to sit down at the table.

"I've been thinking," he said cheerfully.

Bess reached for the mug of coffee with shaking hands, feeling as unsteady as an old drunk after a three-day bender. "What about?" she asked, even though she knew beforehand that she'd regret the question.

"We can file for another three-hundred and twenty acres, once we're married," he said, expertly removing two slices of homemade bread from the oven, where they'd been toasting. "It would only take us a year or two to clear enough for another field of corn, and we could run a few more cattle, too."

Bess knew nothing about clearing land, raising corn, or "running" cattle, nor did she have much of a desire to learn, but she kept the fact to herself. "Who baked that bread?" she asked idly.

"Neighbor woman," Will said. "Her name's Mae Jessine."

Bess sat up a little straighter, intrigued. It would make things so much easier if there were another woman nearby, someone she could talk to and confide in, someone who could help her decide what to do. "I thought you said there weren't any neighbors."

"Well, the Jessines live ten miles from here, beyond the next ridge," Will answered cheerfully, setting the fried eggs and toasted bread on the table, along with the familiar blue-enamel plates and tin utensils. "It's an overnight trip, so I don't see them much. Mr. Kipps comes through every other week or so—that's the circuit preacher—and Mae always sends some fresh bread along with him."

Bess sat up a little straighter. "Does that mean he

won't be through—the minister, I mean—for another two weeks?''

Will sat down and helped himself to a plateful of food. He looked so different, so good, with his shorter hair and his smooth-shaven face, that Bess had to work hard not to stare. He shrugged. "Kipps'll be here when he gets here. Now that more and more people are coming in, he isn't so predictable.''

Bess's stomach rumbled, reminding her that she was famished, and she took an egg and a slice of toast and began to eat. "Your brother said in his letter that he'd send me some money as soon as he got some,'' she announced. "If I decide to leave, maybe Mr. Kipps would see me as far as Onion Creek, so I could catch the freight wagon—''

Will put his fork down; his face grew hard and his countenance seemed to darken. "If you count on my brother for anything,'' he said, "you're likely to be disappointed. I'd have thought you would've guessed that by now.'' He paused and looked away, and a muscle in his jawline bunched and then smoothed out again. When he looked at Bess, his light brown eyes had lost their sparkle. "Should you decide you want to go, all you've got to do is say so, and I'll take you back to town and see you safely on your way.''

Bess felt an ache inside, and wished she'd never left Philadelphia, never come to this far place and met up with Will Tate. Trial that he was, he would be a hard man to leave and, once gone, she expected she'd miss him for the rest of her life. She changed the subject. "Do you think that Indian will come back?''

She is going to leave, Will thought grimly, as he stumbled along behind the plow that morning, heedless of the pleasant scent of the newly turned soil and the warm brightness of the sun. Damn it, Bess is going to leave, even though she has nowhere to go.

He glanced toward the cabin, his brow and chest wet with sweat, and was startled to see Bess coming toward him, making her ladylike way between the furrows with a ladle in one hand and her impractical skirts plucked up in the other.

Will's heart twisted, and he considered ignoring her, but instead he yelled ''Whoa'' to the horse, held the plow firmly, and watched her approach. It was what he'd dreamed of, a pretty woman bringing him water when he was working hard, but if she left, the memory would injure him over and over again during the long, lonely years to come.

She smiled. ''I thought you might be thirsty,'' she said, holding out the ladle.

Will took it, saw that she'd spilled most of the water on the way, and gratefully swallowed what remained. ''Thank you,'' he said, wondering when he'd started to care for Bess and wishing that he never had.

''You won't have to wait for Mr. Kipps to get fresh bread after this,'' she said. ''I found some yeast in your supply cupboard, and I've got a batch rising right now.''

Will wanted to touch her, just lay his fingers lightly to her smooth cheek or her shiny, silken hair, but he didn't dare. It would just be one more thing to remember, and mourn for, after she was gone. ''That's fine,'' he said, and handed her back the ladle.

The happy smile wobbled on her mouth and then fell away.

That was another thing Will didn't want to think about: her mouth. He could imagine only too well what it would be like to kiss her there, to urge her lips apart and explore her with his tongue . . .

''Is something wrong?'' she asked.

Will set his hands to the plow again, and was about to whistle to the horse when Bess laid her fingers lightly on his upper arm. He couldn't scare up a smile, so he simply raised one eyebrow as if to say, What do you want?

''I thought you said we weren't going to hide our feelings from each other,'' she challenged, in a voice so gentle that it made Will want to weep.

Of course he didn't do any such thing. He drew himself up and answered, "That was when I thought you'd be staying on."

She blinked, and Will reflected in wounded amazement that he wouldn't have guessed a woman's eyes could be so blue that it hurt to look into them.

"I haven't decided to go," Bess said, after a long and difficult silence. "I was just thinking out loud."

"You'll go," Will said, and this time he got a whistle out and the horse lurched forward. The plow swerved and made the furrow crooked before he got a good hold on it again.

Bess stumbled alongside him, heedless that the dirt was spoiling the hem of her pretty summer dress. "How can you presume to say such a thing when I don't know myself whether I'm going or staying?" she demanded breathlessly.

Will pretended not to look at her, though he was watching her out of the corner of one eye. "This is hard, lonely country, and you're a city woman," he said tersely. "You'd never last out the first winter, most likely."

Her cheeks reddened. "My being a 'city woman,' as you put it, doesn't mean I'm weak," she said, her strides long. "Damn it, Will Tate, *will you stop?*"

He stopped, and hope filled his heart—hope he couldn't stop himself from feeling.

She put her hands on her hips, the ladle jutting out from one, and glared up at him. "Life can be difficult in the cities, too, you know. There are outbreaks of typhoid, not to mention riots stirred up by union men. Folks get run down by trolley cars and carriages, bitten by rats, and shot by robbers!"

Will hardened his jaw briefly. "What is your point?" he asked.

Bess was seething. "My *point*, William, is that you homesteaders don't have a corner on trouble and hardship, and I'll thank you to stop acting as though you're the only person in the world who has to struggle to get by. We all do!"

He turned to begin plowing again, but Bess ducked under his arm and stood right in his path, between the handles of the plow, so close that she made his skin burn.

"If I choose to leave this place," she said, "it will be because I think it's the right thing to do, and not because I'm afraid of hard winters or Indians or anything else!"

Perhaps it was only her nearness that made Will lose his head, or maybe it was her saucy spirit, he didn't know. Between one moment and the next, he'd closed his big hands around her waist, hoisted her onto the toes of her high-button shoes, and bent his head to take her mouth in the most ferocious kiss he'd ever given any woman.

Bess stiffened, then dropped the ladle into the dirt, wrapped her arms around Will's neck, and kissed him back with an innocent passion that made his blood leap in his veins.

He probably would have lifted her into his arms, carried her into the cabin, and made love to her if it hadn't been for the braying of a mule and a familiar voice shouting, "Anybody to home?"

With a ragged sigh, Will set a blushing, breathless Bess away from him.

"That'll be Mr. Kipps," he said hoarsely, unable to look at Bess because he was afraid he'd see relief in her face, or fury. She was probably ready to scalp him for being so forward, and she'd likely decide she had to ride out with the preacher when he left, just to safeguard her virtue.

Bess was dazed; every nerve and fiber reverberated with the shattering aftershocks of the kiss. She was glad of the visitor's arrival, for if he hadn't come, she might have given herself to Will right there in the field, like some back-street harlot.

She bent down to retrieve the ladle, then smoothed her hair and skirts with her free hand, working up a smile for the old man riding the mule. He was fat as a goose in autumn, with a bushy white beard and long white hair, and he wore a bowler hat, a worn but colorful serape, much-mended trousers, and moccasins.

"Looks like I didn't get here any too soon," Mr. Kipps boomed out, and then he threw back his grizzled head and laughed so hard that the plow horse nickered and tried to bolt.

Will calmed it with a word, but his face was a suspicious shade of pink and his whiskey-colored eyes were narrowed as he regarded the circuit preacher. "I'll thank you to explain that remark," he said, in a taut voice.

Bess elbowed him. It wasn't Mr. Kipps's fault that he'd caught them in an improper embrace, and besides, she already liked the dusty clergyman. "You needn't explain anything," she said sweetly. "You are our guest. You'll come in and make yourself at home, that's what you'll do. Will will see to your mule, and I'll set the table for the noonday meal. You'll join us, of course?"

Kipps looked at Will, raised one enormous white eyebrow, and with a visible effort suppressed a smile. "Of course I will," he said.

Bess glanced at Will, saw that his feathers had smoothed out a little, and felt safe in assuming that he wouldn't be rude to Mr. Kipps in her absence. She started for the cabin, calling back over one shoulder, "Don't be too long now."

Will had killed a chicken that morning and brought it to Bess and, with no small amount of trepidation, she'd dipped it into scalding water, plucked it, and cut it up for frying. The succulent pieces were sizzling away in a skillet at that very moment.

Mr. Kipps and Will both ate heartily of the meal—Bess had mashed potatoes, too, and made gravy—but it was the circuit preacher who did most of the talking. He related news of all the neighbors, saying Mrs. Jessine was about to have her baby any day and would sure be happy to have a woman about when she took to her childbed, and then made the blunt statement both Will and Bess had been waiting for.

"It ain't decent for you two to be living here alone, without benefit of holy words being said over you. Am I right in guessing that you haven't taken the trouble to get hitched?"

Will looked guilty, then exasperated. "There wasn't anybody around to marry us," he said. "She was sleeping on a pile of feed sacks when I found her, and old Sickles sure isn't empowered to perform a ceremony."

"All the same," Kipps insisted, pushing back from the table after a long siege, and laying gnarled hands to his large belly, "I can't leave this place in good conscience if I don't either bring the lady along with me or marry you up whilst I'm here."

Bess's heart started racing again, and she felt her cheeks turn pink. Suddenly shy, she averted her eyes, unable to look at Will.

"We have to talk about this," Will said. "Me and Bess, I mean. Alone."

When Mr. Kipps didn't take the hint and go outside so they could talk in privacy, Will reached across the table, clasped Bess's hand, and dragged her out into the dooryard.

"Well?" he whispered, flinging his arms wide. "What are we going to do? That's a man of God in there, and we can't ignore what he says!"

Bess folded her arms. "What are you suggesting?" she asked, even though she knew, and the idea made her weak and rather breathless. If she married Will, he'd kiss her, like he had in the field, and do other things, too. And she knew she'd like it.

"I want you to stay here and marry me," Will growled. "Damn it, you knew that, but you had to make me say it!"

Bess smiled. "That was the most inglorious proposal I've ever heard of, Mr. Tate—but I'll accept, on one condition."

A grin lit Will's face, but he quickly frowned it away. It seemed to Bess that he was holding his breath, at least until he said, "What condition?"

"We can't be intimate until we know each other better."

Will leaned close, so his nose wasn't an inch from hers. His pale gold eyes snapped with irritation and some other emotion that wasn't so easy to identify. "Just what is it that you want to know about me?" he demanded. "I'll be happy to tell you, right here and now."

Bess shook her head, stubbornly, and the fraction of a smile she allowed herself probably looked a little smug. "I'm afraid it's not as easy as that," she said. "I'm not going to give myself to a man I've known for one day, and that's final."

Will nodded angrily toward the field. "Not an hour ago, you kissed me as if you knew me pretty damn well!"

"Don't push me, Will. Either you agree to my terms, or I'll leave with Mr. Kipps."

He pushed past her and went back into the cabin, where the pious Mr. Kipps was waiting. "We'll be married," he said, sounding as if he'd rather be staked out over an anthill and covered with honey. "Just say the words and be done with it."

Bess interceded. "Now, just a minute, Will Tate. This is my wedding day, and I have to remember it for the rest of my life. I want to wear a pretty dress and fix my hair, and you'll go and find me a bouquet of wildflowers if you know what's good for you."

Mr. Kipps's bright blue eyes twinkled. "You heard what the lady said, Will," he remarked. "I'll see to my old mule, Miss Bess here will fancy herself up, and you'll pick flowers for the bride to hold."

When Will looked at Bess, his face softened all of a sudden, and she knew he didn't mind so much about the flowers as a person would have thought, listening to him before. He wanted her for a wife, even if it meant he had to wait for his husbandly rights, and the knowledge of that thrilled her.

She'd never felt this way about marrying Jackson Reese, she reflected, as she searched through her trunks for her loveliest frock, a pale ivory dancing gown with

delicate embroidery edging the hem and the daring neckline.

When she was dressed, she brushed her hair, and
pinned it loosely at the back of her head, so that it made
a golden aura around her face.

A low whistle of exclamation made Bess turn toward
the doorway and there, on the threshold, stood Will, with
a clump of daisies in his hand and his heart in his eyes.

4

WILL entered the cabin awkwardly, as though the
place were new to him, and laid the bunch of
yellow and white daisies on the table. His Adam's apple
traveled the length of his throat, and then he let his eyes
sweep over Bess's ivory dress and her soft, billowing
coiffure, and swallowed again. "St. Peter will surely
come up one short," he said hoarsely, "when he counts
the angels tonight."

The words struck a chord deep in Bess's heart, in a
region that had never been touched before. She'd heard
enough compliments from men in her time, but most had
been calculated for effect. Will's, she knew, was utterly
sincere.

"Is it time?" she asked.

Will had washed, probably in the icy creek that ran
less than a hundred feet from the house, and his work
shirt was open to his midriff. "Yes, ma'am," he answered shyly, blushing and looking away. "It's time."
With that, he knelt in front of the pinewood trunk where

he kept his personal belongings and took out a clean white shirt. He set the folded garment on the foot of the bed and then dug deeper into the chest, finally bringing out a wooden matchbox. As Bess watched, he slid the box open and reached in for a small object. He closed his fist around whatever it was, shut his eyes briefly, in remembrance or perhaps prayer, and then put that same hand into his trouser pocket.

The brief ritual completed, Will rose gracefully to his feet again and favored Bess with a grin that struck her like a hard wind. "I'll just tidy myself up a little," he said, "and we'll be married."

The wedding took place outside, with the stream and the mountains and the newly plowed field for a church, and it was brief even though Mr. Kipps made an obvious effort to extend the event.

When he reached the part about the rings, Bess had none to offer, even though she'd come out west intending to be married. Will, however, produced a narrow gold band from his britches' pocket—no doubt this was what he had taken so reverently from the chest—and slid it onto Bess's finger.

Tears shimmered in Bess's eyes and her throat went tight, just for a moment, though she couldn't have explained either phenomenon for the life of her.

Finally, Mr. Kipps pronounced them man and wife, and generously invited Will to kiss the bride.

He did so, and with none of the shyness he'd exhibited inside the cabin, when he'd first caught sight of Bess in her wedding dress. In fact, Will kissed Bess almost exactly the way he had in the field that morning, and she thought she'd die of some combination of excitement and suffocation before he let her go.

"I'll make my camp out here, alongside the creek," Mr. Kipps said, after he'd shaken Will's hand in congratulations and offered a courtly bow to Bess. "Me and my ole mule, we favor sleepin' under God's bright stars."

Bess was about to argue that the visitor was welcome

to sleep on the bear rug in front of the hearth, but Will stopped her from speaking with a firm pinch on the bottom.

"I haven't changed my mind, Will Tate," she whispered angrily a few minutes later, when they were inside the cabin with the door closed. "We're not consummating this marriage right away, and therefore there is absolutely no point in making that poor old man sleep on the ground!"

"That poor old man is tougher than boot leather and meaner than Geronimo, and anyhow he never makes his bed under a roof before the first snowfall," Will whispered back, sounding just as irritated. "Besides that, Mrs. Tate, I *will* be alone with my wife on the first night of my marriage, whether or not she allows me to touch her. Anything else would be downright embarrassing!"

Bess thought it was as good a time as any to change the subject. Besides, the bread she'd mixed up that morning was ready for the oven, supper needed to be started, and Will had plenty of chores to finish before nightfall. "If you wouldn't mind stepping outside," she said, turning away with a decisive flourish, "I'll just get out of this fancy gown and put on my morning dress."

She heard the door open and close behind her and was satisfied that she was alone. Humming the bridal march, and feeling happier than she would have admitted to anyone with less authority than an archangel, Bess undid the tiny pearl buttons at the front of her dress and stepped out of it. After that, she discarded the petticoats beneath and wearing only her muslin drawers and camisoles reached up with both hands to let down her hair.

When she turned toward the main part of the bed, she gave a little cry and covered her chest ineffectually with both arms, for Will was standing there watching her, and grinning the broadest grin she'd ever seen on a man's face.

In the next instant, however, his features reflected a sort of solemn tenderness.

"Welcome home, Mrs. Tate," he said gruffly. "I've been waiting a very long time for you."

With those words, he turned from her, took off his good white shirt, and hung it on a peg. The muscles of his back were clearly defined beneath the tan flesh, and Bess felt an overwhelming urge to touch his shoulder blades and kiss the place between them.

"Where did you get the wedding ring?" she asked, because she had to say something and there was nothing else she trusted herself to talk about in that fragile moment. "Was it your mother's?"

Will had donned his work shirt again, and he faced his bride, working the buttons as he spoke. "And her mother's before her," he said.

Again, Bess was touched on some fundamental level of her being. Jackson Reese would have given her a ring with diamonds, costing many times the price of the thin golden band her new husband had slipped onto her finger, but no gift could have been more precious than Will's.

She almost said she loved him, but then the dog began to bark, and Mr. Kipps's mule brayed, and the moment was lost. Will went outside, muttering a curse, and Bess hurriedly put on the dress she'd worn earlier in the day.

At twilight, Mr. Kipps and Will came in to supper, the dog on their heels, and Bess proudly set out a fine meal of canned peas, cold chicken, reheated gravy, and her own fresh-baked bread.

Truth to tell, it nettled her just a little, the way Will acted that night at the table. He wasn't rude or anything like that, and he ate hungrily of the fare, but he talked mostly to Mr. Kipps about the current president and what ought rightly to be done about him. It was almost as though it had slipped Will's mind that there had been a wedding that day, and he'd taken himself a bride.

After the dishes had been cleared away, though, Mr. Kipps brought a mouth harp out of a pocket of his serape and began to play a spritely tune, and Will took Bess into his arms and high-stepped her all around the room. He didn't stop until she was breathless with laughter and so weak that she had no choice but to sag against him.

It was then that Mr. Kipps cleared his throat, murmured a discreet good night, and left the cabin, taking the dog with him for extra company. Apparently, the quality of the mule's companionship was wearing thin.

Very slowly, Will steadied Bess, and set her slightly away from him, though his hands lingered on her shoulders. He looked deep into her eyes for the longest moment, and light from the fire flickered darkly over his features.

Bess thought he was going to kiss her, and she wanted him to, but in the end he drew back.

"I'll be back sometime after you've gone to sleep," he said coolly. He'd been laughing moments before, but now it seemed that all sense of celebration had abandoned him. "Would you be wanting me to walk you out to the privy, just in case you meet another Indian?"

Bess wanted that, and more. She'd hoped that Will would lie beside her, and hold her in his arms, and help her get used to his nearness, but she was too proud to say any of those things. And although she was still as scared of the dark as she had been the night before, she wouldn't let herself ask him to escort her.

She shook her head. "I'll be fine," she said.

She went out, and as she made her way back, she saw the light of a lantern glowing in the gloom, and heard the clanging sound of metal against stone. What on earth was Will doing out there?

Bess suppressed her curiosity, along with the odd sense of disappointment she felt, and went on into the cabin. There, she blew out the lamp, exchanged her clothes for a nightdress, washed her face and polished her teeth, and winded her way through the piles of baggage to the bed.

She'd expected to drop right off to sleep, since the day had been a long and eventful one, but instead Bess lay there, wide awake, listening to the strange sound coming from the woods and wondering. To make matters worse, the cabin and indeed the bed seemed unbearably lonely.

Finally, Bess got up, slipped on her shoes without going through the arduous process of buttoning them, and pulled a wrapper on over her nightgown. Then, hair trailing in a single plait, she lighted the table lantern and set out to find Will.

Mr. Kipps was camped just where he'd said he would be, on the creek bank, and he'd built a little fire to warm himself. He was leaning against his saddle and playing a mournful song on his mouth harp, and Bess hoped he was too intent on his own musings to see her leaving the cabin.

Bess followed the light in the woods for what seemed to her an inordinately long time. Brambles caught at her wrapper and her hair, and more than once some night-sound nearly made her jump out of her skin. By the time she reached the place where Will was working, she was in a somewhat fractious mood.

He was inside a cave of some sort, and by the light of his lantern and the one she carried, Bess saw that her husband was working shirtless in the gloom, swinging a pickax at a wall of solid stone.

"What in the name of mercy are you doing?" Bess demanded. Her patience was taxed to the limit and she could not find it within herself to be gracious, even though that probably would have been the wisest course, as well as the most Christian.

Will set down his ax and wiped his sweaty forehead with one filthy arm. "I might ask the same thing of you," he remarked, without rancor. "Wasn't it you who was afraid to walk out to the privy alone, just last night?"

Bess stomped one foot, and the lantern swayed dangerously in her hand. "Stop your hedging," she snapped. "I want to know what you're doing out here in this— this icy *pit*, on your wedding night!"

He shrugged, leaned down to catch hold of the handle on his own lantern, and then straightened again. "It's no colder than our bed would be," he said, "with you refusing to let me near you."

Tears stung Bess's eyes. She was indeed a living,

breathing paradox, wanting Will to lie beside her on this special night and yet denying him the intimacies a husband expects from a wife. And she didn't understand herself any better than Will did.

"I'm afraid," she said, as surprised by the announcement as anyone. She hadn't consciously formed the words before saying them, but now they were out and there was no going back. "I'm afraid and I need someone to hold me."

Will came toward her, his expression unreadable in the darkness, but she didn't fear him. No, it was the things he made Bess feel that terrified her, the awesome needs and yearnings, the soaring joy and the heart-wrenching sorrow. In less than forty-eight hours, Will Tate had touched her most sacred emotions.

He took her lantern and extinguished the light, then did the same with his own. When he had set both lamps aside, he lifted Bess into his arms and started back along the pathway leading out of the woods, with the bright silver moon leading the way.

Even when they were inside again, Will didn't speak. He just set Bess gently on the bed, took off her unbuttoned shoes and tossed them aside, then left her. She couldn't see him for the baggage and the gloom, but she heard the clatter of the lid on the hot-water reservoir attached to the stove, followed shortly by a great deal of splashing.

She was lying back on a feather pillow, keeping carefully to her side of the mattress and wishing she'd just left well enough alone, when Will got into bed. Still without speaking, he gathered her close against his hard, smooth chest and rested his chin on the top of her head.

His right hand made a comforting circle on her back.

"You're a good man," she said softly, wanting to weep because she'd needed his tenderness so much and he was giving it with no apparent expectation of recompense.

Will's chuckle came from deep in his chest, and it was

rueful. "There are surely times," he confessed, "when I wish I wasn't."

Bess had not wept when word came that Molly and Jackson had run off together, and that there would be no fancy society wedding, nor had she so much as whimpered during the long, frightening trip out west. Not even when she'd had to bed down in Mr. Sickles's dirty store, on a pile of feed sacks, knowing she was soon to be wed to a virtual stranger, had she cried out of the fear, remorse, and homesickness that nearly crushed her . . .

Now, of all times, when she was safe in Will Tate's strong arms, Bess let out a wail and began to sob.

Another man might have panicked, but Will was calm. He just lay there, wearing nothing but the bottoms of his long underwear, as far as Bess could tell, stroking her hair and holding her close.

Only when the storm had been past for some minutes did Will speak. "If you want to go back home to your folks," he said solemnly, "I'll understand."

Bess sniffled inelegantly. "I believe I'll just tarry right here a while, if it's all the same to you."

She felt his smile, like light warming the cool darkness. "I'd like to get on with some of that getting acquainted you're so set on," he said. "What exactly do you need to know about me, Bess?"

She laughed and socked him lightly with one balled fist. "All right, then, here's something. What *were* you doing in that cave out there in the timber?"

"Looking for gold. Or maybe silver."

Bess couldn't have been more surprised if he'd said he expected to chip his way right through to China. "You?" She felt a little disappointed in him, though she was careful to hide the fact. "I thought you wanted to farm the land, and leave the mining business to your brother."

Will kissed the top of her head and, even though the gesture was purely innocuous, Bess felt a hot shiver go straight through her system and tingle in the tips of her toes.

"All I ever wanted was land and a good wife and as many babies as the Lord might see fit to send this way," he said, and he sounded sort of melancholy, like he thought he wasn't going to have those things. "John started that mine, before the wanderlust got so bad that he had to set out for the North country, and he even found a little ore—copper, mostly—but it was too slow for him. I figured if I had more to offer, you might decide to stay here and settle in with me."

Guilt and a piercing stab of something tender and fragile brought fresh tears to Bess's eyes. Will was an intelligent, insightful man; he'd guessed one of her reasons for not wanting to consummate the union too soon—if the two of them hadn't made love, the marriage could still be annulled.

Bess wriggled closer and kissed his warm, Will-scented neck. "Be patient with me," she pleaded. "I need some time to think, and get things worked out in my mind."

He made a comical growling sound, meant to convey his exasperation, and then turned onto his side and arranged Bess to fit against him, spoon-fashion. "Don't expect me to wait too long," he said in a rumbling voice, his breath warm on her nape. "Or I might just go crazy."

Bess's eyes were open wide with surprise, for she could feel Will's desire through the back of her nightgown, and she hadn't once imagined that he could be so big. When—and if—she gave her personal consent, it might be difficult to fit him inside her.

"Will?"

"Hmmm?" He sounded sleepy.

"Does it hurt?"

"Does what hurt?"

"When—when a man joins himself to a woman—isn't it rather a—a tight fit?"

Will gave a low chuckle, but his answer was gentle. "I reckon it's a little snug the first time," he said. "But after that, you'll like having me inside you. I promise."

She turned, propping herself on one elbow, to look

him in the eye. "How can you promise a thing like that?" she asked, out of plain curiosity.

He gave her a nibbling kiss on the mouth that roused another ache in her personal parts.

"I know how to please a woman," he said.

Bess gave him a push and laid back down, though she didn't try to get beyond the warm, steely circle of his embrace. "I'd like to know how you learned, if you're so dead set against fornication!" she whispered, stung by the image of Will lying naked with some other woman.

He laughed. "I never claimed to be anything but a sinner," he told her.

His words were of no comfort to Bess, nor did they calm the minor riot going on inside her. If Will Tate did any sinning, it had better be with her, or she'd take off a strip of his hide.

"Bess."

She lay stiff in her bridegroom's arms, her back to his damnably strong chest. "Leave me alone," she said. "I want to sleep."

"No, you don't," Will answered with quiet confidence. "You want to know what there is to loving, besides taking me inside you." He turned her onto her back and kissed the hollow of her throat. "There's plenty, Bess."

She trembled, and it seemed to her that her skin was going to peel right off, she was so hot. "You promised, Will," she reminded him.

"And I'll keep my word," he assured her, but even as he said the words he was unbuttoning the front of her nightgown. And she couldn't do a thing to stop him, although she knew she was going to regret it if she let herself be wooed. "Relax, Bess, and let me show you what I learned in the big city."

She drew in a quick breath when he pushed aside the front of her gown, revealing one plump breast. He cupped her in a calloused hand and brushed one thumb over the nipple, and the pleasurable sensation made Bess groan.

Will bent his head over her, and touched his tongue

to the sensitive tip, and Bess gasped and arched her back. She had been raised to believe that a man took satisfaction in these tussles in the night, while a woman merely did her duty, and nothing in her upbringing had prepared her for the things she was feeling then.

When Will closed his mouth around her nipple and began to suckle in a gentle but insistent way, she gave a soft, joyous sob and curved her spine into another arch, offering more of herself.

Will was a patient lover, however, and he took his time at that breast, then moved on to the other and attended it with the same languid passion. At the same time, he raised the hem of Bess's nightgown slowly over her knees and thighs until it was bunched around her waist.

She searched her soul for a word of protest, but there was none to be found. She wanted Will to show her more, to lead her to the unknown magic her body instinctively strained toward.

He parted her legs by sliding his hand between them, and she tossed her head from side to side in delirium when he began to caress the moist silk at the junction of her thighs.

"Will," she whispered, pleading for something she didn't understand, "Oh, Will—"

He caught her in a kiss, and at the same time burrowed through to touch the place where her physical passion seemed to be centered. She moaned into his mouth and flung her arms around his neck and he plunged his finger inside her, while still teasing her with the pad of his thumb.

Bess was wild, rushing, careening toward some cataclysm of joy that she had never imagined before Will, let alone hoped for, and still he kissed her.

When she thought she would splinter apart into pieces, when she truly believed she could not feel more intensely than she did then, Will left her mouth, kissed both her breasts as he passed downward over the length of her body . . .

He withdrew his finger and used that and his thumb to part her, and then he nuzzled her ever so lightly with his lips.

Bess made a strangled sound and groped for him, finding his head, entangling the fingers of both hands in his hair.

Will circled the tiny, quivering piece of flesh once, with just the tip of his tongue, and then he began to suck.

Bess bucked under him, grasping the brass rails of the bedstead with both hands, unable to hold back the wild, pagan cries of surrender that rolled up out of her throat and over her tongue.

Something inside her was being wound tighter and tighter, and the pleasure was nearly unbearable, and yet Will showed no mercy. No matter how Bess twisted, he did not let her go, and an invisible sun took shape inside her, flared with sweet heat, and then exploded in a glorious burst of ecstasy.

Bess rode the tide bravely, though the cautious side of her wanted to hide from the dangers of the unknown, and moaned helplessly while her body buckled and arched.

Even when she was still, and Will had raised himself from her, Bess went right on reacting on the inside, for the tremors subsided slowly, leaving a series of small crescendos in their wake.

She knew Will desired her—she could feel the intimidating evidence of that—and she fully expected him to poise himself over her and make her completely his own.

But he didn't.

Instead, he just held her, and sighed again. Soon, he was asleep, his breathing deep and even.

Bess, on the other hand, lay wide awake for a long time, marveling at what Will had learned in the big city, and wondering what *else* he knew.

Bess awakened with a sense of peaceful well-being, and the scents of coffee and frying bacon filled the cabin.

She'd no more than stretched, however, when regret and embarrassment caught up with her.

She pulled the quilts up over her head and remembered, in the most abject misery, how she'd moaned and thrashed in Will's bed the night before. How on earth was she going to face him now, and maintain any semblance of dignity?

Will was whistling happily, and Bess blushed underneath the blankets.

She heard his boot heels on the floor and then, when she knew he was beside the bed, the whistling stopped. In the next instant, the sheet and quilt were flung back, and Bess was revealed, lying there with her bodice open and the hem of her nightgown around her waist.

"Good morning, Mrs. Tate," Will said cheerfully, and it struck her then that that infernal grin of his was not just mischievous but downright sinful. Why hadn't she noticed that before? "Time to get up and bid Mr. Kipps a fond farewell."

Awkwardly, and seething all the while, Bess struggled to right her nightdress. She didn't want to face the preacher, fearing that he must have heard her wanton cries of passion, even through the thick walls of the cabin, and wondered fleetingly if Will would believe she was sick.

His eyes danced with amused perception, as if he'd read her mind. He left the covers resting at the foot of the bed, ran his eyes along the length of Bess's body, leaving her every nerve thrumming with the reminder of all he'd taught her in the night, and then went back to his cooking and his blasted whistling.

Bess rose hastily, fearing that Mr. Kipps would come inside at any moment and catch her dressing, and threw on a brown cotton dress with a high, ruffled collar and a trail of tiny jet buttons going from the throat to the hem.

She had barely managed to brush and pin up her hair before the preacher knocked at the door, which Will had obligingly left open, and stepped over the threshold.

Bess tried, but she could not bring herself to meet Mr. Kipps's gaze.

They were almost through with breakfast, Will and Mr. Kipps talking the whole time like a pair of gossipy old women, when the preacher said something that made Bess look at him at last.

"You might go over and look in on Mae Jessine, Mrs. Tate, if you can manage the trip. She's going to have that baby any day now, and it would lift her spirits considerable to have another woman there to see to things."

Bess put down her fork, her eyes wide as she regarded the preacher and then Will. Did these men honestly expect her to officiate at a birth? Did they think she knew what to do, just because she was female?

"I guess we could manage that," Will said, raising his coffee mug to his lips and taking a sip before going on. "I've got most of the plowing and planting done."

Bess looked away, her cheeks warm, remembering the heat and softness of those lips, and the intimate places where she'd felt their touch. In the attempt to avoid meeting Will's eyes, her gaze collided with Mr. Kipps's gentle, knowing ones.

He nodded toward the bags and boxes, valises and trunks. "Mae is about your age, and about your size, too," he said. "But the Jessines have seen some hard times, and she's been wearing the same dress ever since I've known them."

Bess got the hint, and she was more than willing to share her dresses with the less fortunate Mae, but she needed to clarify another point. "I don't know how to deliver babies," she said.

"It can be a right handy skill, out here in the wilderness," Mr. Kipps said, with implacable good nature.

Bess's heart plummeted to the pit of her stomach, leaving no room for any more of the delicious breakfast Will had made. She hardly heard Mr. Kipps's good-byes, or even her own, and when the preacher had ridden away on his mule, singing a hymn at the top of his lungs, she was still in something of a state. She kept dropping the dishes as she dried them, having to wash them again.

She started when Will stood behind her and laid his hands on her shoulders. He spoke in a quiet voice, but his words were blunt ones.

"Out here, Bess, we survive by helping each other. We'll leave for the Jessines' place as soon as I've finished with the planting."

Bess squared her shoulders and nodded, but she expected she looked a great deal braver than she felt.

5

As it turned out, Will and Bess did not have to go to the Jessines, for two days after the wedding, their neighbors came to them, with their scant belongings carefully stowed in an aging covered wagon pulled by two mules and an ox.

When the sojourners arrived, Bess was in the process of unpacking her trunks, freshening the more practical of her garments by spreading them out on the grass to air in the light of the spring sun. Will was on the far side of the field, planting, but of course he left that off when he saw the wagon coming.

The Jessines were obviously even poorer than Mr. Kipps had intimated at the table—their clothes were ragged, and although both of them were probably in their twenties, like Will and Bess, they appeared to be twice that age.

Mr. Jessine was a wiry, sorrowful-looking man, clinging to a few tatters of pride. Mae was pregnant, and painfully thin despite her protruding stomach. Her skin was sallow and her brown hair lank and dull, though it was plainly clean.

She smiled sadly at Bess as Tom lifted her down from the high wagon seat, but seemed too shy to speak. Will nodded to Mrs. Jessine and shook her husband's hand. "Hello, Tom."

Jessine sounded as though he were on the verge of tears when he replied, "We're givin' up on homesteadin', Will. Fact is, we're headed for Spokane, where I'm hopin' to land myself a job with the railroad."

Bess, who had never known true deprivation in her life, was suddenly embarrassed by her fine clothes, her good skin and shiny hair, and her fancy education. She put the feeling aside, however, and moved toward Mae, wanting to feed the other woman, to embrace her and tell her everything would turn out all right.

"This is my wife, Bess," Will said, when she reached his side. "Bess, Tom and Mae Jessine."

"Won't you come inside?" Bess said to Mae, leaving Tom to Will's care. "I could brew us some tea, and I baked a dried-apple pie just this morning."

Mae looked pathetically eager, and almost too weary to go another step. She stumbled once as she came toward Bess, and Bess automatically put a supporting arm around the other woman's waist.

"Tom and I don't want to be any trouble," Mae said in a small voice, once Bess had seated her on one of the crates that served for chairs. "We just thought we should stop by and let Will know we were leaving, so he wouldn't wonder. Maybe you could tell Mr. Kipps we went to Spokane, when he stops by again?"

"I'll be happy to," Bess said, keeping herself busy at the stove in an effort to bring the pity she was feeling under some control. At the same time, she was coveting a particular rocking chair that sat, unused, in an upstairs hallway of her family's house in Philadelphia. It had soft cushions, that chair, and wide armrests, and it would have been a comfort to Mae in her condition.

Perhaps her mother would ship it as far as Onion Creek, if Bess wrote and asked . . .

"You a store-bought bride?" Mae inquired.

Bess stopped, high color rising in her cheeks, and nodded, still keeping her back to Mae. Before, she'd been trying to hide the pity she had yet to bring under control, but now she had a less selfish reason for not facing the other woman.

"I suppose you could say that," she answered, after a few moments.

"You couldn't have done better than Will Tate," Mae said, apparently seeing no shame in being a mail-order wife. "Now if you'd gotten his brother, John, that would have been a different story. He's got a smile like an angel, John has, but he's up to no good most of the time."

Bess had at last composed herself enough to turn around and face Mae. "The tea's almost ready," she said, sounding stupidly cheerful even to herself.

Instead of answering, Mae gasped and Bess watched in horror as the other woman's stomach contracted visibly beneath the worn blue calico of her dress.

Bess had always understood that the pangs of childbirth came on slowly, but it wasn't so with Mae. She doubled over, moaning in plain agony, and would have toppled off the crate if Bess hadn't rushed over and grabbed her shoulders.

"Come with me now," she urged, gently but firmly, helping Mae to her feet and guiding her to the bed.

There, Bess helped the woman out of her pitiful clothing, which was soaked through with bloody fluid, and put Mae into one of the pretty cotton nightgowns she'd brought from Philadelphia.

While Mae lay writhing and weeping on the mattress, Bess rushed to the door and called out to Will and Tom in the calmest voice she could manage. They had been tethering the Jessines' mismatched team next to the stream, but at Bess's summons they dropped everything and rushed toward her.

Tom, who had probably been through more suffering than any ten people Bess had ever encountered, turned out to be completely useless in the face of his wife's dire need. He muttered something insensible, turned, and stumbled blindly out of the cabin.

Will, bless him, remained. He set his jaw and rolled up his sleeves, his eyes fixed on Mae Jessine. "Is there any hot water?" he asked in an even, quiet voice, and Bess couldn't help admiring his deep-rooted strength.

"I'll get some," Bess said, and hurried to obey.

Mae Jessine began to scream and arch her back in a grim parody of the pleasure Bess had felt in that very bed every night since she and Will had been married. They had not yet consummated their union, but Will had persisted in his skillful ministrations, and introduced his wife to a side of herself she had never known before.

Now, of course, things were tragically different. Bess rushed to the stove and began ladling hot water from the reservoir into a clean white basin. She was shaking so badly that half of it splashed onto the floor.

Mae shrieked, and a flood of fresh blood stained her nightdress crimson.

"Something's wrong," Bess whispered to Will. "You'd better go for a doctor."

He gave her a long-suffering glance, tinged with annoyance. "It would be plain to a blind man that something is wrong, Bess. And there isn't a doctor between here and Spokane. We're going to have to get through this on our own, you and me."

Bess was half-wild with panic. A part of her, one she wasn't the least proud of, wanted to run off into the distance, just the way Tom Jessine had done. On another level, Bess believed that she was strong enough to see the matter through, no matter what happened, as long as Will was there beside her.

Bess stayed, but tears of fear were trickling down her cheeks, and every time Mae screamed, the sound stabbed through her like a lance.

The rest of that day was hellish, and poor Mae seemed

about to be ripped apart by the pain. Finally, though, just at twilight, a tiny, still figure slipped from her tortured figure into Will's waiting hands. The baby was dead, and the sight of its poor, colorless little form fractured something in Bess, something she feared would never heal.

Until that moment, she had not truly known, beyond a superficial awareness, how ugly and unfair life could be, especially in remote places like that one, where medical help was unavailable.

Mae was unconscious but alive, despite an unbelievable loss of blood, and whimpering softly. The merciless pain, and perhaps the knowledge of her loss, seemed to have followed her even into sleep.

Moving like a woman bewitched, Bess gently washed the child and wrapped it in a silken shawl she'd once worn to parties in that faraway world she'd left behind so impulsively. During those moments, she'd have given anything to be back home in Philadelphia, still blissfully ignorant of all the great griefs that could befall a person.

Will had gone out to speak to Tom, and Bess heard the bereaved father's cry of despair—it was a lonely, wolf-like sound that she would never forget. When her husband returned to the cabin, Bess had bathed Mae as best she could and put clean blankets under her, and she was at the washstand, scrubbing her hands and arms with yellow soap. She hardly recognized the grim, frazzled woman staring back at her from the cracked surface of Will's shaving mirror.

He stood with his hands resting on her shoulders for a few moments, Will did, but then, probably guessing that no words had yet been invented to take away her horror or wipe the terrible memories from her mind, he turned away. After gathering the small, silent, motionless bundle up into his arms, he went out again.

Bess knew he was going to bury the baby, and she would have sworn her heart actually shattered with the knowledge, right then and there.

Why had she thought, even for a moment, that she'd

ever be strong enough, brave enough, for this wild, savage country?

It wasn't until Will had collected Bess, made her eat some of last night's supper, and led her to a bed he'd made for them both in the barn, that she gave in completely and dissolved into tears of fury and helplessness and brutal, stone-cold grief.

"That could happen to us," she sobbed into Will's shoulder, when she was finally able to form coherent sentences. "It might be *our* baby you're burying next time!"

"Shhh," Will said, holding her close. "Death can strike anywhere, Bess, you know that."

She shook her head, somewhat wildly. "In Philadelphia, we could have gotten a doctor!"

"Bess, please—you've got to stop tormenting yourself like this. What would or could have happened doesn't matter now; it's all over, and there's nothing for any of us to do but go on as best we can."

Bess was not mollified, but she was exhausted, and soon sank into a deep sleep fraught with dreadful nightmares. She dreamed that Will was shot by Indians, and that she held him in her arms while his blood soaked her bodice and skirts and turned the rich, newly tilled earth beneath them to crimson mud. In another, crueler scenario, they were happy, and the sun was shining, and there were two small daughters working with Bess in the garden, as well as two strapping sons trailing after Will in the fields.

Suddenly, a cloud passed over the sun, and the children closed their eyes, all four of them, and folded to the soil in a slow, graceful dance of death.

Bess awakened, shrieking, and Will had to hold her very tightly and talk very fast to calm her down again.

The next day, Mae opened her eyes, and when Tom gently told her that the baby had never drawn a breath, and was indeed buried some distance from the cabin, in the shade of a cedar tree, her soft weeping made new bruises on Bess's battered heart.

Mae was soon up and around, though she was far from recovered, physically or emotionally—Tom was anxious to reach Spokane before all the jobs were taken, and no amount of pleading on Will and Bess's part would make him stay.

Will burned the old mattress, and made a new one by stitching two old blankets together and stuffing them with straw from the barn. His mood was grim and quiet, and it was plain to Bess that he'd already guessed the direction her thoughts had taken.

Still, she had to tell him what she meant to do, straight-out and face to face. She owed him that much, and considerably more.

She packed just one small bag—her other belongings were stored on a loft in the barn, to be sent for later—and gave that to Tom Jessine to load in the back of his wagon.

Then she went to the mine, where Will had been working the morning through, even though he still had planting to do. Bess knew he wasn't swinging that pickax out of any desire to find copper ore, but because he needed brutally hard, violent work to vent his emotions.

She paused in the yawning mouth of the mine, letting her eyes adjust, for even though Will kept a lamp burning, the place was thick with shadows.

Her heart rose into her throat when she saw Will, shirtless and drenched in sweat, driving his muscles to the point of exhaustion as he swung the ax, striking the hard stone over and over again. The sound rang with despair.

"Will," Bess said softly.

He stopped and lowered the pickax, but he didn't turn to meet her eyes.

"You going now?" he asked.

Bess nodded, her throat thick. "Yes," she said. "I left your mother's ring on the table." She stopped again, willing herself not to break down and cry. "I wouldn't have been a good wife to you, Will. I'm not strong enough, or brave enough, and you deserve someone who can stand up to life just the way you do.''

Will ran one arm across his face and braced himself against the wall of the cave with his other hand, his head lowered. His voice was unusually gruff. ''Farewell, then,'' he said.

Bess tried to speak again; there was so much more she wanted to say, but she couldn't get the words out. Nor could she hold back her tears any longer, so she turned and hurried away, the branches of trees and bushes slapping at her face and grasping at her clothes as she passed.

Mae and Tom had already said their good-byes to Will, and Mae was resting in the back of the wagon when Bess joined her there. The other woman had been scarred by her latest tragedy, of course; sometimes she wept disconsolately, or rocked an invisible baby in her arms, or simply stared off into space as if she were yearning to be called home to some better place.

That day, however, Mae seemed to be in a lucid state.

Now that Bess was aboard, Tom went around to the front of the wagon, climbed up into the box, and shouted to the team.

''You're a fool, Bess Tate, leavin' a man like that,'' Mae said from the pallet Bess had improvised for her earlier, on top of a crate full of tack and harnesses. There was a disturbing singsong quality to her voice, but that didn't lessen the impact of her words. ''If you search from here to China, you'll never find anyone better than your own Will.''

Bess was in no position to defend herself sensibly, since her emotions were still running riot, but she knew one thing: she couldn't endure the hardships that came hand in hand with homesteading. If she had to bury Will, or a child they'd created together, the sorrow would kill her.

''I know there's nobody better than Will,'' she said with a note of petulance in her voice. Bess couldn't figure why self-effacing, retiring Mae had chosen now, of all times, to become assertive in her opinions. ''There's never been a better man and there never will be.''

Mae made an exasperated sound. "What are you going to do after this? Run home to your fancy folks in Philadelphia?"

Bess bristled. "Of course not. I couldn't go back there to live—I've changed too much. I'm going to write and ask Papa for money, and when he sends it, I'll open a rooming house in Spokane, where I hope to find some degree of civilization." She envisioned herself as a spinster of sorts; she could never marry another man, loving Will the way she did, and the future looked long and lonely. All the same, being lonesome would be infinitely preferable to standing next to the grave of someone she loved and aching to jump in after him.

"I still think you're a fool," Mae insisted. She was fading, though, drifting off to sleep. Since Bess had given the other woman a good many of her clothes, Mae was dressed comfortably in a warm, soft nightgown.

Bess had last ridden over that rutted road with Will in his wagon, and the very jostling motion of the Jessines' old Conestoga brought back memories. She tried not to think about all she was leaving behind and to focus on the future, but that proved impossible.

They must have traveled for an hour or thereabouts—the progress was excruciatingly slow—when suddenly Tom shouted and the ancient wagon lumbered to a stop. Mae slept on, but Bess's eyes were open wide as she listened to the nickering of several horses. The hair stood up on the nape of her neck, but she forced herself to grope her way past nail kegs and garden tools to peer out through the opening in the canvas just behind Tom.

Six mounted Indians, clad in buckskins and wearing paint on their faces, blocked the wagon's passage. They were carrying guns, and their expressions were hostile.

"What do they want?" Bess whispered to Tom. She was too fascinated to be really afraid, for the moment at least.

"I'm not sure," Tom answered evenly, keeping his eyes on the Indians. His right hand clasped the barrel of the rifle he'd wisely stowed in the wagon box ahead of time. "They're not talkin' any language I recognize. Best you get back inside, though. Fair-haired women get carried off sometimes."

Bess shrank back into the shadowy confines of the wagon, biting her lower lip and waiting. Every nerve in her body was alive with fear, but not because of the threat of being captured by savages, horrible as it was. No, it was Will Bess was worried about, alone up there at the cabin, unaware of the danger.

By the sounds from outside, Bess knew the Indians were riding around the wagon in a circle, probably assessing it. When one of them thrust aside the canvas flap at the rear of the rig and peered inside, Bess started and slapped one hand over her mouth to stifle a cry.

Faced with the actual possibility of capture, Bess was flooded with insight. If these men carried her off—certainly Tom had a rifle, but he was badly outnumbered—there would be no chance that she would ever see Will again. Furthermore, other men would use her, and even the thought of being touched by anyone besides her husband was intolerable.

Bess closed her eyes and sagged back against a packing crate when the Indian moved away from the tent flap.

There followed more talk, all of it angry, in that strange, guttural language. Then, miraculously, Bess heard the horses retreating, and blood-chilling shrieks trailed back to her on the breeze.

She nearly broke her neck getting to the front of the wagon. "Did they leave?" she demanded of Tom. "Which way were they headed?" Despite her relief, Bess's head was filled with images of those renegades catching Will off guard in the field and killing him.

Tom had taken a kerchief from his hip pocket, and he mopped his sweaty face thoroughly before answering. "Not toward Will's farm," he said, thereby proving himself to be more perceptive than Bess would ever have guessed. " 'Course, they could always double back. Why, I knew a fellow up in Kelly's Gorge who was just mindin' his own business when some injuns came on him unexpected. They done things to him that don't bear thinkin' about.''

Bess grabbed up her valise and scrambled toward the rear of the wagon.

"I'm going back," she announced, after jumping down and walking around to look up at Tom, there in the wagon box.

"We can't turn around now," Tom protested. "And you sure as hell wouldn't be safe walking the whole way."

Bess's priorities had changed greatly, due to recent reflections, and she would not be swayed from her purpose. "I don't care about being safe," she said. "I love Will Tate and I'm going back to him, and no Indians better dare to get in my way, either."

After offering thanks for the ride and a heartfelt farewell, Bess started back up the long, rutted road that led to Will and all the dreams the two of them shared.

Tom shouted for her to come back, and even called her a cussed female, but Bess just kept walking, and pretty soon Mr. Jessine had no choice but to move on. After all, night would come in a few hours, and it was important to keep moving.

Bess was footsore by the time Will's cabin came into view, but when she saw her husband in the field, she threw down her valise and ran.

Calvin came bouncing out to meet her, barking joyously, and the sound made Will stop and turn to watch Bess stumbling over the neat furrows that lay between them. He didn't move or smile, and for an awful moment Bess thought he'd changed his mind and didn't want her after all.

When she reached him, she was amazed and touched to the core of her being to see that his wonderful, mischievous eyes were shining bright with tears.

Bess stood a little distance from Will, feeling shy and hopeful and terrified all at once. "I love you, Will Tate. I want to stay here, if you'll have me."

He smiled, and opened his sun-bronzed, dusty arms, and Bess flew into them, hurling her arms around his neck.

"Thank God," he whispered raggedly. "Thank God." Then he gripped Bess's shoulders and held her away from him. A tear made a streak in the layer of dirt covering his face. "I love you, Bess, with my whole heart, but there's one thing that has to be understood right up front. I've had enough of this waiting business— I want a real wife."

Bess blushed, but her smile was so wide it wobbled and threatened to fall away. "Well, that's just fine," she said, sounding tremulous and brazen, both at once. "I happen to be wanting a real husband."

At last, the familiar grin broke over Will's face. He left the plow, horse and all, and with a great shout of jubilation lifted Bess into his arms and carried her toward the cabin.

Bess was breathless, knowing what was about to happen, but practicality intruded. "Will, we met up with some Indians along the road. They had horses and they could be headed this way."

Will's long stride didn't slow up at all. "It's plain they didn't hurt you. Are Tom and Mae all right?"

Bess nodded, marveling at all she felt for this big man, covered in sweat and field dirt and grinning like a schoolboy. "The red men only wanted to intimidate us, I think. Or maybe they thought the Jessines had seen enough trouble already—that would have been clear to anybody."

A muscle bunched in Will's jaw. "More likely they didn't see anything worth stealing," he said. "If they were on horseback, they must have been northern Indians."

Bess swallowed, feeling perfectly safe in Will's arms, even though she knew that was, at least in part, an illusion. "Do you think we'll see them again?"

Will shrugged. The wind caught his battered old hat

and sent it rolling across the yard, but he didn't make a move to retrieve it.

Instead, he carried Bess over the threshold of his house and set her on her feet with such suddenness that she swayed.

"Before we go any further," he said sternly, "I want to know what changed your mind. What brought you back here, Bess? Was it because of those Indians?"

Bess lowered her eyes for a moment, then met Will's gaze directly. "I didn't come back because I was scared, if that's what you're saying. No sane woman would have walked miles in the sun, with savages abroad, out of *fear*. No, Will, I came home because I realized that, whatever comes, joy or grief, I wanted to share it all with you. And if something bad was going to happen to you, then I wanted to be right here."

His stern face relaxed into another knee-melting grin. "In that case, Mrs. Tate, make yourself at home. I'll wash up a bit, and then you and I will begin our marriage proper-like."

Bess watched, fascinated and filled with love, while her husband took off his shirt, filled a basin, and splashed himself until he was at least partially clean. Then, to her surprise, he took her hand and led her outside, to a shady place on the far side of the cabin, where the grass was soft and fragrant.

"I want to love you here, Bess, this first time—on the land where we'll spend our lives."

She nodded, choked up with emotion and need, and closed her eyes in blissful surrender as Will slowly unbuttoned the front of her shirtwaist. One by one, and ever so gently, he took away her garments and tossed them aside, until she stood bare and vulnerable before him.

His whiskey-colored eyes moved over her in a worshipful sweep, and then he kicked off his boots, unfastened his belt, and came to her as Adam must have come to Eve, so long before, in that distant garden.

His kiss was gentle but hungry, and his skin felt deliciously gritty against Bess's, and she wanted him more desperately than she ever had, even when she'd lain beside him in his bed, and he'd driven her wild with his kisses and caresses.

This was different, somehow holy, and Bess was transfixed with happiness as Will bent to kiss the bare hollow of her throat. She threw her head back, welcoming him, and her blonde hair escaped its pins and tumbled down in a cascade.

Will kissed both her breasts, and made the nipples hard with wanting, and then his mouth came back to hers and together they made fire. Their tongues battled, and Bess felt herself being lowered to the summer-soft ground.

"I can't wait much longer," Will confessed raggedly, when a few passionate minutes had passed, "but I promise I'll be as gentle as I can."

Bess wanted to weep, so deeply did she love this fine man, and so tender was his concern for her. She tossed her head from side to side, her hair spread beneath them like a silken carpet. "No, Will—I don't want you to be gentle. I want to feel the full strength of your passion."

He didn't argue further, but simply positioned himself between Bess's thighs, found her entrance, and plunged inside her in one long, powerful stroke.

Bess felt pain, for Will was big and she had never received a man before, but there was a stirring of pleasure in it, too, a glorious sensation that started as a spark and grew quickly into a blaze.

She closed her hands hard on the sides of Will's strong jaws, drawing his head down and conquering his mouth with a primitive, fevered kiss.

Will groaned, and his magnificent body tensed upon Bess's. Then he began to move, slowly and rhythmically, in and out of her.

Bess broke away from the kiss, unable to restrain her responses any longer, arching her back and clawing at Will's shoulders in the ferocity of her wanting. She began to fling herself at him, and a loving warfare ensued, sweet and violent.

The odyssey ended at the exact same moment for both of them, with Will straining like a stallion claiming his mare, and Bess interlocking her legs with his and shouting his name in beautiful, shameless triumph.

They were both spent, and lay still while the sun waned and the first lavender shadows of twilight strayed across the gently swaying grass. Finally, with her head resting on Will's chest, Bess found the will to speak.

"What if those dratted Indians are watching?"

Will gave a shout of laughter and sat up, though he was careful to keep Bess within the circle of his arms. "Then they're damn rude Indians," he said. He kissed her. "Now, Mrs. Tate, I'd best get my britches back on and go bring that poor old horse of mine in from the field. You'll see about supper?"

Bess beamed at him. "Yes, *Mr*. Tate, I'll see about supper." She watched Will dress and walk away, though, before reaching for her own clothes.

Maybe she and Will had forty years of love ahead of them, she thought, and maybe they had a day, or an hour. Whatever time God had allotted to them, she intended to cherish it, and make the most of every precious moment.

Linda Lael Miller

I am honored to contribute a story to the Avon Books bridal collection for 1993, in part because I believe so strongly in the ideal of true love. It is undeniable that many relationships fail in these modern and skeptical times, but that is, in my opinion, all the more reason to keep the dream alive in the hearts and minds of people everywhere.

We must pursue the shining vision of perfect love, as well as perfect justice and perfect freedom, as distant as the goals may seem, for it is in *moving toward* these very objectives that we grow.

Long live true and glorious love.

The High Sheriff
of Huntingdon

Anne Stuart

The Prophecy

White and black they shall combine
Pure as snow, as blood-red wine
Flame and fire destroy them both
Death and rebirth, blood their troth
In thunder, rain, brought right again.
And all shall be as God's design.

1

"WHERE is my bride?" Alistair Darcourt, the high sheriff of Huntingdon bellowed, his voice thundering through the great hall, stopping all conversation mid-spate.

His second in command, Gilles De Lancey, glanced up idly, his beautiful blue eyes bright with malice. "Why should you care, cousin? It's not as if you've even seen the woman. Have you suddenly developed a lifelong passion for the wench?"

Alistair leaned forward and shoved the crockery from the table with a loud crash. The jug of ale upended on Gilles, who leapt to his feet with a curse.

"Don't try my patience," Alistair snarled. "I'm not a patient man. I've been a bridegroom for more than a week now, and I've yet to see my bride."

"She has a ways to travel," Gilles said, brushing at his damp clothes with maddening calm. "And you have no idea how she's going to respond to the notion that she's been married by proxy. After all, she's been in the convent of the Sisters of the Everlasting Martyr since she was fourteen years old. She might prove a bit intractable. You know how women are."

Alistair Darcourt leaned across the cleared table, fixing his cousin with his odd, golden eyes. Eyes that had been attributed to a legacy from his mother, the witch. Eyes of a madman. "She wouldn't dare," he said simply.

Gilles laughed. "True enough. Your reputation precedes you, cousin. No human, male or female, would dare to stand up to you. I imagine she'll arrive at Huntingdon any day now. It's always possible that she'll be worth the long delay.''

Alistair flung himself away in disgust. "I'm tired of waiting. I'm celebrating my wedding night, and it's a great deal too bad that my bride isn't here to participate.'' He gestured toward a plump young girl whose ripe breasts were spilling out of her soiled red dress. "You there,'' he said, snapping his fingers.

Gilles watched them disappear, no expression on his extremely handsome face. He'd planned to take that particular girl to bed that night himself.

But his cousin was the high sheriff of Huntingdon, and his power was absolute, not merely that of a powerful magistrate. He ruled with an iron fist, and Gilles was only his lowly vassal. The woman could wait. And then he would punish her for his disappointment. That thought made the wait all the more exciting.

Alistair's bride was going to be an interesting addition to the wild tenor of Huntingdon Keep. De Lancey seriously doubted whether a former holy sister would make much of a difference to the controlled chaos of Darcourt's household. Licentiousness and violence were part of their daily fare, as much as brown ale and coarse bread.

Once his impatience was satisfied, Alistair would take no notice of Lady Elspeth of Gaveland. He'd married her for a piece of land, and the none-too-pressing need for an heir. The bride would be lucky if she survived the first night of Alistair's rapacious demands, much less the first year.

It would make life very colorful, De Lancey mused, and usefully distracting, to view the marriage of a holy sister to a man who was generally considered to be the spawn of a witch and the devil himself.

Very distracting indeed.

Lady Elspeth had spent the first three days of the journey with her wrists tied and her mouth gagged. Her esteemed father had grown tired of her shrieks of fury, her calls on God to protect her, and ordered the gag for his own comfort.

By the fourth day she was so weary of trying to breathe through a knotted piece of silk that smelled and tasted of rancid venison that she subsided into a furious silence.

Her father wasn't lulled into thinking she'd accepted her fate. Although he'd been blessedly, peacefully free of his younger daughter's presence in his comfortable household for the last eight years, he hadn't forgotten the lamentably willful streak that ran through such an otherwise unremarkable girl. It was the willful streak that had decided him on the convent for her, that and her talent for managing. She was the kind of woman who did very well with power; even at the tender age of fourteen she'd managed to run his holding and see to his comfort with extraordinary efficiency.

She'd also put a damper on some of his more warlike behavior, and he'd decided the best place for a managing little dove of peace like Elspeth was the convent. Particularly when Sir Hugh still had two other daughters to dispose of comfortably.

The church had been satisfied with a relatively small dowry, and if Sir Hugh of Gaveland had missed the comfort Elspeth was adept at providing, his two younger daughters had made no more than financial demands on his good nature. At least they hadn't wanted him to change his ways.

But now he was stuck with Elspeth again, at least for as long as it took to deliver her to her bridegroom. He glanced over at her pale, furious face, and wondered whether he might live to regret this piece of work.

Not that he'd had any choice. Alistair Darcourt was not a man one argued with. When Gilles De Lancey had arrived with the sheriff's ultimatum, Sir Hugh had told himself that things could have been worse. The sheriff demanded only one of his daughters, and the fact that Elspeth was the least comely and already immured in a convent seemed to disturb her prospective bridegroom not one whit. Or so De Lancey had informed him.

Sir Hugh was a great deal more grieved to part with Dunstan Woods. It was a prime piece of forest, albeit a haunted one, and it held more venison than a household could go through in several lifetimes. Sir Hugh would have gladly married all three of his daughters to the mad sheriff of Huntingdon rather than lose the woods. But he'd had no choice in the matter, he knew that full well. He'd seen evidence of the sheriff's temper and determination; knew about the scores of dead; had seen the burned, blackened villages that had been left in his henchmen's wake. The sight of Gilles De Lancey riding into his stronghold had put the fear of God into him, far greater than any worry about tearing his daughter away from her vocation. Huntingdon had used anything within his reach to consolidate his wealth and power, including some of the most lawless men-at-arms ever known. Sir Hugh knew the alternatives—do what Darcourt demanded or see his own villages laid waste over some trifling excuse.

He preferred to salvage what he could in the face of the sheriff's seemingly insatiable lust for power and possessions. And indeed, Elspeth was no sacrifice at all.

He glanced over at his daughter, who was swaying silently with the motion of the slow-moving carriage. She was a changeling, this first daughter of his, with her tall, willowy body, her straight, flaxen hair and pale face. Her eyes were very blue, like those of his dead wife, and just as reproachful. Her usually gentle mouth was set in a grim, uncompromising line, and her narrow, graceful hands were folded in her lap.

She still wore her pure white habit, though it had clearly seen better days. She was quite strong, and the women attendants he'd brought with him had been no match for her when they tried to force her to change into the beautiful golden gown he'd taken from his youngest daughter Rowena. He hated to think of Rowena's reaction when she got her favorite dress back, after it had been trampled in the dirt by her sister's angry feet.

Sir Hugh couldn't decide which was the better part of valor—to have his men strip Elspeth, or to present her to her husband dressed in holy garb. Either choice made him shudder, and being a man who disliked unpleasantness, he simply refused to decide. If Alistair Darcourt insisted on taking his eldest daughter to wife, then he'd have to accept her in her present clothing.

The heavy traveling coach went over a bump, tossing Elspeth against the side, and her long pale hair drifted over her face. At least they'd managed to destroy her damned wimple during the fruitless battle for clothing. She looked like a witch herself, cool and white and angry. He wondered if Darcourt had any idea what he'd gotten himself into.

A year from now, his stubborn Elspeth would be quiet and tamed. That, or Darcourt would have killed her.

Sir Hugh viewed the possible loss of his daughter with a determined lack of emotion. After all, he'd lost three daughters in childbirth, and two sons. Nothing could grieve him after his second son had died at the age of two, taking his mother with him. He had daughters to spare.

Of course, there was always the possibility that Elspeth could succeed where no man had as yet. Perhaps she would be the death of the sheriff himself. She certainly had nearly been the death of her poor, beleaguered father.

They'd arrive at Huntingdon Castle by evening, if Elspeth didn't play any more of her tricks. Indeed, Sir Hugh fancied the fight had gone out of her, at least temporarily. She looked bone weary and accepting of her fate. It was a good thing she'd been in the convent since the sheriff's rapid rise to power. She wouldn't know the stories circulating about him.

She wouldn't know she'd been married by proxy to the son of the devil himself.

Alistair Darcourt, the high sheriff of Huntingdon, had a headache. Lord, he had more than a headache; he had the vilest remains of debauchery known to man. He lay in the huge bed, alone, naked, waiting for the pain in his head and in his gut to subside.

The girl hadn't pleased him. None of them had for the past weeks, even months. He'd ended up kicking her out of the bed, bored by her attempts to arouse him. The hot flesh of the females of the castle had ceased to interest him any more than the good wine, the dark ale, or the rich food. He'd lost his taste for things, and he could only blame his mother.

She'd warned him about excess, and he'd ignored her. He had little doubt the old witch had put a curse on him just to bring the point home. And since she was the only human being on the face of this earth who wasn't justifiably frightened of him, there was nothing he could do about it.

He rolled onto his back with a loud groan, feeling the pain racket around in his body. He was a fool to let sentiment get in his way. He ought to have Morgana killed. It would be a simple enough matter, and she was the only one with any power over him. Once she was dead, he'd be unstoppable.

But the idea of having his own mother strangled didn't sit well with the faint remains of a conscience he still possessed. Besides, he had a certain fondness for the old woman, despite her less than subservient behavior. At least she stayed out of his way, in the heart of Dunstan Woods.

Then again, it might not be a new curse that was troubling him. There was that other one, the prophecy hanging over his head since his boyhood, one that his mother had repeated to him with a singular lack of tact. She'd heard it from the voices of Dunstan Woods, the forest she called her own with a blithe disregard for its legal ownership. Indeed, no one was going to attempt to dislodge a witch. She'd told him the voices of the night had sang her the prophecy, and he rather wished she'd kept the bloody thing to herself, but the words haunted his dreams, as they had since he first heard the words by the light of a witch's moon.

White and black they shall combine,
Pure as snow, as blood-red wine,
Flame and fire destroy them both,
Death and rebirth, blood their troth,
In thunder, rain, brought right again,
And all shall be as God's design.

He knew those words weren't his mother's. She wasn't very good at rhyming her curses. He knew those words were his destruction, and while he wasn't afraid of death, or another human being, he was afraid of this prophecy. He had no interest in rebirth, or God's design. He liked things as they were, thank you. He liked things by his own design, not some nebulous God's. He rendered unto the hierarchy of the church exactly what he had to, and his new bride was costing him a pretty penny. He wasn't sure why Gaveland didn't want to part with the younger daughters, but he wasn't interested enough to ask. His new bride would provide him with heirs as well as any woman, and she brought him Dunstan Woods. Since she'd spent the last few years in a convent, at least she'd learned to be meek and silent.

He sat up, threading his fingers through his long hair, and began to curse in a low, vile voice. He had no idea what the prophecy meant, but some sixth sense inherited from his mother warned him that the time was close. The years of waiting were over. And he had no intention of surrendering to his fate without a fight.

He knew the knock on the door. It was De Lancey's, a very clever kind of knock, but then, De Lancey was a very clever fellow. The knock suited him, strong yet subservient, ever so faintly sly. Alistair trusted De Lancey as much as he trusted anyone in this world. Which meant that he trusted him not one bit.

"Go away," he shouted, throwing himself back down among the velvet bed-coverings.

De Lancey was a brave man, there was that to be said for him. He opened the door anyway, obviously prepared to duck if Alistair threw something at him. "I hate to interrupt you, cousin," he began.

Alistair picked up an empty goblet and hurled it across the room. It bounced off the door, rolling along the stone floor with a clanking noise. "Get out of my sight, Gilles."

"As you wish, sire." De Lancey's irony wasn't lost on Alistair. "I just thought I might inform you that your bride is about to arrive."

Alistair fell back among the pillows, considering the notion. Now that he'd finally gotten his way, he'd lost interest in the woman. "About time," he muttered. "What does she look like?"

"No one has seen her yet, though it appears she's still dressed in her habit."

"What?" Alistair thundered, furious. He threw himself out of the bed, storming toward his discarded clothes and dressing with a rapid disdain for the frivolities of fashion. "Why the hell is she dressed like a nun?"

"Cousin, she *is* a nun."

Alistair scowled at him. "Not anymore. The girl is my bride. The sooner she realizes it, the better."

"I imagine you're going to enlighten her. That is, if Jenna didn't wear you out."

"Jenna?" Alistair threw his cousin an irritated glance over his shoulder as he fastened his black hose. "Who is Jenna?"

He didn't miss the sudden darkening of Gilles's determinedly affable expression. But he had no interest in deciphering it.

"Jenna was the woman who shared your bed last night," De Lancey replied in a neutral voice.

"Eminently forgettable," Alistair muttered, running his hands through his thick hair.

"She didn't please you?"

"If it's any concern of yours, Gilles, she did not."

"I'll do something about it."

Alistair barely heard him. "See that you do," he said absently. "Where is my bride?"

"I imagine she'll arrive in the front courtyard."

"Very good. You may greet her, take her to her rooms, and get rid of her idiot father."

He'd managed to surprise De Lancey, a feat he seldom accomplished any more. "Where will you be?"

"Looking for someone a little more talented than Jenna. My bride has made me wait for days. Now it's time for her to wait."

"What rooms?"

A small, cool smile played around Alistair's mouth. "Where else? Put her in the haunted tower."

De Lancey's grin displayed his strong white teeth. "You never cease to impress me, cousin. Your bride will feel most welcome."

"That, dear De Lancey, was my intention." Alistair strode toward the door. Only for a moment did he consider that he felt far more lively than he had in months. Marriage certainly did wonders for a man.

Elspeth stepped out of the narrow coach, disdaining her father's supporting hand as her sandaled feet touched the ground. It was early evening, and the courtyard was filled with people. Most of them were men; all of them were evil-looking. Elspeth let her gaze drift coolly around her. The place seemed prosperous enough, but unconscionably filthy. The disarray seemed more from lack of organization than money. Elspeth considered herself very good at organization.

It took her only a moment to realize she was drawing close to accepting her fate. She glanced back at her father, but in the gathering gloom she could see only the anxiety on his bluff, hearty face.

She wasn't certain what was behind that anxiety. Fear that his oldest daughter would somehow shame him. Or fear that some harm might come to her. She suspected it was the former—she never had any illusions about her father's addiction to his own comfort.

"Lady Elspeth!" The voice was soft, musical, yet masculine, pulling her attention from the filth of the offal heap behind what must be the kitchens. She turned, and wondered for a brief moment whether this marriage would be quite so bad after all.

The man hurrying toward her with an affable smile on his handsome face was quite the most beautiful man she'd ever seen in her life. His golden blond locks hung to his broad shoulders, his eyes were a limpid blue, his jaw firm and manly, his gaze steady. As far as husbands went, her new groom was a great deal more appealing than she'd anticipated.

He took her hand in his own surprisingly small one, and brought it to his lips. Soft lips, faintly wet. A chill ran through Elspeth, and she told herself she was being an utter fool. She wondered whether she'd be expected to kiss her husband. Doubtless she'd be expected to do a great deal more before the night was out. At least she'd be doing it with a comely man.

"Welcome to Huntingdon Keep, my lady," the man she assumed was her husband said. "We've been most impatient for your arrival."

Elspeth controlled her instinctive snarl. "My marriage has been most sudden, sire," she said in a low voice not devoid of reproach.

"But not unwelcome, I trust." The golden beauty turned to her father, and there was no lessening of the amity on his handsome face. "You might wish to break your fast before you continue on your way, Sir Hugh. The sheriff has laid on a meal for you, so that your delay will be brief."

Sir Hugh's ruddy face darkened for a moment. "I'd planned to stay a few days. Make sure my daughter's well settled . . ."

"There's no need," the man said smoothly. "My master will make her welcome."

"Your master?" Elspeth said in a startled voice.

If the man knew what she'd been thinking, he didn't betray it. "The sheriff of Huntingdon. Your husband, Lady Elspeth."

She was good at hiding her feelings. She simply nodded her head. "And where is my husband?" she asked. in a cool, controlled voice.

No answer was forthcoming, but she hadn't really expected one. "He's charged me with seeing you safely settled in your new quarters. I'm his second in command, Gilles De Lancey, and your comfort is my most important task. You'll enjoy the rooms your husband chose for you. They have an excellent view of the countryside."

She heard a snicker from somewhere behind her, but ignored it. At least they wouldn't be putting her in a dungeon. "I'm sure I'll find them most charming," she said. She turned to her father, who was surveying their host with doubtful eyes. "You needn't worry about me, Father. Since you saw fit to marry me to the sheriff, I'm sure I'll be well provided for. Don't delay your trip on my account. My sisters await you, and Rowena will want her dress back." Destroying the dress had been her one victory, and she took pleasure in it. Her sister's vanity had been in full flower when Elspeth had left for the convent eight years before. It had probably reached unmanageable proportions by now.

She glanced at her father. She'd been taught forgiveness during her years in the convent, sweet acceptance of a stronger force. Her father was looking miserable, guilty, and eager to escape, leaving his daughter in the clutches of her new life. She wanted to kick him.

She didn't. Pulling her hand free from her new husband's henchman, she crossed the few steps that separated her from her father and kissed his ruddy cheek. "Don't worry," she said in a low voice. "I imagine I'll be fine."

Sir Hugh's troubled expression lightened. "You're sure, lass? I can always take you back."

"Could you?"

He frowned, obviously irritated that she'd called his bluff. "Your husband isn't a man to be trifled with, I'll warn you of that right now. Best learn to keep your eyes down and your tongue silent, or it will go hard for you."

De Lancey was beside her, taking her arm in his.

"Have a good journey, Sir Hugh," he said in a smooth voice.

Sir Hugh opened his mouth to protest, then closed it again with a sigh of defeat. "Take care of yourself, lass," he said heavily.

"That will be the sheriff's job," De Lancey said.

Elspeth didn't miss the look of acute dislike her father cast the handsome lieutenant. Her father was a simple man, accepting of most people. His dislike of De Lancey was both surprising and disturbing.

She didn't have long to consider it. Before her father had left the castle she was being led into the interior of the keep, through dark, odorous corridors lit with greasy tallow candles. Two people accompanied them—a plump, sour-faced woman and an armed guard with a fierce scar across his face. Elspeth wasn't sure which one was the more dangerous.

They climbed forever, up the winding steps of the tower. After the days in the carriage her legs were weak, but not for anything would she allow her energy to flag. She didn't want that mean-looking woman putting her hands on her. And for some reason she didn't want to give De Lancey another excuse to touch her.

They climbed until they reached the top. The door stood ajar on a large, cold chamber with an empty fireplace despite the evening chill, a huge bed, a chair, and little else. The few wall hangings were torn and dusty, and the entire place was filled with cobwebs.

"This is my husband's bedchamber?" she asked with creditable calm, gazing around her.

De Lancey and the soldier were already at the door, leaving the woman inside with her. "You won't be sharing your husband's bedchamber," he said. "Alistair thought you'd be more comfortable up here." He let his gaze drift around the unwelcoming room.

She refused to respond to his mockery. "I'm certain I'll enjoy it here."

De Lancey's bright blue eyes narrowed for a moment. "Someone will bring you a meal. I don't imagine your clothes will be of any use to you. That is, if they're all like the ones you're wearing.''

"I've been a holy sister for eight years.''

De Lancey's smile was charming. "You're in for a rude awakening.''

Elspeth stood very still as she heard the door close behind him. She heard the key turn in the lock. She could feel the woman's eyes on her, but not for anything would she allow her sudden panic to show. She moved to a chair and sank gracefully into it.

"Your husband's a madman,'' the woman said.

Elspeth lifted her eyes. "Is he?'' she said coolly.

The woman nodded, her mouth pursed grimly. "He's the spawn of a witch and the devil himself, and he's without mercy entirely. You'd be better off throwing yourself from yon window than enduring even a night of him.''

Elspeth leaned back. "That would be convenient, wouldn't it?'' she murmured. "He's got whatever dowry he wanted from my father, and he wouldn't have me interfering with his pleasures.''

"You won't be interfering with the sheriff. No one dares to. He'd have your throat cut as soon as look at you,'' the woman said, her eyes small and dark and mean.

"Charming. I get the impression I'm not due for a long and happy marriage.''

Her mild irony was lost on the woman. "Don't you care? Doesn't it bother you that you've been married to a monster?''

"Since there's nothing I can do about it, I don't propose to waste my time beating my breast about it. If he's not interested in having a wife, perhaps he'll allow me to live a separate life.''

The woman shook her head. "You have no idea, do you?''

She could hear the noise of his approach already, the ring of nailed boots on the stone steps, the raucous sound of laughter, both male and female. She didn't move, and she kept her hands folded in her lap to hide their trembling.

She knew his voice when she heard it. Clear and strong and arrogant, bordering on malicious. "Open the door, De Lancey. We want to view the lady of the keep."

It took all Elspeth's self-control not to move when the heavy wooden door was thrust open. All her self-control not to flinch, as the woman did, when the small group of people crowded into the room, staring at her.

He stood in the middle with a buxom redhead firmly attached to his side. Elspeth paid the woman scant heed, concentrating on her husband.

Black, she thought. Black from the top of his long hair to his deep velvet clothes. Like a raven, or a bird of prey. Or a sleek black wolf.

His mouth was wide and cynical, set in a face of narrow, suspicious elegance, and his bright eyes were a curious golden color. He wasn't nearly as handsome as his henchman, nor as broadly built. He was lithe, lean, wickedly graceful, whereas De Lancey was stalwart and beautiful. But next to the sheriff, De Lancey's blond good looks faded into insignificance.

She rose with all the dignity bred into her. Her white robes trailed on the filthy floor as she crossed to the mocking, cynical man who had married her.

She took his hand and sank gracefully to her knees in front of him. His was a disturbingly beautiful hand, with long, deft fingers, a tensile strength. He wore no wedding ring, of course. In its place was a strange golden ring, one that looked like a bird, with black stones for eyes. She pressed her lips against the back of his hand, then looked up at him.

"Husband," she said.

For a moment the rest of the room faded into oblivion as they stared into each other's eyes. His were dark, unreadable, yet there was no missing the fierce intelligence or the disturbing light as he looked down at her.

She knew what he would see. Pale, over-tall, too

skinny, and utterly insignificant. With luck he'd send her back untouched.

He smiled then, a cool, mocking smile that nevertheless had the force of a blow. "My lady wife," he murmured in return, taking her hand and pulling her to her feet. "Welcome to Huntingdon Castle."

And in the distance, Elspeth could hear De Lancey's muffled snort of laughter.

2

ALL in all, Elspeth decided three days later, married life agreed with her. For one thing, since that initial confrontation, she had yet to see her husband again. Apparently he found his auburn-haired companion far more enlivening, for which Elspeth breathed a heartfelt thank God. Or at least, she thought she did. Her life with the Sisters of the Everlasting Martyr had been cozy and communal, with long stretches for meditation and daydreaming. Her life in the haunted tower of Huntingdon Keep was just as peaceful, if a little more lonely.

For one thing, Helva, her sour-faced maid, was not the most cheerful companion. She was a great believer in doom and destruction, and she spent the long afternoons enlivening Elspeth's hours with tales of her new husband's perfidy.

"His mother's a witch, you know," she said, her strong, rough hands busy working on the ugliest tapestry Elspeth had ever seen. She could only hope it wasn't a present for her new mistress. Elspeth had a dislike of dead game, and Helva was using far too much blood red for her tastes.

"Is she?" Unlike most of the people she knew, Elspeth didn't believe in witches. She was also wise enough not to mention that fact too often, since people usually assumed that those who denied the existence of witchcraft were intimately acquainted with its workings.

"Morgana," Helva had said, chewing vigorously. "No one sees her nowadays, and a lucky thing that is. She'd put the evil eye on you, she would, and there'd be no saving you. I heard of a woman who ran into her in the forest by accident, and nine months later she gave birth to a monster."

"I wouldn't think she'd put a curse on her own grand-child," Elspeth said calmly.

Helva lifted her head to stare at her new mistress. "You'll not be saying you're already carrying a child?" she demanded, aghast. "The sheriff hasn't come near you in the last three days. I should know. I've slept at the foot of your bed."

"And snored quite loudly," Elspeth said.

"He hasn't touched you. If you're pregnant, he'll strangle you with his own hands. And you a holy sister."

"I'm not pregnant," she said, leaning back. "Not unless there's to be a second virgin birth." She could see that she'd shocked poor Helva to the depths of her mean little soul. "Don't worry, Helva. There'll be no early children from this marriage."

"Not until he has you," she replied.

Elspeth's fingers tightened into fists. She wasn't afraid of much in this life. She often insisted that her fearless-ness simply came from a lack of imagination, but in recent days her cool temperament was more an act than a reality. The thought of Alistair Darcourt putting those hard, beautiful hands on her was quite terrifying.

"Fortunately, he has yet to show much interest in me," Elspeth murmured. "I imagine there's no hurry. If I'm lucky, he's forgotten my existence."

"He's not the type of man to forget a thing. Special

powers, he has," Helva said, nodding her head. "He'll come to you when he's ready. And God have mercy on your soul."

"Helva, he's only a man."

"That's not what some people think. His mother's a witch, that's for certain, and we all know that witches cohabit with the devil. He's the son of Lucifer himself, you mark my words."

Elspeth was determined not to let Helva frighten her. "I don't believe in devils. Or witches, for that matter."

"You're a foul blasphemer, for all that you were a holy nun," Helva accused her. "If there's no devil, what use is God? Mark my words, the sheriff will teach you to believe in the devil. You'll wish you never doubted. He'll have you killed in your sleep, that he will, if he finds you displease him. He's done it before, and your position won't save you. Have a care for yourself, my lady."

A little frisson of horror swept along Elspeth's backbone. "What do you mean, he's done it before?"

"Not so's anyone would talk about it. But there've been women, women who've shared his bed and angered him. Men who've disagreed with him. Some of them were never seen again. Some of them were found like poor little Jenna just yesterday morning. Her throat was cut from ear to ear. That's how he gets his power. Anyone opposes him, they die."

"You mean he creeps around in the dark and murders people? I find that hard to believe," Elspeth said firmly, wishing she weren't so gullible.

"He doesn't need to soil his own hands. There are people, there are powers that do his bidding," Helva said darkly.

"He's not about to kill me. He could have just left me in the convent."

"That's as may be. If I were you, my lady, I wouldn't be wasting my time locked up here. I'd be planning my escape."

"What would your omniscient master say to that?

Aren't you worried about waking one morning with your throat cut?''

"I hate to see a poor innocent like you at the mercy of a depraved creature like the sheriff," Helva announced with righteous indignation.

Elspeth didn't believe her for a moment. In the past three days Helva hadn't shown the least bit of concern for her new mistress. "I hardly think escape is possible. I can't imagine who would take me in. The convent let me go quite willingly, my father would scarcely provide me shelter, and it sounds as if the sheriff has everyone too terrified to risk offending him. If I try to run, I'll be signing my own death warrant. I think it would be a much better idea to see whether I could advance my marriage. Whether I like it or not, I'm wed in the eyes of God and the Holy Roman Father, and if it's till death do us part then I'd like to do what I can to put off that eventuality. Could you send word to my husband that I'd like to see him?''

Helva's horrified intake of air was the only answer she needed. "You're as mad as he is," she wheezed.

"No," said Elspeth. "Just practical."

"He'll be the death of you, sooner or later."

"I'm not a great one for patience. It was ever my failing. If he's going to murder me, I'd just as soon he'd hurry up and do it. Maybe if I'm killed before he exerts his conjugal rights I could end up a martyr."

Helva's heavy brows beetled in confusion as she considered whether Elspeth was serious or not. Since Elspeth herself wasn't quite sure, it was an amusing sight.

She'd gone through the last three days in a kind of limbo, waiting for her husband, hearing nothing but nightmare stories about his evil excesses, stories that would have terrified a braver soul than she. Stories of such magnitude that some kind of numbness had set in. She wasn't about to believe the ghost stories Helva tried to frighten her with, either about the headless lady who wandered the north tower, or about her husband, purportedly a monster in the guise of a dark angel. She didn't believe in ghosts, devils, or witches. But she did believe in evil.

She was going to find out for herself whether her husband was truly as wicked as everyone insisted.

Not only did Helva snore quite loudly, she slept more soundly than anyone Elspeth had ever met, with the possible exception of Sister Mary Frances or Sir Hugh after his fourth bottle. It was a simple enough matter for Elspeth to extract the heavy key from the braided gold rope around her ample girth; simple enough to unlock the door and start down the winding stairs, following the noise of revelry and abandon.

It was a warm, clear night, with the moon shining through the slotted windows, enabling Elspeth to find her way slowly downwards. "It's a good thing I have eyes like a cat," she announced aloud, pleased by the companionship of her voice in the dark, lonely tower. "Otherwise I might end up with a broken neck at the bottom of the stairs, and my esteemed husband would have no need to murder me."

There was no answer, of course. The headless ghost, if she even existed, was of course silent, her head and her mouth long gone. Elspeth was still dressed in her habit, the rough white material tight around her slender throat, though she'd dispensed with the uncomfortable sandals and was now going barefoot. She only wished she could make a suitable covering for her hair. It hung down her back in a fall of silver white, giving her her own ghostly appearance, and she half-hoped she had the slightest ability to frighten Alistair Darcourt as much as he terrified her.

She could only guess that she was drawing nearer the great hall. The noise and the smell were overpowering. Roasted mutton, spilled ale, and fresh bread made a medley of scents that teased her nostrils, reminding her of the thin, tasteless gruel that had been delivered to the tower room for the last three days. Her stomach rumbled almost loudly enough to be heard over the shouts of encouragement, the shrill feminine laughter.

She could imagine what kind of debauchery was going on in the great hall, and for a moment she contemplated running away, back to the dubious safety of her tower room. And then it was too late. A crowd of people spilled into the corridor, and in the light of the torches high on the walls she could see the raven dark figure of the sheriff himself.

Two women clung to him this time, neither of them the buxom redhead. One of them was scarcely dressed; the other looked both dazed and slatternly. Darcourt seemed totally engrossed in the fairly obvious charms of both women, and Elspeth considered whether she might be able to fade into the darkness, letting them pass by without seeing her.

In the end the choice was taken out of her hand. Gilles De Lancey stood behind Alistair, and his sharp eyes had seen her hidden in the shadows. He touched the sheriff's shoulder, whispering something against the long black hair, and a moment later her husband had shrugged the women away with complete disdain and was advancing on her, moving like a huge black cat, sleek and graceful and impossibly dangerous.

His golden eyes impaled her, and she was only vaguely aware that the crowd behind him had disappeared at some unseen order, leaving them alone in the cavernous passageway. Her eyes dropped to the knife at his waist, and she wondered whether she'd made a very great mistake. And whether she'd live to regret it.

He stopped within inches of her, so close that she could smell the spirits on his breath, the heat of the fire, and a faint, intoxicating scent that was so foreign to her that she could only vaguely define it as male.

"Who the hell are you?" he demanded, his voice deep and arrogant and totally devoid of dissembling.

For a moment she was speechless with shock. She'd expected rape, murder, or any milder form of abuse from the man. She hadn't expected him to simply forget her.

''Your wife,'' she blurted out, then could have bitten her tongue.

His eyes narrowed as he considered the notion. ''I'd forgotten,'' he said simply. ''As it is, you'll have to wait your turn. I have other plans for tonight.'' And he presented his back to her, preparing to desert her.

Elspeth had learned to control her temper early on. Rage in a world ruled by men was usually a waste of time, and she chose to be diplomatic whenever possible. She looked at her husband's elegant, retreating back, and hissed, ''So do I.''

It was a mistake. She'd spoken softly enough, but the man had hearing like a cat. He whirled around, catching her shoulders in those hard, beautiful hands of his, and she knew her first moments of real panic. ''I don't believe I heard you correctly, my lady wife,'' he said in a silken, menacing voice. His long fingers flexed into her soft flesh, almost but not quite painfully. ''Clearly everyone has failed to warn you about me. You would be wise not to cross me. I have a temper that is not a pretty sight, and I can be most lamentably rash. If you wish to enjoy your married life, you'd best learn to watch your tongue.''

He did frighten her. Something about the glowing intensity in his golden eyes, the fierce strength in his hands, the warmth of his flesh burning into hers. What would happen if he touched her even more intimately, pulling her against his elegant, black-clad body? What would happen if he kissed her?

She lifted her head, fighting the panic, determined not to be cowed. The man was a bully, pure and simple. ''I never have,'' she said in a voice that barely shook.

His hand slid down her arm, capturing one of her strong white hands in his. ''Not the hands of a lady,'' he said, running his thumb over the palm.

''I wasn't a lady. I was a holy sister,'' she snapped, emotion seeping through. His touch unnerved her as no man's had. But then, there were few who'd dared to touch her in her cloistered years. "I was busy with works of charity."

"Something I know little about." He glanced up, and one might have thought the upturning of his wide, sensuous mouth was a sweet smile. One would have been wrong. "You may reserve your charitable acts for your husband. Your clothes displease me. Have them burned."

"I have nothing else to wear."

He shrugged. "I'll endeavor to see that you don't miss them."

Again came that insidious trickle of fear. She tried to tug her hand away, but his grip tightened. "I sent you a wedding ring," he said abruptly, his eyes narrowing in displeasure. "Did your greedy father steal it?"

She yanked at her hand again, but to no avail. "I had no need of a ring," she said. "I already have my own. I am a bride of God."

"Yes, but He never consummated the union."

She should have been horrified at the outright blasphemy. Instead, unfortunately, she laughed, a small, reluctant chuckle that she quickly tried to swallow.

The effect on Alistair Darcourt was electrifying. He stared at her with something close to shock, and he dropped her hand as if it was burning him. "White," he murmured in a dazed tone. "White and black."

She glanced down at her snowy white habit, at the white-blonde hair trailing down to her waist, to her strange husband's face, the darkness inherent in everything about him. "Poetic," she said. "And not without a grain of truth. Wouldn't you rather send me back to the convent? I'm certain you could keep the dowry. That way I wouldn't interfere with your pleasures."

He pulled himself out of his momentary trance with something akin to a snarl. "You won't interfere with me in any way."

"Then send me back." She couldn't deny the pleading in her voice, she who'd never pleaded in her life.

But she was dealing with a man who apparently prided

himself on being a stranger to mercy or pity. His smile was small, cool, and savage. "Not until I'm done with you," he said. And before she realized what he intended, he'd taken her shoulders and pushed her up against the stone wall, and his mouth was hot and wet and hard on hers.

Shock reverberated through her body, holding her still. Through the heavy folds of her habit she could feel the length of him, pressing against her, the solid strength of bone and muscle almost distracting her from the devastation of his mouth on hers.

This was nothing like the kisses she'd received from family and friends. Nothing like she'd ever imagined. His hand reached up and caught her chin, and his long fingers held her face still as he plundered her mouth, forcing her lips apart, pushing his tongue between her teeth. She tried to shove him away in sudden panic, but he was strong, much too strong, and she was no match for him. She couldn't breathe, her body felt crushed, and for the first time in her life she considered whether she might faint.

It was almost an abstract notion. She thought about it, and as she let her mind drift, his kiss changed ever so slightly. He slanted his mouth across hers, and there was less brutality and more wooing. No longer was she shoved against the wall; instead he'd slid his arm around her shaking shoulders, pulling her up against him, into his arms, and for a moment she began to melt beneath the unexpected sensuality of his kiss, the heat and strength of his body. She wondered if she was supposed to kiss him back, and how she would go about doing such a shocking thing.

"There you are, cousin." A familiar voice broke through the faint roaring in her ears. It took her a moment of dreadful coldness before she realized that he no longer held her. She was leaning up against the wall, her knees shaking, her hands trembling, her eyes still shut. She opened them to see the handsome, ever-smiling face of Gilles De Lancey.

Alistair had turned his back on her, and she had no idea whether he had suffered any reaction to the power of that kiss. "What do you want, Gilles?" he said in a bored voice.

"I hadn't realized you were . . . er . . . occupied. The ladies were asking for you. I can tell them you are otherwise engaged."

The sheriff waved a negligent hand. "That's the thing about wives, Gilles. They'll keep. Make sure she finds her way back to the tower with no side trips. And see what you can do about the crone who was supposed to watch her."

He sauntered away with deliberate nonchalance. Elspeth stared after him, furious, affronted, relieved. She put a trembling hand to her mouth, realizing it was damp and swollen. She never knew men kissed like that. She wasn't sure she liked it.

The only answer was to have him try it again. Half the problem had been that she wasn't expecting it, and he was furious with her. Maybe she could get him to kiss her again, this time when he wasn't angry, when she was ready for it, so that she could decide whether she cared for it or not. She suspected she could grow to like it very much indeed.

However, it seemed as if the high sheriff of Huntingdon was always in some sort of rage. And if that first kiss was anything to go by, it was uncertain whether Elspeth would ever be quite ready for it.

"Ready to return to your rooms, my lady?" Gilles De Lancey said in his mellifluous voice, all gentle concern.

Elspeth glanced up at him. He was a very handsome man, with his blond hair, his strong body, and his pretty face. Much more handsome than her husband. Yet Elspeth had not the slightest interest in seeing how his soft, slightly plump lips tasted.

"Ready," she said coolly, moving out in front of him with all the grace of a queen. They traversed the keep in silence, climbing the long winding stairs with deliberate care. It wasn't until they reached the landing outside her rooms that Gilles De Lancey finally spoke.

"I worry about you, my lady," he murmured, pausing to take her hand. His own hands were so different from the sheriff's. Strong and calloused, but oddly small against her own. "My cousin is not quite . . . sane. I would hate to see you suffer for his . . . oddities." He kissed her hand, and she had the strange urge to snatch it away. "I am at your service, good lady."

She was being foolish. De Lancey was the only friend she had in this castle of enemies. She didn't dare offend him. "There is nothing to worry about," she said calmly, letting her hand rest in his.

"Forgive me, my lady, but I know my cousin far better than you do, and there is a very great deal to worry about. I will do everything within my power to keep you safe. You must trust me, my lady."

She didn't. It was that simple. Despite his warm smile, his handsome face, and his earnest, affable manners, she didn't trust him at all. He reminded her of one of her father's stewards, a man who had been found guilty of crimes too numerous to mention, both financial and social, a man whose hideous death Elspeth didn't care to remember.

Carefully, gently, she detached her hand. "I appreciate your offer," she murmured, slipping in the door as Helva's snores continued to fill the landing.

"I won't let him hurt you," Gilles swore. "I'll help you escape before I would let that happen."

She should have jumped at the hint of an offer. If Alistair hadn't kissed her with that odd blend of anger and desperation, she might have.

But he had kissed her. And for the time being, she was in no rush to leave.

"Good night," she murmured, closing the door behind her.

And from beyond the heavy wood she heard his voice, shy and earnest and just faintly breathless, "Good night, dear lady." Just before he turned the heavy lock.

Alistair Darcourt was getting very drunk indeed. He'd dismissed the two women, though he had little doubt he could summon them back if he were to change his mind.

He wasn't about to. He had other things to deal with, things a great deal more troubling than climbing between the legs of a pair of overly willing wenches.

White and black they shall combine. The words rang in his head, and he stared at his reflection in the polished silver goblet with moody rage. There wasn't a soul much blacker than his was, from his midnight black hair to the black velvet clothes he favored, all the way down to his undeniably black heart.

And there wasn't much whiter than a flaxen-haired, white-robed nun who was still as pure and virginal as the day she came into the world. *White and black they shall combine*. He didn't want to combine with her. If he had any sense at all he'd send her back to the convent, as she'd begged him to.

It wasn't as if he had need of a woman. There were dozens around eager to do his bidding if he so much as nodded in their direction. And there would be no need to give back Dunstan Woods. They were his now, and if it hadn't been for his cursed mother he never would have bothered with this farce of a marriage but simply taken the woods from Gaveland in the first place.

But his mother was firm in her demands, and he was to get the woods by peaceful means, with no bloodshed. He was used to the shedding of blood, to taking what he wanted. It was a violent time, and the only way to rise in the world was to play the game. He'd risen rapidly in King John's employ through his cunning and daring, through his ability to make himself invaluable to his lord and liege. He'd been suitably rewarded. Huntingdon was one of the richest fiefdoms in all of England, and he was the sheriff, serving under King John's absent rule, and the profits and power that came to him were enormous.

Not that he was a man condemned to use brute force to achieve his ends. He was equally adept at threats and manipulation. There had never been a time when he hadn't gotten what he wanted; settled a score, waged a battle, and won. He was all-powerful, and he intended to stay that way.

But that pale, flaxen-haired wife of his was a definite danger. He wasn't sure what had made him kiss her. Maybe the thought that she dared stand there, still in her nun's clothes with the ring of Christ on her finger, not his ring. She looked at him out of those cool, defiant blue eyes, and he wanted nothing more than to take her. To show her that when he cared to exert his power, she'd have no chance against him at all.

But Lord, she was innocent! She'd never felt a man's tongue in her mouth, she hadn't even realized the almost painful arousal she'd burned into his body, something more overwhelming than he'd felt in months. Perhaps years. Her struggles hadn't daunted him; her acquiescence had only made the fire burn hotter. He wanted her with such a fierce, angry need that he didn't dare touch her.

He knew what he had to do. There were two choices. Perhaps three. He could send her back to the convent, out of his sight, and hope he'd never have to think of her again. It would be the sensible alternative, and if Sir Hugh were fool enough to try to take Dunstan Woods back, then bloodshed would be inevitable.

Or he could keep her locked away indefinitely. He'd almost forgotten her in the three days she'd been in residence—De Lancey had seen to it that he'd never wanted for distraction. But then he'd seen her, standing like a pure white flame in the shadowy corridor, watching him with those deep, dreamy eyes.

There was another choice, the most logical one, the one he most wished to avoid. He deeply distrusted his mother. She saw too much, knew too much, interfered too much. But she would know how to free him from the insidious effect his bride was having on his senses.

He had no intention of entering the bridal bed until he was more in command of himself. He could always rape her, but he'd never had much taste for the sport, leaving it to people like his cousin and his men-at-arms. He needed to bed her, briskly, efficiently, plant his seed in her cold, unwilling body, and then leave her. He didn't want to be tempted to bring that body alive, with his hands, his mouth, his tongue.

His mother could take care of it. She had a potion for everything. She was adept at concocting love philtres for the smitten men and women whose love was not returned, who dared to find her hovel deep in the woods. Surely she could produce a spell or potion that had the opposite effect.

But how was he to explain that her implacable, omnipotent son was feeling endangered by a slender reed of a girl. *"White and black they shall combine . . . And all shall be as God's design.*

What did it mean? His death? Or simply the destruction of the power he'd amassed for himself? She was his nemesis, he knew it deep in his bones, with the faint trace of intuitive power he'd inherited from his mother. Elspeth was his destiny. And he refused to submit to any destiny but that of his own choosing.

If he had to, he'd have her killed before he'd succumb to the ancient curse.

But for a moment, a brief, errant thought slipped into his mind, and he remembered the shock of her sweet, untutored mouth beneath his. And he wondered whether the reward might not be worth the danger.

3

"SHE'S eager for you," Gilles hissed in his ear.

The sheriff barely heard him. He was watching the men training. Savage, cunning animals, all of them, and quite the most elite fighting force in the whole of England. It was no wonder King John had chosen to reward him mightily. To do less would be to endanger his own security.

Not that Alistair had any desire to disrupt the throne. King John was efficient enough, so busy worrying about the nobles in the north that he left Alistair alone, the master of Huntingdon with no one to interfere. His men guarded the western border from the bloody Welsh, who were more savage than human in the opinion of most people. Only the savagery of Alistair's own men could match theirs.

"I doubt it," he said absently a few moments later. He turned to glance at Gilles. "I assume you're referring to my wife? I imagine the only thing she's eager for is a return to her nice safe convent."

"You might consider letting her go."

Suddenly Gilles had his full attention. "That's an odd suggestion, coming from you. What would you have me do, annul the marriage and send her back with an armed guard?"

"I'd make certain she arrived safely," Gilles said in a suitably modest voice, his blue eyes downcast.

"Would you now? I wonder." Alistair turned back to

watch the men. It was late afternoon, two days since he'd accosted his wife in that deserted hallway. He'd dreamed about her since. The first night he'd drunk so much wine he thought he'd ensured that he wouldn't think of her. Instead she'd haunted his dreams like a white ghost.

The second night he'd been sober, and accompanied. It had been no better. When he pushed the clothes off the girl's shoulders, he hadn't seen the overripe body, the sagging, full breasts exposed for his entertainment. Instead he'd seen *her* body, as pale and white as her habit. Pure, untouched, as he'd never been in his long, dissolute life. He'd ended up kicking the woman out, having lost his taste for her. If he were any less powerful, his recent lack of bed partners would bring forth gossip. As it was, no one would dare whisper about him. His capacity for women, for wine, for warfare, was legendary. If he had temporarily lost interest in the obvious pleasures of the flesh, it wouldn't reflect on his ability to control his men.

But sooner or later they would talk. Even his reputation couldn't keep wagging tongues silent, and women who were rejected tended to complain. He was feeling edgy, frustrated, nervy as a cat on a hot stone wall. He needed to take action, to do something about the white woman living in the haunted tower, haunting his mind more powerfully than any headless ghost had ever haunted Huntingdon Keep.

"There's no need for you to provide an heir," Gilles was continuing in his persuasive voice. "You're barely thirty, and it's my responsibility to keep you safe."

"Do you really think," Alistair said in a meditative voice, "that I need you safeguarding me?"

As always, it was his most gentle tone that had the strongest effect. He didn't need to glance at Gilles to know his ruddy color had paled considerably. "Of course not, cousin. I would hope my efforts on your behalf would not go unappreciated. I enable you to concentrate on other things while I—"

"I'm quite able to concentrate on a great many things at one time," Alistair said softly. "It's one of my gifts."

Gilles was never a coward. "It has always been the case," he agreed. "But I wonder about recently. This woman has unsettled you. I think you should get rid of her before she weakens you completely . . ." The words were strangled in his throat as Alistair hauled him up by his pale blue tunic and slammed him against the parapet.

"Your worry is misplaced, Gilles," he said in a silken voice. "And I have no intention of disposing of my lady wife, at least not yet. She amuses me."

"Alistair . . ." Gilles protested in a choked voice, and belatedly Alistair realized he was strangling him.

He released him abruptly, and Gilles put his small, strong hands to his throat, gasping for a moment.

"And if you think I might be likely to share her," the sheriff continued, "then you fail to appreciate my deep respect for the sacrament of marriage."

"You have no respect for anything, sacrament or not," Gilles said in a raspy, sulky voice.

"True enough. But what's mine, I keep. Until I'm ready to dispose of it. The girl belongs to me. Me alone. If you put your hands on her I will cut them off. Along with other parts of your anatomy if you feel like trespassing."

Gilles flushed, but he managed a shaky grin. "I wish you a long and happy marriage, cousin," he said.

"Better to wish me a short and fertile one." His rage had subsided to a more manageable level. "Which reminds me, Gilles. Have you come any closer to finding out what happened to the girl? Jenna, I think her name was."

Gilles's handsome face settled into lines of sorrow. "I haven't been able to discover a thing."

"They assume I killed her," Alistair said thoughtfully.

Gilles didn't bother to deny it. "Does that trouble you?"

"Not particularly. Having people afraid of me has its own special merit. Has my bride heard the rumors?"

"I imagine she has."

"So presumably she believes me capable of cold-blooded murder if a female fails to please me. All the better. Mayhap she'll lie there docilely enough when I take her virginity. I'm not in the mood for a battle," he added, summoning forth a convincing yawn.

"When will that be, Alistair?"

He hesitated for only a moment. "I hardly think it any concern of yours, cousin. But I imagine the sooner I take care of that little issue the better. You aren't, by any chance, enamored of the woman? Because I would find that extremely distressing. You're a useful man to have around. You accomplish things quite easily, and you don't bother me with petty details. I would be sorry to lose you."

"But if it came to a choice between me and your wife?" Gilles asked, and there was no missing the intensity in his usually smooth, light voice.

Alistair gave his most charming, ironic smile. "There would be no choice whatsoever, dear boy. It's simple enough to find a local bully, even one as deceptively charming as you are. A wife with an impeccable blood-line and Dunstan Woods is a great deal harder to come by. Besides, I think I might have developed a taste for pale virgins."

"You never have before."

Another man might have missed the fury burning beneath Gilles's determinedly light voice. Alistair never missed a thing. "But I've become jaded in my old age," he said. He moved away from the parapet. "There's a full moon tonight. A witch's moon, my mother used to call it." And he saw in the corner of his eye that Gilles hurriedly crossed himself.

"I have quite an evening planned for you, Alistair. There's a young woman in the kitchens, quite untried, but with the most spectacular set of—"

"I'm afraid I have other plans tonight, dear cousin," Alistair said. "You'll have to avail yourself of the kitchen maid this time. Keep her warm for me."

"What could you possibly have that is more pressing?"

Alistair gave him his sweetest smile, the smile that made strong men cower, the smile that he was purported to have inherited from his father, the devil. "I thought that would be obvious, cousin," he said gently. "I need to beget an heir."

Helva hadn't been best pleased with Elspeth's escape three days ago. She'd expressed her displeasure with one or two extremely hard pinches, a general air of hostility, and by refusing to talk to Elspeth.

Elspeth could have accepted that with equanimity. She longed for a brief moment of peace, of serenity. But Helva never left her, not even for a moment. Not when, after much pleading and arguing, she'd managed to secure herself a shallow bath of lukewarm water and dried rose petals. Not when she stripped down to her fine linen undergarments and waited pointedly for Helva to absent herself. Not even during her prayers, which were allowed to take far too little of the day.

It was a beautiful evening, with a warm summer breeze dancing through the windows, a full moon silvering the inky dark sky, the cries of night birds echoing around the tower. The heavy white habit had grown uncomfortably warm, and Elspeth had unfastened part of the overdress in a vain effort to cool off. Her husband seemed to have forgotten her existence once more, including his orders to burn her clothes, and for that she could only be grateful. She'd never been overfond of the heavy white habits favored by the Sisters of the Everlasting Martyr. But since her sojourn at Huntingdon Keep, she found the familiar garments comforting.

She heard the sound of the key in her door with complete disinterest. It was doubtless the servant come to remove her empty bowl of gruel. It was a good thing she'd never paid much attention to the overrated pleasures of the flesh. But after a week, gruel was getting slightly wearisome, particularly when the scent of roast mutton drifted up to her window on the warm night air.

Or her visitor might be Gilles De Lancey. He'd come every night and stayed a decorous few minutes, asking after her welfare, kissing her hand, making sure the glowering Helva was always within hearing. But Helva didn't see the burning promise in his undeniably beautiful blue eyes, didn't feel the pressure of his soft lips against the back of her hand. Helva didn't see what Elspeth could see full well: that all she had to do was ask and Gilles De Lancey would spirit her away from this place.

She still wasn't sure what had kept her there. Certainly not fear of her husband's revenge. Everyone had gone to great pains to inform her that Alistair was mad, dangerous, and evil. If even half the stories about him were true, her time on this earth was already nearing its end. Her only chance of survival was to escape.

But something kept her from taking that step. Perhaps it was her instinctive distrust of men who were too handsome. Perhaps it was the unforgettable disturbance of Alistair's kiss. Or perhaps she was simply going as mad as her new husband purportedly was.

She was standing in the window, staring out into the night air, when the door opened. She had come to a decision—if De Lancey offered a means of escape she would take it. To be sure, she'd been married in the eyes of God and her church. But she'd been miles away from the ceremony, completely oblivious, and while no one had ever suggested that a bride had to agree to being wed, it only seemed fair that she at least be consulted in the matter.

The Sisters of the Everlasting Martyr might offer her sanctuary from the sheriff's rage and her father's bullying, though they hadn't been much help originally. Or perhaps De Lancey himself knew of a place where she might hide until the sheriff forgot about his runaway bride.

She turned, plastering a welcoming smile on her face, one that froze when she saw the black figure of her husband filling the doorway.

"You there," he said contemptuously, nodding at Helva. "Make yourself scarce."

It was only slightly gratifying to see the sour-tempered Helva scurry to do her master's bidding. Elspeth held herself very still, leaning against the stone casement, considering whether she had any reason to be frightened. The answer, unwelcome as it was, was definitely yes.

"I'll wait outside," Helva murmured deferentially.

"You'll get your fat, useless carcass downstairs and out of the tower," the high sheriff of Huntingdon said in his cool, silvery voice. "I don't wish to be interrupted." And he started toward Elspeth, casually unfastening his doublet.

She was determined not to flinch, though she was suddenly very cold. This was her husband. It was her duty and God's will that she submit to him. Despite the disturbing power of his kiss, she had a hard time remembering that. "I wouldn't think anyone would dare interrupt you," she said in an admirably calm voice.

He didn't even bother to check to make sure that Helva had left. "People are surprisingly foolhardy," he said, watching her with his strange golden eyes. He glanced around him. "Is there any wine in this place?"

She shook her head. "I've been kept on a ration of cold gruel and brackish water since I've been here."

"And you haven't liked that one bit, have you?" he murmured, stripping off the heavy velvet tunic. He was wearing a loose black shirt beneath, and black hose, and his long black hair was a mane around his face. "You must have been used to more luxurious treatment in the convent."

"The accommodations were a slight improvement."

"I'll see to it that you're better fed," he said, not moving any closer. "You're far too thin for my taste. I prefer my women with curves."

Elspeth thought back to the various women in their states of undress, clinging to his arm. "So I've observed," she said dryly. "Why don't you come back in a few weeks and see if I measure up to your standards then?''

The silence in the room was ice cold, and Elspeth would have given anything to call back her mocking words. She'd always been a bit too free with her tongue, speaking her mind when she should have been meekly, dutifully silent, but now was the worst time of all to be flippant. Alone in a tower room with a purported madman who had total power over her body and her life, she ought to be quiet, subservient, and totally docile.

"Your mistake, my lady wife," he said in a soft, menacing voice. "There's only one thing I despise above all others in this world, and that is being bored. You've just made the fatal error of piquing my interest."

"Fatal." Her voice shook as she echoed that word.

His smile was scarcely reassuring. "So you've heard the rumors about me? That I'm the son of the devil, that I eat little children, that I murder anyone who displeases me."

"Actually I hadn't heard the one about the children." She slapped a restraining hand across her mouth, horrified at her own indiscretion.

His eyes gleamed in the evening light. "I might suggest that you shouldn't believe everything you hear," he said. "But I think I prefer you quivering in terror at the thought of my unregenerate evil. However, you don't appear to be quivering yet. I suppose I ought to do something about that." He started toward her.

There was no place to run. The thick stone wall of the castle was hard at her back, and not even to escape a madman would she throw herself from the battlement. She never had much use for melodramatic gestures, and life was far too interesting to be dispensed with so lightly. She pressed against the wall, feeling like a cornered doe as the ravening wolf advanced on her.

The touch of his hand against her neck made her flinch. Slowly, he began to unfasten the neck bindings of her habit, his golden eyes impaling hers, and she could feel the sudden, terrified pounding of her heart.

"I've never been interested in taking virgins," he said in a dreamy, almost abstracted voice as the overdress came apart beneath his deft hand, exposing the white column of her neck, the pale skin of her breasts. "But in your case it might prove entertaining." And he put his mouth against her neck, tasting the pulse that beat wildly there, his teeth sharp against the tender skin. The heavy white overdress fell to the floor at their feet, leaving her clad only in her light linen chemise.

She shivered, both hot and cold. She didn't dare move, afraid that if she did, it would bring her body closer to his. His other hand slid up the thin material, moving between her small breasts, pressing against her heart. She could feel the outline of his hand burning against her flesh as her heart clamored for something she couldn't begin to understand.

He lifted his head, looking down into her bewildered face with cool satisfaction. "Your heart is pounding, bride. Is it because you're frightened? Or is there some other reason why your pulse is racing?"

She tried to shake her head, to deny the evidence of her body, but his mouth caught hers, silencing her argument. He kissed her, deep and full and hard, allowing no escape. Indeed, she wasn't sure she wanted to escape. Her arms came up of their own accord, around his waist, and she held on, suddenly afraid she might faint. He was overwhelming, devouring, taking her mouth with a fierce hunger that stirred an answering, slumbering fire within her. She was no longer able to think. Even if her body was still within the tower room, trapped against the strong, powerful body of her stranger husband, her mind had taken that flying leap out onto the battlements. She made a helpless, longing little sound, half of panic, half of desire, and when he lifted his head this time there was no disguising the triumph in his amber eyes.

No denying the smug sound of his laughter, either, as he released her, moving back across the room and untying the laces of his shirt. "Get on the bed," he ordered casually. "This won't take long."

The haze of confusion vanished as abruptly as if someone had thrown a bucket of cold water over her. She leaned back against the stone wall, staring at him, her breasts rising and falling with a sudden burst of rage.

He glanced over his shoulder, clearly impatient, and his cynical, dark beauty made him look like the son of Lucifer himself. "What are you waiting for?" he demanded in a bored voice. "Take off the rest of your clothes and spread your legs."

He turned away from her, stripping off the black shirt and tossing it on the table. She took several silent, barefoot steps toward her husband, admiring the smooth, muscled line of his back, the sweep of shoulder, the elegant, wiry strength of him. Then she picked up the almost empty jug of water and slammed it over his head.

He went down hard. The rough crockery was in shards around him, and there was blood pouring from a gash in his cheek. His eyes were closed, and Elspeth stood over him, wondering whether she'd killed him. Widowhood might have a great deal to offer.

However, she didn't want to have killed him. She leaned down, putting a careful hand against his neck, feeling for a pulse. Within seconds her wrist was grabbed as his hand wrapped around the fragile bones like a manacle, hauling her down so that she was sprawled halfway across him, her face inches from his. "Bitch," he said. And he pulled her down so that her mouth met his.

She kissed him then. Inexpertly, furiously, with full abandon, opening her mouth to his, pressing her hands against his shoulders, pushing him down against the broken crockery and spilled water. When her tongue touched his, the shock almost made her veer away, but his hands were too strong, too determined, holding her in place as she felt the dampness seep into her thin linen skirts, felt the sharp bite of broken pottery beneath her knee.

She wanted to sink down against him, to drown in the spilled water and the heat of his mouth. It took every last ounce of pride, of self-preservation, to yank herself away from him before he could pull her back. And this time, when she coshed him on the head with a second pottery jug, he stayed down.

She didn't dare check to see if he still lived. The man was incredible—if she put her hands on him again, he'd probably have her spread-eagled beneath him. She scrambled away, eyeing him warily, terrified he might once again surge forward and capture her. But this time he was still, motionless.

She struggled to her feet as new panic swept over her. Her only chance was to escape before anyone saw her, before her bridegroom returned to his senses and demanded her blood. Huntingdon Keep was on the edge of Dunstan Woods—surely on a warm summer night she could find a place to hide. The woods were ancient, haunted, inhabited by demons and witches and sylvan creatures. She'd have to trust in the God who seemed to have deserted her lately to carry her safely through the dangers of the woods.

She reached for her discarded overdress, then let her hand drop. Pure white was not the best choice for someone who was trying to be inconspicuous. Instead she picked up the sheriff's rich black cloak and draped it around her slender body. With one last worrying glance at Alistair's comatose body, she turned to slip through the tower door, only to come smack up against Helva's solid body.

"He's not dead," the old woman said, more a statement than a question. "It would take more than the likes of you to stop him. He's got protection from his mother, the witch, and from his father, the devil. No puny little weakling like you could harm him."

"I haven't done badly so far," she said, her unrepentant tongue getting the best of her once more.

"He'll kill you. He'll cut out your heart and feed it to the crows," she hissed. "He'll slash your throat from ear to ear, just like poor Jenna, and the stones will grow red with your blood."

Elspeth controlled her queasy reaction to such an image with a strong effort. "Then I'd better get out of here,'' she said in a practical voice, wondering whether Helva would try to stop her. Wondering whether she stood a chance in hell of overpowering such a mountainous woman.

But Helva made no move toward her. ''Run,'' she said in a low, evil voice. ''It will do you no good. He'll find you. He will, or his mother. Your body will be staked out at the crossroads, the flesh flayed from your bones as a warning . . .''

''Please!'' Elspeth protested. ''I can imagine the rest.'' She pushed past her, starting down the winding stairs as quickly as she dared.

''He'll find you!'' Helva shrieked after her, standing on the landing like an avenging angel. ''And you'll die a slow, terrible death. You'll die, you'll die . . .''

Elspeth closed her ears to the shrieks and curses, increasing her speed in the dark tower. Though the noise from the great hall was thunderous, so was Helva's voice, and she didn't dare run into any of Alistair's men. Not if she hoped for a chance of escape.

She heard the noise of booted feet on the stone floor just as she reached the bottom of the stairs, and without hesitation she slipped into the shadows, grateful for the darkness of the pilfered cloak. She could see Gilles De Lancey's blond hair, his stalwart body as he paused at the foot of the stairs, and she almost called out to him, asking for help.

Something kept her silent. Something stilled her hand as she was about to reach out to him. Something quieted her tongue as he started a slow, steady climb to the tower. When he moved past the first circle, she stuck her head out to peer at him. The torchlight glinted on the jeweled knife at his belt, and she stared at the weapon with something akin to fascination.

All men were armed nowadays, even priests. Of course De Lancey would wear a knife at his belt. Why did she think there was evil attached to it, any more evil than came attached to most weapons?

He might have felt her eyes on him, or he might simply have been naturally cautious. He stopped, whirling around to stare down into the darkness an instant after she'd flattened herself against the wall, her breathing and her heartbeat stilled.

A moment later she heard his footsteps continue moving upward until the sound vanished into the darkness. A noise drifted down, an eerie, gurgling sound, like a voice being cut off mid-sentence. And then all was silent once more.

She didn't dare hesitate any longer. It took her precious minutes to wrestle with the heavy door, and then she was outside for the first time in almost a week, the soft night air swirling around her.

The moon hung high overhead, and the courtyard was deserted, shrouded in shadow. Elspeth moved swiftly and silently along the wall of the keep, running one hand against the rough surface to guide her way. She passed no one but a cat intent on his round of night hunting, and for a moment she thought of her husband, a sleek black cat looking for a juicy white mouse.

He wouldn't find her, not if she could help it. No one would find her deep in the heart of Dunstan Woods. She could hide there forever, and be safe.

The smoke was billowing forth, filling Morgana's rheumy old eyes, making her blink furiously. There were no tears, of course. Witches cannot cry.

She stirred, tossing a squirrel's tail into her loathsome brew, muttering beneath her breath in a cheery little singsong.

> *White and black they shall combine*
> *Pure as snow, as blood-red wine*
> *Flame and fire destroy them both*
> *Death and rebirth, blood their troth*
> *In thunder, rain, brought right again*
> *And all shall be as God's design.*

Morgana took a sip of the broth, shuddering with pleasure. "God's design, bah," she muttered. "This is no curse of mine. Bring me my daughter-in-law. Bring her to Dunstan Woods. Bring her to me." And the smoke whirled upward, giving her the answer she sought.

4

ALLISTAIR Darcourt was in a towering rage. When he finally staggered to his feet, blood still seeping from the cut on his cheek, his fury was so overwhelming that he thought he might explode.

"De Lancey!" he bellowed, stumbling toward the winding stairs.

"I'm here, cousin." De Lancey's cool voice came from the doorway. "Where's your bride?"

Alistair glared at him, wondering whether he might vent some of his rage by pummeling his sly cousin into repentance. "Wipe that smug smile off your face, Gilles," he snarled. "I'll deal with you later. Unless you can tell me you've already managed to stop her."

"I've seen no sign of her," De Lancey said. "Nor her maid."

"Saddle my horse." Alistair spat the words, yanking on his black shirt, ignoring the blood on his cheek.

"I'll go after her . . ." De Lancey began, but the sheriff cut him off.

"She's mine," he said. "And by God, she'll learn that before the night is out. I want no man touching her but me."

"It's late. You'll need help," Gilles protested.

Alistair's smile was chilling. "I have all the help I'll need," he said, and once more Gilles crossed himself in superstitious terror. "Get my horse ready."

De Lancey raced down the winding tower stairs, and Alistair followed him, his black shirt flapping as he stormed into the deserted courtyard.

"Where is she?" he howled to the night air.

There was no answer.

De Lancey appeared, leading the sheriff's huge gray gelding. Alistair leaped onto the back of the horse and wheeled around in the courtyard, almost trampling his cousin in his passionate fury. A moment later he'd raced from the castle yard and out into the windy night, without a backward glance.

Elspeth ran until her breath caught in her chest, and still she ran. The tree branches pulled at her clothes, tore at her hair, scratched her pale skin. The wind had picked up, tossing the huge, ancient trees overhead, and in the distance she could hear the faint call of an owl.

Dunstan Woods was no place for a woman alone at night. She had heard the stories all her life. It was no place for anyone unprotected from fairies and creatures of the dark. Demons lurked there, witches and trolls and monsters that stole the minds of innocents and left them witless, that tore flesh into pieces and left nothing but bones and bits of rag to bear witness that a mortal soul had once passed this way. Elspeth refused to panic. She ran, her bare feet bleeding, her long hair flying out behind her, her skirts tripping her up. The sheriff's cloak was slipping from her shoulders, and she pulled it more tightly about her, finding some odd comfort in the rich black folds. Had she killed him? Did she care? If she was a widow, her problems were now solved—until she was hunted down and killed for the murder of the high sheriff of Huntingdon.

The sky was dark and fitful overhead, the full moon dancing behind scudding clouds. Elspeth sank down on a soft hillock, trying to catch her breath, to still her panic. She'd escaped Huntingdon Keep, where the greatest danger lay. Surely she was safer alone in Dunstan Woods than in the possession of a madman. A man who now had every reason to want her dead.

Her father's lands lay to the north of the vast, sprawling wilderness, and he and his men had always done their best to skirt the forest, leaving it to the creatures of the night and their spawn. It had belonged to her father, but the demons had claimed it long ago, those seen and unseen, and Sir Hugh had been helpless to fight the powers of darkness. Indeed, her father had probably been just as happy to pass it over to Alistair Darcourt and let him deal with it. A fitting dowry for the son of the devil.

Shivering, Elspeth huddled beneath the rich velvet cloak. She was hungry, bone-weary, and dangerously near despair. All that she had trusted and counted on in this life seemed to have abandoned her, and now her husband probably lay dead from her own hands. Yet the taste of his mouth lingered disturbingly on her lips.

She should move deeper into the ancient forest, clutching the silver cross that hung to her waist beneath her thin linen chemise for whatever protection it might offer. The sheriff's men would come after her, hunt her down in the forest like a wild boar. She didn't want to die at the end of a dozen lances.

· She pulled herself to her feet, gritting her teeth against her moan of pain. Deeper, deeper into the woods. was where safety lay. It was her only hope.

The trees were thick, ancient, with no discernible path in the inky darkness. She could rely only on her instincts. They pulled her to the left, into the very heart of the forest. To the left lay warmth and safety, she was sure of it. Forcing herself, she moved onward, deeper and deeper into Dunstan Woods.

She lost track of time. It might have been minutes or hours or days that she wandered through the darkness where no light penetrated. All she could do was keep moving slowly onward, stopping only to catch her breath before continuing. When she first saw the dim light coming toward her through the thick mist, she stopped, fighting back the superstitious terror that filled her weary heart. She'd heard tales of goblins luring people to their doom in the swamps with faerie lights. What sane, God-fearing person would be here in the heart of the forest, welcoming her? If she had any sense at all, she would turn and run back the way she had come.

But she no longer had any sense. She no longer cared if she lived or died. She was too weary to continue. If that light signaled death, then she was ready for it. The fight had left her.

It was no faerie light. No will-o'-the-wisp luring her to her doom. It was simply a cottage; small, rough-hewn, overgrown with moss and branches, and the light spilled out into the darkness like a beacon.

"There you are, my pretty," a cracked, ancient voice said from within. "I'd almost despaired of you finding your way here." Silhouetted in the doorway was a broad, bent-over figure.

Once more her superstitious terror threatened to overcome reason. "Who are you?" she demanded, her voice deceptively steady.

The woman stepped back slightly, and Elspeth could see her face. It was beautiful, for all that it was aged and seamed. Her hair hung to her waist, thick and gray and flowing; her clothes were soft and shapeless; and her eyes were bright and intelligent and curiously light in her narrow face.

"There's nothing to be afraid of," she said in that hoarse, gentle voice. "I've been waiting a long time. For a while I was afraid you were too strong for me. I rather think you would be if you weren't so weary. What have they been feeding you up at the castle?"

It was too confusing. She didn't bother to think about how the woman knew she was from the castle, or how she'd happened to end up here. She simply answered the question. "Thin gruel."

The old woman's mouth curved in a mocking smile,

one that was eerily familiar. "How like them," she murmured. "Come in, child, and let me give you something to eat. I've a pot of stew on the hearth. It should put some strength back into you."

Elspeth followed her into the tiny hut. It was small, cramped, redolent of herbs and other foreign smells that were strangely beguiling. For the first time since she'd been informed that she was now a married woman, Elspeth felt curiously at peace.

"He's not a bad boy, you know," the old woman said as she handed Elspeth a bowl of rich, dark stew. "He has a temper, that's for certain. He always was too quick, even as a child. He doesn't suffer fools gladly, and the world is full of fools."

The stew was thick and savory, warming the empty knot in Elspeth's stomach. She ate slowly, dreamily, content to watch as the old woman brought a basin of herbed water for her bruised, bleeding feet. "*Who* doesn't?" she murmured, the spoon scraping the bottom of the earthenware bowl.

The woman moved beside her, dried flowers in her hand, and she shook them over Elspeth's weary head. "My son, of course," she said. "Your husband."

For a moment Elspeth's lassitude lifted. "You're the witch," she gasped.

"Not the most tactful thing to call your mother-in-law," the old woman said, "but accurate, nonetheless. You may call me Morgana. Unless you'd prefer something a little more intimate."

Elspeth tried to move back on her seat, but there was no where to go and she was feeling so deeply weary. "I don't believe in witches," she said, wondering if she still meant it. "How did I get here?"

"I summoned you. After all, I couldn't let you wander around the woods with no protection. These are dangerous times, and despite everything, Alistair is too trusting. My son would never forgive me if I let anything happen to you."

"He wants to kill me himself."

"Nonsense. And you seemed like such a level-headed girl. Don't believe all the things that are said of my son. To be sure, he's a bit wild, a bit dangerous, perhaps even a bit mad. But you could be the making of him." And she began to mutter something beneath her breath, something Elspeth couldn't quite hear, about white and black, blood and snow, and fire and rain.

She tried to struggle to her feet, but her body refused to obey her, and her mind began to spin. "I won't . . ." she murmured, and felt herself begin to fall moments before Morgana's unusually strong arms caught her with surprising gentleness.

"Of course you will," she said. "There's no denying the prophecy. It came to me on the wind the day he was born, and there was no turning away from it. Let me make you some of my special tea, and you won't mind it at all."

"No!" Elspeth screamed, but the sound came out as an agonized whisper. She raised her hands to ward off any more potions. "You've poisoned me."

"Of course not. Just given you something to help you sleep. You're weary, child, you need your rest. We have time. Alistair won't realize where you are until tomorrow at the soonest. When you awake I'll brew you some tea."

"No," she cried again, but there was no sound. She was helpless to resist as Morgana pulled her through a curtained doorway into a small, dark room.

Moonlight streamed through a window in the roof, illuminating a bed covered with velvet and animal skins. The old woman pushed her gently down on it. Elspeth felt herself fall from a great distance, landing on a cloud of luxuriant softness, her hair spilling around her as she stared up at the creature who was her husband's mother.

"Rest now, my child," Morgana murmured, pulling a velvet throw around her, and for one bizarre moment she reminded Elspeth of Sister Mary Frances.

Elspeth needed to escape. She was tall for a woman— perhaps she could climb out the hatch in the roof and disappear into the forest before Morgana realized she was gone. She had to lull the old lady into thinking she was asleep. Indeed, her eyes were so heavy it would be a relief to close them, even for the moment needed to trick the old woman. She let them drift shut, only for a moment, only because she had to.

When Morgana checked on her three hours later, she was still sleeping. She'd shifted in her sleep, making small, whimpering sounds at the back of her throat, and Morgana contemplated trying to tip some of the warm tea down her throat. She truly didn't expect Alistair to realize where his runaway bride had disappeared to, not for another twenty-four hours at least, but it would never do to underestimate her formidable son.

The cottage was deep in Dunstan Woods. The wind seldom penetrated beneath the ancient oaks, but overhead the leaves shivered in the warm summer breeze, and the night-flying birds called out a warning. The moon had risen, a witch's moon, one whose silver light would lead Alistair straight home. She didn't dare wait.

The tea didn't take long to brew. Indeed, she had more call for love philtres than anything else. There was no challenge in making them, no challenge at all in seeing a reluctant maid succumb or a reserved swain fall prey to the lures of the flesh. She'd grown tired of brewing them. But this was a special instance. Her son's destiny lay sleeping in the bed, and Morgana had no intention of waiting any longer. There were too many things out of her control. This much she could ensure.

Elspeth lay sleeping more lightly now as the dark hours of the night passed. Her white-blonde hair spread around her like a bridal veil, and her face was still and beautiful in repose. She really was a lovely child, Morgana thought dispassionately. Willful, too. There weren't many brides who'd cosh their husbands on the head and take off into the depths of a haunted forest. Particularly when her husband was the feared high sheriff of Huntingdon.

She'd do well for him. She'd bear him strong babies. Her body was narrow, but her hips were wide enough to bring forth boys, lots of them. Girls as well. And Morgana was ready to be a grandmother. Kneeling on the soft bed, she took Elspeth's narrow shoulders in her strong hands and pulled her upright.

"Here, sweeting," she crooned, reaching for the bowl of tea. "Drink this, and you won't be troubled by these silly doubts. Just a taste, love, and things will be ever so much better."

Elspeth felt herself struggle through the fog. She opened her eyes, staring up into the woman's face with dawning horror. "Leave me alone," she gasped.

"Just a sip, and you'll never—"

"Get away from her, you hag!" The high sheriff of Huntingdon stood silhouetted in the doorway, his voice thundering through the tiny cottage.

"Fine talk for a son." Morgana rose with affront. "Here I am, trying to help you, and—"

"Trying to dose her with your filthy potions," Alistair said, shouldering his way through the narrow doorway. He looked dark and dangerous in the cramped quarters of his mother's house, with his inky black hair, his wild eyes, his tall, lean body vibrating with rage. "I don't need your help."

"You haven't done too well yourself. You've had her for almost a week now and she's still as pure as the day she was born."

"Did you touch her?" His voice was icy cold, deadly, and as Elspeth lay still and silent she wondered that his mother didn't quail before him.

But the old lady was apparently the only human, or semi-human, not afraid of Alistair Darcourt. "Of course not," she scoffed. "I don't need to check her maidenhead to know she's still unawakened. What have you been doing the past week, boy? Toying with your harlots? I want grandchildren."

"You'll have them," he said, as his eyes met Elspeth's in the dimly lit room. There was an unspoken threat in them, and Elspeth wondered where her panic had disappeared to. Perhaps she'd run so far and so fast that she could no longer fight him. If he wanted children she'd at least be expected to survive another nine months in reasonably sound health. She should take that as a good sign.

She could see the cut on the side of his face. It hadn't been stitched, and it would leave a scar. One more thing he could blame on her, she thought, wanting to burrow down beneath the heavy fur throws that covered the soft bed.

He moved further into the tiny cottage with disdainful, elegant grace, entering the tiny bedroom, dwarfing it with his presence. "She's the one, isn't she?" he asked almost absently. "White and black . . ."

"Aye," his mother said.

"She'll destroy me."

"Perhaps."

He moved closer to the bed. He was wearing a loose black shirt, black hose, and tall black boots. He looked impossibly evil, and his black-gloved hand reached out and took a strand of her pale hair. "She hardly looks lethal," he said in a deliberately bored voice, which was belied by the gleam in his golden eyes.

"If you can't bring yourself to touch her," his mother said, "I could brew some tea for you as well. That is, if you don't want her . . ."

"Oh, I want her," he said softly, dangerously.

"Well," said Morgana briskly, taking a step back. "Then that's that. The marriage bed awaits you. I've strewn it with lavender and tansy, wolf's bane and thyme. There'll be a son from this night's work, you'll see."

He didn't even glance her way. Slowly, he began to strip off his heavy black gloves, watching Elspeth's expressionless face. "Make yourself scarce," he said. "I've no desire for an audience."

"I expect you know what you're about," the old witch cackled. "I've got some herbs to gather, and they're best picked by the dark of the moon. Mayhaps I'll head over toward the north ridge. Won't be back till midday, or later.''

He nodded, untying the laces of his black shirt, not moving as the door closed loudly behind the old woman. In the still night air they could hear her voice mixing with the sounds of the other night creatures, the cry of the owls, the song of the nightingale. She was muttering something in a singsong voice, familiar words that made no sense, and slowly they faded away in the distance. And Elspeth was alone with her husband in the heart of the haunted forest.

He sat down heavily on the end of the bed, not touching her, and began to strip off his tall riding boots. She watched him, wondering if there was any way to distract him from his goal. When he'd pulled off his boots he rose and looked at her, and the moonlight speared down through the hole in the roof, silvering his midnight hair, giving the odd and totally inappropriate effect of a halo.

"Why should I destroy you?" she asked suddenly, the first words she had dared speak.

They halted him in his steady advance. "You couldn't," he said flatly.

"Then why are you afraid of me?" Not the wisest choice of words, but Elspeth had recently discovered she was very far from wise. After twenty-two years of practical, celibate living, during which she'd viewed men as overbearing tyrants who were at least tolerated, and at most shunned entirely, she was suddenly irrationally vulnerable to a man who seemed to combine all the worst traits of the species. She hadn't needed Morgana's love philtre. She'd somehow managed to imbibe one of her own.

"I'm not afraid of anyone," he said. "Or anything of this earth or of other dimensions. My mother has seen to that. It's part of my power."

"What about your father?"

He laughed softly. "Ah, yes, my father. The devil himself."

"Was he?"

His smile was small, bitter, but not without amusement. "I doubt it. If he were, I wouldn't have had to work so hard to get where I am. Indeed, I think Morgana would remember if she'd managed to couple with the prince of darkness himself. As it is, I imagine he was a handsome tinker. Or even a landholder. Someone who has no memory of what a tumble with a witch brought forth."

He was standing very close to the bed. She could smell the herbs, mixed with the warm summer breeze and the wondrous scent of the forest. She could lie back and stare at the moon and try not to pay attention to what he was doing.

She glanced at him with a doubtful expression. "You are going to do it, aren't you?" she asked, wishing she could think of a better euphemism but failing entirely.

"To be sure."

"And it's going to be painful. I know that full well. Even with the tenderest of husbands, the act is uncomfortable and degrading for women. It was ordained that it be so, so that we should pay for the sins of Eve. And you aren't," she added boldly, "the most tender of husbands. I imagine you're planning to pay me back for coshing you on the head with the water jug."

He finished untying the shirt and stripping it from his strong, lean body. "Oh, I don't know if I need to go that far. Mind you, I'm not about to turn my back on you again. But there are other ways of ensuring your future obedience."

She looked at him uneasily. She could endure pain. Her father had been quick to punish a recalcitrant child, and the Sisters of the Everlasting Martyr had lived up to their name. She could kneel for endless hours on a cold stone floor, eat nothing but thin gruel and drink foul water. She could survive ritual whippings and beatings and solitude. But she wasn't sure she could survive that intent expression in Alistair Darcourt's golden eyes.

"Please," she said, sudden degrading fear filling her voice.

His smile was unnerving. He knelt down on the bed, leaning over her, and he seemed huge and dark and smothering as he blocked out the moonlight. "Indeed, I do just as I please," he said softly. "You're my destiny, Elspeth of Gaveland. Or my curse. It remains to be seen."

"I don't understand."

He picked up a strand of her hair, running it through his long fingers, and once more she was mesmerized by the beauty of his hands. "White and black, they shall combine," he murmured, bringing the long, silky strand to his lips. "Pure as snow, as blood-red wine." He moved down, settling his long body over hers, the heavy animal furs between them, and yet she could feel him, every bone, every muscle, hot against her tender flesh. She could feel the pulse racing through her body and his, feel the thudding of her heartbeat matching his. "You're white," he whispered, his voice only a breath of sound. "Pure as snow." His mouth drifted over her brow, her cheekbones, and she shut her eyes, feeling his lips feather against her trembling lids. "And I'm black and evil, darkness personified." He kissed the tender spot behind her ear, his tongue hot and damp.

She was having trouble breathing. She was burning up beneath the mountain of covers; she was freezing cold, shivering. "Is that all there is to the prophecy?" she choked out.

He levered himself off her, his mouth traveling down the side of her neck as he tugged the heavy covers away from her. "Flame and fire destroy them both," he whispered against her skin. "Death and rebirth, blood their troth."

"It sounds a little extreme to me," Elspeth said in a strangled voice as his hand drifted back up the front of her thin linen chemise. His skin was hot, burning through the material; the fingers deft, sliding, reaching, and covering her breast. She jerked, arching off the bed in silent protest, but he simply pushed her back down, holding her shoulders pinned against the rough mattress as he put his mouth where his hand had been all too briefly.

She'd never paid much attention to her body before. Her breasts had simply been there, small, in the way, with no earthly use since she'd never intended to marry or bear children. Alistair's mouth on her breast was an astonishing revelation of feelings so overwhelming that she wasn't sure she could bear it. His mouth pulled at her, hotly, wetly, his tongue circling her nipple, and she felt it grow hard in his mouth, felt her other breast tighten in sympathetic response, and she made a low, helpless sound of protest.

He lifted his head to look down at her, and there was no denying the cool triumph in his eyes. "I thought it a little extreme myself," he said, his slightly labored breathing the only sign that he was moved by her reaction. "But there's hope. The prophecy goes on." And he touched the tip of his tongue to her other breast through the thin cloth, dampening it, teasing it, and Elspeth found she was clutching the heavy velvet beneath her, fisting it in her hands to keep from touching him.

"Does it?" She couldn't even manage a pretense of calm. Her voice came out in a quiet gasp.

He sat back, staring down at her, and his sleekly muscled chest was rising and falling more rapidly now. "Yes," he said, reaching to the high neckline of the thin chemise. With one deft yank he tore it open, ripping it down the middle from neckline to hem, pulling it away from her pale white body, exposing it to the moonlight and his cool, deceptively dispassionate gaze. "In thunder, rain, brought right again," he said, and it took a moment before she realized he was still quoting the prophecy. "And all shall be as God's design."

"God's design?" She watched him, wary, waiting. "You think God has blessed our union?"

"Or the devil. It makes little difference to me." He reached out and took her heavy silver cross in his hand. "Is this supposed to protect you from the likes of me?"

"It's failed."

"Indeed." He yanked on it, and it broke free, to disappear in the tumbled bedclothes. He leaned forward and put his mouth hard against hers, his body pressing against her undressed one, pressing her into the warmth of the bed, settling between her long legs. She searched for one last defense, one trace of pride, of self-discipline or protection. None remained as she released her grip on the bed beneath her and put her arms around his neck, slanting her mouth beneath his, kissing him back.

His chest was hot, sleek, and strong against hers, his arms muscled and tight with self-control. He slid his hand between their bodies, between her thighs, and her shock this time was even more intense. As was his determination, his fingers threaded through the thick tangle of hair, touching her, pressing against her, sliding deep into the damp, throbbing heat of her. She tried to tighten her legs, but he would have none of it. He was strong, more than she realized, and very determined, and he broke the kiss, panting slightly. "Don't fight me," he said. "I don't want to hurt you."

She stared up at him, baffled, her mouth tingling, her body trembling with fear and longing. "Why not? I thought you enjoyed hurting."

He cursed then, a low, foul curse that made her flinch. His eyes were mesmerizing, watching her. "Do I terrify you, then?"

She wanted to say yes. And yet if he left her now, sent her back to the convent, she might be very willing to die.

She just managed a smile. "Do I terrify you?" she countered in a rough whisper.

He shook his head, more in wonder than denial. "You astonish me," he said. And sliding down the length of her body, he shocked her still further by putting his mouth between her legs.

She tried to hit him then, but he ignored her, his hands clasping her thighs, holding her in place. She squirmed against him, but it only brought his mouth tighter, hotter against her most secret places. This was his revenge, his torment, his degradation, and she hated him, she hated him, she . . .

Began to like it. Her breath caught in her lungs as a tight, spiraling sensation curled in the pit of her stomach and fanned outward. She wanted to cry, she wanted to scream, she wanted to die; she wasn't sure what she wanted except for him to stop, to keep on. Her heels dug into the pile of velvet beneath her, the soft breeze danced across her skin, and she knew he had to be the son of the devil himself. And then her body exploded, splintered into a thousand stars, and she heard a low, animal-like shriek, and knew, to her shame, that it came from her own throat.

He slid up, covering her, his hips resting between her legs as he threaded his hands through her thick hair. "Did you like that, my pretty little nun?" he murmured.

She couldn't catch her breath. Her face was wet with tears, and she was lost, confused. "You're a monster," she gasped. "A devil, a cruel, rapacious beast . . ." His mouth stopped hers, and without hesitation she kissed him back, fiercely, her arms sliding tightly around his neck, holding him hard against her body.

He lifted his head. "We're not finished yet," he said. "No," she answered.

He levered his body away from hers a few scant inches, and she felt chilled to the bone. "No?" he echoed in a mocking, reasonable voice.

She was a good, holy woman, a keeper of the faith, one who had never blasphemed in her life. "God damn you," she said. "Yes." And she pulled him back against her.

5

ALISTAIR Darcourt had bedded many women in his life, so many that he'd long ago lost count. But all those faceless, nameless women hadn't had the power to move him like the small, slender woman lying beneath him, staring up at him with a mixture of anger and desire.

He threaded his long fingers through her silken hair, molding her skull beneath his hands. So fragile, so deceptively meek. He'd been a fool to marry—he simply should have taken Dunstan Woods for taxes. Sir Hugh of Gaveland wouldn't have dared to defy him, and the woman who'd already begun to twist and turn into the fabric of his life would still be safely in her convent.

He could send her back. Keep her immured there, away from the sight and touch of men. It was almost an acceptable alternative. As long as no other man touched her, he could forget about her.

But priests were men, despite their vows of celibacy. And he'd seen his own cousin's reaction to her.

He had two choices. He could bed her, take her body until he tired of it. He could get sons from her, wear her out, and then send her back to her convent, or stash her in one of his own smaller houses, away from temptation. Or he could save himself a great deal of trouble and simply kill her now.

People said he had witch's eyes: his mother's eyes, an eerie golden color that could look into people's souls and ferret out their secrets. They were nothing compared to the limpid blue of his pale bride. She lay beneath him, her white-blonde hair fanned out around her. The cool intelligence in her eyes disconcerted him, particularly when she made no effort to disguise her confused desire for him.

"Are you going to do it?" Her voice was little more than a whisper, but unnervingly calm.

He pressed against her, wondering if she even recognized his arousal. From the faintly shocked expression in her eyes, he decided she had a fairly good notion. "I thought we already made that clear."

"I mean are you going to kill me?"

It was almost enough to unman him. "What makes you say that?" he countered cautiously. He wanted to kiss her. He wanted to cover her soft mouth with his and drink deeply. He wanted her body, her heart, and her soul.

"Do you deny you were considering it?"

"I don't have to deny anything." Damn his mother! She must have dosed him when he didn't realize it. There had to be something to explain his mindless reaction to the pale wench. "You're my bride, and my property. I can do anything I please with you."

She didn't even flinch. Lying naked beneath him, her body still racked with faint tremors of reaction from what he'd just done to her, she accepted that information without pause. "If you're going to kill me, you might consider doing it now."

She sounded so reasonable as she discussed her death. He didn't want her reasonable. He wanted her panicked, silly, dismissable. Not fascinating. "Why?"

"Because if I die a virgin there's a good chance I'll be considered a martyr. Perhaps even a saint, eventually."

"Ambitious, aren't you?"

Her lashes were surprisingly dark, fanning over those clear blue eyes. "I always have been. At the very least, if I die a virgin I'll be guaranteed a swift entrance to heaven."

"Sorry," he said.

"It would be very simple," she said, her voice low and persuasive. "You're strong—you could just squeeze your hands together and crush my skull. Or you could strangle me—it wouldn't take long."

"Bloodthirsty little creature, aren't you? Haven't you heard—I prefer to use a knife?" he mocked, thinking of the young woman he'd turned from his bed, who'd turned up dead two days later.

His meek little bride winced. "I'm not over-fond of blood," she confessed. "Perhaps your mother could poison me?" She sounded hopeful.

He laughed then, unable to help himself. "By the time she got around to it you'd no longer be a virgin." He rocked against her again, lightly, reveling in her little shiver of response.

"Wouldn't you rather kill me?" she asked in a sweet, plaintive voice.

"I'm afraid not." And he gave in to temptation, setting his mouth against hers, thrusting his tongue inside her mouth roughly, trying to still that ember of desire that burned brightly, paradoxically within her.

He didn't want her to want him. She was dangerous, all purity and gentleness and seductive goodness wrapped up in a serene, beautiful body and a betraying sense of humor. He'd never met a woman who dared to mock him. He doubted there was anything Elspeth of Gaveland wouldn't dare.

Not even taking the black, dangerous high sheriff of Huntingdon into her bed, her body, her heart. She had a heart, there was no doubt of that. It was beating madly against his. She would take him and love him and weaken him. The thought was unbearable.

He put his hands on her throat, feeling the pulse throbbing. It would be so easy. He lifted his head to stare down at her, trying to will himself to take the blackest, darkest step of all.

He couldn't do it. It was already too late. Instead, he put his mouth against her neck, biting it lightly as his hands slid down and covered her small, perfect breasts.

He felt the fight leave her body, the acceptance wash over her, followed by a new tension when he lifted his body off hers and stripped off the rest of his clothes.

She was right. There would be pain for her the first time, but she seemed untroubled by the notion. She was damp from her own desire and from his mouth, and she writhed when he touched her, his fingers testing her.

She was small and tight and virginal, and he couldn't wait any longer. He nudged her legs apart, resting in the cradle of her thighs, and told himself he didn't care, he'd simply thrust into her and claim his release.

For some reason he wanted to kiss her ear. She had perfect ears, small, delicate. He nibbled one soft lobe and felt her shiver.

He pushed into her, slowly, knowing he was hurting her. Her breath came in shaken little pants, yet she arched off the bed to meet the slow, steady thrust of his hips. Her arms were tight around his sweat-slippery back, clinging to him, and the little choking sounds she was making were ones of desire as well as pain.

He said what he never thought he'd say. "I don't want to hurt you." The words were torn from him in an agonized gasp as he tried to control the powerful urges of his body. His muscles were clenched in iron will, his forehead was beaded with sweat, and he didn't know how much longer he could stand the torment.

"It's all right," she said in a whisper. "I'm your wife. Your destiny. Take me." And she arched up against him, seeking him.

He lost control. For the first time in his life, a woman overpowered him. He thrust against her, breaking through the frail barrier of her maidenhead, sinking deep into the glorious tightness of her. She cried out then, a small, soft sound, and he kissed her, his mouth covering her face, drinking her tears, tasting her soft mouth.

And then he noticed she was still clinging to him. Instead of turning cold, she was holding him tightly, and if her desire had faded with the pain, it hadn't vanished entirely.

He was at her mercy, yet there was one way he could still salvage his pride. He reached between their bodies and touched her, hearing her choked gasp with male satisfaction.

He began to move then, thrusting slowly deep inside her, determined not to lose all control until she'd grown used to it. He half-expected a protest, but she was beyond speech, melting in his arms, meeting him in the eternal advance and retreat of desire.

And then he could no longer protect her. Red-hot passion ripped away the last of his epic self-control, and he surged into her, again and again. He barely heard her choked gasp, the tiny scream of fulfillment he'd managed to wring from her. And then he followed, thrusting into her tightly welcoming body, giving her his essence, his soul, his love.

Giving her his son.

Elspeth lay on her back in the soft bed, Alistair spread-eagled over her. His long black hair was entwined with her silver-blonde strands. His arms and legs were wrapped around hers. His body still rested within hers.

The soft breeze dried the tears on her face. She hadn't even realized she'd cried. Her breathing was taking forever to return to normal, and her heart was still racing, shuddering inside her.

Was it a witch's curse? Or was it an act of God? It didn't matter. She lay in her husband's arms, and was content.

It couldn't be true. Surely she wasn't content to lie beneath a dangerous madman. She was deliriously, wildly happy, alive for the first time in her life. It made no difference if he was everything they said he was. She must be fully as mad as he was purported to be. She loved him.

Destiny, he'd called it. A prophecy. She was too pragmatic to believe in such things. Too pragmatic to believe in falling in love with a dangerous man who happened to be her husband.

But practicality didn't alter things. She loved him. And she would let nothing short of death tear her from his arms. Until he grew tired of her.

He would, of course. Helva and Gilles had been more than happy to tell her stories about his legendary appetite for women and debauchery. An untutored nun would soon lose all appeal to a man of his sophisticated tastes, and while she'd been willing to do anything he wanted, she doubted he'd have the inclination to teach her more. For all she knew, this last hour might be all she'd ever have of him.

The memory, and something else. The old woman had told him there'd be a son from this night's work. Elspeth had no doubt about that whatsoever. Whether it made sense or not, she knew. She carried his seed, his child, within her.

She heard a guttural, unromantic sound, and she turned her face from the moonlit sky to stare at him. He was asleep, obviously sated. She must have pleased him, at least a little bit. How could something that was so astonishing, so cataclysmic, be mundane for him?

Of course, he'd done this a thousand times before. And suddenly Elspeth, who considered herself relatively meek and charitable, wanted to scratch the eyes from every woman who'd ever lay beneath him. Starting with that brazen hussy who had been clinging to his arm when she first saw him.

How had the prophecy gone? *White and black they shall combine*. They'd certainly done that, in marriage and then in the flesh. *Pure as snow, as blood-red wine*. Not so pure any more. It had gone on with something about death and destruction, fire and thunder and rebirth.

His head lay on her shoulder. He looked like a boy, innocent, unsullied. Not the creature of legendary rages and awesome excesses. Simply a man. Her man.

For however long he chose to keep her. And when he dismissed her she'd have little choice but to take her leave, go back to the haven of the Sisters of the Ever-lasting Martyr, or wherever else he chose to send her. And she'd go meekly.

Like hell she would! She'd been brought up to be dutiful; in this life she had little choice. When she'd proven too willful, too intelligent for her father's peace of mind, he'd simply shipped her off to the convent.

She wasn't going to be dismissed again. She wouldn't relinquish Alistair Darcourt without a fight. While she'd taunted him with it, she had never actually believed him capable of killing her. After last night, it would be the only way he'd be able to be rid of her.

His destiny, his prophecy, his curse. She was his. And she wasn't going to let him go.

The room was filled with the faint gray light of approaching dawn. Elspeth shivered, trying to burrow deeper into the soft furs, only to find them ripped unceremoniously from her.

Her husband towered over her, dark, distant, clothed once more in black. "Get dressed," he said in a lazy tone that she didn't quite believe. "It's time to go back to the keep."

She reached for the covers, but he jerked them out of her way. She had to content herself with wrapping her arms around her body. "I don't have anything to wear," she said in a husky, practical voice. "You ripped it off me last night."

He looked momentarily daunted. He wheeled around, disappearing into the outer room, and a moment later he was back, a blood-red dress over his arm. He tossed it on the bed, barely glancing at her. "It'll be too big for you," he said. "It must have belonged to my mother in her wild youth. It will have to do."

Still Elspeth didn't move. She hadn't expected tenderness or affection. Being brought back to the keep was almost more than she'd hoped for. But that didn't mean she didn't still long for something else.

"Are you witless?" he demanded, deliberately trying

to goad her. "Was the shock of last night too much for your delicate sensibilities? You'd best get used to it. I'm far from through with you."

She couldn't help it. A smile wreathed her face. "Good," she said flatly, reaching for the dress, which lay across her bare feet.

His hand caught hers, hauling her naked body up against his. He threaded one hand through her thick hair, holding her face still as he pressed her up against his rich velvet clothes. "You've heard the stories, Elspeth of Gaveland. Only half of them are true. But that's enough. I'm the son of the devil, in spirit if not in fact, and running away from me was probably the wisest thing you ever did. You just didn't run far enough."

"Should I run now?"

"I'd find you," he said flatly. "You'll never get away." And he pressed his mouth against her, a hard, possessive kiss.

She endured it patiently, waiting. And to be sure, his mouth softened, coaxing, teasing, nibbling at her lips, and his tongue danced across the soft contours of her mouth, seducing with an unexpected tenderness.

Then he thrust her away from him, as if he suddenly realized what he was doing. "I think you're the witch," he said in a cold, bleak voice. "Get dressed, or I'll haul you back to the keep naked."

She picked up the dress, holding it against her, waiting for him to leave. "Is there any water? I need to wash."

He didn't answer as he strode from the room, from the cottage, leaving her alone. She climbed off the bed, feeling stiff and sore, only to find an earthenware bowl of herb-scented water on the rude table by the wall. A soft dry cloth lay beside it, and when she touched it she realized the water had been warmed for her.

She washed and dressed as swiftly as she could, marveling at her sense of well-being. The dress was long enough, but built for a more voluptuous frame, and it had a tendency to fall off her narrow shoulders and expose far too much of her chest. Not that there was much to expose, she thought with deliberate self-mockery. She was hardly endowed with the necessary curves to delight a man.

But the odd thing was, she felt as if she were. She felt voluptuous, sensuous, ripely sexual. Her extremely bad-tempered husband would probably laugh if he knew what she was thinking.

When she stepped out into the main room, he was lounging in the doorway, staring at her with a brooding expression on his dark face. "There's tea for you. Drink it swiftly, and we'll be on our way."

She glanced at the small bowl on the table, the steam drifting upward. "Where's your mother?"

"Somewhere on the other side of Dunstan Woods, I suspect. Why do you ask?"

"I wanted to thank her for warming the water for me. And for brewing the tea. But you must have done it."

He obviously didn't like it that she'd taken notice. "Anything to speed you along," he snapped. "I need to get back to the castle. I'm not certain I trust De Lancey."

"But he's your cousin," she said, shocked. "Your closest friend! Your second in command."

"Exactly," he said dryly. "Drink your tea."

She took the small bowl in her hands, noting that they trembled slightly, and brought the hot brew to her lips. It smelled sweet and savory, and sudden doubts assailed her. She set it back down again without touching it.

His mockery was back in full force. "Afraid I'm going to poison you, Elspeth? It wouldn't be very practical of me, and I am a very practical man. What would we do with your body? If I want you dead, you'll know it. It's simply an herbal brew to strengthen your blood and ease your discomfort."

"You reassure me," she said with a faint mockery of her own, ignoring the blush that rose to her cheeks as she reached for the tea and took a small, delicate sip. It warmed its way down her throat, spreading more well-being through her body.

"Of course I could be lying to you," he said casually, stepping into the small room. "It could be a love philtre. Just to keep you pliant and amenable, I could have had my mother brew you a potion that would convince you that you were in love with me."

"There's no need for a potion."

She might as well have hit him. His indrawn breath was sharp and pained, and then silence filled the room. She drained the tea, set the bowl back down on the rough wooden table, and met his golden eyes. Fearlessly, she told herself.

And then he was prepared to fight back. "You're too easy, Elspeth of Gaveland. One night with me between your legs and you're ready to believe you've found true love. You're in for a rude awakening."

She pushed her long hair from her face. "You mean you're not always so tender and romantic?" she teased gently. "I'm doomed to be disillusioned?"

"Don't!" he said, and there was real pain in his voice. Elspeth's teasing faded. "Don't what?"

"Don't make me care for you. It will come to a bad end." And without another word he strode from the cottage, leaving her to follow after him as best she could.

She sat behind him on the gelding, her arms around his waist, feeling the warm skin beneath the thin black shirt. She rested her head against his broad back, closing her eyes and listening to the sound of his breathing, the steady beat of his heart as they rode through the woods.

It was further into the day than she would have thought when they finally emerged from the darkness of the virgin forest. The sun was already past noon, and the sky was bright blue, marred only by thick white clouds that presaged a harsh storm to follow on the blessing of hot summer air.

She could feel the eyes watching as they rode back into the castle yard, but no one said a word. The air was almost unnaturally silent, broken only by the sound of the animals, the chickens running loose, the whinny of a horse, the squeal of a pig.

Elspeth wanted to keep her face buried against Alistair's back, but her pride had always been a source of difficulty for her, and for the time being, she was the lady of the castle. She lifted her head, looking about her, hoping to convey a mixture of friendliness and self-assurance, neither of which she was feeling.

It happened so quickly it was over almost before it began. The people of Huntingdon were still and silent in the presence of their lord, but the children were not quite so wise. A filthy, tow-headed child streaked out of an outbuilding, shrieking with laughter, unaware of the tension in the courtyard. He raced directly in front of Alistair's gray gelding, and Elspeth tightened her grip, turning her face against his back, horrified at the certain collision of beast and child.

It took amazing reflexes to avert it. It took considerable strength to make the horse rear away from the child, to bring him down again out of harm's reach. It took a certain amount of caring for the unknown child even to make the effort.

Alistair stood up in the saddle, and she released her stranglehold around his waist, letting out her pent-up breath when she realized the danger was past. Alistair had averted certain tragedy. "Whose brat is this?" he bellowed.

The child had fallen in the dust, and with tears rolling down his filthy face, he was crying, almost as loudly as the sheriff was shouting. No one moved to comfort the child, everyone too terrified of their lord and master to move.

Elspeth didn't hesitate. She slid off the back of the restless horse and scooped the child into her arms as she struggled to keep the over-large dress decently around her. Alistair cursed as he wheeled the horse away from them, and then he jumped off the back of the gelding, arrogantly certain that someone would take control of his horse.

He came up beside Elspeth as she held the weeping child, not touching her. "I asked a question!" he thundered. "I expect an answer."

In return came Elspeth's voice, loud and clear. "Stop it, my lord. You're scaring the child."

The shocked silence was deafening. The assembled inhabitants of Huntingdon Keep watched with horror, expecting to see their new lady struck down.

There was no reading the expression in Alistair's golden eyes. For all she knew, he would do exactly as his people feared he might. But she wouldn't let him hurt the child. She tightened her grip, and the filthy little mite shrieked in protest.

"You might show a bit more gratitude to your lady," Alistair told the boy in a deceptively mild voice. He took the struggling child from Elspeth's grip, and she was too shocked to try to hold on.

The child looked up at the sheriff in fascination. "Devil," he observed pleasantly, and began to howl again.

Alistair set him carefully on the hard ground, and as the child raced off on chubby little legs, he gave him a good swift smack on his bottom. And then he caught Elspeth's arm in his, a little more forcefully than was strictly necessary, but she decided she'd let it pass this time. "Come along," he said beneath his breath, giving her a jerk.

She stumbled after him, plastering a calm expression on her face. He was in a fury, that was certain, but then she was growing used to his furies. As she struggled to keep up with him she stumbled over the dress, almost falling.

He caught her expertly when she hadn't even thought he was aware of her. He scooped her effortlessly up in his arms, striding into the keep as his body vibrated with tension.

Gilles De Lancey was awaiting them, a welcoming smile on his handsome face, a guarded look in his perfect blue eyes. "We wondered where you were, cousin," he said pleasantly.

Alistair fixed him with a cool stare. "Were you unable to discharge your duties during my absence, De Lancey? You could be replaced."

De Lancey flushed. "Everything is in good heart, my lord sheriff. I was simply concerned . . ."

"That touches me, Gilles," Alistair said, shifting Elspeth in his arms. "And I do know how to reward loyalty." He started through the hallway, his arms too tight around her.

"Where are you taking me?" she asked. "My rooms are in the north tower."

"Your rooms are wherever I say they are. If you try my patience any longer, they'll be in the dungeon."

"Yes, my lord sheriff," she said meekly.

He cursed her under his breath. "Between you and De Lancey I'll never have a moment's peace."

"And were you looking for peace, my lord?"

The hallway was deserted. Deliberately, Elspeth knew. Though De Lancey wouldn't be far away, he'd be silent, watching, spying.

Alistair let Elspeth down, her body sliding against his, her bare feet cool on the stone floor. "If I am," he said, "then doubtless I married the wrong nun. You'll sleep with me, wench. Until I tire of you."

"Or I of you."

He caught her chin in his strong hand, and his fury blazed. "Don't push me too far, Elspeth of Gaveland. You're mine, and what is mine, I keep."

It was a clash of wills. If she had any sense at all, any decorum, she would lower her eyes and docilely agree.

Instead she lifted her hand and gently touched his cheek. He flinched, trying to pull away, but she simply wrapped her hand in a lock of his thick, dark hair. "My name is Elspeth of Huntingdon. And you're mine, Alistair. Remember the prophecy."

He stared down at her in mute frustration. "I only wish I could forget."

6

"**Y**OU aren't going to abandon me here?" Elspeth demanded when Alistair dragged her into a huge room and then started for the door.

He paused, staring at her. "Would you prefer my company? I have five minutes to spare. Get on the bed and lift your skirts."

He watched the faint color rise to her cheeks, but she managed a steadfast expression. "There is no need to be crude, my lord."

"There's every need. I am ruler of this castle, lord of this domain, placed here by his highness, King John. I have complete power over everyone, your family included, and I can do anything I damned well please. I can be crude, I can be vicious, I can be completely murderous if it takes my fancy. Get on the bed."

She had a temper, his bride. That much he'd discovered early on. She turned to look for something to throw at him.

He was at her side, catching her arm before she could heft the heavy candelabrum. His fingers wrapped around her wrist so tightly he numbed it, and she dropped the heavy metal with a cry of pain.

He released her instantly, squashing the flash of guilt as swiftly as it came upon him. "You will learn not to defy me," he said. "Unless you relish pain."

"I was never particularly obedient," she said quietly, rubbing her aching wrist.

He took her hand again, and he could see that it required all her willpower not to flinch as he brought her wrist to his mouth, kissing the red marks his long fingers had left.

He felt the hot chill run through her, and she shuddered, closing her eyes for a brief moment. He stared at her, obsessed, wanting her with an intensity that made him forget everything, including his suspicions, his desperate need for power. He stared at her, and all he wanted was her, her gentleness, her temper, her stubbornness, her humor. The thought terrified him, he, who had never known fear.

"De Lancey," he bellowed, his eyes not leaving hers.

"My lord?" he said, appearing in the open doorway.

Alistair still looked at her, and his fingers were caressing her wrist, unable to help himself. He had no choice. He had to send her away while he still could. "You will take Lady Elspeth back to the convent."

"No!" she cried, trying to pull away from him in sudden despair.

He didn't let her go. "The marriage will be annulled. Inform the bishop."

"No," she said again.

"By your command," De Lancey said, and there was no missing the satisfaction in his voice. "I warned you, cousin. She'll weaken you, and there's no way you can hold your power if a woman gets in your way . . ."

"Silence!" Alistair thundered, still staring down at Elspeth's miserable face, his fingers caressing her. And then he threw her hand away from him and stormed from the room without a backward glance.

He didn't stop until he reached the courtyard. The people were scurrying away from him, as always, and he told himself he was pleased to have such a reputation for harshness. Doubtless they thought him capable of witchcraft at the very least, and no one dared disobey him.

Except for the man who'd killed Jenna. The man who professed to be his devoted servant, his best friend, his cousin. The man he'd left alone with his bride.

It had been a simple enough matter to find who'd spent the last night with Jenna. De Lancey was possessed of any number of useful qualities—brutality, charm, deviousness, and a certain slyness that stood him well in the place of intelligence. But he was also cursed with an overweening vanity, one that threatened to rival Alistair's own, and he had failed to realize his cousin knew him far too well.

He wouldn't dare harm Elspeth while Alistair was close by, Alistair knew that much. Gilles would wait until he got her away from Huntingdon Keep. But she would never make it back to the convent. Some accident would befall her, and De Lancey would return alone, sorrowful, smirking when he thought no one would notice. And if Alistair had any sense at all he would allow him to do so, turning a blind eye while De Lancey did the dirty work.

But Alistair's cool common sense seemed to have evaporated. De Lancey had been a useful tool, but now his usefulness was at an end. He would send Elspeth away from him, someplace distant where he could swiftly forget about her. But first he would kill De Lancey. Before De Lancey killed him.

Elspeth didn't move. Misery and despair formed a tight ball inside her heart, burning through her soul. He couldn't dismiss her so readily, so abruptly. She couldn't let him do it.

"We'll leave within the hour," De Lancey said gently.

She turned to look at him, her eyes bright with unshed tears. "I won't go."

"Yes, you will, my lady."

"He'll change his mind," she cried, certain of no such thing.

But De Lancey suddenly looked unsure. "It's possible," he said. "It could be made to happen." For a moment the notion didn't look the slightest bit pleasing to him, and then he put his usual affable smile on his handsome face. "We could make it happen, my lady," he continued. "If you love him, I will do everything I can to help you."

Through her misery Elspeth still retained a trace of suspicion. "Why?"

"Why, because he's my lord and my cousin. I want only what's best for him," De Lancey said smoothly. "But we'll have to be circumspect. He's ordered me to take you back to the convent, and we'll have to make him think we're leaving. He doesn't like his will to be crossed."

"So I've observed," Elspeth said faintly.

"You'll need to change for the journey. Act as if you're willing to accept his decree. I'll send one of the serving women with clothes for you."

"Not Helva," she begged, remembering the woman's sour old face.

"No," said De Lancey, with commendable sadness. "Not Helva. She's dead."

A sudden icy fear trickled through Elspeth's body. "What do you mean?"

"Someone cut her throat last night. She was found in the tower bedroom, hidden behind some furniture. Someone butchered her in a mindless fury."

"Not Alistair," she said fiercely.

"Of course not," De Lancey agreed softly, his eyes full of pity for her obvious naivete. "Are you certain you don't want me to get you safely away from here? While you can still go?"

"Very certain."

De Lancey nodded, a certain grimness around his fine mouth. "Meet me in the outer chapel. If anyone questions you, say you're going to make confession so that you may reenter the convent absolved of any worldly sins." There was a pregnant pause. "Were there any worldly sins, my lady?"

She looked at him with a haughty expression worthy of her husband. "What business is it of yours, my lord?"

"None, of course," he said hastily. "Remember,

we'll meet in the chapel. No one will be there at this time of day. We can talk privately.''

She watched him leave as she pulled the loose dress up over her shoulders again. She didn't trust him, never had. But he was her only hope against her husband's sudden decree, and she was willing to use anything and anyone to keep from being dismissed like so much unwanted baggage. She wouldn't be sent away from him, back to the living death of the convent. She wouldn't leave him, and she'd accept help from the devil himself to accomplish that.

Gilles De Lancey was almost angelic in his beauty. She was mad not to trust him. Mad not to want to escape with his help when she had the chance.

The chapel was a thatched wooden structure outside the keep, unpleasantly adjacent to the pigsties and the kitchens. Most castles the size of Huntingdon Keep had a chapel inside, but Alistair had turned it into a gaming room, relegating whatever religious observances he tolerated to the older church building.

Elspeth half-expected someone to stop her as she made her way across the littered courtyard less than an hour later, but if anyone watched her, they did so covertly.

No one had ever shown up with a change of clothes for her, and Elspeth had grown tired of waiting. If worse came to worst and she returned to the Sisters of the Everlasting Martyr in the blood-red dress of a witch, it wouldn't be her fault. She wouldn't even care if Reverend Mother refused her admittance.

The chapel was deserted when she stepped inside, closing the door behind her. Dust motes floated in the air, and the smell of incense almost overpowered the smell from the kitchen pits. Almost. Elspeth glanced around her, but there was no sign of Friar Parkin, no sign of anyone at all. She knelt at the ornately carved altar, crossing herself, trying to concentrate on prayer. But all she could think of was her husband.

''There you are.'' De Lancey's voice seemed to come from directly above her, and it took all Elspeth's self-control not to jump. She forced herself to keep her head down, to continue the prayer that had only a fraction of her attention, before crossing herself again and looking upward.

"Where is Friar Parkin?" she asked, sitting back on her heels.

"You didn't really want to see him, did you? I thought we were going to make plans for your future."

There was something about the smug expression in his bright blue eyes, the faint swagger in his muscular body, that sent a chill of apprehension through Elspeth. "I had wanted to make my confession."

"Make it to me, my lady. I'd delight to hear the details. You must have hidden talents, to turn Alistair into such a wreck. I've never tried a nun."

Her back stiffened. "You said you would help me."

"And so I will. I want you to come away with me, dear lady. Alistair doesn't want you anymore, but I do. I have no objections to taking his leavings—I've done so often enough. My home is small but snug, and I'm certain I can keep you well distracted. I'm considered a talented lover."

The man was actually preening. Elspeth held her hands together tightly, afraid he might see she was trembling. There was something dark and evil in the ancient chapel, something she'd felt before, and never in the presence of her supposedly wicked husband.

"I have no need for a lover," she said calmly. "I wish only for my husband."

"But he doesn't wish for you."

She tried not to flinch at his bald pronouncement. "I think he does. He just doesn't want to admit it."

De Lancey sauntered into the chapel, coming up close to her, and once again she noticed the long, jeweled dagger at his belt. "It makes no difference, dear lady," he said. "He's not going to have you. You weaken him, and he must be strong, merciless. I intend to see to it."

She saw his move coming bare moments before he made it. The jeweled knife flashed out, but she had already ducked, rolling along the dust-laden floor, her blood-red dress wrapped around her.

She wasn't fast enough. He leaped for her, and she felt the sudden stinging pain in her neck before she kicked him, hard, scrambling away on her hands and knees as he howled in rage. She made it only a few feet before she was brought up short, the ample material of the dress caught in the intricate carving of the altar.

"Little bitch." Gilles panted, crawling after her. "I'll cut your throat like I did those other whores. Everyone is terrified of the high and mighty sheriff of Huntingdon, but little do they know it's me they're frightened of. I'm the one who's made a pact with the devil. I'm the one who will do what needs to be done. Including getting rid of you. I'm the real power here, the terror. And those fools don't even begin to realize it."

"Most edifying, cousin." Alistair's bored voice came from the back of the chapel. "You may be far more merciless than I am, but you lack one essential ingredient for success in this life."

It took Gilles only a moment to recover from his shock. He scrambled to his feet, the knife still gripped in one hand, and Elspeth could see the bright red of her blood on the shiny blade. "And what's that, my lord sheriff," Gilles said mockingly. "A sense of humanity? Decency? Honor?"

"Heavens, no," Alistair replied. "I've never been troubled much by those. What you lack, dear Gilles, is intelligence. Had you been blessed with it, you would have known that I haven't trusted you for months. I was waiting for you to betray yourself. I knew you would sooner or later. I rather thought I'd catch you with that poor girl, but unfortunately, I was distracted by my bride. That will be remedied."

"Cousin," Gilles said, suddenly persuasive, "I've done it all for you. You rule by terror, yet you've been able to keep your conscience clean. I've done your dirty work for you, and been glad of the chance to serve you. You don't want to be burdened with this wench, you said so yourself. A man of your discriminating tastes can't be satisfied with a skinny nun, no matter how many forests she brings you. I was simply going to take care of the matter for you, as I've taken care of so many in the past. I've punished them all, for you. Even Helva, for letting the wench escape. You haven't wanted to know the details, you've just wanted results. Turn your back, return to the keep, and forget about this afternoon. You'll be a widower, wealthier by one of the finest forests in this part of England, and no one to trouble you.''

"As I said, Gilles," Alistair remarked pleasantly, "you are most definitely a fool."

Elspeth had been tugging at the dress, trying to rip it free, but for all that the material was ancient, it was still very strong. Her neck was wet, and she knew the dampness came from her own blood, but she refused to think about it, too intent on freeing herself, too intent on the confrontation between the man who looked like the devil and the man who was the devil.

She saw Gilles move, the knife slashing, and she screamed out a warning, but Alistair was already out of range, disappearing into the darkness in the back of the small chapel.

Gilles laughed, a pleasant, benevolent chuckle. "So be it," he said. "I'll do you both, you know. People know the prophecy, cousin; I've made certain they've heard it. 'Flame and fire destroy them both, death and rebirth, blood their troth.' I only wanted to serve you. You and I shared so much. The same love of power, the same lack of weakness. I never would have been distracted by a woman. Perhaps I'm better off without you interfering.''

"How are you going to manage the flame, Gilles?" Alistair's mocking voice floated forward.

"Oh, quite easily, dear cousin. I was already planning it for your lady wife. I will simply send you to your doom along with her. You can't escape, you know. There's no way out back there, and I'll be waiting by the front. I'll run you through—it won't matter. No one will find your body until you're too blackened and burned for people to know what actually killed you."

"Don't you think my people might notice if the chapel goes up in smoke in the middle of the day?" Alistair sounded as reasonable as Gilles did, as if they were discussing the proper deployment of troops, or where the best fishing was to be had. "I've tried my best to rid them of their foolish, sentimental religion, but I'm afraid I've failed. They do cling to the old ways, and they would do anything to keep their shabby little chapel from burning. And who's to say it won't spread to the stables, and on to the kitchens?"

"There are other horses. Other kitchens. And I'm afraid there's no one around to come to your assistance. They have orders—from you, I told them—to keep to their houses, no matter what. They're too terrified of you to disobey. Even if they hear your wife's screams for help, they won't interfere."

"You're probably right, dear cousin," Alistair reflected. "Then I expect it behooves me to save myself."

"You can always try, dear Alistair," Gilles said gently as he slipped out the door, slamming it behind him.

In a flash Alistair hurtled out of the darkness, throwing himself against the door, but it was already barred. He pounded on it, his formidable voice raining curses and imprecations at De Lancey's golden head, but the smoke was already seeping through the door, crackling noisily with the hungry sound of dry tinder.

"Damn!" Alistair said, whirling around and storming to the darkened end of the chapel.

"He said there was no exit there," Elspeth called after him, still yanking at her dress.

"He's an idiot," Alistair shot back. "I'm not about to be a roasted pig for his delectation." And he began slamming his body at a spot in the far wall.

The flames had spread rapidly, licking up the sides of the wall and edging toward the thatch. Elspeth gave one more mighty yank of the dress, and the material ripped. Instead of freedom, however, it brought the ancient altar down on her leg with a painful crash, trapping her even more securely.

The smoke was filling her lungs and her eyes, and she could no longer see. She could hear Alistair cursing, however, and the sound was oddly reassuring. Flames were filling the dust-dry building, blocking any possible exit. But Alistair would escape. It would be a small victory.

"Where the hell are you?" His voice snarled through the thick smoke.

"I'm trapped," she said between fits of coughing. "You go ahead and save yourself."

"For God's sake," he snapped, "get on your feet and get out of here."

"I can't."

The thatch had caught, setting the entire ceiling ablaze. It wouldn't be long, and Elspeth expected it would be painful, and she only hoped she wouldn't scream. Despite Alistair's protestations of cold-bloodedness, she didn't think he'd want to hear her scream.

A shape loomed up out of the smoke with such suddenness that she did scream. The heavy altar was shoved off her leg, and she was hauled to her feet, then up into her husband's arms. "Hide your face against my chest," he ordered, and started through the flames.

The noise and heat were unbearable, suffocating. She wanted to push him away, but she knew further argument would only endanger him. "Stupid man," she whispered against his chest, certain they were both about to die.

A moment later they were out of the inferno, into air so fresh it hurt to breathe it. Alistair sank to his knees, Elspeth still clutched in his arms, and she raised her head to see embers burning on his dark velvet sleeve. She slapped at them, ignoring the pain in her hands and in her neck until he stopped her, holding her hands in his, staring at her out of his wild, golden eyes.

"He cut you," he said, his voice hoarse from the smoke. He touched the blood on her neck and it glistened bright red with life. "I'll rip his heart out." He tried to pull away, but she caught his hands firmly. Her strength was no match for his, yet he didn't pull away.

"Why didn't you leave me in there?" she demanded. "You could have been killed."

"Foolish sentiment," he snapped.

"Is that all?"

"Practicality," he added. "You might be carrying my child."

"Your son," she said, saying it aloud for the first time.

He looked startled. "You're not the witch. There's no way you could know."

"I know." She looked up, realizing with sudden shock that it was raining quite heavily, soaking down upon them as they knelt in the courtyard. Thunder rumbled in the distance, and lightning streaked across the leaden sky. "You had no other reason to save me?" she asked.

"Perhaps I didn't want the prophecy to come true. I detest being a whim of God."

She smiled then, and released his hands. "If you say so," she said, sinking back.

Whatever threats De Lancey had used to keep the inhabitants of Huntingdon Castle in their homes had long since lost their power. A crowd of people were congregating around the burning chapel, muttering darkly. The heavy rain was soaking everything, keeping the fire from spreading.

"You, there," Alistair called in his lordly, arrogant voice. "See to my wife. She needs tending. The rest of you, there'll be a reward of forty marks for the man who brings Gilles De Lancey to me."

"He's right here, your lordship," one of the men-at-arms said in an uneasy voice.

Alistair surged to his feet, instantly dismissing Elspeth's existence as he followed the voice, but she managed to struggle to her feet, hauling the heavy wet dress around her to trail after him.

"Where?" he demanded.

"He's dead, your lordship. Looks like he fell on his knife."

Elspeth came up behind her tall, rain-drenched husband and stared down at the dead man, trying to keep the bile from rising in her throat. In death, Gilles De Lancey was no longer a handsome man. He lay on his back in the mud, his bright blue eyes wide and staring, his jeweled knife skewering his manly throat.

She could feel her husband's rage, his tension as he took a step toward his enemy's body, and she decided now was as good a time as any. She swooned, deliberately graceful, prepared to topple onto the ground if need be to stop her husband from committing an act of savagery.

She never made it to the ground. Alistair caught her, cursing loudly, holding her with infinite gentleness. She closed her eyes and let him carry her out of the rain and into the warmth and safety of the keep as he cursed all the way, issuing orders and then countermanding them. He was a rare handful, her husband, she thought, hiding her trembling smile against the wet velvet of his tunic. He smelled like rain and smoke and Alistair, and she wanted to cry.

The eventual silence came as a shock. She finally lifted her head, plastering a wan expression on her face, only to find that he'd brought her back to his rooms. None of the servants had followed—he must have dismissed them or scared them away with all his ranting and raving, and now they were alone. He stood with her over the high carved bed and stared down at her, an enigmatic expression on his face.

"Liar," he said, and dropped her.

She landed with a tiny yelp. "What do you mean by that?" she demanded, affronted.

"You didn't faint."

"I felt dizzy."

"You didn't want to see me cut out Gilles's heart."

She sat up, fully aware that the neckline of the blood-red dress gaped attractively. At least she suspected he found it attractive, judging from the way he was looking at her. "Well, no," she admitted. "I told you, I don't like the sight of blood. Would you have done it?"

"Yes," he said flatly. "What about this?" He touched her neck, and she winced. "Doesn't he deserve to pay for this?"

"Considering that he is already dead, I think the debt is paid in full," she said. "What are you going to do now? Continue to terrorize the poor people of Huntingdon? Send me back to the convent? Find another madman like De Lancey to commit your crimes?"

He stared at her, and there was no reading his expression. "Things have worked well so far," he said. "In my short life I've amassed enormous power and wealth. People will do anything I tell them to. I see no reason to change the way I do things."

"You have everything you could ever want. There's no need to frighten people into doing your will. It's just as easy to inspire their love."

"Why in the devil's name would I want to do that?" he demanded.

"If not for God, then for me," she said simply. "And for the sake of your children."

He looked horrified. "I could always gag you," he said, half to himself. "You must have taken a vow of silence in the convent. There's no other explanation for your being quite so vociferous now."

"I'm not as meek as I should be."

"That," he said calmly, "is an understatement."

"You don't need a mousy wife."

"I don't need a wife at all."

"But you've got one."

"It's nothing I can't remedy. I've broken the prophecy. We weren't destroyed by flame and fire. I have nothing to worry about by getting rid of you."

She shook her head, feeling her long hair flow around her. "You didn't break the prophecy. You made it come true. 'Flame and fire destroy them both, death and rebirth, blood their troth.'" She touched his fingers, which were still marked with her blood. "A part of me died in that fire. A part of you as well."

He jerked away. "You're fanciful."

"No, I'm not. You try so hard to be wicked. A truly wicked man would have let me perish in the flames. You came back and saved me."

"It was a mistake," he said sourly. "If I'd left you there, at least I wouldn't have to listen to your infernal yammering. And I would have caught up with De Lancey before Morgana got to him."

"Morgana?"

"Somewhere in the heart of Dunstan Woods she's sitting with a little doll in her hand. And there's a sharp pin stuck right through the center of that doll's neck. I may not have had revenge, but my mother has."

"I don't believe in witches," Elspeth said, shivering.

"Fortunately, De Lancey did."

"You can't send me away," she said desperately, rising to her knees in the bed.

"Why not?" He seemed no more than casually interested in her argument.

"You've forgotten the rest of the prophecy. 'In thunder, rain, brought right again.' It's still raining, isn't it? Keeping the fire from spreading?"

"And?" he prodded.

"'And all shall be as God's design.'"

He closed his eyes wearily, and cursed. "Elspeth," he said with great patience, "I have no interest in God's will. I have no interest in anyone's will but my own. I'm a very bad man. Perhaps not quite so bad as Gilles, but I expect I've come close in my time. I'm not a fit husband for a child like you. I release you from your wedding vows."

"I never made my wedding vows!" she cried in frustration. "So how can you release me? I'm your bride, Alistair Darcourt, and you can't dismiss me so easily. I'm your prophecy, your destiny, your fate. I'm God's will, and not even you can deny it."

He caught her shoulders in his hands, pulling her up

to him. He was trying his best to glare at her, and he was failing. "Damn you," he muttered under his breath, and kissed her hard.

She didn't hesitate. She kissed him back, twining her arms around him, pulling him off balance, down onto the bed beside her. She tore at his clothes, he tore at hers, both of them desperate with need.

When he finally rolled off her, he was panting, breathless, and still fighting it.

"I'll never be a good man," he warned her, his voice severe, at odds with the gentleness of his hand as it trailed down her arm.

"You're probably right," she agreed cheerfully enough, snuggling up against his chest. He put his arm around her, pulling her closer, probably without even realizing it. "I suppose I'll just have to be a good example for everyone, to make up for your unparalleled wickedness."

"They'll tell you you married a monster."

"They'll be right," she said sweetly.

"I won't be tamed."

"Alistair, my love," she said, raising herself on her elbow and smiling down at him, "you already are."

Lady Elspeth of Gaveland never made it to sainthood, or even an early martyrdom. She lived an unheard of eighty-nine years, all of them spent at the side of her recalcitrant husband, the high sheriff of Huntingdon.

People still crossed themselves when he looked at them askance. And they thanked providence that all but one of the twelve children Lady Elspeth brought forth and raised to healthy adulthood took after their mother and not their father, nor his mother the witch, who was purported to still live deep in the haunted depths of Dunstan Woods, singing her wicked songs and planning her evil deeds.

And in the end, the lord high sheriff and his bride were buried in the fine new chapel at Huntingdon Keep, Alistair's reluctant gift to Lady Elspeth on the occasion of the birth of their first child, a son. And if Morgan, that first son, had golden eyes, and if wicked things tended to befall anyone who happened to cross his will, neither of his parents made mention of it.

After all, who really believed in witches?

Anne Stuart

When Avon Books asked me to write a short story for this bridal collection, I wasn't sure about it. I've never found brides and weddings that romantic. After all, the chase is over, the couple is in harmony, and the best thing about it is the bride gets to wear a nice dress.

However, in the past, brides weren't quite so predictable or weddings so ordinary. There were marriages of convenience, stolen brides, proxy marriages, arranged marriages, marriages where the principals were strangers, and all that luscious stuff. In the past, the excitement of discovering love came after the wedding, not before.

So I took one of history's most colorful villains, the wicked Sheriff of Nottingham, changed him into the High Sheriff of Huntingdon, matched him up with a stubborn ex-nun and then watched the sparks fly. I had a great deal of fun with the two of them, and I hope you did too.

And needless to say, they both lived happily ever after.

Avon Romances—
the best in exceptional authors
and unforgettable novels!

THE LION'S DAUGHTER Loretta Chase
76647-7/$4.50 US/$5.50 Can

CAPTAIN OF MY HEART Danelle Harmon
76676-0/$4.50 US/$5.50 Can

BELOVED INTRUDER Joan Van Nuys
76476-8/$4.50 US/$5.50 Can

SURRENDER TO THE FURY Cara Miles
76452-0/$4.50 US/$5.50 Can

SCARLET KISSES Patricia Camden
76825-9/$4.50 US/$5.50 Can

WILDSTAR Nicole Jordan
76622-1/$4.50 US/$5.50 Can

HEART OF THE WILD Donna Stephens
77014-8/$4.50 US/$5.50 Can

TRAITOR'S KISS Joy Tucker
76446-6/$4.50 US/$5.50 Can

SILVER AND SAPPHIRES Shelly Thacker
77034-2/$4.50 US/$5.50 Can

SCOUNDREL'S DESIRE Joann DeLazzari
76421-0/$4.50 US/$5.50 Can

Avon Romantic Treasures

Unforgettable, enthralling love stories,
sparkling with passion and adventure
from Romance's bestselling authors

AWAKEN MY FIRE *by Jennifer Horsman*
76701-5/$4.50 US/$5.50 Can

ONLY BY YOUR TOUCH *by Stella Cameron*
76606-X/$4.50 US/$5.50 Can

FIRE AT MIDNIGHT *by Barbara Dawson Smith*
76275-7/$4.50 US/$5.50 Can

ONLY WITH YOUR LOVE *by Lisa Kleypas*
76151-3/$4.50 US/$5.50 Can

MY WILD ROSE *by Deborah Camp*
76738-4/$4.50 US/$5.50 Can

MIDNIGHT AND MAGNOLIAS *by Rebecca Paisley*
76566-7/$4.50 US/$5.50 Can

THE MASTER'S BRIDE *by Suzannah Davis*
76821-6/$4.50 US/$5.50 Can

A ROSE AT MIDNIGHT *by Anne Stuart*
76740-6/$4.50 US/$5.50 Can